THE PERSIAN

ALSO BY DAVID McCLOSKEY

The Seventh Floor
Moscow X
Damascus Station

THE PERSIAN

a novel

DAVID McCLOSKEY

W. W. NORTON & COMPANY
Independent Publishers Since 1923

This is a work of fiction. Names, characters, places, and incidents are the products of the author's imagination or are used fictitiously. Any resemblance to actual events, locales, or persons, living or dead, is entirely coincidental.

Copyright © 2025 by David McCloskey

All rights reserved
Printed in the United States of America
First Edition

For information about permission to reproduce selections from this book, write to Permissions, W. W. Norton & Company, Inc., 500 Fifth Avenue, New York, NY 10110

For information about special discounts for bulk purchases, please contact W. W. Norton Special Sales at specialsales@wwnorton.com or 800-233-4830

Map by Michael Borop
Manufacturing by Lakeside Book Company
Production manager: Julia Druskin

Library of Congress Cataloging-in-Publication Data

ISBN 978-1-324-12319-4

W. W. Norton & Company, Inc., 500 Fifth Avenue, New York, NY 10110
www.wwnorton.com

W. W. Norton & Company Ltd., 15 Carlisle Street, London W1D 3BS

10 9 8 7 6 5 4 3 2 1

As always for Abby, my love
And for the people of Israel and Iran, for hope, and a new way

Love comes with a knife.

—RŪMĪ

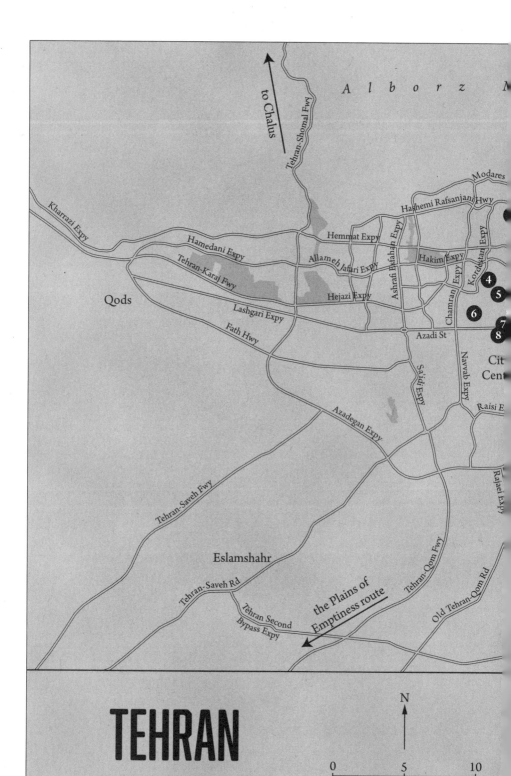

PROLOGUE
Tehran, Iran
Four years ago

IT DID NOT ESCAPE the Israeli watching through the hijacked phone camera that this very scene had unrolled that morning at his own breakfast table in Tel Aviv. His daughter was about the same age—even the nail polish had been pink.

―――

ROYA SHABANI BLEW ACROSS her daughter's freshly painted fingernails. Alya, ever a mimic, took a deep breath and huffed as hard as she could across the bright pink polish.

"Who's coming to my party?" Alya asked, watching her mother screw the cap onto the polish.

"Everyone you wanted. The list we made, sweetie."

She began to stand, but Alya held her wrist tight. "How many?"

"Six," Roya said.

"Will there be cake?"

"You and I made the cake," Roya said. "We are bringing that."

"Can I bring my lamby?"

"Of course," Roya said. "Your lamb can come."

Roya stood and glanced at the clock. "Why don't we draw while we wait for Papa to finish working? Go get your paper and crayons." As Alya hustled off, Roya strode over to Abbas's office and raised her fist to knock on the door before she thought better of it. They were going to be late, even if traffic was light, which in central Tehran it never was. But why bother Abbas, and add his agitation to the mix? So she turned around, and headed for the bathroom to check the rings of kohl around her eyes and reapply the bright red lipstick that Abbas had once complimented.

Back in the living room, Alya slid her mother a few crayons and a sheet of paper, and Roya aimlessly began drawing. Something had been wrong for a few months now—late nights in the office, overnights, last-minute travel, always to places he would not name, and always with Colonel Ghorbani, his uncle. When he was home, he was joyless and distracted. At dinner he would stare off into the distance, as he'd done in the thick of his dissertation, which meant he was trying to work out a problem. Then, it had been amusing, endearing. Now it was worrisome. Abbas was not the cheating type, but Roya could not help but wonder if he was having an affair, or had taken a temporary wife.

Halfway through Roya's second distracted attempt at drawing a fountain, with Alya's ire rising that Maman could not do it right, the door to the office swung open and Abbas walked out while sliding on his jacket and trying his best to smile.

Alya darted to him, hands outstretched, and said, "Papa! See my nails?"

"Absolutely beautiful," he said, making a show of admiring them while gathering her into his arms. "Are you ten today?"

"I'm five, Papa!" He kissed her head. Roya heard his phone buzz, and when he set Alya down he was back on it. An hour earlier, while getting ready, Roya had entertained a brief fantasy that the night would offer some connection with Abbas, a chance to talk at dinner, to admire their daughter, and, if lovemaking wasn't in the cards, at least to go to bed at the same time. But she could see his mind was elsewhere, and that made hers itch for cigarettes, which Abbas hated. He wasn't a prayer-and-fasting type—though both Shabanis occasionally had to put on a show for his job. No, his objection was rather the smell, which he said made him queasy. Though maybe after dinner, and once Alya was asleep, he would return to the office? She hated that, which was where the cigarettes came in . . .

TRAFFIC WAS A GRIND as they inched northbound from Yusef Abad up to the restaurant off Jordan Avenue; not a drive any Tehrani wanted to make in rush hour, but this was where the Shabanis went to celebrate birthdays. Not the sort of ritual a newly minted five-year-old girl was likely to let you break. Alya was singing to the stuffed lamb in the backseat, occasionally interjecting, "Ugggh, why so slow, Papa?"

"Traffic, love," Roya said. "Papa is going as fast as he can." As they were passing a sycamore-lined median, Alya began singing again. This time it wasn't nonsense, it was a nursery rhyme, the one about the little chicken and the pool, a bathtime favorite. For a moment, with all of them together in the car, the singing made Roya feel warm and cozy. Tonight they might actually have fun.

Abbas's phone began to light up and buzz with incoming messages.

"I'm picking up the shoes tomorrow," Roya said, while Abbas typed out a message on his phone.

No response, except a few angry honks from the car behind them.

"Abbas?"

"Oh, what?" Face still fastened to the phone.

"I said I'm picking up your shoes tomorrow. The ones I had made for your birthday."

"That's great. That's great."

No sooner had he put his phone down than it would blink and buzz again. The traffic, the toddler singsong—which was growing quite loud—the honks... Roya rifled through her purse and tossed it back at her feet in a huff. A mistake, she thought, not to bring the cigarettes.

"Does your uncle know it's her birthday?"

"What? I don't know."

The traffic was loosening; the car in front puttered ahead. Roya looked at Abbas, who was looking at his phone.

"Abbas, go."

"Oh." The phone clattered into the cupholder, Abbas jerked the car forward. They drove in silence for a few moments. Alya had stopped singing. All Roya could hear was the beep and buzz of his phone.

"Colonel Ghorbani," Roya said, emphasizing his uncle's rank, which Abbas hated, "told me at *your* birthday dinner that you might be his nephew, but you're like a son to him. So how does he not know it's her birthday?"

"I told you, Roya, I don't know what he knows."

"Maybe you could tell him, then? When the car stops again and you pick up the phone? So we can enjoy dinner."

"Only some of it is my uncle," Abbas said. He looked down at his phone and then seemed to catch Roya glaring at him. He drifted his eyes back to the road, chastened.

There had been plenty of times in the past month when Roya had wanted to take her husband by the shoulders and shout: *You're a scientist! You're supposed to be sitting alone in a lab!* She regretted his decision to reject the postdoc opportunity in Paris in favor of Colonel Jaffar Ghorbani and whatever his group was doing. "I design materials that radars can't see," Abbas had said once. That was all she knew. That was all she was going to get.

When they exited the highway they made a right and then, after a few blocks, turned down a road that would send them right back the way they'd come, but this time on the same side of the street as the restaurant. Roya looked out the window at a van up on the curb. One front tire was missing and it was up on a jack. Abandoned. Another Tehrani driver throwing in the towel.

"Auntie will be there?" Alya said.

"Yes, sweetheart, she's already there. Auntie's waiting for us."

"I can have cake now?" Roya turned and saw Alya eyeing the cake, sitting beside her in the backseat.

"Not now, sweetheart," Roya said. "We're almost there."

Abbas slowed the car for a speed bump, the restaurant just ahead. Alya began singing again. *"Lili lili hozak..."*

Roya spotted a little market she knew carried packs of cigarettes smuggled in from Dubai. Maybe she could send her sister, Afsaneh, to snag one for her, assuming Roya couldn't slip away while pretending to use the bathroom.

Her thoughts were interrupted by a loud crack as the windshield spiderwebbed, and Roya thought someone had thrown a stone into the glass. Abbas let out a strange yelp. The car had been rolling so slowly that it bounced to a stop against the speed bump. There were pieces of glass on her lap. Air was rushing in.

"Abbas!" she screamed.

"I can't see," he yelled, "I can't see." Abbas yanked off his seat belt and smacked wildly at the door handle. Then Roya saw it, a shard of glass protruding from his eye, glimmering under the streetlights. Blood was trickling down his face.

"Abbas!"

When he got the door open Abbas fell out into the street. Alya was screaming in terror. Roya was, too, but their screams were drowned out by the roar of more gunfire. Abbas was flailing and jerking around, and then she saw a ruddy brown spray jet loose from his body, she didn't know what it was, but the shooting stopped and the car was momentarily quiet except for Alya's screaming. "Abbas!" she yelled, but he didn't move, didn't speak, and then she'd opened her own door and was crawling, reaching up to grasp around for the handle of the back door. The gun thundered again, a short burst, and then stopped. Roya was splayed across the cake, wrenching Alya free from her car seat, pulling her out. "Abbas!" she called. "Abbas!" The only response was another round of gunfire.

Papa, Papa, Papa, the girl was screaming. Roya was turning and twisting, trying to figure which way to run—she didn't know where the shooter was—when her eyes fell on a blue Zamyad pickup. She felt the explosion in her teeth, in her bones. She was staring at its white-orange center, and it felt like the light was searing her eyes. A hulk of metal lifted from the bed of the truck, shooting skyward like the takeoff of a rocket.

With Alya slung over her shoulder, Roya turned and ran.

IN AN UNMARKED limestone building outside Tel Aviv, the Israeli squeezed the shoulder of a woman sitting at a computer terminal, and said she'd done well. A small group was clustered in the operations room, and no one was talking. The only noise had been the sound of gunfire in Tehran, nearly two thousand kilometers away. The woman lifted her hand from the joystick that was tethered, by satellite uplink, to a Belgian-made FN MAG machine gun. The kill order had been clear, as they always were: No collateral damage. And that included the young scientist's family.

The Israeli watched the survivors run. In the grainy feed he made out a stuffed pink lamb flopping against the new widow's back, clutched tight in the little girl's pink-painted grip.

The Interrogation Room
Location: ███████

Present day

"WHERE AM I, General?"

Kamran Esfahani loads his questions with a tone of slavish deference because, though the man resembles a kindly Persian grandfather, he is, in the main, a psychopath.

The General is looking hard at Kam. He plucks a sugar cube from the bowl on the table, tucks it between his teeth, and sips his tea. Kam typically would not ask such questions, but, during the three years spent in his care, hustled constantly between makeshift prisons, he has never once sat across from the General, clothed properly, with a steaming cup of tea at his fingertips, a spoon on the table, and a window at his back.

Something flashes through the General's eyes and it tells Kam that he will deeply regret asking the question again. It has been over a year since the General last beat him or strung him up in what his captors call the Chicken Kebab, but the memories are fresh each morning. Kam can still see the glint of the pipe brought down on his leg, can still remember how the pain bent time into an arc that stretched into eternity, and how that glimpse into the void filled him with a despair so powerful that it surely has no name, at least not in Persian, Swedish, or English, the three languages he speaks. And he's got more than the memories, of course. He's got blurry vision in his left eye and a permanent hitch in his stride.

What is the spoon doing here? A spoon!

Two thousand seven hundred and twenty-one consecutive meals have been served, without utensils, on rubber discs, so Kam can't help but blink suspiciously at the spoon. A mirage? An eyeball scooper? A test? Perhaps the General plans to skin the fingers that pick it up? The General calms his fears with a nod, a genuine one, which Kam knows looks quite different from the version he uses for trickery, for lulling him into thinking there will be no physical harm. Kam puts a lump of sugar into his tea and slowly picks up the spoon. He stirs, savoring the cold metal on his fingertips. He sets it down on the table and waits, listening to the soft metallic wobble as the bowl of the spoon comes to rest.

"You will write it down again," the General says. He is rubbing the gray bristle on his neck, and Kam follows his eye contact as it settles on the portraits of the two Ayatollahs looking down from the wall above. When Kam was a child the sight of the Ayatollahs frightened him—it still does. He looks away.

How many times has he written it all down? Dozens, certainly. A hundred is probably closer. As if reading Kam's thoughts, the General lowers his eyes from Khomeini and says, "One more time."

Only once more? Are they finally going to kill him?

"May I use notes from my past testimonies?" Kam asks.

The General clicks his tongue. Translation: *Hell, no.*

"General," Kam says, with a slight bow of his head, "I have already confessed to my crimes. I've hidden nothing."

"Those," the General says, wagging his finger, "are not the same thing." And he gives a great laugh. Kam does not feel the cup slip from his fingers. He only feels the warm tea seeping into his pants and for a moment believes he's wet himself. Kam has never heard the General laugh. He had assumed the man lacked even the lunatic's sense of humor. Together they watch more tea run off the side of the table. Kam knows better than to stand without permission, so he just looks at the mess, and the General looks at him, more from curiosity than anger. The General could motion to the camera for a rag, but he does not. Nor does he motion for a new cup.

He instead pops a sugar cube in his mouth and chews on it as if it were a cracker. The General is the only person Kam has ever seen do this. A few times he has seen the man eat entire bowls of sugar cubes and once Kam even dared to suggest, from his long experience as a dentist, that the General give it up. But, for a man who asks so many questions, the General is also a terrible listener. He eats one more, licks a few grains from the corner of his mouth, and says, "You have confessed, yes. And what a list, eh? Sowing corruption on earth. Serving as a witting agent for the Zionist Entity. Breaking-and-entering. Robbery. Impersonating an official of the Islamic Republic. Wire fraud. Assault. Accomplice to murder. Fornication." He begins to chew on another sugar cube and stares down Kam with the look of a man who despises fornicators because he desperately wants to be one. "You will write it again. And you will leave nothing out. It will be comprehensive, and final."

Final? Kam considers another question. The General's silent gaze screams: *Do not.*

"You will be clear on the chronology," the General says. "You will be more careful than last time." Kam knows that one of the surest roads to punishment is to throw fog around what happened when. The man is a real stickler for dates.

Kam nods, and makes it a nice, meek one.

Then the General motions to the camera hung in the corner.

It has been at least a year since the General's last request for testimony; since then, Kam has worked diligently to forget the more painful parts, the ones that lock him in the past, in fantasies of endings he will never write.

Colonel Salar Askari, one of the General's underlings, enters the room. He wears a patch over his left eye. Bizarrely it very nearly matches the color of his own skin, but that is only one of the reasons Kam does not like to look at him, and it's not even close to the top. Around Askari floats the smell of rosewater and a predilection for forms of violence that in most places would be seen as sadism but here are treated more like paintings, with great potential for innovation and beauty. The muscles in Kam's arms and legs and back clench tight, but then he sees that Askari's hands are mercifully free of pipe, razors, cords, mystery creams, knives, leashes, terrariums, belts, vials, bags, rodent traps, sandpaper, or—the darkest possibility—lugging a bucket of water.

Unless it is contained in a small rubber cup, Kam no longer likes water. There's been unpleasantness with water. In here, certainly, thanks to Askari's buckets, big enough to submerge your head but not so big that there's room to move it around. But more than anything, water reminds Kam of how he got here. And most days he'd take the General's pipe over thoughts about that.

Instead of a bucket, Askari is carrying a thick stack of A4 paper and a shoebox filled with crayons, all the same shade of dark blue. Crayons are used for the writing drills because it is tricky to kill yourself with one. Kam suspects it is not impossible, though, and in his first grim months he nearly summoned the courage to give it a try. He might attempt it now, but for the knowledge that however they choose to kill him, it will be swifter, gentler, and far more certain than jamming a sharpened blue crayon into his eye socket, face-planting into the table, and plunging it into his brain. Also, now he's got the spoon.

To his relief, the General dismisses Askari. Then he says, "Remember: this is your masterpiece, your magnum opus, your Nobel Prize winner."

The General has variously accused Kam of representing the intelligence services of Israel, America, Britain, and Sweden. Kam finds the Nobel mention, with its nod to Sweden, land of his childhood, a good sign. The General tends to be less violent when he pretends to be interrogating a Swede. Kam's optimism soars when he remembers that the Nobel cannot be awarded posthumously, and then, not for the first time, he realizes he's overthinking it. That happens a lot in here. He's got way too much time.

The General stands and claims one more cube. Kam hears the crunching of teeth on sugar and then the click of the door and the man is gone. Kam sorts through the box for a good crayon. Three years of writing, and he's got standards. It's the one spot in his life where he's got some control, so he's developed strong opinions on the proper tools for a confession. The crayon must be long enough. No nubs! When your big toenail is the crayon sharpener you don't want to look at the nubs any longer, much less be forced to write with one. So it cannot be dull from the start. But it also cannot be so sharp as to risk a premature fracture. After Kam finds the one, he slides a piece of paper off the stack.

The first drafts, right after his capture three years ago, were utter shit, like all first drafts. To call them stories would be like calling the raw ingredients spread across your counter a meal. No, they were just a bunch of facts. Information wrung from his tortured lips and committed to bloodstained sheets of A4. But he knows he's being too hard on himself. As a dentist, his writing had been limited to office memorandums and patient notes. As a spy, his cables adopted similarly clinical tones.

Just the facts, Glitzman, his handler, the man who'd recruited him to work for Mossad, liked to say. Leave the story to someone else.

Mossad had preferred he write in English, not Swedish. The General, of course, demands that he write in Persian. And it is in Persian that Kam has found his voice.

In those early months the torture and the writing were coiled together. When Kam was tortured, or deprived of sleep, or put into small boxes, he fantasized about writing, and when he was writing, he fantasized about torture. That hothouse produced the story. Or, more accurately, the stories. Kam has written his confession so many times that he's developed a few different styles.

His first attempt at offering more than just the facts was a piece of faux-literary garbage that dragged on for about two crayons before an editorial session in the Chicken Kebab set him straight. Sometimes you get to finish the stories, and other times they finish you.

There is a spy version, of course. He hadn't read much spy fiction before becoming a spy, but he'd binged crime thrillers and figured the guts of the two genres were probably not so different. The General was very determined to get the spy story out of him straightaway—that is why the literary attempt drew such fury. The spy stuff is what the General wants most of all, and Kam's polished it to pure gold over who knows how many drafts.

There is also a love story, though lots of it is made up. That one can easily devolve into supermarket erotica, with multiple romances strewn across scenes as toe-curlingly salacious as they are pure joy to write. Though the General demands the spy story above all, Kam believes part of the reason he is still alive is that the General enjoys these spicier offerings.

As time went on, Kam grew foolhardy, and one week got a good many crayons into a Scandi crime version. Though the political and social commentary was appropriately sharp, and the crime at its center was darkly warped, the General did not appreciate that Kam had written in the first person from the General's perspective as the investigator. A visit from Askari dashed all hopes of completing the draft.

The storytelling, though, was not the only blade to sharpen, so to speak. Kam's fingers would shake constantly, rendering the handwriting illegible, he often bled on the papers, and would forget the basics—no page numbers, for instance. That incensed the General, who said it was a great disappointment to his readers. Kam was soon flogged to new levels of professionalism and clarity in his writing.

Now the cell becomes Kam's scriptorium. In his dragging, tedious Persian script, he writes the Quranic inscription, "*IN THE NAME OF GOD, HONESTY WILL SAVE YOU,*" across the top of the cover page. Kam knows that the General appreciates this self-talk reminder right up front. Beneath it Kam titles this as the first part of his sworn confession and then signs his name. Someone will fill in the date later, because, though he does not know the date today, he also knows not to ask. The General's men will fill in the location, for their own files. He writes the number one in the top left corner.

But which story should he tell?

The General said it was to be his masterpiece. Perhaps the best of each, he thinks. Though not Scandi crime. If this is to be the last thing he writes, it cannot be as a Swede, because he fucking hates Sweden. He would also like to write something the General will let him finish. He would like to reach the end.

The end.

Across hundreds of drafts, no matter the type of story, Kam has only managed to write one version of the end. It is the part he fears the most.

Someday, he has told himself, someday he will write a new beginning to the bleakness of the end. Will he find it here, on this last attempt? A prisoner can dream, he thinks.

As always, Kam completes a final ritual before he starts this draft.

He imagines writing down his last remaining secret, in crayon, on one of these A4 sheets right in front of him.

One secret.

Three years in captivity, Kam has held on to only one.

Then he pictures a wooden cigar box. He slides the paper with the secret inside. In the early days of his captivity, he locked the real secret written on imaginary paper in the imaginary cigar box into an imaginary safe, but the General's men broke into every physical safe in his apartment, and Kam thought he should also improve his mental defenses. He now pictures the cigar box with his secret incinerated on a monstrous pyre, the light and heat so fierce that every dark corner of his brain burns bright as day. This way Kam's not lying when the General asks him if he's been truthful. If the story is complete. He's written it all down, has he not? The prisoner cannot be held responsible for how management handles the papers.

Kam presses the crayon to the paper and begins.

النجاه فی الصدق
بخش اول از شهادت‌های من

.... Number
.... Date
.... Attachment

The power
is with
those who resist
1979

The Islamic Republic of Iran

In the name of God
Honesty will save you
The **first** part of my sworn confession
    Kamran Esfahani

CHAPTER 1

Tehran, Iran

Four years ago

MY ANCESTORS BEGAN their journey to Persia as slaves. We left as dentists.

Though it must be said, General, that dentistry is its own form of slavery, even if its entanglements are more benign. When I returned to Iran, I was still a dentist, but it was really more of a cover. I had high hopes of making myself something more.

THE NIGHT BEFORE I conspired in a kidnapping was nine months to the day before I was kidnapped myself. Though, General, regarding the latter, I know that you prefer the term *apprehended*.

That evening I swung into the bedroom of the hotel suite, three glasses of Mr. Chavez Blended Special Whisky in hand. Anahita stood to fetch her clothes while Amir-Ali lit his pipe. He was sprawled across the bed, and the sheets were stretched across his chest, the rest of him uncovered and hairy. Anahita was what the mullahs called a "special" woman, or temporary wife. She was Amir-Ali's favorite, and we were celebrating because it was his birthday. We were also blowing off some steam because the next day we had to help with the kidnapping. It wasn't our first time, but still: It's kidnapping. In the run-up it can be hard to think about anything else.

Amir-Ali made no move for the drink, so I stood there, glasses in hand, watching Anahita sort through the pile of her discarded clothes. She moved slowly, seemingly disinterested in putting them back on. Amir-Ali took a long drag of opium. The habit is far more common among older men in the countryside, but my friend was a passionate collector of all vice, no matter how alien. I distributed the whiskey. Amir-Ali pronounced it Iraqi piss, though he still downed half of it in the first gulp.

I took a seat in one of the chairs by the bed. Anahita, apparently deciding against the clothes, joined me, taking a seat in the facing chair. She crossed her legs and gave me a look laced with suggestion and mischief, the sort of practiced stare that had doubtless prompted many men to lose small fortunes. I might have, too, if I'd had one. Chip in on a few more kidnappings, and I'd be on my way.

"A mullah finishes a sermon on the merits of good hijab," I said, forcing myself to look Anahita in the eyes. "Covering your head is a badge of honor. A sign of your obedience to Allah. On and on. It's a long sermon."

Amir-Ali put his head back on the pillow and shut his eyes with a snort. He always liked this one.

I continued, "After the sermon, a woman runs up to the mullah and says, I'm so pious, I even wear the hijab inside my own home. How will I be rewarded? And the mullah tells the woman that the keys to Paradise are yours. And right behind this woman there is another."

"Of course there is," Anahita cooed.

"And this second woman says to the mullah, Sir, I wear the chador. I even wear it in my own home. I wear it to sleep. And the mullah says that she will also be given the keys to Paradise."

"Is there a third woman, my friend?" Amir-Ali asked, momentarily lost behind a cloud of smoke.

"There is a third woman," I said. "She is last in line to speak with the mullah. And she says, Sir, I don't bother with any of it. When I'm at home I strut around naked. And the mullah says, Madam, here are the keys to my house!"

Amir-Ali belly-laughed, sending more smoke our way. Anahita was also laughing as she stood up, stretching provocatively. This time I could not look away. Catching my eyes, she grinned: "I like the last woman."

There was a rough knock on the hotel room door.

The kind of knock that in Tehran immediately has you thinking about where the exits are. "Guidance Patrol, open up." The voice was gruff.

We all looked at each other. The Hanna was a favorite haunt in Tehran. We'd given the usual "tip" to the guy at the front desk and shown him the temporary marriage certificate to allow us upstairs with Anahita in tow, no problems. So what was this?

"Guidance Patrol," Amir-Ali muttered. "What the hell are they doing here? They're supposed to be on the streets."

"Maybe someone downstairs reported us," Anahita whispered.

I offered a bewildered shrug. Amir-Ali began hiding the pipe. Anahita hurriedly pulled on her clothes. I flung open a window to help with the smell and then hustled to the door. "Yes?" I asked.

"Open the door now!"

I did as the voice asked and was greeted by two men wearing the dark green uniforms and black berets of the Guidance Patrol. They were staring, wide-eyed, at Anahita, who'd drifted into the living room behind me. "What's going on?" I demanded.

"Who is this?" the smaller guy said, jerking his chin toward Anahita. His wispy beard and baby face made the uniform seem absurd.

Amir-Ali, clothed but reeking of opium, came to the door and assumed his power stance. "She is my wife," Amir-Ali said.

Oh boy, I thought.

"And who are you?" the smaller officer demanded.

"I am a surgeon," Amir-Ali said. "Here—" He pulled out a business card and his ID and waved them in front of the taller guard's stubbly face. "Have a look at this. My name is Amir-Ali Mirbaghri. *Doctor* Amir-Ali Mirbaghri."

"Mirbaghri..."

"Mirbaghri!"

He just kept on repeating his name, hoping it would register, because one of his brothers was a bigwig in the Interior Ministry, to which the Guidance Patrol reported. Another brother did something inside the Central Bank. The third was a judge. His sister had married an up-and-comer in Tehran's mayoralty. Amir-Ali, after losing his medical license, had been trying to make money for this well-known clan—times had been tough as of late—but the downside of his backstage role was that these two Guidance Patrol goons had no clue who he was.

"Let's have your IDs," the tall officer said to me and Anahita. The two officers studied the papers and then the tall one studied me. "You are a Jew, yes? This name isn't Jewish"—he smacked my national card—"but there is something about you . . . I don't know. I can feel it."

Before I could respond, the small guy was waving documents at Amir-Ali: "You said you are married. Yet this woman doesn't have your name."

"*Sigheh* marriage," Amir-Ali said smugly. "Just for tonight."

The drink and opium had made my friend forget that it was my name on the temporary marriage certificate, not his. The drugs had also apparently convinced Amir-Ali that he had the certificate in his jacket pocket. He patted for a while and then turned sheepishly to me. Anahita put her face in her palms. From my own pocket I removed the forged certificate and then handed it to the tall guy. One look at the names, and he bared his teeth into a nasty smile while handing the paper to his comrade.

"Well, well," he said, leering at Anahita. "Hello, Mrs. Whore."

The short guy took a threatening step toward Amir-Ali and tore the certificate to shreds right in front of his face. Then he looked around at each of us. "A Jew, a whore, and an opium addict."

An opening to a bad joke. And, unfortunately, true.

"A shameless breach of public morals," the tall one snarled, glancing at Anahita, then forlornly into the bedroom, like a man left out.

"He's not a Zionist," Amir-Ali said, gripping me resolutely by the shoulder. "He's not even really a Jew." Apparently, my friend believed this to be the most serious of the three labels, the one to nail down first. I did wonder where his rebuttal was going, but he never got the chance to explain. The short guy, who had wandered into the bedroom, now returned along with the handle of whiskey and a triumphant smile. Alcohol meant not only fines or jail time, but lashings.

Amir-Ali was shouting that this was a quiet evening of backgammon among friends, what the hell was going on anyhow, and didn't they know who he was? They responded by way of bagging his head. They cuffed me and Anahita, and before they could get the hoods on us, I caught a glance of her stoic face. She'd been arrested before, she knew the drill. And then she disappeared as one of the officers slipped a hood on me. In the darkness I heard Amir-Ali droning on about the backgammon. Then it was light again, and the taller guard was tossing my hood to the floor before yanking off Amir-Ali's.

"Backgammon, you say?" he asked. "Show me the board. Who was playing?"

I wasn't sure whether to laugh or cry. Amir-Ali looked to me. I don't know what my eyes must have said, so I murmured, "Second drawer down, under the TV."

The tall officer bulled across the room and retrieved the board that the hotel kept there. "Why is it in a drawer, then?"

Anahita's chin drooped to her neck. She made a strange noise.

"We finished playing before you knocked," Amir-Ali said, with the confidence of a practiced liar. "Just a few minutes ago, in fact."

The tall guy ran a hand across the case. What he saw on his palm made him smile. He made a fist and brought it close to Amir-Ali's face. My friend's nose twitched, from fear or irritation, I did not know. The officer unfurled his hand and blew a cloud of dust into Amir-Ali's eyes.

CHAPTER 2

Tehran

WE RODE IN hooded darkness and silence broken only by Amir-Ali's occasional protestations. We couldn't see where we were, but after maybe a half-hour ride in a Guidance Patrol van, Anahita was separated from us, and we were hustled into a building that smelled of dust and ancient photocopiers. When the hoods finally came off, Amir-Ali and I were in a windowless room, seated across the table from the two officers. On it was a regulation one-meter-long leather whip and a Quran. Something inside a large bucket on the floor had caught the short guy's attention. I peered over and saw the bucket was teeming with cockroaches.

"What the fuck is this?" Amir-Ali said. He was also looking at the bucket.

"If we properly arrest and try you," the tall officer said, "you'll be given ninety-nine lashes apiece for the drinking. Guaranteed. The judge will sort out the fornication."

"What about my wife?" Amir-Ali said. I was proud of my friend. Stick to your guns, I thought. Good for you.

"Your whore," the short one said, "will be dealt with separately."

"But why have it all processed formally?" the tall guy said, then he smiled at the roach bucket. "Let's instead do fifty lashes and you each stick your head in that bucket for a few minutes."

Amir-Ali looked at the whip and the bucket and then the tall guy. "Are you serious?"

"Where's Anahita?" I heard myself say.

"The whore is elsewhere," the short one said.

"How much do you want for a tip?" Amir-Ali said. "Let's settle this and be done."

The short one leaned forward and said, "You're in too deep for that. This is beyond money."

"Beyond money," Amir-Ali shouted incredulously. "Are you insane?"

They did look insane, I must admit. They looked like a couple guys who were going to have a hell of a time flogging us.

Amir-Ali's desperation sharpened to anger: "If you want to play it this way, you're both going to lose your jobs. You think I was inventing my brother at the Interior Ministry? And then, once you're on the street, I'm going to find you and take your balls. You are making a huge mistake. So how about this: You let us go, plus the girl, and you keep your balls, eh? I have ways of getting to you people."

The officers, undeterred and tiring of Amir-Ali's threats, decided that he'd volunteered to go first. But, perhaps a bit queasy about the prospect of jamming a man's head into a writhing mass of insects, the tall officer picked up the whip and tucked the Quran into his armpit.

The short one stood Amir-Ali up, stripped off his shirt, and made him kneel, facing the wall. I sat there, frozen, as he begged for mercy at the top of his lungs.

"Fifty lashes," the tall one pronounced. "Half-price." And now Amir-Ali was hollering about lawyers and judges and the tall one was saying that's the point, we're going to save the lawyers and judges the trouble. I was so entranced I didn't even hear the cell door open. A woman in a black chador swept by me. She took a position between the officers, right behind Amir-Ali, who had not stopped shouting. The woman raised a leg to expose her studded Valentino heels. She stuck one into Amir-Ali's upper back, as if requiring leverage for the flogging to come. She withdrew something, pink and poufy, from inside her chador.

"This is for your corruption," the tall one said. "For your sins, Amir-Ali Mirbaghri."

The woman lashed her poufy whip across Amir-Ali's back. He was tense, twitching, waiting for pain that never did come. "One," she said, imitating the low voice of a man. Then she dangled the whip over his head so the pink poufs bounced through his field of vision.

"Happy birthday," I cried out. I stood and smacked Amir-Ali's bare back. "Happy birthday, you sinner. You sower of corruption on earth."

The two officers also laughed.

Anahita laughed. Amir-Ali spun around, looked at me, then up at Anahita in disbelief. He laughed, at first in relief, then in joy. Pure joy.

Back then, before all that was to come, I could laugh at such things. The maw of your Islamic Republic chewed up other people, not us. Jokes and sporting fun are possible at such a distance. No longer, of course. But that night none of us stopped laughing for a very long time.

WE ALL WENT BACK to Amir-Ali's place and kept the party going, though this time, with Anahita in the car, we kept our eyes peeled for the actual Guidance Patrol. We all had whiskeys in Amir-Ali's garden, and I settled up with the two guys while Amir-Ali and Anahita retreated for another romp in the bedroom. They were wannabe actors, currently employed at my favorite bakery, probably homosexuals, and I told them—quite honestly—that I thought they had great potential. Two gay bakers had managed to impersonate the fanatical floggers of the Guidance Patrol. "Great things," I told them. "I foresee great things for you."

Near dawn, after we'd bidden Anahita farewell, Amir-Ali filled our glasses once more and said he had something to show me. We went out through his courtyard, the trees covered in a thin layer of Tehran's smog brought low as dust. In his garage he flicked on the lights and I saw that he was beaming.

I whistled and jokingly smacked his shoulder. "You shouldn't have."

He laughed, running his hand over the silver hood. He thunked open the driver's door. "A gift to myself."

"It's beautiful," I said. And it was. The coachline was a delicate blue, there were four proud rear exhausts, its shoulder line was sharp and well-defined, and the rear lamps, I saw, floated in the visual trickery of a transparent panel. Like Mirbaghri himself, with his scattered streaks of gray hair, the car sported only the gentlest whispers of patina: wrinkled, faded leather on the seats, a few places where the light glinted off the imperfections of dents. But mostly it was a thing of beauty.

"It's a Khamsin," Mirbaghri said, sitting in the front seat like a little boy, " '72."

"Khamsin," I said, letting the name gently roll off my tongue.

Amir-Ali smiled. "Named for an Egyptian desert wind. Guess who owned it."

"The Ayatollah," I said immediately, and with confidence. "He drove it to the airport in Paris on his way to Tehran. I've seen the videos."

Mirbaghri's confusion melted into a long laugh when he caught a glimpse of my eyes. I bent down for a better look inside. The interior was all blue. The dash was edged in blue leather and trimmed in gray. Below was an absolute riot of switches, slide controls, vents, and knobs that resembled the cockpit inside an Apollo space capsule.

He brought the engine to life. It was throaty; a deep, sonorous hum.

"This was part of the Shah's imperial garage," Mirbaghri said, his hands caressing the steering wheel. "The headlights pop up. Hydraulics. Look."

He flipped them up. The beams brightened the white stone walls of the garage.

"Are we going for a ride?" I asked.

"I'm too drunk," he said, quite sadly, and killed the engine. "It's a bitch to drive here in the city. But on an open road? Paradise."

"You should be saving your cash," I said. "What would Glitzman say?"

"He'd scold me, too. He'd ask how anyone would think a failed doctor could afford such a thing."

"And?"

"I'm too alive for this place," Amir-Ali said, his hand stroking the wheel. "You've got your California dream. I've got right now."

"What you've got is a problem holding on to money," I said.

With a chuckle he wrapped his palm around the stick. "First you channel Glitzman, now my maman. Shame on you. Plus, once you buy a place in California, why would I need to? I'll just sleep on your couch when I visit. How close are you to the number?"

"Two more years," I said. "Give or take."

We exchanged a quick glance that said, *If we make it*, and we broke eye contact because that was a grim and pointless subject, and why spoil the afterglow of a fine evening?

Amir-Ali whistled, rapped his fingers on the wheel, and lurched unsteadily out of the car. "Let's go inside for some tea. Sober up and toast the morning. We've got a big day." I helped him stand, and took a good long look at the Khamsin, though it was really more of a leer. A fantasy gripped me: I am driving this car, southbound along the Pacific Coast Highway. The windows are down. The air is silky, the palms stooped and proud all at once. Dusk burns orange and pink and the sea is glass. There is a woman beside me, faceless as she is beautiful. I am listening to the engine's mellow voice, the road and its possibilities opening before me.

With a chuckle at my obvious lust, Amir-Ali killed the garage lights.

IN THE KITCHEN I put water on for tea and camped at the counter with my phone. I clicked into my calculator app, the one Glitzman's people had loaded onto my phone during our training in Albania the previous year. I entered a seventeen-digit alphanumeric code which opened the partitioned hard drive.

"What does Glitzman have to say?" Amir-Ali asked, laying out a spread of flatbread, white cheese, and jam.

I read the short message. "We're on," I said, thinking I'd have to pass on the tea because there were threads of nausea coiling in my throat.

As if mirroring my thoughts, the kettle began to scream.

CHAPTER 3

Tehran

THE MORNING OF THE KIDNAPPING, the weather was so pleasant, Tehran's usually smoggy skies so clear and open to the mountains, that after cleaning up at home I decided on a leisurely walk to my dental practice.

I often consider Tehran my foster home because it has kicked me around so much. But the analogy doesn't quite work because I was actually born here. It is my native home, even if I am a Persian Jew raised in Sweden, and even if by that sunny morning ten thousand American dollars were flowing monthly to an escrow account established by a maze of shell companies created by the State of Israel.

And, quite honestly, Tehran is more alive than any home I've ever known.

It is hewn into the mountains, obnoxiously loud, and covered by a jagged skin of brutalist buildings. It smells of smoke and diesel. Developed haphazardly, growing in disorganized spurts, Tehran, like most of us, lacks any coherent center. And like us, it is also unpredictable. That morning I hoped the city would behave otherwise. That things would go to plan.

The breeze meant the smell of diesel and dust was instead baking bread, ripe fruit, and dried herbs piled in stall baskets. I passed a Super Star Fried Chicken and then crossed under one of the government-funded billboards urging Tehran's bitchy citizens to stop bitching so much. This one read: LET'S NOT SPEND SO MUCH TIME DISCUSSING SOCIETY'S PROBLEMS IN OUR HOMES. But where else, really, could we complain? Not out here in the street, that's for sure.

The buildings around my practice were that classic Tehrani jumble of concrete slabs, gaudy marble, and the occasional faux-Grecian pillars. My office was the concrete slab varietal, enlivened by a few scrawny sycamores that stood sentry along the sidewalk. Amir-Ali was working on a cigarette outside.

We went in and headed straight for the storage room. It was Friday, first day of the weekend, and the place was empty.

During one of our meetings in Sweden, before I'd opened the practice in Tehran, I'd drawn the proposed office layout on a napkin, and Glitzman had asked where the storage room would be, and how large. What size crates might it hold? What, he asked, would you say is the capacity? And I'd pointed to where we might install supply closets and he'd shaken his head and said that won't do at all.

And so exam room three had become storage space. None of my employees had the key. I unlocked the room and we went inside and shut the door behind us. On the floor were a dozen or so boxes that had arrived in recent weeks. All were covered in shipping labels denoting European points of origin (Brussels, Paris, Frankfurt) and if anyone had bothered to investigate the sender, they would have found them to be dental suppliers with legitimate, if rather sparse, websites. Some of the packages had been delivered through the actual post. Others by unmarked vans at strange hours near an industrial park on the eastern rim of Tehran, where either I or Amir-Ali would duly collect them. I'd invented alibis for what might be inside based on the shape and weight, imagining conversations with a curious hygienist who might spot them, or, worse, with a nosy inspector arriving to make trouble for a bribe. Oh yes, sir, that bulky one there is a stool. That smaller one is a new chair-mounted kit for exam room two, here, I can show you, yes, the one in there is getting old . . .

As I peeled open the flap of the first box, I saw the glint of gunmetal and that nausea again began to climb my throat. I wasn't exactly thrilled to be part of anything kinetic, to use a term Glitzman was fond of. Amir-Ali peered over my shoulder and whistled. There were five guns packed tightly inside. AK-47s or some variant.

In another box we found the banana-shaped magazines, hidden in individual brown packaging. There was a satellite phone in another. A case with vials of a clear liquid and syringes. Handguns. Another box with the magazines. Four cattle prods. Three sets of license plates with Tehrani registration. I did appreciate that they were pre-weathered, splattered in mud. There were three first-aid kits. A box of push-to-talks. A Toughbook laptop. Body armor. An assortment of duffel bags and a Pelican case. Microphones. Three webcams. Following the instructions in Glitzman's cable, we packed everything up and then locked the storage room.

Both of us wanted a smoke, but Glitzman had told us not to loiter around outside, so we went into my office, where I had an ample supply of duty-free Swedish *snus*, and dipped while we waited. Stuffing one of the packets against my gums, I looked at Amir-Ali and could tell we were thinking the same thing.

We should have asked Glitzman for a raise.

THE OFFICE LINE RANG a few minutes later. When I picked it up I heard three clicks.

Amir-Ali and I went downstairs into the parking garage. The opening roller door slowly revealed an idling gray van, which clipped inside soon as it could, parking near the white Toyota van and the Peugeot sedan that Amir-Ali and I had bought two weeks earlier at Glitzman's behest, in cash, from a smuggler out in Kerman.

Two Israeli women I did not know hopped out, both cloaked in chadors. I pegged them for Persian Jews, like me. They gave us aliases; only later would I learn their true names and scraps of their biographies. The short one with gunfighter eyes was Rivka Sadegh; she was Glitzman's favorite, a bruiser, a Persian Jew of the self-loathing varietal. The tall woman, lean and beautiful with cheekbones high as heaven, was Yael. Next came her husband, Meir, who would ride with me and, I presumed, manage the eventual interrogation once our target, one Captain Ismail Qaani, fell into our grip.

The two Kurdish brothers in the front seat had trained with me and Amir-Ali in Albania.

Aryas, the driver, greeted me with his typical serious demeanor twinged with bitterness—scar of having recently lost the love of his life to another man back in Erbil. Unbuckling his seat belt, he stepped down from the van. I handed him keys for the Toyota that Amir-Ali and I had secured.

Kovan, his brother, was not one for seat belts. He was thick, in the transitional decade where he was no longer muscular, but not yet truly fat. When we opened the back of the van to toss in one of the Pelican cases, Kovan snickered when I startled at the sight of a dead goat wrapped in plastic. Kovan was a man who took pleasure in others' discomfort—the sort who relish eating sandwiches in front of the family dog, or who don't warn you about dead goats in the backseat.

Glitzman, finished barking in Hebrew over a satphone in the van, now jumped out and greeted us.

Glitzman. What to say of Arik Glitzman, the man who recruited me? By then I'd come to learn that he was Chief of Mossad's Caesarea Division, the group responsible for sowing chaos and mayhem in Iran.

Glitzman was rather Napoleonic, short and paunchy with a thatch of black hair and a round face bright with a wide smile. There was fun in his eyes and if they had not belonged to a secret servant of the State of Israel, they might have belonged to a magician, or a kindergarten teacher. Nothing in his mouth was really straight; his front teeth, the implants, were blazing white, while the rest were quite stained. I had assumed the implants to be the result of an accident, perhaps a tumble down the stairs, and only later would I learn I was half right: it had been stairs, but he'd been pushed. Also the stairs had been in Dubai.

"You feel good?" he asked. Though we had everything planned, Glitzman was fond of looking his assets—people like me and Amir-Ali—in the eyes before a collective leap off the cliff.

"I feel good," Amir-Ali said, putting on his body armor.

"And you?" Glitzman asked. "All good?"

"I feel how I feel," I said.

"And how is that?"

"Ready to get on with it."

"Are you going to be okay?"

"I'll be fine," I said. "But I'd like to know why we're after him."

"What's the point of you knowing?"

"I'll feel better."

Glitzman gave me a piteous look bleeding to anger. "That's what the money is for. Keep your eye on the work, and soon enough you'll have your waves and sun and surfer girls. Let me keep it simple for you. I'll handle the questions." He'd begun smiling, but it was one I did not like.

"Something," I said. "Give me something, Arik." I unzipped my jacket to slide on my body armor.

"Something would be nice," Amir-Ali said, "for a change."

For a moment Glitzman watched the two women inspect the cattle prods. At the zap of electricity he turned to us and said, "Captain Ismail Qaani, as you know, is a member of the Qods Force. A new group called Unit 840. It's run by a colonel named Ghorbani. His unit is out to kill Jews. I'm out to stop him."

Glitzman walked us a few paces away from the van while the team loaded the gear. His arm was on my shoulder, and he spoke to both of us with the intensity he can muster for conversations when he wants you to believe there's no one else in the world but you and him. "Captain Qaani has been tasked with supporting operations to kill Jews in Turkey and Europe. And we'd like to ask him a few questions about that."

"How do you know?" I replied, and immediately wished I hadn't. Glitzman treated me to a look of sadness bordering on condescension.

"Special collection," he said, and hit my shoulder, flashing that same unkind smile.

All of us huddled briefly around the vans, and we went through it all once more. Meir ran a final check to confirm that the feeds from the cameras hidden in the blue Peugeot were linked to the Toughbook that Glitzman would operate from the back of the Toyota. I was going to drive the Peugeot, Meir my passenger. Our job was to pull off the road right by the patch of scrub in the roundabout, the one I'd been studying so intently that it had begun appearing in my dreams.

As we finished loading everything, I caught a final glimpse of goat hooves entombed in plastic. Glitzman, monitoring the target's phone from a tablet he'd brought with him, barked that it was time.

The three engines kicked to life. Meir and I went first, in the Peugeot laden with hidden cameras. Amir-Ali drove the gray van, Kovan beside him, the two Israeli women wearing chadors and sporting cattle prods behind, alongside the goat carcass, a couple buckets of blood, and most of the guns. Aryas drove the Toyota with Glitzman and his command center, link to unseen masters in Tel Aviv, hidden in back. We clipped out of my parking garage and set off to kidnap a bad man bound for a pleasant weekend with his family in the countryside. A few more of these, and soon enough I'd be trading the thrilling anxiety of espionage and the tedium of dentistry for the warmth of the California sun.

My midlife crisis was shaping up nicely, I thought.

CHAPTER 4
Tehran / Absard

THE JOURNEY TO ABSARD wove through a landscape of brown-green hills and mountains, some wrinkled and naked, others thatched with scrubby bushes and trees. Wispy clouds scudded along an otherwise brilliant blue sky, untainted by smog, and I imagined Glitzman pronouncing the weather perfect for a kidnapping. Not a single reason for Qaani to stay in his car, he would say, or something like it. Traffic was light, mostly families on their way to weekend picnics or hikes, and I was glad no one I passed paid us much mind, because I was white-knuckled and sweaty for most of the ride, feeling that if anyone looked me up and down they'd have reasons to think I'd just fled some gruesome crime scene back in the capital. Wrong, I thought (and even then the thought felt insane). I'm *going* to the crime scene, not *coming* from it.

Meir and I did not exchange more than a few words but there was a softness to him, a candle of amusement brightening his face, and in less awful circumstances we'd have found much to share. While I drove, in his flawless Persian Meir occasionally mumbled shreds of Rūmī and Hafez, the poets my mother had read to me when I was very young. Meir ejected each verse with his arms pretzeled across his chest, searching the scrubby hills and passing orchards for enemies that never did show themselves.

The drive took ninety minutes. It felt like a thousand. I spent a lot of it thinking about Captain Qaani, who at this point I knew well from the surveillance package we had assembled over the past few months. He was a workaholic, but at home he was affectionate and attentive to his family. He had two younger brothers and their WhatsApp thread was full of what I found to be genuinely hilarious ribbing and fraternal comradery. He despised Israel, Zionism, and, more particularly, Jews. According to Glitzman's special collection he was working feverishly to kill more of us.

Captain Qaani also liked to take his wife and two sons to their home in Absard for the weekends. He was not senior enough for a bodyguard or security detail, and, critically, Qaani liked to drive himself. The family always took the same route.

All along this route Aryas and Glitzman had duly—and clandestinely—followed, keeping the vehicle in sight the entire way. Meir and I stayed well ahead, out of view.

Outside Absard I pulled the Peugeot onto a patch of dirt at the far end of a roundabout the Qaanis would whirl through in... I checked the time... an hour. Maybe an hour fifteen depending on bladders. I positioned the car so the cameras snuggled into the left rear brake light, headrest, and dash would have clean views of the road. Meir clicked the push-to-talk three times and received three in return.

"Back up about two meters," Meir said. I did, and once they'd run the checks and confirmed the view, I sat there on my phone until four cars had gone by, and Glitzman was satisfied that the angles worked. Then Meir and I put the sedan up on the jack, waving off a kindly older man's offer to help. I wiped down the steering wheel, gearshift, console, dash. When I was done I slid on sunglasses and stood there soaking in the neighboring lemon orchard framed under the vault of blue sky. Why didn't men like Qaani just stop killing Jews? Then they could enjoy their lemons. They could watch their sons grow old. I'd have to find another way to finance my move to California, but I'd take that trade.

Four clicks on the push-to-talk this time, Meir nodded my way, and I pretended to scroll my phone while we waited. In truth I was churning through the hundred ways an op like this might go wrong, and kicking myself—again—that we'd not pushed Glitzman harder on our bonus.

Every now and then my mind wandered to the ultimate mystery: how the Kurds had gotten the poor goat.

AFTER TWENTY MINUTES Amir-Ali's van pulled to a stop beside the Peugeot. Meir and I jumped in the side door and took our seats on covered plastic buckets across from Rivka and Yael. As we turned a corner I heard liquid sloshing below me and when I looked up Yael was smiling. At the time I was a wreck, and trying desperately to hide that from everyone. I thought that if I tried a smile my lips would quiver, so I gave Yael a grim nod instead and, without another word, we began breathing through our mouths to unwrap the goat.

GLITZMAN REPORTED that the Qaani caravan was making slow time—three bathroom stops for the boys instead of the usual one—and so Amir-Ali circled the van twice through Absard on a preplanned holding route that, without traffic, required eleven minutes per loop. Halfway through our second pass, Glitzman hit the push-to-talk five times. Then he did it again.

Translation: *Get into position.*

We swirled back through the roundabout and then Amir-Ali banked the van right, down the road that led to Qaani's house. After the second speed bump, when we were about five hundred or so meters from his drive and all alone, Amir-Ali screeched the van to a halt, right on the road. For all the discomforts and sartorial sins of a chador, they are good for hiding things. Rivka and Yael's were swaddling the cattle prods.

We held there for a sticky moment while Amir-Ali and Kovan scanned for onlookers.

"We're clear," Kovan said, and ducked into the back.

I grabbed the goat's horns, Kovan its haunches, and we swung down from the van and threw the carcass under the front tires. Rivka had picked up the blood bucket I'd commandeered for a seat. She spread it on the road and across the front of the car, then she and Kovan had a quick spat over whether she'd used enough until she relented and tossed out a bit more. Plenty of details are now lost to me, some combination of time and torture, but I remember the staged bloodstain on that road clear as day because its outline bore a spooky resemblance to a map of Iran, that of a distended ovary yanked crosswise.

"Three minutes," Amir-Ali called out. Kovan popped the hood and inside turned a valve on a small canister until smoke began to leak. Then he jumped into the back with Meir. I slid into the passenger seat. Amir-Ali was in the driver's seat, door open, legs dangling outside, phone in the crick of his neck, as if he were handling the emergency call. Rivka and Yael milled outside. *Look at us*, the scene screamed, *we've had some bad luck on the road. This damn goat came from nowhere, and one of its nasty little horns plunged into some critical piece of mechanical equipment and now we're stuck.*

I remember admiring the setup, even as I was having trouble swallowing like maybe I had a few coins lodged in my throat. Amir-Ali's hand was resting on the bulge of the handgun tucked into his waistband, hidden beneath a light jacket.

Warbling through Kovan's push-to-talk came Glitzman's voice, firm and clear. The brief, garbled code meant that Qaani's car had passed my abandoned Peugeot, and that the Mossad facial recognition algorithms (or analysts) back in Israel had confirmed it was him. Even though it was *Qaani's* BMW, and even though *Qaani's* personal phone was traveling inside, I understood from Glitzman's grumbling in the cables that Mossad required visual confirmation before initiating an operation that might very likely end in a killing.

"One minute," Kovan called. He shifted into position at the back of the van, rubbery club in hand. I saw that he was smiling. Meir was mumbling verse again. Then I did not know Yael was his wife; now the anxious glances her direction make more sense, though I don't expect that from back there Meir could make out more than a patch of the black chador through the dirty pane of glass in the divider.

"One minute," Amir-Ali called out to the two women.

Did Qaani carry a gun? A weapon?—Glitzman had put the question to us in a cable responding to the first surveillance logs. We'd been looking, and we'd never seen one.

The only slower minutes I have lived have been lived in these rooms and cells. My vision narrowed to the smoke curling from the engine. I didn't even have a weapon on me—and Glitzman had good reason for that—but I felt naked, and scanned into the back for what I might use if things went sideways, but there were no good options. Plus, Meir's poetry was beginning to remind me of those scenes in war movies where some poor bastard is muttering prayers before everyone goes over the lip of a trench, or the landing craft kisses the beach, and then the doors swing open and everyone dies. I turned to face the front.

Qaani's BMW had turned right off the roundabout and was headed our way. Rivka waved him down.

He might just keep on going, Amir-Ali had said, when we'd first hatched the general concept for this snatch-and-grab.

He'll stop, I replied. He'll be with his family.

What does it matter? asked Kovan.

Tell me you're a narcissist without telling me you're a narcissist, I thought, and sighed.

Because he'll look like a prick in front of his wife and kids, I said. That's why. Imagine the conversation with his sons when they get to the house. *Why were those people stopped, Papa? Why didn't we help?*

I'd just keep on going, Kovan had said, laughing. And none of us doubted him.

Qaani's BMW crunched to a stop about ten meters from us. He and his wife exchanged a few words.

I leaned back in the seat and put my phone to my ear and loose hairs must have gotten stuck between the phone and the case, because my hand was shaking so badly it yanked a few strands right out.

Qaani stepped out. He had on a light jacket maybe a size too large. While he walked toward our van he looked back at his family—the boys had started fighting in the backseat—and put up a hand to say: *All is well. All is well.* He did look calm, and why wouldn't he? We were in his neighborhood. We were innocents with car trouble.

Amir-Ali, now approaching Qaani, had begun chattering about the crazy goat that ran into the road, how it had come from over there, how his brother had seen it first—he pointed up to me, I waved back with as much nonchalance as I could muster—and whether Qaani lived around here, and knew of any mechanics nearby who might be willing to have a look?

Down the road, maybe a few hundred yards behind Qaani, I saw Glitzman's van kicking up dust. The commotion inside the Qaani vehicle caught my attention. And it also caught Qaani's. Amir-Ali had been coaxing him closer to the dead goat and a look at the engine, with the Israeli women encircling him, but even I could see that Yael didn't look natural. Her hand was gripped outside her chador around the cattle prod beneath. What was going on inside that car? Dusk was gathering, I had to squint, and I saw that one of the boys had lofted himself over the center console from the backseat. Their mother was shouting at them to stop, and Qaani wasn't paying attention to the smoking engine any longer. He'd retreated a few steps toward the car. With his back turned, Yael was trying to retrieve the cattle prod, and my adrenaline was pounding, and time stopped moving at its normal pace. Much of the chaos I never heard or saw. Meir's mumbled poetry faded. My senses had banked into a narrow tunnel.

A horn was blaring.

When my head jerked toward the noise I saw the outline of one of Qaani's kids leaning over his mom, mashing the steering wheel. At the time I thought it was a warning, that someone had spotted Yael's cattle prod. Now I think it was horseplay.

In any case, the horn sent Kovan rushing out the back door of the van. And it sent Yael's cattle prod to the dirt. The clatter of an electrocution stick at his feet had Qaani reaching for something beneath his jacket. Rivka's chador ruffled and churned, slow-motion, Marilyn Monroe's dress in the wind, as she tried to bring the prod into Qaani's ribs. Amir-Ali was drawing his gun. What was Meir doing? Where was he? I don't remember.

In Albania we'd all been coached that in this sort of operation the margin of error was slim: it was basically whether the target's still in shock by the time you've got hands on him. One mash of the horn had turned the tables and ruined our surprise. Kovan wasn't quite there yet and Amir-Ali's gun wasn't quite out. But Qaani's was. His vision was tunneling, too, and he went for the nearest threat.

I think the first shot hit Amir-Ali high in the upper thigh, below the body armor. There was another shot. My friend fell.

At almost the same time, Yael and Rivka got their prods into Qaani's side. There was a dogpile on him, a scrum, and I couldn't make out what was happening other than to see, as I jumped out of the van, that blood was pooling around Amir-Ali's neck and head. Kovan and Meir and the two women were simultaneously zapping and zip-tying Qaani.

Glitzman's van was hurtling toward us. I was kneeling over Amir-Ali. His hand was on his neck and his eyes were moons looking up at the sky and his face was draining to the color of milk. There was a lot of blood coming out of his neck and when I looked over the rest of him I saw that there was more oozing from below his waist.

The others dragged the now-zip-tied Qaani into the van. They threw him in back, where the goat had been.

There was another gunshot, which sounded quite faint to me, and only later did I learn it was Aryas, firing a warning shot into the air to frighten off Qaani's wife from making a run at her husband. Aryas rushed over, and with one look at Amir-Ali, said: "Oh fuck, fuck, fuck."

I hauled him into the command center van, Glitzman sweeping gear aside to make room, tearing open the first-aid kit, screaming at Aryas to drive. Aryas scrambled to the front of ours, gunned the engine, and spun the vehicle around. I lost my footing, hit the back door, and nearly crashed on top of Amir-Ali.

I knelt by him again, rummaging through the first-aid kit for the syringes loaded with the cellulose sponges, the ones Amir-Ali had called tampons back in Albania—back when all of this was just plain fun. When it was a way to feel alive, make some money, and raise our middle fingers high at this sinister clown show of an Islamic Republic. Now it was my friend's blood all over the floor of a van. It was Amir-Ali looking through me with his mouth open. It was me saying that it was going to be okay, that after this we'd take the Khamsin out for a spin. We'd go see Anahita. We would—

The Interrogation Room
Location: ███████████

Present day

"I CAN'T WRITE IT AGAIN," Kam yells. "I've written it a hundred fucking times!"

He's shouting up at the cameras. Two guards burst into the room, holding clubs. Kam puts up his hands, the right one still clutching the crayon. "Please," he begs, "please."

But the interruption has the guards giddy. They've been bored as hell in that room behind the mirror, which is probably a copycat of his cell minus the locks. Now there's action. The shorter lieutenant comes at Kam. He feels the whack of the club on his back, but it's a glancing blow and not so painful. The next one connects with a kidney, and the pain is just incredible, the kind that turns piss to blood. Though all of this is somehow less awful than finishing this part of the story. The bigger one brings the club down on his back a few more times, and he's heaped there against the wall, pain riding on each breath.

There is a debate about whether to call Colonel Askari. Kam shuts his eyes and begs please no, please do not, and in the end they decide a call is more trouble than it's worth. They lug him to his cell and throw him on the floor.

"One hour," the bigger one shouts. "We'll be back in one hour."

The lights vanish as Kam crawls onto his mattress.

Moving on in the story, he thinks. Fast-forward a bit.

The next part always comes in fragments, though quite often they are out of order. Kam thinks about how he will write them down.

There is, of course, the moment when Kam realizes Glitzman is dropping him off, time to say goodbye, no need for you to risk the border. He'd spoken more gently than usual, but Kam could tell how deadly serious Glitzman was that Kam get the hell out of the van. There was a play to run. They had Qaani somewhere. They had questions for him.

There is the cinnamon, nutmeg, and walnut smell of *ferenjan*, a dish Maman made for his birthdays, which Kam cooked in his Tehran apartment that evening worried what might happen to him if he did not do *something* and it was clear he could not see anyone, should not go out. That meal usually smells like soul, but that night all he could smell was copper, all he could taste was metal. He scooped it into the garbage and gulped moonshine vodka until he blacked out.

There is the message, arriving from Glitzman next morning, encouraging (ordering) Kam to hop on a flight to Sweden, dish his patients to the hygienists for a few weeks, shutter the practice if necessary, at least temporarily. Shouldn't be hard. It's not that busy.

One day later Kam was in Stockholm, doomscrolling California real estate listings in an odd mixture of a fantasy and a reality check. Does he really need Glitzman's money? He would like to think he does not. That, after what happened in Absard, he can just walk away. But he's signed up for this in large part to finance his California dream, and if he bails now it will never begin.

And soon enough, Kam becomes distracted by thoughts of himself. He is not scraping by in a dental practice, nor is he in slushy Stockholm, anxious land of the dim black winter. He is weightless and free. He is floating into the California sun, cherishing the warmth until it consumes him. To think of anything else is to think of Amir-Ali in the back of that van, and when that happens—

Kam rolls over on the mattress in his cell.

He decides that he's going to skip some things when he returns to the writing.

First, he'll pass on describing Glitzman trying to tourniquet the leg, all the cursing and screaming that the wound was too high, near the groin. There is the frenetic call on the satphone, asking about the doctors on standby in Kurdistan or a patch-through to Tel Aviv for someone to talk them through options, though Amir-Ali's leaking blood counts down like sand rushing fast through an hourglass. Kam will skip the part where he injects that sponge-loaded syringe into the wound, praying that it quickly closes up and clots, but the bleeding doesn't stop, it barely slows. Kam now knows that the bullet nicked open Amir-Ali's carotid, but at the time he was in shock, squeezing his palm into his friend's neck, trying to keep that blood inside, but it just kept rushing out to slicken the floor. Kam will certainly leave out this detail: The ends of his shoelaces were painted by Amir-Ali's blood. Here with his eyes shut Kam's mind still rolls that film in all its bright red color.

The compress was soaked and no matter how hard he pressed, no matter how much he squeezed, blood kept on draining out. Same as the goat, the smell was coppery, and a few drops of it must have found a way into Kam's mouth, because when the memory strikes he always tastes metal. Right now, in the darkness of his cell, there is a sickening tang on the tip of his tongue.

When Kam goes back to the writing, most of all he will not write this: at the end Amir-Ali lifted a limp hand to nowhere and moved his mouth a little, trying to say something, or maybe to smile.

Kam believes now that Amir-Ali died for him. Insane? Years of thinking about it, and he's decided it's true. Kam won't have it any other way.

When he's hauled back to write again, Kam will leave all this out.

If the General asks about this part, he'll make up something lighthearted, maybe about him and Amir-Ali in the Khamsin. A drive they never did take, but one they'll finally get around to in the story. Maybe Anahita's in the backseat. They're on the Pacific Coast Highway. The windows are down. The air is silky, the palms stooped and proud all at once. Dusk burns orange and pink and the sea is glass.

What happens in this story?

Kam doesn't know yet, but he knows that whatever they get into, it'll be trouble. And this, most of all: it'll have a happy ending.

CHAPTER 5
Tel Aviv, Israel
Three years ago

ON SHABBAT AFTERNOONS Arik Glitzman took his usual nap with his daughter Oriana.

He did not sleep during these naps, he could barely sleep at night, much less in the middle of the day—it did not help that Oriana was also a restless napper—but he approached the nap with a zeal he wished he could muster for his faith or his marriage.

That particular afternoon, after the kidnapping, with Oriana breathing rhythmically beside him, Glitzman did not think of the last moments of Captain Qaani's life, after they'd finished interrogating him in that makeshift prison in Erbil. They had sweated the man for all he had, and in the end it was less than they'd have liked. They'd squeezed only a name, Hossein Moghaddam, another officer in the unit, along with yet more confirmation that those Jew-killers were now aiming for Jews inside Israel.

In those naps Glitzman did not question whether killing Qaani—or any of the others he'd killed throughout his career—had been right or wrong or made them all safer. He did not experience the numbing fear that he was one of history's last Jews, that the world Oriana should grow old into might instead be sharpening its knife for her. That it might have other ideas. When he was snuggled up with Oriana he felt less alone.

And he felt something otherwise missing from his life: a foreign mix of hope and joy. So he thought of Oriana's dance recitals. Her silken monkey-print pajamas. Her riotous smile. How she would delicately unsheath frozen chocolate from her Häagen-Dazs before moving to the ice cream. At first he had wished he might fall asleep. Rest like his daughter. But now he was grateful he did not, because instead of relishing that lack of fear, he'd waste the time sleeping. Awake, whorls of Oriana's hair a scarf on his neck, Glitzman could convince himself, for anywhere between thirty minutes and two hours, that the future was not lost. That he was not alone. That there were things to look for in this world.

Before he had married Tzipi, before Oriana, before he'd set up the Caesarea Division, Glitzman had served at the Mossad Station in the Israeli Embassy in Washington, D.C. He had spent three years among the Americans, and had been shocked—though he knew he should not have been—to find them entirely unburdened from history. The Americans he knew best possessed a rosy nostalgia about the past and a preposterous hope for the future.

When I nap next to Oriana, he thought, I am an American.

Maybe he was in Nebraska, which he had visited once, and found enchanting. The fields, the prairies, the pancake-flat land a sea of dirt and grass and cornstalks stretching away in every direction. Drive two hours and you're in Des Moines, not Damascus.

But when Oriana stirred, and the day resumed, he felt the weight of history hit him like a hammer on an anvil. He had spent his adult life hoping Israel might become a normal country, that Jews might be normal people. His uncle had said once he'd like Israel to make peace with the Palestinians and in the region so it could be treated like a boring country, like New Zealand, but given everything that had happened on the Land, it was surely too much to ask. What could you do with so much history?

He'd be up from the nap, and then he would feel tired, and Tzipi, if she noticed his yawns or his exhausted eyes, might ask what exactly he'd been doing in there for two hours that he was so spent, and he couldn't quite manage to say. She already thought him borderline insane, and he could not gift her the certainty she craved. So he'd go outside and history would roar back while he readied the grill.

Everyone had scars and stories and all were shared on the nightly television broadcasts, to reverberate, again and again, through the national psyche. Meir's nephew, a reservist, had driven a bulldozer inside Gaza for almost six months during the war until he sustained damage to his hand and leg from an explosive. When he came back, Meir said the kid couldn't return to his old construction job because he could no longer put his feet on the stairs of a bulldozer without convulsing or urinating. He also refused to eat meat, which Meir discovered when his sister confiscated the kebabs he'd brought over for a barbecue. What had the kid run over? What had he done? What had he seen? Everyone knew. No one asked.

Glitzman was not so blind as to deny the terrible destruction of Gazan life, the settlements that slowly devoured the West Bank, and yet... yet... yet he felt, above and before all, that Israel must prevail. Power brought a loss of innocence, but what would weakness bring? When Jews went to their knees, they didn't get a compromise. They got shot.

And yet, all this trauma, all this history, Glitzman, who liked to spend his Shabbat evenings in front of that grill with a beer in hand, could not help but feel that despite it all: Life went on. Life, mundane life, crashed through history. Above the layers of trauma, there was simply too much to do.

Ben Gurion Airport: open. Tourism, though deflated, waned but never did seem to dry up. Glitzman's twentysomething nephews, who had fought in the Gazan war and had returned without apparent psychological wounds, told him the clubs were still open—and they were full, Uncle, full of girls!

Pharmacies: open.

Auto mechanics: open (and Glitzman, who had just taken the family Kia in for a tune-up, could report that parts were available, lead times light-speed).

Hotels: open, though sometimes crowded with northerners, fleeing Hezbollah's rockets and missiles.

Roadways: open, though dangerous as ever. For Israelis, in war and peace and everything in between, seem to work out their demons on the nation's chaotic roads.

The salon where Tzipi had her hair cut and colored shuttered for a while, but that was only because a Palestinian boy from East Jerusalem had blown himself to bits outside the café two doors down. He'd killed only himself, but his head had rocketed through the salon window, where it came to rest on one of the chairs—or that was what her friend Fania claimed had happened. Tzipi hadn't been there, no one was harmed, other than the bomber. Two weeks later the salon reopened: glass repaired, chair replaced or bleached to hell, fresh and new. And not a day too soon, Tzipi said, running a brush through her newly blackened hair while Glitzman plated the steaks. "Did you notice how streaky and gray I've gone?"

"No, dear," he said, with conviction, for Glitzman was a man who'd seen a few traps in his time, and who understood that the deadliest were the ones laid in plain sight. She blinked, smiled, and playfully slapped his cheek just before she kissed it. Oriana came onto the patio carrying the silverware, and this time she did not drop it all.

As they sat for the meal, Glitzman was mildly embarrassed to say that, above all, he was grateful for the simple fact that while most Israelis contributed to the onward grind of daily life by practicing law or medicine, or trudging into dreary office jobs, Glitzman and his Caesarea Division cashed their checks with revenge. Their craft was targeted killings, cyberattacks, and sabotage inside Iran.

When Iranian scientists perished in mysterious explosions?

How about when Qods Force officers were tossed from fifth-floor balconies?

Or when the hard-copy documentation of Iran's nuclear progress was lifted from storage safes at a warehouse in Tehran, and carted over the border on trucks?

Yank the thread back far enough on each, and it's Glitzman wearing those sweaters. Was Israel the victim or some nouveaux colonial aggressor here? *Neither,* came the answer from his Caesarea Division. *We are killing those trying to kill us. Colonel Ghorbani is after us, so we go after him. We are doing what normal countries do when enemies strike.*

Three Directors ago, Glitzman established the unit to slow the Iranian nuclear program, and over fifteen years it had morphed into a more general-purpose instrument Israel might wield against a messianic Iranian regime intent on strangling the present incarnation of the Jewish State.

Others would doubtless consider his work strange. Glitzman did not.

If prostitution was the oldest profession, he imagined killing to be a close second, particularly the targeted variety. There was tradition here, lineage; he was fond of a story from the Book of Judges in which a woman, maybe a prostitute herself, had killed a Canaanite general by hammering a tent peg through his skull. Glitzman took pride in scarring Israel's enemies, returning what they got blow for blow. And usually far worse than that.

"Mine's undercooked, Arik," Tzipi said, holding up the slit-open flank.

"That's how a steak's supposed to look," he grumbled, "that's medium rare." Though he fought the urge to roll his eyes and duly accepted the outstretched plate to char the meat to hell the way she liked. Tzipi whispered something he did not quite catch. Oriana giggled.

When dinner was done, he sprawled on the floor and built a Lego tractor with Oriana while Tzipi drank wine and read a book on the couch. On Shabbat, Glitzman was the administrator of bedtime, and after the chaos of the bath, the second change of pajamas, and the dogged resistance to teeth-brushing, the air raid sirens felt like a relief. A time-out. They went into the safe room for a few minutes. After, Oriana surrendered to the toothbrush and they settled into the easy chair beside her bed to read a story. They were slowly working through *Watership Down,* and that night had reached a particularly gripping scene in which one of the stouthearted rabbits fights the psychotic General Woundwort in a tunnel inside the warren. Oriana had a tight grip on his arm and a few times he saw her lips shiver.

"Will the story have a happy ending, Papa?" she asked.

"I'm sure it will," he said.

"How do you know?"

He hadn't read the book, so he supposed it was possible the tale ended in the wholesale slaughter of the good rabbits, but he said, "This is the sort of story that's got a happy ending."

He kissed Oriana once more, flipped off the lights, and shut the door, careful to leave it, as agreed, cracked open. Amid those layers of loneliness and trauma, pride and determination, Arik Glitzman that night remained blissfully unaware of this seemingly mundane fact: In a safe tucked into Colonel Ghorbani's office at a pleasant home in north Tehran, Glitzman's name, and those of many of his friends and colleagues, had been put on a list labeled "Zionists Who Must Live Secretly."

Which is to say, they were marked.

CHAPTER 6

Tehran

THE WIDOW ROYA SHABANI ran freezing water over the burn while Alya drew a bird.

"You are too young to forget where you put the pencils," chided her sister Afsaneh, dropping a few pieces of *sangak* into the searing pan as though nothing had happened.

"You are too young to forget you've left on the burners," Roya snapped, watching the frigid water course over her hand.

"Nothing of the sort," her sister said, in that cheerful singsong she used to deflect all criticism, or any topic of serious conversation. "I merely stepped away."

Roya shut off the sink, dried her hands, and forced a reassuring smile at Alya, who had been frightened by her mother's pained yelp. Roya kept close watch on her daughter's terrors, and the night before had been the first since Abba's death that Alya had not woken in one.

And the truth of it? When Roya awoke after dawn and realized there'd been no visit from Alya, she had felt great loss. Yet another death of their old life, which seemed, each day, to discover new ways to die. Alya shuffled over from her seat to kiss her mother's burn before returning to her bird.

At the cooktop Afsaneh was humming a tune that Roya did not recognize. Roya wanted to tell her sister that one should not step away from hot stovetops with a five-year-old around, but what was the point?

Needless to say, Roya did not like leaving Alya with Afsaneh while she went to work. She also had no choice. She really did need the money.

The past few months had been a numbing slurry of shock and dread; the typical routine of staying in bed, or watching television with Alya, or leafing through magazines and books she would not remember, had been snapped by occasional smacks of reality that mostly made her want to crawl under the covers, shut her eyes, and vanish.

Her husband had been murdered. How could this be? Abbas was not a soldier, not a nuclear engineer. He was materials scientist! With an incomprehensible doctoral thesis on something to do with nanostructures and radar absorption to prove it.

As with so many pseudo-arranged marriages in Tehran, they'd fallen in love after they got married, their lives glued together through their shared love of books and movies and, eventually, after much trying, with the arrival of Alya two years after Roya graduated from university. By then Abbas had been recruited by his uncle. That meant she'd had less of Abbas, but there was security, there was money, and there was love.

And now?

She was the wife of a martyr, but unlike martyrs who died in impossible-to-cover-up explosions, or on some foreign battlefield, his uncle, Colonel Ghorbani, did not want to publicize what had happened. It was not good for morale to advertise that your best scientists might have their brains spilled by Zionist spies on their way to birthday dinners. Under no circumstances was she to speak of what had happened that night. Silence would cash Abbas's pension.

But gossip in Persia spreads like fungus, so within weeks even casual acquaintances—her mechanic, the widower who ran her favorite produce shop—knew that she was a widow, and a twenty-seven-year-old widow at that, a position most Persian men would consider the second most sexually predatory species of female, just behind the divorcee. Once married, a woman's chastity is no longer the responsibility of her male kin. Roya was fair game, and the propositions—for sex, dates, and marriage—had been constant. She had stopped making eye contact with men. Forget about smiling. Head down. Keep moving.

The chirp of her phone broke her thoughts. Glancing over, she saw it was a message from Hossein Moghaddam. She was not late, but still.

Roya threw on her coat. She kissed Alya on the head, told her to be good for Aunt Afsaneh. Alya insisted on a wet kiss on the lips, which Roya was happy to give. She thought of Hossein on the way. She hurried.

THE OFFICE WAS a large two-story home in Niavaran. Had Abbas lived, the Shabanis someday might have been able to afford a place in this peaceful neighborhood of leaves and wide streets and views of the Alborz, rising up like the points of a snowcapped crown. Here, on Tehran's far northern flank, Roya had always found the smog less hellish, the traffic less violent.

Roya entered the code for the front gate while a camera watched her overhead. Inside, she walked through a small, unkempt garden to the front door, where another camera stood sentry.

When Hossein had asked her to find a suitable property, she had asked what it was for, and he had not laughed, not out loud, but she had seen his face rearrange.

"Logistics," he had said. "Business." He might well have winked, so transparent was the lie.

"And you want me to find a house?" she had asked. "A residence?"

"A property for a small team," he said, "who will come and go."

"Why do you want *me* to arrange it?" she said.

"Because you are competent, and this is a highly sensitive matter. I need someone outside Qods to help me. Help us. I trust you. And Colonel Ghorbani trusts you, the wife of his martyred nephew."

Trust? She had heard nothing from the colonel since Abbas's funeral.

"We will pay you at the rate of a sixth-year administrative officer," Hossein said, "in light of your sacrifice. There would be occasional travel. Mostly to Istanbul. Maybe Dubai. But that is all for later. First, you will find a house, here in Tehran. Will any of this be a problem?"

No, she said, no, it would not. In her entire life she had left Iran only twice. The thought made her giddy. And it must have shown on her face, because Hossein would twice more mention Istanbul in particular, that his group used a lovely villa there, and that sometimes, if enough of them traveled, the women would stay there, as there were three bedrooms.

"This house you would like me to arrange," she had said. "Where should it be?"

"In a fine neighborhood, among other homes," he replied. "Far from any official buildings. With plenty of children running around."

CHAPTER 7

Tehran

ROYA'S SMALL OFFICE was upstairs. The neighbor's fence was just below her window. On the other side, young boys occasionally played or scuffled outside, pretending to shoot each other or kicking a soccer ball. Roya conducted a quick tour for a head count, then went to the kitchen to prepare tea. Each day was a collection of seemingly random jobs; she did not understand this team's purpose, nor did she really care. She enjoyed her rhythm of discrete tasks, of lists she could cross out.

Mina entered the kitchen. The woman, a few years Roya's junior, was responsible for "analytics and research" (according to Hossein). She also doubled as the house cleaner because Ghorbani had refused to allow anyone else into the property, even cleaners from one of the approved services used by Qods. He was also concerned about loose paper. They'd created separate bags for the sensitive stuff, which Mina, poor dear, was responsible each week for burning.

"Good morning," Roya said, and tried to hand the woman a cup of steaming tea.

"Why did you go through so much trouble?" Mina asked, eyeing the glass eagerly. "I could not."

"Please go ahead," Roya said. "I insist."

"I simply could not."

"I insist. I am your servant."

Mina completed the ritual *tarof* with an exclamation of her embarrassment at the kindness of Roya's cup of tea, thus completing the dishonest yet civil pleasantries, that death struggle for the lower hand that lubricates Persian social exchange and ensures that for brief snatches of time unequal people may deal as equals. Mina took a long sip of her tea and said, "I need Bitcoin. We're buying a dataset, and the seller won't take any government currency."

Roya arranged the teapot and glasses on a tray. She handled purchasing through a front company incorporated in Turkey. If someone on this team wanted to acquire something, clandestinely, and outside Iran, it fell to Roya to make the purchase. So far that had mostly meant phones, foreign currency, hotel rooms, and long-term rentals. Never crypto. Her literature courses and housewifery had prepared her for none of this. Her indentured servitude to a place that had gotten her husband killed did not sit well with Roya, nor did she enjoy long stretches away from Alya. But new problems? Figuring things out? Spending time with adults? Making Hossein happy . . .

"Hossein—" Roya began.

"He approved it," Mina cut in. "It's in your inbox."

Roya nodded. "I'll get into it this morning."

Mina finished her tea, but instead of placing the glass on the tray, she left it on the counter for Roya to clean up. Roya made a note to dump a few glasses of water in her trash can before Mina completed her rounds that afternoon.

Next Roya brought tea to Major Shirazi. His room, one of the largest in the office, was always locked, and she brought the tea regardless of whether he wanted it. A keypad had been installed on the door, and she did not have the code.

Tea tray in hand, she knocked, and called through the door, "Major?"

"Roya, why did you go through so much trouble?" Then the major carefully swung open the door to wave her in. The room—which had been a generous study—included a window but the shades were always drawn. One wall was covered in columns of servers, another by a long desk with six computer monitors, which the major and his team always flipped to blue screen savers when she brought in the tea. After they had denied their thirst, and she had insisted, the major's two lieutenants accepted. The major wore a headset with goggles. She had wondered what it was, but she knew better than to ask. Indeed, she'd yet to speak a single word to the major that was not about the tea. Today was no different.

The final stop, her favorite, was Hossein's office. His door was open. He waved her in, asked her to take a seat, have tea with him while they managed the list. She slid his cup off the tray.

"How is Alya?" he asked.

"She is well, thank you. Full of energy. Happy."

Hossein had not touched her; he had not officially propositioned her. But—and he was doing it right now—from his gaze it was plain how he felt. What she did not know was what he planned to do about it. In her experience he was a decisive man. Direct, clear, respected by the others, including Colonel Ghorbani. And what did she want him to decide?

"A few things for this morning," he said. "Maybe take notes?"

She fetched a pen and notebook from her office and returned to take a seat in front of Hossein's desk. A strand of hair had slipped from her hijab; she tucked it back in.

"The colonel is making a trip to Basra next week. He will need twenty million Iraqi dinars before he leaves. Can you get that by Monday?"

"I will handle it today. It will be done." She scrawled the command, shorthand, on her sheet, and looked up at him with what she hoped was a decisive nod.

Hossein looked at his own notes. "We will need an apartment in Paris, for two weeks, from the ninth through the twenty-third." Her heart fluttered. Would she travel to Paris? Her hopes had risen so quickly that she might have dared to ask had he not immediately shot them down.

"No prep visit will be necessary. Everything else is sorted. Just be sure that the major has the relevant details. No later than Tuesday morning, let's say."

"Certainly." She was focused on her notes, but her mind was in Paris. Paris!

More than anything she wanted to see Paris. Or maybe Los Angeles, where one of her uncles lived, but that would never happen. Paris could, one day. She felt a sudden wave of hopelessness, but she tried to brighten her eyes so it would not show.

"The major has neighborhoods in mind. Talk to him before you book anything. Yes?"

"Yes." Bookings, unlike requests for money—to say nothing of cryptocurrency—were relatively straightforward.

"And let me know if you run into any problems with the crypto for Mina."

"I had no idea data was so expensive," Roya said, meaning nothing by it.

Hossein smiled kindly, but he seemed to harden. On the Niavaran compound, questions were not encouraged. They turned officemates to ice.

Hossein said, "When the sellers have stolen it, be it from the police, or their employer, they tend to charge a premium."

"Of course."

"Now, in fact, let's go have a chat with the good major. We can collect his thoughts on neighborhoods. Get a head start."

They walked back to the major's room. One of the major's men answered, ushering them in with what Roya thought was a look of extreme annoyance. Roya hesitated, but Hossein motioned for her to come in, too. The major was standing, facing the bank of servers, wearing the headset. In his hands was a controller with several joysticks. The other men were watching the screens, no longer static blue but bright with color. The view was beautiful—a city from a great height. Then, swiveling: a surrounding countryside of hills, olive groves, and limestone. She did not know where it was, but it was not Tehran. When the camera turned, she glimpsed a golden dome that . . . was it? . . . the sight prickled her arms to gooseflesh. Hossein should not have brought her in here; the major's men had become tense. Please, she thought, time to go. Hossein was oblivious. She looked down at her shoes and fussed with her blocky manteau.

"Paris, Major," Hossein said. "We're going to book it today. You have a location in mind?"

"One moment," he said, irritated.

She saw Hossein roll his eyes.

"Three," the major said. "Two. One."

The major flicked the joystick. One of his men, seated at the computer, said: "Tilt observed at eight-eighteen and twenty-one-point-two seconds local."

The other one scribbled numbers on a paper. Roya felt sweat gathering on her upper lip. She wanted to leave.

"Three-point-one-second delay," the one doing the math said. "The cluster is tight at this point. All within a tenth of a second."

"Good," the major said. "I'm going to land it."

"You're busy. I'll come back," Hossein said. The major did not respond. The dome had vanished from view. On the screen she saw a billboard advertising something to do with cars, the message written in a language which she could not read, but, as with the dome, thought she recognized. The knowledge in here was dangerous; she resolved to return only for tea deliveries. She beat Hossein to the door, and when they were out, it clanged shut behind. Shuffling through the hallway, she wiped a finger over the sweat beading on her upper lip and contemplated the blissful experience of working through her list, ignorant of the purpose behind the team here in Niavaran, most of all whatever the major was planning for that strange and lovely city.

CHAPTER 8
Tel Aviv

IN THOSE DAYS *King Ahasuerus sat on the throne of his kingdom, which was in Shushan the capital. In the third year of his reign, he made a banquet for all his princes and his servants, the army of Persia . . .*

The string on Glitzman's mask was digging into his ears, the plastic was running with his sweat, and the air was stale with his hot, trapped breath. Tugging it off, he set the mask in his lap so that its face—the bland face of Mordecai—pointed at the synagogue ceiling. The service was dragging. For him, anyway, and by all appearances for Oriana, who was fidgety, all hopped-up on candy. He sighed, and Tzipi shot him a look. Though he was bored, Purim was one of the few services he could tolerate. Glitzman did not believe in God, but could see value in a holiday devoted to reminding everyone of the enduring threat of Persian annihilationism. A bonus: the megillah, in a tip of the cap to Glitzman's atheism, itself did not once mention God. Earlier in the day, he had tried to arrange a deal in which he would attend the reading and skip out on the carnival in favor of a night working in the office.

"What sort of message would *that* send Oriana?" Tzipi had scolded.

"The right one," he'd said. "That history will repeat itself if we Jews are not vigilant, if we're out drinking at carnivals and toasting the past." Arik Glitzman's belief in parties was thinner even than his belief in God.

The look he'd received had been so withering, the debate—most unusual for the Glitzman home—had stopped right there. Tzipi, whose beliefs included both God and parties, and not in that order, had spent the rest of the afternoon drinking wine and baking prune-filled treats for Oriana to pass out to their neighbors.

Drink, the Purim injunction went, until you cannot tell good from evil. Your right from your left.

Well, Glitzman thought, sitting on the bench between his wife and daughter for the evening reading, feeling very agitated, it's a fucking Tuesday. He figured that half of Caesarea Division would be hungover tomorrow, and they had ops to plan and run, did they not? We're going to spend a day slamming booze to celebrate our escape from genocide at the hand of a Persian lunatic a few thousand years ago, are we now, even as we inch closer to the same fate today?

Had Glitzman said all of this in the office that morning? He had. Had he been booed, loud as the congregation was hissing and booing now, to drown out the mention of the vizier, Haman? He had. The service, Glitzman saw, was going to dribble along for a good while.

...wherefore Haman...

"Boo, boo, boo!" shrieked Oriana, who in place of a more traditional Purim mask was wearing a unicorn tiara and a ballerina costume.

...sought to destroy all the Jews that were throughout the whole kingdom...

Glitzman's thoughts drifted to Amir-Ali bleeding out in that van; to Qaani's final cry for mercy...

And Haman...

"Boo! Boo! Boo!" cried the congregation. Oh damn, thought Glitzman, get on with it.

...said unto king Ahasuerus, There is a certain people scattered abroad and dispersed among the people in all the provinces of thy kingdom; and their laws are diverse from all people; neither keep they the king's laws: therefore it is not for the king's profit to suffer them. If it please the king, let it be written that they may be destroyed...

A totally unoriginal plotline, Glitzman thought. Were it a movie, it would be part one of a blockbuster franchise—sequels upon sequels upon sequels—and with each installment the director would be forced to ratchet up the gore as compensation for the rehashed, overworked storyline: madman sets out to kill all the Jews. Though, he must admit, the scale of Haman's threat seemed laughable in comparison to the present circumstance. Caesarea Division had Kurds and a Swedish dentist—there were no assets nearly as well-placed as Esther, who'd been consort to the king. Plus, back then the Persian despot hadn't gone along with the madness.

... And the letters were sent by posts into all the king's provinces, to destroy, to kill, and to cause to perish, all Jews, both young and old, little children and women, in one day, even upon the thirteenth day of the twelfth month, which is the month Adar, and to take the spoil of them for a prey ...

Glitzman, after a yawn, rearranged his mask. He tuned out for a while, thinking of reasons he might concoct for skipping the parties, and drawing only blanks.

... And in every province, whithersoever the king's commandment and his decree came, there was great mourning among the Jews, and fasting, and weeping, and wailing; and many lay in sackcloth and ashes ...

At Oriana's age, Glitzman's parents had witnessed this very scene in Poland. Two of his four grandparents had not survived.

... Then said the king unto her, What wilt thou, queen Esther? And what is thy request? it shall be even given to thee if it be half the kingdom ...

Half the kingdom to a concubine? Glitzman smiled to himself. You had to appreciate the historical consistency of this Persian bullshit. Glitzman could recall meeting with an Iranian agent in Istanbul, complimenting one of the guy's rugs hanging on the wall, and the Persian told him to take it, please, I insist, I insist, I am your servant, it is yours, and Glitzman—who then had been green as could be, this was a hundred years ago—had relented, and his old boss and mentor Zohar had said, after the meeting, are you crazy, accepting that? He insisted, Glitzman said. He kept on insisting. And Zohar said: That doesn't mean it's true.

Glitzman tuned back in with Esther's plea to save her people, the plot twist of hanging Haman on his own gallows, and, finally, the revenge of the Jews against their enemies, which was Glitzman's favorite act in the story, in no small part because it was near the end.

... The Jews had light, and gladness, and joy, and honor. And in every province, and in every city, whithersoever the king's commandment and his decree came, the Jews had joy and gladness, a feast and a good day. And many of the people of the land became Jews; for the fear of the Jews fell upon them ...

Glitzman was pretty sure most of the story was not true, but this part? Lunacy. "If such things were possible," he whispered to Tzipi, "Gazans would be rabbis by now." He could sense a menacing glare forming even under her Esther mask. He quickly turned away.

... Thus the Jews smote all their enemies with the stroke of the sword, and slaughter, and destruction, and did what they would unto those that hated them.

Amen, thought Glitzman. Amen.

CHAPTER 9
Jerusalem

WHILE PURIM REVELRY UNROLLED outside, Glitzman's deputy Meir Ben-Ami and his wife Yael sat in their study in Jerusalem. He was reading a Persian novel, trying desperately to focus over the noise from the carnival, and contemplating whether earplugs might be necessary to properly cocoon. Having abandoned a last-ditch attempt to convince her husband to join a party at her cousin's, Yael, curled in the chair, was subjecting her notebook to a withering series of venomous pen strokes. Hacking at the paper was more like it.

"You really should go on to the party," Meir had said. "I'll be fine here."

Yael's reply was a noise that seemed to stay lodged in her throat, the words perhaps too vile to show themselves. Then she fired off what Meir thought was a several-hundred-word message to someone on her phone, so long did she stand there glowering while she typed. Now ensconced in the chair, Yael's invective had become longhand in that notebook, though still at an impressively blistering pace.

Disengagement, Meir knew, was the surest road to recovery and eventual redemption. Burying himself back in his book, he pinned a lump of sugar in his teeth and raised the small glass teacup gingerly to his lips. They had moved to Jerusalem a few years earlier, suffering the traffic to be closer to his elderly parents. Turned out that in addition to Yael's frustration with his antisocial tendencies, he was also suffering the neighbor's dog, a mutt whose barks and howls—a regular annoyance—were now rising above the din of the party.

His flow again interrupted, Meir laid the book on his desk and stepped out the front door, where he listened to the shouts of partygoers, the thump of the music, and the yowls of the damn dog. Outside, despite the noise, his thoughts briefly drifted to wonderment at how close it all was. Israel was so cut off from its neighbors and yet his grandparents' old home in Aleppo would have been less than a day's journey, were it still standing.

Though he had not heard his neighbor's shouts or scolds, the dog had stopped barking.

Meir made his way back to his desk, where the book stood waiting like a cold meal. Yael, still in the chair, had traded her notebook for a novel. Meir opened the small safe under the desk and slid out a trim notebook containing his first attempts at a short story. A work of fiction, at least to Meir's mind, though he was not sure Glitzman would agree.

Meir had helped kill a lot of Persians—he put the number at fourteen—but lately he had come to believe that the price of walking about without feeling guilt or shame was to write it all down. At first he'd considered going chronologically, and he'd written a few grafs about the day Glitzman had appeared at Meir's desk and they'd gone for coffee at GREG. Glitzman had explained that he'd been tasked with standing up a group to do things inside Iran, and he wanted someone who was "just the right amount of Persian." Meir was a lifelong student of Iran, and was afflicted by a strain of Persophilia that had him entering romantic entanglements exclusively with Persian Jews (Yael the capstone), writing his university thesis on the *Shahnameh*, and joining Mossad to devote his life to targeting Iranians. Meir had been flattered by Glitzman. He still was.

This story took place well before the development of satellite-linked robotic guns of the sort used to kill Abbas Shabani. In those early days of hunting Iran's nuclear scientists and engineers, Mossad relied on operatives who would glide through Tehrani traffic on motorbikes and smack magnetized limpet mines on the side of the victim's car during the morning commute. Glitzman liked to call the operations "divine interventions." Meir's story concerned the fifth such smiting.

The scientist's wife had not once been in the car during the entire three weeks of surveillance, and the kill order was clear: no collateral damage. That was what distinguished Mossad from the Qods Force. The Office would not approve an operation that killed a target's family. Qods would greenlight anything, the more dead Jews, the better.

But that day, as the operative puttered by the scientist's car and slapped the mine on the driver's-side door, he saw—too late—that the wife was sitting in the passenger seat. The scientist would die instantly. His wife would nearly die, too, from massive blood loss, but in the end she would only lose her left arm from the elbow down.

Because she had survived, the Office conducted no formal review, and as time went on, the operation was lost to the files and no one in Caesarea spoke of it again. Now Meir was trying to write his story from the perspective of the wife, but as he looked over the first page, he was worried he had no talent for it. The opening lines read a lot like one of his cables.

He was contemplating starting over when he first heard the high-pitched buzz. His brain, fixed on the story, processed the noise first as racket from the festival, then the whine of distant machinery. Yael, he saw, had not even glanced up. Meir took a sip of the now-lukewarm tea, looked out the window, then picked up a red pen and crossed out a few lines of clinical prose. Should he write from the standpoint of the assassin instead? But the thought was interrupted: the buzzing sound was growing louder.

Not two weeks earlier he and Glitzman and Yael and a few others had seen a demonstration of a prototype exfil drone, nicknamed the Escape Pod, down at one of the test sites in the Negev. This high-pitched buzzing whir was not as loud, but it struck the same chord in his mind. As the buzzing grew louder and louder, Meir stood. Yael arched her neck toward—

And the window exploded.

The air above him was sucked from the room, and a black shape thrummed overhead, so close he might almost grab it. The drone struck the bookcases behind him, and the blast sent him flying over the desk and he found himself on the floor, looking up at his own blood painted across the ceiling. Strips of paper and mangled bookbinding floated through the air like a flock of birds. He was struggling to say something, to call for Yael, but blood came out of his mouth instead. He felt no pain. He felt nothing. Heard nothing. He tried to lift his right hand and he could not. He could not move his fingers. He tried to lift his left hand, and he could not, and then he saw that it was gone, along with the arm.

He could not see as far as his legs, and he blinked a few times and realized he could no longer see the ruined bookshelves, nor his blood on the walls and ceiling. He could not see Yael. He let his head rest on the floor and turned to see a ball bearing, glistening with blood, rolling into his cottony field of vision. It came to rest against his chin. He'd grown accustomed to the air raid sirens after such attacks. At Meir's last breath there was only silence.

CHAPTER 10
Tel Aviv / Jerusalem

TO HIS CREDIT, and—he hoped—Tzipi's gratitude, Glitzman had kept his promises: that evening he'd gone out to Purim parties with the family. His behavior, in fact, had been so good that he had resisted answering Cohen's first phone call. The second, though, arrived within moments of the first voice mail, and when Tzipi saw his face, after he'd yanked off the mask, an explanation for bailing on the parties hadn't been necessary. Glitzman barely remembered what Cohen had said. Later, on the drive to Jerusalem, he realized the Mordecai mask was still on top of his head.

No bystanders, no civilians.

Only Meir and Yael.

Glitzman found the lack of collateral damage more ominous than if Meir and Yael had died in a crowd of civilians, blown to bits by a suicide bomber on a bus. They'd wanted them alone. It made Glitzman think of Qaani's warnings. It made him think of this mysterious Unit 840, out to kill people in Israel. And would it soon be coming for him?

Around midnight Glitzman was standing beside a beanpole of a Shabak captain under harsh overhead lights, the wreckage arranged in trays across a long table like dishes at a grim banquet. Three techs were poring over twisted pieces of metal, plastic shards, and boxes with protruding wires.

Picking up a wrecked length of black plastic, the captain remarked, "Russian-made quadcopter. A VT-40 model fabricated by the Sudoplatov group. They make about a half million of these annually, primarily for use in Ukraine."

"Cheap," Glitzman grunted.

"They cost about two hundred dollars," the captain said. "Given a few hours, my nine-year-old nephew would be capable of flying one. The captain paused, though Glitzman was not sure if it was for effect or out of deference, but he nodded for the captain to continue. "They can fly around eight kilometers on a single battery charge. Payload limit is three kilograms, these guys say, plenty for the commo equipment and a small munition." The captain handed the plastic to Glitzman, who turned it over in his hands.

Glitzman said flatly, "It wasn't picked up by any of the air defense systems? Any cameras?"

The captain snorted. "Do you know how many cameras we have in Jerusalem?"

"Plenty."

"More than plenty. Have a look at this." The captain took a laptop from one of the technicians and spun it to face Glitzman, who quickly realized he was watching a video of a drone whizzing above the streets of Jerusalem.

The view changed frequently, it had been spliced together from different cameras, but the storyline was consistent: it was on its way to Meir and Yael's home.

"None of our air defense systems would pick this up," the captain said. "It's flying too low."

Glitzman saw the drone artfully dodge a streetlamp. "Skilled pilot," he said.

"There's probably some basic AI on it," the captain said, tapping the screen. "Nothing revolutionary, but I don't think a human pilot would have dodged it so quickly."

"It was autonomous, you think?"

"No, no, no," the captain said, "I doubt it."

"Doubt, or know?"

"Doubt. Certainty is impossible, what with the hardware having been destroyed in the blast. But if there was an operator, they could have been a ways away."

"They wouldn't even need to be in Israel," Glitzman said. And he thought about gunning down Abbas Shabani with a machine gun fired by satellite.

"Have a look at this," the captain said, motioning for Glitzman to follow.

They stopped behind a gaunt technician snapping photographs of a box. "This was sitting on a rooftop about ten blocks from their home. It looks like cardboard, doesn't it?"

Glitzman nodded.

"Exactly," the captain said dryly. "Now feel it."

Glitzman ran his hand over the box—it was smooth as plastic.

"It's waterproof." The captain opened the top flaps and jabbed his finger at a piece of hardware. "Clasped shut with three of these, and do you know what they link to?" He held up a thin white box.

"Transceiver?" Glitzman asked.

"Exactly," the captain said, now shifting his eyes to another piece of equipment, this one on the floor beside the technician, whom he waved off. "See this? It's a remote-operated lift table. Chinese-made. Also wired up with a transceiver. Someone flicks a switch and the top flaps unlock, they hit another button and the lift table rises, and here I'm speculating, but it's just the right size for our drone. How about that? Drone rises up, above the box, then it gets flicked on and flies off."

"You found the box and all of this by tracking the drone flight on the cameras, yes?" Glitzman asked, one eyebrow raised.

"Yes."

"So then your video can tell me when the box was placed? You must have video of that?"

The captain shook his head, and Glitzman thought he saw the man's face redden ever so slightly. "Well, that's the problem," the captain said. "Because whoever placed this knows something about the camera networks. The building in question, well, it's being built, as it happens. It's a construction site. No cameras inside yet, at least none that are operational."

"The entrances?"

Again the captain shook his head.

"Fingerprints on anything? Hair? Blood?"

"We have not found anything yet. But it's too early to be definitive about it."

"Goddammit," Glitzman said after a long pause.

"Yes," the captain said. "On that we can be definitive. One more thing."

Glitzman followed him to a table littered with mangled metal. On it sat a plastic bucket. The captain plucked a ball bearing from inside and handed it to Glitzman.

"It's a FRAG-05-975 munition," the captain said. "Got a bunch of ball bearings in it. Manufactured by the Ukrainians, probably had to be smuggled in. A Russian drone coupled with a Ukrainian explosive."

"Volatile marriage," Glitzman said.

"Less than a kilo of explosives," the captain replied, plinking a ball bearing back into the bucket. "The munition could have been smuggled into the country inside . . . well, pretty much anything. A book, a bottle of wine, a lamp. The hull is fabricated on a 3D printer. Kills anything within about fourteen meters. They could have purchased the lift table in-country—we're trying to run that down."

Glitzman was turning over a ball bearing in his fingers. "They would need someone inside Israel to place the drone," he heard himself say, before growing quiet. In the silence came a dozen questions, each unanswerable, and none of which needed to be spoken aloud.

Glitzman tossed the ball bearing back into the bucket. "You wouldn't need many people. A cell to receive shipments, conduct basic surveillance. They would require only a small network."

"I agree," the captain said. "But who is *they*?"

MEIR AND YAEL'S HOUSE was taped-off and still crowded with National Police and Shabak officers. Glitzman hadn't been here before, but even if he'd not known who owned the place, within a few moments of entering he saw that he would have guessed correctly.

The floors were a tapestry of Persian rugs. He walked across them into the kitchen, where he glimpsed a half dozen Persian cookbooks perched on a small wall shelf. He followed another rug from the kitchen, pushing through a crowd of National Police, and then another down a hall, past the office, which the captain said was still a mess, probably best to steer clear. Glitzman came to the bedroom. The walls were cluttered with photos and paintings; old travel lithographs; a portrait of a striking woman wearing a chador; a photo of someone (Meir's father? Yael's?) posing for handshake photos with a crop of the Shah's generals. His two friends and Persia. More proof, Glitzman thought, that inside life's loop hate and love are joined together at the hip.

Glitzman left the bedroom. The living room was spacious and bright, cheerful even, in close proximity to a gruesome murder. And there was a garden, Glitzman saw.

Jerusalem, terraced across cramped limestone hilltops, overrun by religious nuts, cut in half (divided, in Glitzman's mind, between those who hated him for being a Jew and those who hated him for not being Jew enough), lacking any space or room whatsoever to breathe—with the real estate prices for receipts—and his friends had found themselves a nice little garden. How Persian.

Glitzman shut the door behind him, leaving the captain and the crowd inside.

A high limestone wall hemmed in the garden on three sides. There was the pleasant sound of running water but he did not see it. Olive trees, myrtle, rosemary, lavender, mint, and sage mingled together in a gray-green landscape that made Glitzman feel something he had not expected: peace. He took a seat and looked around and thought about Meir sitting here, soaking in something he could never enjoy. Something to which, Glitzman might have added, Meir, like everyone in Caesarea Division, had no *right*. A man such as Meir, whose moments of peace had been few, if he'd ever decided to experience one, coming out to this patio in the evenings . . . to do what, exactly? Enjoy nature? The fruits of his labors?

Unthinkable.

Would Yael have sat out here? Glitzman didn't have a clue. He was struck by the strange feeling that in fifteen years of working with Meir, and five with Yael, he'd managed to learn a great deal about the two of them, except for anything that mattered.

He thought of Meir's old apartment in Tel Aviv, which boasted a view of the sea, or would have, had the shades ever been open.

"There's a sea out there," Glitzman had said.

"I've seen it before," Meir had said. "And too much sunlight... it's not good for the older books."

Glitzman would've wagered that he'd already put more mileage on this garden in five minutes than Meir had in five months. Meir would have found the peacefulness unsettling, like a bone-chilling silence settling over a room while you are trying to sleep. Meir, Glitzman thought, would have been more comfortable being blown to pieces than being alone with his thoughts in this garden.

There had been a time, a hundred foggy years ago, when Glitzman would have registered the myriad insanities of life in his chosen profession, and those in particular of the organization he served, but, now, in late middle age, that impulse had decayed along with his strength and libido, and his moment of reflection soured to resentment that Meir and Yael had left him behind. That he would have to avenge their deaths alone.

Meir was a bastard. Yael, too.

For the garden, certainly, but most of all for getting themselves killed.

CHAPTER 11

Tel Aviv

THE SHADOW WAR'S playing field is not level, Glitzman understood, not by a long shot.

If the Iranians possessed certain advantages in the available stock of military-age males (the Office's analysts put the ratio at ten for every one Israeli), and perhaps also in the spiritual domain, which Glitzman termed "death-wish commitment," it was Israel that dominated in the most technologically advanced patches of this arena's bloodstained dirt. The Caesarea Division could fly people and cargo in and out of Iran unseen by its air defense systems. Caesarea could plant worms and viruses on computer networks inside Tehran's nuclear program, electricity grid, and water transmission networks. And, through sneakily placed fiber-optic splices, Caesarea owned the Islamic Republic's telecommunications networks.

The tilted playing field meant that Arik Glitzman's political masters expected him to solve problems, and fast. "Why, Arik," a somewhat menacing phrase his bosses had grown fond of while preparing for the meetings after Meir and Yael's murders, meetings in which Glitzman had been offered to the Prime Minister as a blood sacrifice, "why is it, Arik, that you can find terrorists all throughout Iran, but you cannot find the tendrils of a network killing our people here?"

The month since the murders had featured an endless loop of these meetings, among the worst of his career. The Shabak investigation grew cold, and yet there was unmistakable evidence that the Iranians—or whomever was behind the killings, this was a matter of some debate—had accomplices in Israel. After all, *someone* had placed the drone. *Someone* had ingeniously camouflaged it inside that waterproof, remotely opened box. *Someone* had smuggled all of it into the country.

Every Iran source had been tasked. Mossad Stations had put the question to every logical service, from the CIA all the way down to the Russians, and no one had anything crunchy, or, if they did, they would not share.

From the kidnapped (now dead) Captain Qaani, Glitzman had the name of a Qods Force operations officer, Hossein Moghaddam.

He had the outlines of a unit targeting Jews in Israel, run by the shadowy Colonel Ghorbani.

He had facts. He had leads. And he followed them all, each to its cold, dead end. There were so many questions Glitzman could not answer, and that day, headed up to Cohen's office, he suspected all of them were coming his way.

WHEN ONE OF Amos Cohen's people hustled Glitzman into the office, his old friend was fiddling with a bright purple Post-it note stuck on his desk, staring as if it reminded him of some bothersome, uncompleted task. When Glitzman took his seat, he saw that it was blank. Cohen, frowning, dropped it into the brown bag beside his desk, the one for the classified material.

Glitzman eyed the write-up on Cohen's desk. His friend was a physical-paper guy, that's how old they were getting. There was a tidy executive summary on top and a page, which Glitzman had typed, on what he wanted to do next. Down the right-hand margin bled a squiggly red line pointing nowhere and a doodle of what was maybe a duck.

Glitzman didn't mind that his line on the org chart traced up through Cohen. Glitzman didn't care about org charts. Nor did he mind that Cohen's office came with a girl who sat outside to send people away; Glitzman liked doing that part himself. The present Director was a political master, and like all political men he had a servile dog at his disposal. Enter Amos Cohen: lapdog, bulldog, sheepdog—whatever was required. Glitzman had the instincts of only one of those breeds, and it happened to be the one most unwelcome on the executive floors. Which was why Amos summoned Glitzman, and not the other way around.

Glitzman stared at the picture hanging behind Cohen's desk, snapped sometime in '41, of Amos's grandfather kneeling before two Nazi soldiers seconds before he was shot in the head. They both knew Mossad only as the Office and it was decorated accordingly bland, the furniture and décor all forgettable, but no matter how many times Glitzman came here for meetings, the picture could not be ignored. It loomed over everything.

"I know there's nothing new," Cohen said. "I just wanted to talk it through. I have the Director in the morning."

"You have the Director every morning, Amos."

"Tomorrow it's about you."

"Which of my successes, in particular?"

"Your utter lack of actionable leads in Iran to help us find Meir and Yael's killers. Remind me, why no action on . . . what was the name of the ops officer Qaani gave us?"

"Hossein Moghaddam," Glitzman said. "And the boss of Unit 840, Colonel Ghorbani, he—"

"Ghorbani." Cohen almost spat out the name. "He's the one with his sights *inside* Israel, that right? Fits the pattern, I'd say."

"It does," Glitzman said. "The Iranians have been more aggressive inside Israel as of late, and they've had some success, so it all tracks. There was a cell in Jerusalem last year surveilling bases, planning to kill our scientists. A separate cell ran damage assessments of the Iranians' drone and missile strikes. All for cash."

"Wasn't there someone the Iranians paid to start a forest fire?" Cohen asked.

"There was," Glitzman said. "That guy was recruited over social media. He lit a few cars on fire and then tried to burn down a park. And don't forget that he was also preparing to kill the CEO of a defense tech firm. All roads lead to murder, Amos. The Iranians start small, see what these cells can handle, then they aim to kill. That is almost certainly what's happened to Meir and Yael."

Cohen had looked up. "Wasn't there another case where the Iranians recruited a guy who left a severed horse head on someone's patio?"

"It was a goat," Glitzman said. "The Iranians also tasked him to burn down a forest. I forget which one."

"Why are they keen on forest fires?" Cohen asked.

"Some holdover from their Zoroastrian fire worship, maybe, who knows?" Glitzman replied, and thought that Meir would have some quip, probably a relevant poem, or some obscure piece of cultural history, and it would agitate Amos to no end, and that made him smile, and he dearly missed his friend.

"The point is that Ghorbani would be the sort of man you bring in to break through this drought," Glitzman said.

"Drought?"

"All of these spy rings have been rolled up," Glitzman said. "They've not killed any of their marks, until now, at least. Perhaps Ghorbani has been brought in to change this. There are a few hints, nothing more, that he's craftier than the Iranians out hiring mercenary Jews to burn down their own forests."

"You mean that he's a ghost now?" Cohen asked, tapping Glitzman's memo sitting on the desk.

"It's astounding," Glitzman said. "Ghorbani and Hossein Moghaddam have vanished from our collection. We've even sent a few of our surveillance resources in Tehran to scope out the home address we had on Ghorbani. And—"

"Let me guess," Cohen said. "Doesn't live there anymore."

Glitzman tapped his nose. "The selectors we had for him are no longer active. We're not picking him up on internal Qods Force comms, either. You're right to call him a ghost. You might mention this to the Director tomorrow."

Cohen said, "Theories?"

"Ghorbani's targeted killing operation is so sensitive, and he knows that we've penetrated them so fully, that he's running it completely off the grid, so to speak. No old phones. No Qods Force email, faxes, cable traffic, any of that."

"We found Qaani," Cohen said.

"He made a mistake," Glitzman said. "He ran his mouth on an old phone. Same as Abbas Shabani."

Cohen was fiddling with his kippah. With his other hand he danced fingers across a line of Post-it notes as if they were piano keys. "The Prime Minister wanted to leak some of the tapes of your interrogation of our kidnapping victim, Arik. Of the questioning, I mean, before we had to eliminate him. Embarrass the Iranians. Make them feel nothing and no one is safe. I have so far prevented this from happening, the Director has cautioned against, and the Prime Minister has listened. But no one likes it, and—"

"Amos, if we leak any of this, we tip our hand. We put our people in Tehran at risk. No, we must give Ghorbani some doubt about what's happened. Look, Qaani's given us a start. We have a name: Hossein Moghaddam. We have a structure run by Ghorbani that we're targeting. It's not nothing. I don't want Ghorbani changing up his staff now. I don't want him to know what we know."

"You need to find Ghorbani. Or Moghaddam. I need something to take to the Director."

"We are working on it. People in Tehran are working on it. It's the only priority, Amos."

Cohen, nodding, opened a folder on his desk. "Speaking of your people in Tehran. The support asset we lost, this Amir-Ali Mirbaghri—"

"The Kurdish brothers have handled it," Meir said.

"What does that mean, exactly?"

"Our priority, Amos," Glitzman cut in, "was to avoid formal investigations. Amir-Ali was a recreational drug user. He drank. He'd just bought a fucking sports car owned previously by the Shah. We've connected dots."

"How is his friend doing, our Swedish dentist? He recruited Amir-Ali. They were friends. Is he still in the game?"

"He still hates being a dentist and wants to retire in California," Glitzman said.

"A dentist," Cohen's chuckle and slight shake of the head signaled acceptance of Glitzman's assurance at face value. "I was skeptical of him, Arik—and that was a progressive view inside the Office at the time. Others thought you were insane. Recruit a dentist? To do what? Well, you showed us what."

"You saw the report on how Kam celebrated Amir-Ali's birthday, yes?" Glitzman asked. "The one we got from his phone? Most people would think his plan too risky, they wouldn't be able to predict Amir-Ali's reaction. But Kam knew he'd love the prank, the theater, the whole bit. Kam knew him better than he knew himself. Back when Kam was asking Amir-Ali to get involved with us, he had the guy recruited before he'd even made the pitch. My Kamran's good with people. Knows how they work. He's still in the game, Amos. He'll find his way through."

CHAPTER 12

Tel Aviv

IN THOSE DAYS the formidable structures that formed Arik Glitzman's mind would fold in on themselves under the shock of the stress, creating a rigid warren of thought that impressed his colleagues, annoyed his few friends, and utterly dismayed his family. The secrecy made it all worse. Tzipi, despite her status as a long-suffering wife of a Mossad official—a member of Caesarea, at that—desired a certain degree of situational awareness. To Glitzman's great irritation, she expected to be told the why of things. She wanted clear answers to questions he could scarcely acknowledge in the first place.

So when Glitzman drew a map depicting a spiderweb of potential driving routes between home and school, home and Oriana's piano lessons, home and the dance studio, Tzipi fought to comprehend why, in god's name, Arik, is this necessary? Is this to do with Meir and Yael? Glitzman's answer was to open the fridge. By the time he'd shut the door, deciding against another egg, she was gone.

When, one Tuesday, a four-man, two-car security detail materialized outside their apartment, to Glitzman's profound gratitude Tzipi, though bristling, submitted to the intrusion without questions or a fight. When Oriana asked who was in the car, Tzipi said that Papa's bosses decided to help us out a bit, though when the inevitable toddler questions followed ("*Why?*" "*With what?*"), Tzipi commanded Oriana to pipe down, this is all part of having a father who protects people, not another word. It worked, at least for a day or two. Later, when Oriana wondered about the shiny black cars, Tzipi would tell her they might pretend they were carriages, and she a princess.

One Saturday morning, Glitzman happened to look out the window to see Tzipi shoveling Oriana, clutching her wand, clad in tights, a tutu, and a tiara—all pink—into a jet-black armored Land Cruiser, the befuddled security officer doubtless insisting his orders were to remain on the premises. Tzipi and Oriana wore him down, because by the time Glitzman made it down to the street, the car was speeding off. To Glitzman's great satisfaction they took the third left, following one of his suggested alternative routes to the dance studio.

But everyone has their limits, and Tzipi's were found the day a crew arrived to install windows of ballistic glass and to upgrade their security system with cameras covering the entrance to the apartment building and their interior front door. The security upgrades were, to be fair, less of a disruption than the security detail. The new windows looked identical to the old, and the cameras weren't even visible from inside the apartment itself. But the security detail and their serpentine routes had felt temporary. Now, when Glitzman watched his wife glaring up at the camera outside their apartment door, uncertain who was watching her, she looked affronted. Like a woman who had permanently lost something. That her fate was no longer her own.

That night, after Oriana had gone to bed, Tzipi joined him for a smoke on the balcony and asked, quietly and directly, if she should be alarmed.

"And why not?" she asked, before he'd even had a chance to respond. "Because it seems that your office is alarmed."

"Absolutely not," he insisted. "There is no reason for any alarm whatsoever."

A merciful oddity of the Glitzman domestic compact was that Tzipi always forgave her husband's first lie. Such sins were absolved instantly and easily, features as they were of his chosen trade. The lies were treachery only if they went on, and they never really did, because Tzipi would stop asking the questions that generated the lies in the first place. But she was spooked, and Glitzman felt that she was on the verge of submitting Meir and Yael's murder as the compelling evidence it was.

"Then, Arik, why"—there again, that damnable word—"why are Meir and Yael dead? Why are we suddenly putting ourselves under surveillance"—she jerked her cigarette up toward the glowing red dot of a new camera above them on the wall, pointing down at the street below—"and why can I not drive Oriana to Ms. Dagan's studio as I always have, on a route that does not cast me into grinding traffic, or sling me on a ridiculous loop? Why do we have men outside in armored SUVs? Why are you telling me that I should sometimes leave ten minutes early, other times twenty, and still others not take Oriana at all? Maybe your office can send babysitters? They've sent everything else. What am I supposed to do with her on Tuesday afternoons?"

A rare failure of Tzipi's tactics, he thought, to exchange the *whys* for the far more manageable *whats*. Glitzman pounced. "Take Oriana for ice cream," he said. "I will draw you several routes."

Tzipi sucked in a sharp breath through her nose, a noise that could only mean she was weighing the merits of slapping him. He duly lowered the cigarette from his lips in anticipation. And then, regaining her verve, she delivered one of the few *what* questions he could not answer: "Arik," she said. "What is going on?"

The Interrogation Room
Location: ▮▮▮▮▮▮▮▮▮▮▮▮▮▮▮
Present day

"ARIK GLITZMAN," the General says, from nowhere, as he reads. "Chief of the Zionist Entity's so-called 'Caesarea Division.'"

He licks his pointer finger, turns over the page, and pops another sugar cube into his mouth.

Kam has been watching the General read through an earlier draft of his confession, and there's some blood spatter on these pages, which means it might even be a first edition. While waiting, Kam has counted the white-painted bricks that form the wall by the door a dozen or more times. (There are 347.) He's had a brief staring contest with Khomeini. (He lost.)

"What do you think of Glitzman?" the General asks. His eyes are still buried in the papers.

Kam thinks too many things of Glitzman to effectively summarize. In the past this question—or those like it—has tended to start the ball rolling toward beatings. Kam chooses the one answer that he has learned will direct it elsewhere.

"Arik Glitzman is a competent intelligence officer and formidable recruiter," Kam says. "He is also a Zionist madman."

Proof, right there, that honesty absolutely will not save you.

Glitzman's not a madman, but it's really important that the General hears the lie from Kam's lips. As befitting someone in the position of running an interrogation center, the General is utterly devoid of empathy. In the written confessions nuance is tolerated. But here, face-to-face with the General, Glitzman cannot be painted as Kam sees him: a manipulative yet honest recruiter, loving yet absentee father, fearsome yet elegant operational planner. And above all as a ruthless killer—and yet one who saves lives.

Killing to save lives, Kam thinks.

Why not fuck for chastity while you're at it?

But Kam's not sure Glitzman is wrong. You can't really promote chastity through fucking, but he wonders if you might be able to save a few people by killing the right ones. Take the General. Kam has fantasies about Glitzman killing him. And he knows damn well it would save lives, starting with his own.

"I want the stuff before the kidnapping and the death of Amir-Ali," the General says. "Before the murders of your Zionist friends. Take us back to your recruitment story, Kamran," the General says, baring his teeth. "Plus the training in Albania." Mention of that Balkan shithole brings a flicker of amusement to the General's eyes. "You should consider this your final word on how the madman Glitzman convinced a dentist to play spy games."

The General motions to the camera, and soon an underling Kam does not recognize has dumped a stack of A4 and a fresh box of crayons on the table. The General stands to leave.

Albania. Hard pass, Kam thinks. The General likes to hear about Albania because it is embarrassing to Kam, and the General is a major fan of embarrassing his prisoners, staff, and probably his family. (Does the General have children? Kam has wondered. And if so, where are they institutionalized? He does believe there is a Mrs. General, and he worries about her. He feels they would have a lot to talk about.)

The General's delight in shame carnivals is the reason why, years ago, once the spy story was written down, they backtracked to tackle embarrassing and operationally useless questions such as:

Why did Malin leave you, only to marry a Swedish orthopedic surgeon within the calendar year?

Why did the Stockholm dental practice you inherited from your father begin failing? (And do you believe your father had hints that you were a failure before he died?)

Why is your brother Sina's annual income seven times your own? (And, given his financial situation, why did he not bail out your failing dental practice?)

Why did your father favor Sina, despite you following in his footsteps as a dentist?

With these for options, Kam must admit that his recruitment and Albania are relative softballs. Even so, one of the silver linings of this final testimony is that soon Kam will no longer be forced to answer such questions. Soon he'll be dead.

شماره: ....
تاریخ: ....
پیوست: ....

النجاه فی الصدق
بخش دوم از شهادت‌های من

.... Number
.... Date
.... Attachment

In the name of God
Honesty will save you
The _second_ part of my shown confession
—Kamron Esfahani

CHAPTER 13

Stockholm, Sweden
Six years ago

THESE EVENTS, GENERAL, took place in the months before I returned to Iran, in service of the Zionist Entity, to commit espionage and sow corruption on earth.

MY SCHEDULE ON THAT fateful morning had an appointment blocked for one "Pluta, P."

Peter Pluta, it turned out, was a Polish furniture salesman from Kraków.

The nationality was the only part that wasn't really cover, or at least the bit nearest the truth. Some of Glitzman's family indeed hailed from Lvov, back when it had belonged to independent Poland, before the war. His forebears had learned how to survive in this hostile territory, their potential enemies, depending on day and season, some mix of Germans, Poles, Ukrainians, and Russians. Arik Glitzman had swapped that European cocktail for Arabs and Persians. The dance for survival, though, was mostly unchanged.

Peter Pluta was my first appointment on that Monday morning six years ago, and I was terribly hungover. I'd arrived at my practice a half hour late, my hair still wet from the shower. Upon seeing my face, my lone remaining dental hygienist, Astrid, treated me to a look rich with that peculiarly Swedish mix of condescension, shame, and anxiety.

"Perhaps you go home and rest?" she said.

"I'm fine. Just tired. Long weekend."

She nodded, unconvinced, and told me that my first appointment that summer morning was a routine cleaning for a Pole. He'd shown up at the office around eight forty-five, asking for a same-day cleaning. My nine a.m. block was open (as were nearly all the others), and Astrid had already done the cleaning. She said: "You might not even bother with the check."

"What do you mean?"

"That Pole's teeth look like they were cleaned last week. Though I can't see any record of it in the system, so if they were, it wasn't in Sweden."

I lathered my hands in antibac. "And no X-rays?"

"He said he didn't need them." (That was too bad—we could have used the cash.)

"And he doesn't speak Swedish?"

"Right. It's English, unless you've got Polish."

"Na zdrowie!"—and I laughed, as I mimicked taking a shot. Astrid was unamused. The records she shoved into my hands had his name as Peter Pluta.

Months would pass before I called him Glitzman.

I went in, introduced myself in English, and squeaked alongside him on my stool. I poked around and noticed some chipping and significant wear on 1:2 and 2:2. Bruxism, teeth-grinding on the lateral incisors. Later, when I was to learn of the stress borne daily by Arik Glitzman, I would come to believe it was a minor miracle that he hadn't already splintered the teeth in his sleep.

"You are visiting Sweden?" I asked, making conversation as I found similar chipping and enamel wear on 1:6, 1:7, and 1:8. It was the same for their opposite numbers on the left side.

"Jaaaaas," he grunted.

"You picked the right month. It's miserable most of the year. How long will you stay?"

"Maaabeee a few muh... few muh months."

"You are fastidious about your dental cleanings, then?"

"Vaaarry."

Not that I was going to complain about unnecessary work. It was an easy appointment, which was about all I could handle in my slightly hungover state. I'd just repositioned the mirror for a better look when Glitzman gently grasped my wrist and pulled my hand back from his mouth. He wiped the corners of his mouth with the blue paper bib. "Water."

I readied the syringe to give him a squirt, but he raised a hand. "A cup, thank you."

I filled a paper cup and handed it to him. He swirled and spat into the cuspidor. And then he sat up, turning to face me.

"You are really a dentist?" Glitzman asked.

An odd question, to be sure, from a man sitting in a dental chair, speaking to the guy whose name was on the diploma hung on the wall, and who had been examining his teeth mere seconds earlier. I replied with an equally odd answer, though it happened to be true. "Mostly," I said.

"I understand there's a spot of trouble," Glitzman said.

"Oh," I said, "I don't think there's too much trouble with your teeth. Some abrasion and cracks from grinding, you need a night guard to—"

"No," he cut in, "I mean that *you* are in a spot of trouble." Your men are quite talented, General, but they usually need pipes and belts to make their points. Glitzman does not. "And I know that sounds threatening," Glitzman went on, "but you must know this: I am here out of love and concern."

"What?" I said dumbly. He was looking at me with a familiarity that I found remarkably disconcerting.

Glitzman had begun fussing with a scaler. Stillness, I would learn, was not one of his strengths. "My dentist also tells me I should wear a mouth guard. Same as your hygienist. Says if I don't, I'll grind my teeth down to nubs. I have been procrastinating."

"He's not wrong."

"She." He carefully returned the scaler to its spot on the tray and faced me again, his hands flat on his knees. "I am a keen observer of your recent extracurricular work in Iran, your attempts to import medical equipment and the like, to compensate for how poorly this place"—he motioned around the office—"is doing. But it's a little risky, isn't it? Sanctions and all. Plus it all seems to have fizzled out. I don't normally think of dentists as gamblers. Certainly not Swedish dentists..." He trailed off, but his eyes had not. "But you're not really Swedish, are you?"

I'd gotten this line, or a version of it, plenty of times from blond-haired, blue-eyed Svensson Swedes, most of whom thought I was an Arab, one of the hundreds of thousands of Syrian or Iraqi refugees who'd fled their civil wars for Stockholm. Maybe this Pluta was a pissed-off right-wing Pole who didn't care for brown people in Europe? I considered telling him off, or issuing another denial, but my heart was running at a gallop. There was something all-seeing and frightening and comforting about Arik Glitzman, all at once. I dipped my head to absent-mindedly nip at a fingernail. "Who are you?"

"A friend," Glitzman said.

"A friend?"

"A friend." Here Glitzman, straightening his back, scooted closer to me. "A comrade who understands the spot you are in."

"And who might this comrade be, exactly?"

He sighed. "Peter Pluta, but you already know that, seeing as you have the name on your chart, do you not? But if you must know, I work for a furniture manufacturer out of Kraków. I'm here in Stockholm on business." He sighed again, as if the identity, though false, were still a great burden on him. "And perhaps I will explain who you are, eh, for my bona fides? You are a dentist, yes, as you say. Your paternal grandfather started the line. Glory days of the Jews in Iran, the sixties and seventies. Your father was a dentist, too. It's the family business, after all. There was a practice in Tehran, in Yusef Abad, not far from the synagogue. There were side businesses in Europe, my analysts tell me. Family did well. There is a house a short ways off Vali Asr, with a large garden. Of course, in those years Vali Asr was known as Pahlavi Street and your family's home wasn't occupied by the Sheep Butchers' Union. You've no memories of the place back then, I imagine?"

I was not actually sure if it was a question, and I was growing conscientious of the sweat blooming in my armpits.

"I have another appointment," I said feebly.

Glitzman, hawklike, was waiting on his answer.

"Really," I said.

His nose twitched. "Kamran, your next appointment is at two p. m. with Mrs. Liza Backstrom."

I blinked a few times and waited for my heart to stop.

"Do you remember the old place?" Glitzman inquired.

"I wasn't a year old when we left Iran."

"But you went back with your father often, didn't you? On his quixotic quests to recover the home. Once your brother had a choice in the matter he stopped taking the trips. But you've got one foot in Tehran, Kamran, haven't you?"

I wanted to send him away; I wanted to run; I wanted to hear him out. Astrid knocked softly on the door, said the paperwork for Mr. Pluta's mouth guard was ready.

"I'll grab it in a few minutes," I called back. I heard Astrid's footsteps padding away, then, loudly, for her benefit, I said: "You won't have any enamel left if you don't start wearing a mouth guard soon."

Glitzman smiled. Because his head was still back in the chair and the smile was gleeful, I noticed, with growing interest, yet more wear on the cuspids. That happy glint was back in his eyes.

"Most Iranians would kill to come to Sweden," Glitzman said. "And yet you seem keen to travel the other direction." He picked up a plaque scaler. "Why?"

There was a very long answer to this question, but it was already blazingly obvious that Glitzman preferred short ones. "I want out," I said. I folded my hands into my armpits to see if the warmth might stop my fingers from shaking.

"There is a California dream here, is there not?" Glitzman said. "Maybe I can help you find it. Plenty of lovely Persian girls in Los Angeles." Confirming my fears, Glitzman then slipped me, from his pocket, a piece of paper bearing the address of a bungalow off the Pacific Coast Highway, near Corona Del Mar. A bit of a fixer-upper, it must be said, decidedly not on the ocean side, and also entirely out of reach, given my finances. It had been one of my more frequent web searches in recent months. I'd mentioned this to no one. I'd never sent a message about it. I'd searched for it. On my phone. Only my phone. I'd read news stories about Israeli malware with punch lines like this. At that moment, I would have been more comfortable in the throes of a vigorous colonoscopy.

"You could call this a threat," Glitzman said, with a glance at the paper, "but you'd be wiser to see it as an opportunity. I think you will find the work complementary to your talents. In addition to being lucrative."

"Complementary to the dentistry?" I asked.

Glitzman belly-laughed. He held up the scaler. "Is this clean?"

Astrid, in truth, could be uneven in the sanitization department, but I said: "Absolutely."

Where Glitzman had been running his tongue, he now brought the scaler along his front teeth.

"How do you know about California?" I asked.

"Let me help you dig yourself out of this mess."

"If I say no?"

He shrugged.

"Are you threatening me?" I asked.

He heaved that great sigh once more. "Don't be foolish. I want to help," Glitzman said. And I could see that he meant it.

CHAPTER 14
Stockholm

THAT SAME EVENING I arrived at the appointed restaurant, a cozy place in Gamla Stan, at precisely eight o'clock. At Glitzman's insistence I'd powered through my singular remaining appointment with Mrs. Backstrom, though Astrid quite obviously knew that something was wrong, because when I waved goodbye at the end of the day her studied gaze held far more pity than condescension. At home, in the intervening hours, I'd sat in the darkness of my living room, wondering if there were cameras in there. After thinking about that for a while, I realized if they had wired up my apartment the cameras were surely infrared, and the darkness would do me no good. I flipped on the lights to search. I found nothing, and at the time that was encouraging, but now I know that if there were cameras, I'd have never found them. My phone now felt radioactive in my hands. I powered it down and set it inside my safe. Though they obviously still had access to the phone, I felt better with it in the safe, which I figured would dampen the impact of any explosives they'd hidden inside.

I briefly considered ignoring Glitzman's instructions, but he doubtless knew where I lived, and it felt less violating to walk along with his leash than to have him show up here to toss me in his pound. Having been marinating in my own sweat for hours, I grew conscious of my smell. After my shower, I went out, and by the time I reached the restaurant—Glitzman was waiting—I could smell myself again.

In front of him were plates of pickled herring and smoked salmon.

"Better than the lox in New York," Glitzman said as I sat down, his mouth full. "Though to find a good bagel here"—he made a smug noise—"well, I'd have to be the Jew to make it."

Though he was perhaps chummier in the casual setting of the restaurant, he was still full of that same brew of mirth and menace that had filled the examination room that afternoon.

I ordered the plain roast chicken, fearing I might not keep down anything more complicated.

"You need to explain yourself," I said, rehearsing the speech I'd worked on facing my bathroom mirror an hour earlier. "You're spying on me. You know things... You show up at my office. You say you can help. I need to know what's going on." I considered a threat about involving the Swedish authorities, but held back for the insane—yet very real— reason that I did not wish to anger him.

"My name's not Pluta, of course," he said, through a mouthful of herring, "but it's no help to either of us to give you the real one. I work for the State of Israel, for an organization that worries day and night about Iran. And we weren't spying on you. At least not to start. We *were* keeping an eye on a few of the people you've met in Tehran. We—"

Glitzman hushed as the waiter brought my chicken and mineral water. I pushed it aside as soon as he'd left us. Glitzman and I studied each other for a moment. In a gigantic bite he finished off the salmon.

"You were spying on me," I muttered.

"Not on purpose," he said. "Just listen. I have a proposal for you."

I picked up my fork, looked at the chicken, and set it back down. I tried a sip of water and the bubbles crackled and popped in my mouth as I struggled to swallow.

Glitzman went on, "Work for me—for a good cause, I should add— and I'll put you on a monthly retainer. For your services, not to Israel, let's say, but to international Jewry."

"A monthly retainer?" I asked.

"Indeed," Glitzman said. "In exchange for shuttering your practice here and opening one in Tehran. Taking the plunge. Reconnecting with your homeland. All that."

"Move to Tehran," I repeated.

My eyes must have said it was a question, because he sighed and stared at me as if this should have been obvious by now, even to a humble dentist. "You go in and out of Tehran, you have valid Iranian documents, you have never been to Israel, though you are a Jew. Not a Zionist, let's say, but a Jew. You are a Persian first, are you not? Of course you are. You are a Persian and a Jew, and where is the contradiction in that? Nowhere. Jews had been in Persia for over a thousand years when the Arabs showed up with their Islam."

My grandfather had been a prominent Tehrani Jew at a time when Israel had a de facto embassy in Tehran, when Israeli engineers and agronomists and businessmen and intelligence officers were all over the country, pitching in on the Shah's doomed effort to modernize. I had heard one story—and only slivers, at that—of an approach Mossad made to my grandfather at some point in the early seventies. He was a wealthy Persian who had never been to Israel, who, unlike my father, spoke barely a word of Hebrew. He had everything to lose. As I remember the story, my grandfather had politely told them to fuck off. But here his grandson was, listening.

Glitzman leaned back in his chair, folded his legs, and fussed with a stray thread on the cuff of his pants. "They wrote me a speech to give you. Would you like to hear it?"

"Who's they?" I asked.

He ignored this. "When our agents or officers are Jews, particularly those without much history in Israel, there is a general belief in my organization, including a few of our more senior, dimwitted mandarins, that these people would benefit from a reminder of the importance of their work to the long-term security of the State of Israel."

"Do you think I need that speech?" I asked. I had my own problems that needed working out before I could tackle those of the Jewish State or the Islamic Republic. Two entities, which, as the names alone suggest, are drowning in problems, and will be forevermore.

"No," Glitzman said. "But I need to give it. You think I sit at the top of the food chain? Sometimes someone else tells me how it is, or how it's going to be." The loose thread on his pant leg had him enraptured for a moment. "In a generation's time," he said, with some theater in his voice, "the Iranian regime has stoked the ring of fire that burns around Israel now." He nudged his head toward the window. "You think we'd all feel good here in this little Nordic paradise if the Norwegians had one hundred and fifty thousand rockets and missiles pointed at Stockholm? You think you could enjoy a night like this, fearless and bright, if the Finns were a month away from having a nuke and run by a death cult keen to turn your fjords into bathtubs of blood? How about if the Danes were arming and funding a bunch of the Arabs in Stockholm to blow themselves up inside your goddamn IKEAs? What if attacks like what happened on Drottninggatan a few years back were happening every few weeks? A madman hijacks a truck and rams it into pedestrians and department stores? No? Damn straight. And . . . end scene. There you have it, albeit with some of my own flair. What do you think?"

"Norway's got the fjords," I said, "not Sweden."

"Ah, they have it all, don't they?" Glitzman said. "I'll pass that along. Otherwise?"

"It's fine."

Glitzman made a strange noise; it had come from his mouth but was more flatulence than sigh. Leaning into the table, he pointed a finger my way. "It's shit. They wrote that for a Swede."

"I am a Swede."

"Are you?" Glitzman sized me up as a tailor might a client who has rapidly accumulated a great deal of weight. No judgment, but there was work to be done. "Not denying the passport, but you're too brown to be a Swede, even if you're a dentist. You're too foreign to be an Iranian—and what's more grotesque than a foreign-born Iranian? You hate the mullahs and the regime, but then again, so does everyone else. And you're a Jew but you're not an Israeli, and I have my doubts about your commitment to Zionism. Which, by the way, I've kept to myself inside the organization. You've got no family in Israel. You've never even visited. Everyone who fled Tehran came here or went to Los Angeles or New

York. You don't speak Hebrew; your father never taught you. Your bar mitzvah was...shall we say, a subdued affair. I hear there is a saying among Persian Jews: Iran is my homeland, Jerusalem is the direction of my prayers. But you don't even pray."

"It has been a while," I confessed.

"I think," Glitzman concluded, "that you believe Israel is a fine idea for *other* Jews. That you're mostly bored. That you want a new life."

I might have applauded, but I couldn't congratulate him for spying on me. So I said, "That's not so far off the mark."

Glitzman went on, "What could be more exciting than opening a dental practice in Tehran, particularly one with very different—some might say, more exciting—objectives from your failing operation here? A practice that sends and receive goods inside Iran. A place I might park cars for a while, or run money through. A little outpost in the heart of enemy territory, one that might have interesting patients, people whose trust you might win? I'm not describing a dentist, am I?"

"You're describing a spy," I said.

"You say that scornfully, like it's a dirty word," Glitzman scolded. "I rather like how it sounds, especially on you. Better than *dentist*, am I right? Spies retire to California to play in the sun. But do you know what happens to Swedish dentists?"

For a brief moment, I felt a strange desire to defend the Swedish system, and shot back: "They probably have a comfortable retirement and a summerhouse in Gotland."

"The successful ones, sure," Glitzman said, jabbing his fork into another piece of herring, "But the rest, the ones like you? Well, my analysts say that those dentists drink themselves to death in the darkness of winter."

THAT NIGHT, and the next one, Glitzman and I got frighteningly drunk as his pitch shifted from cold logic to the realms of emotion. He wanted me to feel that this wasn't just business. He wanted me to trust him, and he'd clearly done his homework: I like drinking, and after two sessions of drinking with pretty much anybody I'm going to like them, too.

    Those nights are a fog except for one encounter. While leaving a bar right around close, a tall, blond, and very drunk Swedish guy shouted at me, called me a Syrian like he was describing a fungus, and then, approaching us, said something that must have been quite nasty, though I honestly did not hear what it was. I'd only just turned to face him when, with one fearsome blow to the face, Glitzman put him on the floor. We hurried out of the bar, laughing, Glitzman's arm around my shoulder, and mine around his.

CHAPTER 15
Tehran / Tirana, Albania

ONE YEAR AFTER Glitzman's visit, a Persian Jewish dentist from Stockholm and a disgraced Tehrani doctor were headed to Albania for two weeks' training in small arms, surveillance and countersurveillance, agent handling and recruitment, covert communications technology, breaking-and-entering, and the construction of explosive devices, on the dime of the spy agency of the State of Israel.

Try and tell me the world makes any sense.

AMIR-ALI, that disgraced Tehrani doctor, had become one of my new dental practice's first patients when I'd settled back in Iran to work for Glitzman. Amir-Ali found me because his previous dentist had retired and he had severe tooth pain (cavities on 3:5 and 3:6), which, as it turned out, were the least of his problems.

When I met him he was also under fire from the medical board because a patient had died of a heart attack during a routine hip replacement surgery. The board investigator, a real true believer, perhaps sniffing atheism on Amir-Ali and also hints of actual moonshine, had turned the hearing into an ideological exam. Amir-Ali could only name seven of the twelve imams and he couldn't put them in anything close to the right order. He could not recite the Quranic verses that did not begin with *in the name of God*. He atrociously misquoted Khomeini. These days the ideological tests are mostly box-checking exercises, but Amir-Ali found an examiner looking to make an example of his inability to check any of the boxes. So by the time Amir-Ali had decided to do something about the cavities, the poor guy had been dumped from his orthopedic practice, his funds for wine and women were running dangerously low, and he was spending his spare time, when sober, trying to convince his more successful siblings to coinvest in various financial schemes. We became fast friends. We had much in common.

One weekend in that first year back in Tehran (I think it was winter, I remember wearing coats), at Glitzman's instruction, I took Amir-Ali to dinner at a new Italian place in the Palladium Mall, and we traded jokes about the mullahs, and when we got drunk together from there on out, which was often, we commiserated about the sad reality that the Islamic Republic could flood the region with advanced weaponry but couldn't tend to the sewers in Tehran. Or thin the smog. Or save the Persian cheetah. Or maintain the water levels on Lake Urmia. The regime was, however, quite good at hurting its own people. In a few months' time, Amir-Ali, on his way to rock-bottom, was beaten by a militia during a traffic stop. Thankfully, I'd not been with him.

The next weekend, on Thursday night, I sent Anahita to his house. Then, on the Friday morning, I took him, bleary-eyed, into the mountains for some sheep hunting on the theory that, having been humiliated by his government, he would enjoy killing something. On our way into the mountains I pulled over, slid a duffel from the car, and gestured for him to follow. We walked a ways up into the hills, straight to the coordinates I had from Glitzman. At the drop site I opened the bag and held it there for Amir-Ali.

"Go on," I said. "Have a look." He looked excited, like if the bag had been larger he might have expected Anahita to jump out.

Instead there were Ziploc bags with handguns in them. An AK-47 wrapped in plastic. A brick of cash: American dollars, and lots by the look of it. A laptop. An electronic box that resembled a battery. I wasn't even sure what it was. Two manila envelopes, probably stuffed with identity papers—they were sealed and we didn't open them. He spread everything across the ground and we stood there for a moment, looking at it. It was windy that day and the bags were fluttering in the breeze. We got our cigarettes lit under the cocoon of our hands. Amir-Ali hadn't taken his eyes off the guns.

"Not for hunting?" he said, tapping his foot on the AK-47.

"Not for hunting sheep," I said.

"Who's it all for?"

"Friends."

"Your friends?"

"They could be yours, too."

"I'm not so sure they could."

"Why not?" I said. "I think you'd get along well. We all hate the same people."

We loaded everything back in the duffel, then I found the spot on the ground and together we pried up a board covered in dirt and convincing synthetic long grass. Beneath it was a box. I put the duffel in the box and covered it back up.

"How well does it pay?" he asked.

A FEW MONTHS AFTER THAT, and Amir-Ali and I were on our way to Albania.

The man waiting for us at the hotel in Dubrovnik was older, maybe mid-fifties, with a white shock of hair, the roughened hands of a farmer, and an English accent I could not place then, but now understand to be Albanian. Though at the time his accent was mysterious, I took it to mean we were trading the charming warmth of Dubrovnik for something far more austere.

From Dubrovnik he chauffeured us down the craggy Adriatic coast. In about six hours we reached a remote farm outside Tirana. There we met the Kurdish brothers, Aryas and Kovan, for the first time. The four of us were classmates.

Glitzman selected Albania because on the other side of the capital there was another encampment, really a small town: Camp Ashraf 3, headquarters of the People's Mujahedin Organization of Iran, the MEK.

The MEK are the only people who like killing mullahs, soldiers, and nuclear scientists more than the Israelis. Those crazy fuckers have buckets of Iranian blood on their hands. All of which to say, in the Middle East, the enemies of your enemies are terrific friends, and Mossad has built up quite the partnership with them. Though we weren't to mix with any of the MEK fighters, I am sure the farm where we lived and trained had been used by the Mossad to train those cultists in the not-so-distant past.

Amir-Ali and I felt a certain inferiority around Aryas and Kovan, who had fought against the Islamic State inside Iraq while I had been running a dental practice into the ground and Amir-Ali had been in medical school.

Thankfully, we began in the classroom. First day we sat in a prefab room, soaking in sweat from balls to brow, learning at the feet of our principal instructor, a Marseillaise Jew named Maurice. We spent ten hours on how to use the communications software they'd hidden on our phones. Maurice gave us sample scenarios ("You've just cased a house, here's what you saw . . .") and had us type out the messages. It quickly became clear that, if Aryas and Kovan possessed any structured thoughts whatsoever, they were unable to put them to paper.

We soon shifted to more active subjects.

Steady dental or surgical hands, it turns out, are quite useful for picking locks and capturing crystal-clear photographs on a wide range of subminiature cameras, many of which are smaller than a thumbnail and fidgety as a five-year-old sitting for a cleaning. I will also submit for this official record that when it came to the spy's ultimate sword—the pen—I was as superior to the Kurds behind a desk as they were to me behind a scope. Amir-Ali landed somewhere in the middle.

Maurice also put us through a defensive driving program in which, for a finale, I may have fractured my collarbone (though it was never X-rayed) when Amir-Ali T-boned the hood of my Land Cruiser.

Injury aside, I was beginning to have some fun learning at the feet of the vaunted Mossad, which Maurice called only "the Office." I got to pick locks, learn surveillance techniques, crash cars, and use freaky-small cameras in the relative safety of what was basically a spy amusement park. It was camaraderie and fun and games. And absolutely zero risk. Amir-Ali and I thought this was going to be fun. Easy money.

Soon, though, things turned more physical, more kinetic, and more embarrassing. A new instructor arrived for this part, a Sayeret Matkal sergeant, a wall of a man with a thin mustache and a thicket of curly hair, whom we called only Sarge.

Sarge took us out to the farm's shooting range. There was a buffet of weapons spread across the table. We started with a small handgun. He demonstrated how to load and aim, then handed it to me. It was a smallish pistol, and yet I felt intimidated. I'd fired hunting rifles a few times, and always missed horribly.

"You ever fired one of these?" asked Sarge, though I think he knew the answer.

"Why do I need to know how to shoot?" I asked. "If it comes to that, I'm dead."

"We'll practice how you properly shoot yourself in the head in a few minutes," Sarge said, and he was deadly serious. "But for now let's work on how you might defend yourself before it comes to that." He sent one of the paper targets out about five meters.

This was no answer, but Sarge wasn't the sort of man you argued with, certainly not on a gun range.

I squared up as he'd demonstrated, aimed, squeezed the trigger. The recoil surprised me. Kovan laughed. I peered downrange, no clue where it had gone. "Where did that one go?"

"Wide left," Sarge said.

"Was it close?" I asked.

"Not really."

"I don't really like guns."

"I can see that."

I shot another round.

"How about that one?"

"Wider left," Sarge said.

"What kind of gun is this?" I asked.

"A Makarov. Russian-made."

"Well, there you have it," I said. "It's a piece of shit."

Amir-Ali winced. The brothers laughed, more at me than with me. Sarge did not. "Again," he said.

I shot another round. When I looked over, Sarge was squinting downrange, a look of utter disdain on his face. At the time I thought he was being a dick, but in retrospect I suppose my performance was the equivalent of attempting your first dental cleaning and missing so horribly that the scaler goes wide of the teeth to prick an ear. Even Amir-Ali looked horrified.

"Maybe," Sarge said, "your left arm is shorter than your right. In any case, try to shoot more to the right. Aim right."

I shot again. "Did that one go right?"

"Why are you closing your left eye?" Sarge asked.

"To see better."

"You see better with one eye shut?" he asked. "Do you drive with one eye shut? Or clean teeth?"

This time I kept both eyes open. "I'm seeing double," I said. "I'm sort of dizzy."

Aryas whispered something to Kovan.

"Shut the fuck up," I said, turning around.

Sarge gave me a pair of sunglasses and stuck some tape on the left lens and asked if I was still seeing double. I was not. "This time keep your eyes open."

I shot the rest of the magazine, then another, and missed every single shot. "Maybe you show me where to put it against my head?" I asked. "For the suicide option."

Sarge ignored this. He handed the gun to Kovan, who had told us the first night there that he and his brother had killed a bunch of Islamic State headchoppers during the war. Some at point-blank, certainly, there had been executions of course, but others at great distances, with all sorts of guns. All thoughts that this might be bluster evaporated as he sent three rounds into a tightly packed cluster clean through the target's head.

"Tell you what," Sarge said, turning to me. "If you need to get yourself shot in the head, have him do it for you."

THE LAST BIT was pure torture, and I am still not sure what purpose it served other than as a bonding exercise, or perhaps amusement for the Israelis.

One evening Sarge fed us a gigantic meal of meatballs, *byrek*, and black bread washed down with beer, and I am now convinced it was poisoned, because from what had seemed like a modestly pleasant social interaction with Sarge—a rarity—the four of us were hustled, in various diarrhetic states, into a rusting shipping container with a small pail for a toilet. I sat inside with Amir-Ali and those Kurds for who knows how many hours, Sarge pumping on repeat, through speakers above us the size of twin beds, a putrid song called "Truck Yeah" by the American country singer Tim McGraw. While in the box we guessed, correctly, at the title—the lyrics more than gave it away—but I only discovered the artist later, and I wish, perhaps more than anything, that I had not included this anecdote in my original confession, General.

There have been days, dozens of them, in which my anger toward Mr. McGraw has eclipsed the loathing I feel toward your men, and yes, even the hatred I reserve for myself.

The Interrogation Room
Location: ▉▉▉▉▉▉▉▉▉▉
Present day

KAM PUTS DOWN THE CRAYON, massages his wrist, and straightens the papers. He startles at the door, and Colonel Askari's rosewater scent fills the room.

Oh no, Kam thinks. Oh god no.

Kam wrote this for the General. At the General's prompt! He is expecting the General. Honesty will save you, my ass! Dumb, he thinks. Dumb, dumb, dumb. Why did you write all that? A mistake. You've made these mistakes before, but you're not a rookie anymore. You're a veteran prisoner. There's just no excuse.

Maybe Askari will just collect it and . . . oh no.

Askari has joined him at the table.

Askari picks up the papers and reads the confession all the way through. It takes longer than you'd think because Askari's bum eye makes reading difficult. Or so he once told Kam. In truth, Askari's never been big on reading the confessions, more on the beatings that get them rolling in the first place.

"We're done with this section," Askari says, still reading. "When we bring you back, we'll revisit your long con. The batch of deceit that landed you here."

Askari turns over the last page with a satisfied laugh. The tone makes Kam instantly unwell, and the shine in Askari's eyes doesn't help. Askari brandishes a few more chuckles and then he stands, collects the A4 and crayons, and leaves the room. Kam wants to cry. He is too numb to cry, but he would really like to let it out. He counts the bricks three more times and tells himself that Askari has been called away on some other business. Surely he won't have any time to rig things up.

Two of the underlings arrive to take him back to his cell. Kam moves slowly, his steps so heavy and hesitant that once or twice the guards jerk his shoulders to move faster. They turn a corner, and . . .

Kam hears the first pounding twangs and thumps of the music. It's surging through the shut metal door. He stops, digs in his heels. The underlings, who are smiling broadly, drag him onward. He tries to grab a door handle, the frame, anything, but they smack his hands away and pull him along. One of them opens the door to his cell and just before they fling him onto his mat the voice of Tim McGraw attacks Kam like a horde of bats sprung from a cave.

CHAPTER 16

Tel Aviv

Three years ago

SIX WEEKS AFTER Meir and Yael had been murdered, on a bright April afternoon (though no one knew if the sun was shining—the Caesarea offices had no windows), Glitzman's new Deputy, Rivka Sadegh, brought a single sheet of paper into his office, and with great theater propped it up against a framed photo of Oriana in a tutu.

Rivka's father had been tortured and hanged by the mullahs in the bloody afterbirth of the Revolution. The rumor mill figured him for a blown Mossad asset, but Glitzman thought it more likely he'd been hanged for his vocal opposition to Khomeini. In any case, Glitzman had never gone looking for confirmation in the files, both because he'd never been fond of history, and also because he knew the files were the last place you went for the truth. It was Meir who'd known all the details, and he was dead.

What Glitzman knew for certain was that after making aliyah in '81, Rivka's mother, a hopeless Persian romantic, chose to forsake the country and language that reminded her of her beloved husband, the language that made such romanticism possible in the first place. So Rivka had not been raised speaking Persian at home. Her birth name, in fact, had been Nazanin, but in a bid to out-Sabra the Sabras during those first months in Israel, her mother had gone for Rivka. The girl was young and would not remember, her mother figured. She hadn't even been able to walk.

Glitzman knew all of this because, when Rivka had been recruited, the Office had been disappointed that she did not speak her country's tongue, and private immersion had to be paid for, and it had been Glitzman who'd signed the papers. Rivka had studied the language (though she spoke with a lilt), not for love of Persia, but because it would help in separating other troublesome Persians from their heads.

"We caught a break." Rivka grinned, pointing to the document.

"Hossein Moghaddam, the name Qaani gave us, well, he's traveling to Istanbul. One of his aliases appeared on an Iran Air booking."

Glitzman snatched up the document. Israel's signals intelligence gurus, Unit 8200, regularly hoovered up airline booking data. He saw the alias, circled, on the list, alongside a passport number.

"Business class," Rivka said. "I guess Ghorbani likes to send his people out in style."

"In Iran, the terrorists wear Rolexes," Glitzman replied. "The Americans passed us an address linked to this alias, didn't they?"

"Villa in Bebek, near the water," Rivka answered. "Nice place. Ankorion's surveillance crew checked it out. They've been watching it on and off. It's been quiet."

"Ankorion still runs an asset at Istanbul airport, that right?" Glitzman asked.

"That's right," Rivka said. "You and Ankorion still hate each other?"

WHAT GLITZMAN AND COHEN had worked on together in the field could fill a (highly classified) history book, but, as with his friendship with Meir, what they knew of each other's lives outside the Office could have scarcely fit on the colorful sticky notes Cohen taped on his desk. ADHD, Glitzman suspected. Cohen was affixing one to a bare quadrant of his desk when Glitzman took his seat. From a distance Cohen's sticky notes were humorous, the butt of lighthearted jokes, but up close, while planning an op with the man, the scattershot approach drove Glitzman insane.

"We have an opportunity," Glitzman said.

Cohen seemed to wince. Then, in another agitating Cohen trademark, he paused for an uncomfortably long time before he spoke. "You've said this to me before, Arik."

"Did I?"

"Yes. And then we almost died. In Erbil."

"When the Iranians lobbed a missile? That was unrelated."

"Sort of related, seeing as it blew up the safe house, yes?"

"They weren't aiming for us specifically."

Glitzman's eyes wandered to Cohen's dark blue kippah, where a fly had crash-landed. Cohen smacked, smushing the fly, then scowled at the mess on his palm.

"What were you expecting?" Glitzman said.

"To miss." Cohen collected a tissue from the box on his desk. "What's the opportunity, Arik?"

"We have a lead on one of Ghorbani's men traveling to Istanbul. Hossein Moghaddam. It's the name that came out of the interrogation we conducted on Ismail Qaani. Moghaddam is booked on an Iran Air flight to Istanbul next Friday," Glitzman said. "Or I should say, one of his aliases has been issued a ticket. We have an address in Istanbul. We have a photo. We have . . . grist."

"Who's he meeting?" Cohen asked.

"The point of the trip," Glitzman said, "would be to answer that question."

Cohen smoothed the adhesive strip of a purple sticky note against the desk. He'd gone completely gray since taking the new job, and though Glitzman had no firsthand intelligence to confirm it, he suspected the kippah, which Cohen had sported unevenly in years prior, had made a comeback for the operational purpose of concealing a rapidly developing bald spot.

"And you want what?"

"Surveillance resources. In Istanbul. I have a flight number, a photograph, a passport number, and an address. I want to stick him in Istanbul, see where he goes, who he meets. Ankorion's got a unilateral team in Istanbul and I want you to unlock them for me. Best-case is we get a juicy lead on an Iranian hit squad. Worst-case is we get nothing."

"Not true," Cohen said. "Worst-case is that this goes south in Istanbul, someone gets themselves killed, and the mop-up becomes an international incident."

"You were more optimistic in your youth, Amos."

"I certainly was not."

"You could copy-paste that dreary little worst-case scenario to anything this organization does," Glitzman shot back.

"Precisely," Cohen said, leaning back in his chair. "I often do."

"Look at it this way," Glitzman said, thinking it was time to close the sale. "If it goes sideways, who's holding the shovel, and who's getting heaped with the shit?"

"Ooooh . . . I like that," Cohen said, sitting back up. "I like that." He pulled another sticky note from the stack and began to jot something down. His chicken scratch was impossible to read, but Glitzman dearly hoped he was being quoted.

AT BREAKFAST, Glitzman had told Tzipi he would be home by six-thirty. That was three hours ago. He had spent those three hours in the office, planning for Istanbul with Rivka, waiting for Cohen to sign the authorization papers, and trying to mollify Tzipi, who was not quite happy, judging by the frequency of the calls to his open line. Oriana, he imagined, was being kept awake, fueled by sugar and television and promises that her father would put her to bed when, if ever, he made it home, all flowing from Tzipi's belief that the punishment always fit the crime. Miss a dance recital and receive a video of Oriana in tears. Come home late, and exhausted, and your daughter is hurled at you. Arik Glitzman, who had overseen operations of immense tactical complexity, could not fathom the tradecraft required to deal with what was coming to him. He was sure, in fact, that it did not exist.

"What do you think of it all?" Glitzman asked.

"Which part?"

"Yael and Meir being killed, the people after us."

Rivka had her hand over her mouth, thumb massaging one cheek, four fingers massaging the other, which meant she was deep in thought about what not to say. "They are hunting us, Arik. We killed their people, they are killing ours. I'd like to do something about that."

Glitzman had once put the problem to Meir, who quoted Rūmī back at him: *Don't try to put out a fire by throwing on more fire.* And Glitzman had asked what the hell else he might throw on the flames, then, seeing as water also seemed to encourage the blaze. Meir literally threw up his hands, said he didn't have a damn clue. A smile hovered over Rivka's mouth but did not land. Glitzman, feeling a wave of fatigue wash over him, swallowed a yawn. "There is a cold simplicity to it," he said. "I give Ghorbani that."

"We find the network," Rivka said. "And . . ." She aimed a finger gun into the middle distance and fired.

Another yawn bubbled up, and this time he could not suppress it. "Killing them won't stop it," Glitzman said, "not really, but we've got no other choice, do we? We've just got to keep on killing them."

Rivka caught the yawn. And when she nodded, her sad smile, at last, touched down.

CHAPTER 17

Istanbul, Turkey

THOUGH HOSSEIN HAD NEVER said as much, Roya had come to believe she had been chosen for the Istanbul trips because the Turkish security services—though competent, capable, and suspicious of Iranians—were also packed with chauvinists (What bureaucracy was not? she wondered), and therefore far less likely to pay attention to an Iranian female traveling under the auspices of the Ali Emiri Efendi Cultural Center. This was her third visit, and the schedule for the morning would be identical to that of the first two. The stops would be dreary, the traffic somehow worse than Tehran's. And yet, as she sat in the taxi moving south from the airport at a slow crawl, Roya felt a pang of excitement at the city before her, and then a twinge of guilt at her brief separation from Alya. Someday, she thought, to comfort herself, someday we will come here together.

The ride was two awful hours. The center itself, occupying a nondescript town house near Sultanahmet, was her first stop. Her suitcase clacked over the tiles as she walked toward the dour Imad's office.

"How was your flight?" Imad asked, in a tone of abject disinterest.

"It did not crash."

This earned a grunt from the man, who swiveled his chair around to begin dialing the combination lock on the safe. Three trips, and he'd yet to reveal a single emotion. Roya was relieved, actually, to interact with a man so completely disinterested in her marital status. Kneeling on the floor because his office was so cramped, she unzipped the main compartment on her suitcase and set aside the two plastic bags holding her clothing. On her first trip to Istanbul she'd not bagged her things. Her underwear had been visible from the desk, and she was fairly certain Imad had seen it. Now she covered everything, careful to leave plenty of spare room, so she would not be embarrassed when he loaded in the money.

She felt around for the two buttons that Hossein's men had added beneath the plastic bottom of the suitcase, which popped when compressed. She wedged her fingers in a corner and peeled back the plastic to reveal a hidden compartment. Imad was placing rolls of U.S. dollars on his desk. Roya stood dumbly, waiting, Imad's concentration totally absorbed by the count. He made a few notes on a pad, which disappeared into the safe. He folded his hands on the desk and reviewed the bills as if hoping they might one day make him proud. At his nod she slipped them into the concealed compartment in her case. One hundred thousand, as expected. No wonder Hossein himself was traveling to Istanbul for this meeting, whatever it was about. She did not ask questions, though. She merely did all the work. The zipper on her case caught, and after a frustrating minute, Imad retrieved a pair of pliers from a desk drawer. Then, with the money packed and wheels clattering across the tiles, Roya was gone.

NEXT: ON FOOT toward the water, suitcase clanging behind, swirling through flocks of tourists in Sultanahmet to an equipment storage facility for one of the ferry operators, a firm owned by a man that Hossein said was "a longtime friend of Iran." She had to huff to the warehouse on foot because Hossein had been explicit: no taxi rides here, they did not want Turks linking this address to an Iranian, even if she was a helpless woman. Here she would collect phones with a variety of SIM cards and International Mobile Equipment Identity, IMEI, serial numbers, and, occasionally, boxes with contents that mostly remained mysterious, even to Roya. On her last visit, when the tape had peeled from the top, she had spotted cartons of assorted electronics and mechanical parts that might have been for a motorcycle, or perhaps a model airplane.

The small warehouse sat on the water on the Golden Horn, in the shadows of the Galata Bridge. She did not like coming here. Wild dogs were a problem throughout Istanbul, and a crumbling, dusty industrial building down near the water was prime real estate: there were plenty of rats to hunt. The dogs mostly left you alone, but some of them, watching her stroll toward the main storage facility, were quite large. Cats also creeped through the alleys and atop crumbling loading docks. Her suitcase smacked loudly on uneven pavement and a few times she had to jerk it free from large cracks. But there were no cameras; there was no one around at all. The emptiness, save for the feral dogs, made her feel supremely vulnerable. She came to a metal door wearing a skirt of rust and a plate that read EMPLOYEE ENTRANCE.

She entered a code, the light blinked green, and she went inside. Alongside the main storage room floor there was a dusty kitchenette, a few empty offices, and a conference room. Dust covered everything except the small boxes in the corner, left there by Hossein's friend a few days earlier. She placed them into her case, rearranging her things a few times to make room for it all. Then she left, hustling through the awful loading docks, careful to move quickly, but not so quick as to spook the party of dogs, watching her with lazy interest from beneath a rusty jungle of strewn pipe.

FROM THE DOCKS she rode the ferry north to the first bridge at Ortaköy, then took a taxi into Levent for some shopping to provision the house where Hossein would conduct his meeting. Between a grocery, a minimart, and a high-end deli, Roya worked through the list Hossein had given her in Tehran—cigarettes, lighters, tea, empty black duffel, three bottles of Coke, bag of sugar, a few boxes of Turkish sweets, a prewrapped *mezze* platter—ticking items off her list as she trudged through Istanbul's salty dusk, her head down and her thoughts fastened to Alya, and her sister, and Hossein, and the nagging fear that she was hopelessly adrift and wouldn't even recognize land when she saw it. Life was the next patch of never-ending sea. Life was the next twenty or so minutes.

Shopping done, she caught a taxi into Etiler, and had the driver drop her a few blocks from the house. She turned onto a leafy side street and recognized the small freestanding rental. With great relief, she went inside, where she immediately dumped her suitcase and the bags. She walked the property to be sure it was clean and to check for obvious cameras—the rentals were different on each trip, and last time she'd found a nanny cam one of the hosts had left behind. In one bathroom she flushed a urine-filled toilet.

Satisfied with her search, she laid the supplies and the phones on the dining room table. The food went into the refrigerator, the bricks of cash into the newly bought duffel, which she plopped in one of the dining room chairs. A string of messages from her sister pinged through to her Turkish phone number: pictures of Alya at the park, close-in shots of her drawings, most of which appeared to be misshapen bunnies, and in each her toothy white smile was aglow, filling the camera. One last tour of the house to be sure everything was in order, then she texted Hossein the code for the key box. *All ready.* But before she could even slip the phone in her pocket, she saw the ripple of three dots indicating he was responding. Had his flight already landed?

Come meet me tonight? We will debrief.

She thought for a moment about their last trip here, in January. He'd been a gentleman—a hand on her arm when he became animated at dinner, a keen look in his eyes, a few not-so-discreet glances at her bottom. But no more than that. Did she want more? There were worse matches; there were probably better. But he was here, in Istanbul, and it had been so long since Abbas . . .

She stared at the phone for a moment before choosing a curt reply: *You will be at your villa?*

Yes.

She did not know who Hossein was meeting in Istanbul. Mostly, she did not care. She was thinking, as always, about the money she would leave behind. Roya assumed Hossein would take a cut, presuming that whomever he was meeting did not know how much had been withdrawn, that Imad at the center did not know where the funds were going, and that Roya, the only other person sitting in the middle of this game, would have no inclination to push or prod on why she was muling bricks of cash in a suitcase, over the broken sidewalks of a fishy-smelling Istanbul street, past curious dogs, through the billows of cigarette smoke the Turks threw up in every direction, all in service of a Qods Force officer who, if it came to it, could quite easily tell his superiors that Roya had taken the money, that he was shocked—shocked!—at the thievery of his lovely yet devious subordinate.

ROYA'S USUAL HOTEL in Ortaköy was near enough the safe house and Hossein's villa to be convenient, but not so close that she wouldn't have time to check if anyone was following her. The training Hossein had provided in Tehran was rudimentary—with only a few hours of classroom instruction and no time on the street, even she knew that—but he'd stressed that when she performed her duties in Istanbul she must always "zigzag four or five times between stops, and duck into stores whenever possible." The words were in her mind as she browsed a few clothing boutiques and a sweets shop. She did not think anyone had followed her that morning, and she felt similarly now, on the way to her hotel.

The tile in the lobby had gotten dirtier and more chipped since January. A man sat in a stiff-backed chair looking through the front windows with such attention that he might have been gazing upon some other world, instead of a group of fat, tired-looking businessmen smoking cigarettes. She stowed the suitcase in the closet, kicked off her shoes, and lay down on the bed. Resisting the temptation to close her eyes, she pulled out her Turkish phone and called her sister on WhatsApp.

"Hi," Afsaneh said when the video connected.

"Is Alya still down for her nap?" Roya asked.

"She is. Shall I wake her?"

"No, no," she said. "How are you?"

"We are fine here. We went to the park. Did you get the pictures?"

"I did, thank you."

"She misses you."

"Why does that sound like an accusation?"

"Because you have a guilty conscience and an overactive imagination. It was a statement, Roya."

Roya glanced around the quiet room and felt a sudden rush of familiar shame: I am glad to be alone, she thought, just for a few days I am glad to be away. I feel terrible, and yet I am a little glad to be away from the chaos of expectation and responsibility and ... the noise. God, how she loved Alya, and, god, how she had come to relish a few days away.

"Is he there with you?" Afsaneh asked.

"Who?"

"You know who."

"Who?"

"You know who."

Roya whispered: "Hossein is my boss, Afsaneh. And he's fond of me. What can I do? I work for him. It's not like I have much of a choice..."

Her sister slammed down the phone, so Roya could see only the kitchen ceiling. There was a clatter of pots and kitchenware, followed by Afsaneh's sigh, which, aimed at nothing in particular, hit everything all at once. When Afsaneh again picked up the phone, they cradled each other in a heavy silence, in which Roya felt that her elder sister had again appraised her, fully and completely, only to find her utterly wanting, as always. Roya heard the rush of water filling the teakettle. Afsaneh brought the phone close to her face, looked around to be sure no one was in earshot, and said, quite calmly: "Roya, don't be a whore."

A bright smile then flashed across her sister's face, and Roya, dumbstruck, saw that she was trotting, phone in hand, down the hallway, toward Alya's room. "She is awake!" Then Roya could hear Alya shouting: Mama! Mama! Mama!

"Wait, Afsaneh," Roya said. "I need to go. I'll call later."

The video jerked around until it found her sister's face, backed against a wall in the hallway.

"Remember—don't be a whore," Afsaneh said in strangely affable tone. She was looking off toward the racket behind Alya's door when Roya ended the call.

CHAPTER 18

Istanbul

BECAUSE, FOR MOST OF its modern history, Israel has not had diplomatic facilities in much of its near abroad, Mossad's operational playbook does not rely on formal embassies, officers sporting the paper-thin veneer of diplomatic cover, or state-sponsored smuggling conducted through the diplomatic pouch. Operational teams are cobbled together based on the mission requirements, surged to where they are needed, and then disbanded when the work is done. The plane is built as it flies.

This was the case in Istanbul, where, with Cohen's blessing, and that bastard Ankorion's consent, Glitzman had assembled a safe house and team of surveillants in just shy of forty-eight hours.

The operations room was a freestanding town house rented by a French-Jewish officer under non-official cover—NOC—not far from Moghaddam's villa in Bebek. The divans in the sitting room were covered in musty velvet pillows and the table was decorated by a crop of foo lions. The eight people cloistered in that room, now pounded by the smell of cigarettes, body odor, and grease, were a wildly eclectic blend of nationalities.

The surveillance team leaders were Santiago and Hanna Cervantes, who had lived in Istanbul for decades. Everyone called the guy Santa (the Jewish Santa Claus, he would grumble.)

There was also an American Jew named Milt Bradley, a name that sounded familiar to Glitzman, though he was not quite able to place it. Milt carried a tablet that held Mossad's primo intel on Istanbul's CCTV camera networks and, with a pen, began marking zones where the team had noted recreational drone activity.

"Where's the coffee?" Glitzman called into the kitchen.

No one answered. The rest of the surveillance team were reviewing a map spread on the table, the foo lions moved aside to make space. Glitzman had taken note of an old Turkish Jewish woman everyone called Nene, but he had already forgotten the names of her son and grandson. The son was about a head taller than the father and the father looked about the same age as the son and Glitzman decided he would ask nothing more about this family. It was, after all, unlikely he would ever work with any of these people again.

The parts of the surveillance team made zero sense when summed together, and that was precisely the point. But this crew had Glitzman wondering if Ankorion had poured him the dregs from his cup. Nene was nearing seventy, Rivka had said, while scanning the team's profiles in Tel Aviv, and Glitzman had actually managed to get out a laugh, though only after he'd flung a few curses at Ankorion.

Glitzman checked the flights: Hossein Moghaddam was arriving right on time.

MOSSAD'S MAN at Istanbul Airport shuffled into the back of the sterile room while the on-duty lieutenant droned on during the evening shift briefing. Looking around the room, Colonel Alp Fidan noted ten officers present, each stealing uneasy glances his direction, pondering the appearance of the second most important customs officer at the airport, which could, under no circumstances, be construed as a positive sign.

Fidan had worked at Istanbul Airport for twelve years, the last six of which he'd found a lucrative side hustle doing favors for Mossad.

Sometimes this meant ensuring pallets of cargo were loaded onto trucks without submitting to the scanners; others (and these were trickier than you might think) he arranged for the hauling of people—always Arabs or Persians—into secondary, where their electronics could be briefly confiscated for clandestine imaging. So, on the spectrum of their requests, this one graced the simpler end. No need to bribe the knuckle draggers on the ramp or physically touch the Iranian or his belongings. No—flags were uncomplicated. To earn a €10,000 bonus, Fidan merely had to concoct a reason for the on-duty customs officials to notify him when the Iranian appeared in their lane.

Directly beneath the NO SMOKING sign Fidan lit a cigarette, burning through it in silence while the lieutenant finished the bland security update, assigned lane numbers and break times, and bickered with several of the officers about the value of an online training module, a refresher on the facial recognition software installed last year, which had been glitchy. As the argument rolled on, Fidan crushed his cigarette out in the trash can, careful to be sure he did not light the plastic on fire, and growled, "Enough. The training is mandatory. We have a request in from the National Police for a flag. An Iranian. His name is Farzan Jamshidi. If he appears in your lane, you are to let him through, you are to notify me immediately, and you are to send me his information. Are we understood?"

STOOPED OVER ONE OF the duty officers in the control room, Fidan watched as the 184 passengers of Iran Air Flight 082, direct from Tehran, deplaned and shuffled toward passport control. The lines this morning were relatively short—there had been a rash of inbound cancellations due to weather in Germany and the Gulf—so the queue for Flight 082 would be ten minutes long, at most. *A thousand euros a minute if this goes well*, Fidan thought. Cash he could put toward jewelry, or perhaps purses, for—in order—his two daughters, his wife, and his mistress, who was sadly beginning to remind him of his wife.

He walked out onto the floor, where he milled around making chitchat with two of his officers while keeping an eye on the line. Five, then ten minutes passed. Then his phone trilled. It was Amina, down in lane three. He looked up and saw that she was hustling toward him.

He refreshed his email, dragging the screen down, releasing, dragging. Nothing appeared. Had she sent anything?

"What is the matter?" he said tersely.

"Colonel!" she breathed heavily. "He just passed through. I could not..." She paused to catch her breath. "I could not send his information. The stupid system crashed. It is rebooting now. It takes maybe ten minutes...it..."

Fidan looked off at the trickle of Iranians headed toward baggage claim. "What did he look like? Tell me now."

"Gray suit, tan shoes"—another gasp—"blue shirt."

Fidan swore, then began trailing the Iran Air passengers out toward baggage, walking as fast as he could without running. On the app he texted off a brief description and the approximate time the still-faceless Farzan Jamshidi had cleared passport control.

IN THE COMMAND CENTER, Glitzman was listening through the microphones to the heavy mouth-breathing of Milt Bradley, waiting at baggage carousel five, where passengers for Iran Air 082 were assembling. "Any bags yet?" Glitzman asked in English.

"None," Milt replied. "Carousel is inert."

Treating the phone to a look of unmitigated hatred, Glitzman muted the line and looked to Rivka, who said, "It's not moving."

Glitzman was about to unmute the phone when a message arrived through the group's Signal chat with a thin description of Moghaddam and a passport-control timestamp that meant the guy would be showing up any second, if he wasn't there yet.

"Gray suit, tan shoes, blue shirt," Glitzman called out. "Anything?"

"Not yet," Milt said. "But I'm sweating buckets out here."

Glitzman knew the sweat was not from nerves, but from the thirty pounds of commo equipment and a deck of three external batteries humming inside his hiker's pack. Milt's tech gear was running a Pineapple: inside his backpack, every second a ping went out, masking itself as the airport's open Wi-Fi network, scanning for the lone phone selector that Mossad possessed on Moghaddam.

"Is the carousel still inert?" Glitzman asked.

"It's still not moving," Milton replied.

ANOTHER MAN MIGHT HAVE let it go, but Alp Fidan had scattered vague hints of purses and shoes and jewelry across the women in his life, and he worried that if he took his foot off the gas in this operation, there might be less work in the future, and that simply would not do. So Fidan edged into a run, slowing down only once he entered the baggage claim hall and looked around, conscious that he could not appear overly anxious or perturbed. The hall was not particularly busy, crowds milled around perhaps half of the fourteen claim carousels. He thought he spotted tan shoes on a man walking toward the taxi line. Fidan followed, glimpsing him approaching one of the black taxis. Speed-walking, cursing under his breath, phone at his ear in a desperate bid to appear preoccupied, Fidan closed the gap to bring the man into sharper view.

Same shoes, Fidan thought.

He was sure it was him.

Or was he?

He was fairly sure.

As the man ducked into a cab, Fidan caught a slash of blue collar peeking out from beneath the coat. Now that he thought about it, the guy hadn't been wearing a coat at customs, had he? Maybe it had been in his bag. The taxi door shut. Fidan, now fifteen meters from the car, but with a clean view of the license plate, stopped dead in his tracks to memorize the number. Turning away, Fidan typed the vehicle description and plate number into his chat and sent it off to the Israelis. Deep breath. Another. The air was exhaust and made him cough. He found Amina in the breakroom.

"Did you find him, Colonel?" she said.

"Yes, I believe so," Fidan replied, pouring himself a thimble of coffee. "The system's back up, so I sent you his information."

Fidan pulled up the photo, set down his coffee, zoomed in. He thought about the face for a while, then sent the passport information and photograph off to the Israelis. Was it him? He thought so, he was at least pretty sure, but each passing minute drained Fidan's confidence he had it right.

RIVKA TYPED INTO THE CHAT: *Black Mercedes taxi van. Turkish plates. 34 DC 17851.*

"We can split the atom," Glitzman muttered, "and still it takes ten fucking people to follow one Persian through the airport."

THE MESSAGE BROUGHT to life the three cars waiting in the parking lot. In a silver Renault, the Cervanteses made for the street approaching the terminal, where they hoped to intersect, then swing behind, the black taxi. Nene's grandson made the same move from his black Kia.

Nene and her son, in a weathered white Fiat Egea, bumped away from the pump at the airport petrol station. If all went to plan, they would tag the mark first because they were on a natural chokepoint: the airport had a single exit.

Next to the flag inside the airport, this was the most delicate move in the entire dance, because the rabbit, the surveillance mark, had been dark for almost a full minute. Accidents and happenstance, to say nothing of errors of tradecraft, could cost them everything. Glitzman once had an op go sideways because one of his surveillants, a Rhodesian mercenary, had set his disguise beard aflame while lighting a cigarette, and in his panic had lost the mark.

"There," Nene said to her son, nodding up the road. She turned the Signal chat into a call and said, in stilted English, "Spot him."

The black taxi shot past. They swung onto the road, muscling around two other vehicles to claim a spot directly behind the cab. The license plate number matched. And there was a head in the backseat.

The cars left the airport in a convoy. Moghaddam's taxi in front, next

Nene and her son, then her grandson, and finally the Cervanteses in the rear, keeping their Renault out of sight as long as possible. Through the dash-mounted camera in Nene's car, Glitzman watched the bumper of Moghaddam's cab. The convoy headed toward downtown, crawling through grinding traffic, careful to keep Moghaddam's taxi near enough to follow, but not so close that he might spook.

THE SURVEILLANCE CARAVAN followed the cab until it stopped outside a pharmacy a few blocks from the water, in Arnavutköy. On the map Glitzman saw that the Cervanteses' car had overshot Moghaddam, goaded on, Santa jabbered, by the sudden undamming of traffic in their lane. A half block up they were refolded into the mess, and the radio chatter became a Spanish-language argument between husband and wife, Glitzman supposed, over the availability of parking. Hanna jumped out of the car, leaving her husband behind, and Glitzman listened in horror as it became clear the Cervanteses had lost sight of him. Where is he, Hanna kept muttering, where is he? I don't see him.

His heart rate spiking, Glitzman watched the dash cam as the car bearing Nene and her son pulled to the opposite side of the road and parked in a tight spot on the sidewalk. When they'd stepped out, Glitzman saw Nene clandestinely snapping several photos of the man who had exited the cab. She began following him.

Glitzman muted the mic on his phone and turned to Rivka. "The seventy-year-old is now the point. Fucking great."

"She's sixty-six," Rivka said.

Nene huffed farther uphill, trailing Moghaddam, breathing into the earpiece as if she might soon die. Her son was trailing behind, gaining ground. After a few minutes, Nene made a small noise and said, in thickly accented English, "Oh boy. Oh boy. Oh no."

"What?" Glitzman shouted. "What is it?"

"He go alley," Nene huffed out. "Hold on. Oh boy."

"I'm behind him," said Nene's son. Glitzman heard heavy breathing, and then the man's mic cut out and he could only hear Nene.

She was breathing like she had glass in her lungs. Like she was running uphill through a forest fire. "Oh boy," she kept saying.

Then Glitzman heard a lot of barking.

"Fuck's that?" Rivka said. "Dogs?"

Glitzman became aware of a great tension in his jaw. Then he heard a clatter. There was more barking. Nene screamed. She was shouting in Turkish and now her son was shouting back, and though none of it sounded good, Glitzman couldn't make out a word. He said, to everyone, to no one, "What the fuck? What's going on?"

"Dog knock him down," hissed Nene. "I go see."

"Who's minding the rabbit, then?" Glitzman shouted into the mics.

He watched on the dashcam as Nene's grandson decided to abandon his car in the street. Glitzman tracked his beacon as the kid plodded off, on foot, toward the alley where they had lost Moghaddam.

Glitzman hung his head. "We're fucked," he said to Rivka, who made a noise of affirmation.

They listened to Nene's grandson choppily narrate his fruitless stroll down the side street.

The gist of it: plenty of ways in and out, no sign of Moghaddam. Nene had helped her son onto a bench, where he was moaning, in Turkish, that something was broken. The dogs hadn't been after him, of course. They were after a rat. The rodent had squiggled right under his feet and then a few larger dogs had bowled into his legs. Hanna and Santa scoured the neighborhood for signs of Moghaddam, to no avail.

Glitzman was staring at a map of Istanbul, cigarette pinned in his teeth, phone in the death grip of his right hand. The map confirmed his worst fears: Moghaddam's route made little sense if he were headed to his apartment. Could be bound for an operational meet, a restaurant, his favorite whorehouse, who knew? There were almost twenty million fucking people in this city and Moghaddam was going somewhere to meet with one of them. Glitzman lit a fresh cigarette with the embers of the one in his mouth, which he then crumpled into a bowl, along with all the others.

"A shot at cracking up Ghorbani's network," Glitzman said, muting the chat, "dashed by a pack of wild dogs."

Glitzman wanted to smash one of the foo lions into the wall but thought better and unmuted the chat. "Search the neighborhood for another half hour, then we'll take up our positions outside his villa. Wait for him to come back, and take it from there." The surveillants chimed their acknowledgments.

Glitzman gave the map another smack. "Big fucking city," he mumbled.

"Big fucking city," Rivka agreed.

CHAPTER 19

Istanbul

WHEN YOU'RE A NOBODY, you can do anything.

Roya had a modest per diem available for reimbursement, and an Iran Air return ticket that could not be punched until after the weekend. She was in a city with water and boats and freedom offered by a mass of people who did not know her at all.

But what to do until she met Hossein that evening? And what, exactly, was going to happen during this debriefing—to say nothing of afterward?

OPTIONS, ROYA THOUGHT. So many wild options in Istanbul.

Rent a motorbike! Too dangerous.

Drink whiskey! Not the greatest idea. Remember the headache next morning? Abbas didn't scrape himself out of bed until lunchtime.

A tattoo! As if Afsaneh needed more material.

In the end Roya decided, rather unambitiously, on a walk. She dressed in Turkish gray scale: sensible black walking shoes, a plain charcoal-colored dress, and a white hijab. Tucked inside it was each unruly forelock of her hair. At a *tekel* a few blocks north of the hotel, she bought a pack of Marlboros and a lighter. A few blocks later she bought a Turkish coffee so sweet it seemed to melt her teeth. She sat there with her cup and her cigarette, watching women walk past, some in hijabs, others in short skirts, no one paying her any mind, and then her thoughts drifted to Alya, and she felt a pang of loneliness that made her get up and leave. She stopped when she reached the tram.

Was someone following her?

She did not think so, and yet she also knew she did not truly have the means to know, nor had she been particularly attentive this afternoon. She was finding herself homesick.

At Eyüp she switched to the *teleferik*, the cable car, which she rode up, up, up. As a girl she had sometimes wondered how the men who ran Iran felt. Now she felt she had a feeble taste of it, effortlessly ascending the heights of this hill.

At the top Roya exited the cable car. Then, walking in the pure light of day, she tore off her hijab and thrust it into her purse. A dozen Iranian women had completed this same act in the bathroom on the airplane, but Roya had not. She had been afraid. She was finding, more and more, that she was afraid.

But now she ran her fingers through her matted, sweaty hair, relishing the breeze and the brilliant light. A gust of wind blew her hair off her shoulders, sending it back into a cape and then upward, weightless, into an anarchic corded crown. The fingers of the air were scratching an unreachable, infuriating itch. Roya tussled her hair and then gave it back to the wind.

She claimed a seat at a windblown café. The table was covered in a green-and-white patterned tablecloth anchored by a rock conscripted to be a centerpiece. Spreading out from the hillside were the spires of mosques and the tops of pines prickling the city; the swoop and drift of seabirds; and, just barely, in the distance, the bluish gold bubbles of the Hagia Sophia. She ordered a coffee and *simit* and thought that in another world she would stay here until dark, until the city flickered on and she could watch over it all. But that was not her world, so she gave each patron a rather conspiratorial side-eye. Even after she was certain she was not being followed, Roya sat for a few moments in a submissive hunch, sipping her coffee, picking at her bread, hair playing in the wind, just waiting to be proven wrong.

CHAPTER 20

Istanbul

THE STREETS BRIGHTENED on Roya's circuitous journey back to Bebek. The sidewalks grew smoother. The smell from the shops less oily, less greasy. Clothes on the pedestrians became slimmer, more well-cut, brighter, more Western. The crowds smelled of alcohol and smooth tobacco and perfume, and she was hit, again, by the homesick desire to fly back to Tehran early. Or at least to call Afsaneh and check in.

Later, Roya would also recognize fear mingling in the cloud of unease settling around her. Fear of the meeting with Hossein. But on the walk Roya just pushed it aside. And she put her hijab back on.

Hossein had given her the job.

He had created chances for travel. For freedom, however ephemeral.

He had use of a beautiful villa in this cheerful neighborhood. And, after all, things only worked because everyone took what they could get. Abbas had, too, and that was just so they'd have a little extra pocket money. He'd been an honest man. Here was the upside-down nature of the system: you could only be trusted if you were corrupt. It was the honest ones who had problems.

The thoughts flashed like rocket fire through her mind.

Hossein was suave, capable, a highflyer. He'd reach heights Abbas never would have. She heard Afsaneh's voice: Then, Roya, why is he not married? It was a good question.

He'd been a gentleman, mostly.

Mostly.

He would not force it, he would not make her, would he?

No, he was kind. Handsome.

The text messages her sister had seen over the past few months... Roya knew she should not have responded—but what choice did she have? He was her boss. Also she had kind of enjoyed herself.

She turned the corner and looked up: Moghaddam's villa was three stories, painted bright green, with cheerful flower boxes perched on the wrought-iron balconies of the second floor. Warm light from the windows smiled on the Bosphorus below. His neighbor on the right was an empty art gallery; on his left was a soiled stone town house, its windows dark. Her phone trilled.

I'll open the gate.

Don't be a whore, she heard her sister say. I'm not a whore, Roya whispered to herself, just because my sister envies me.

The gate clicked. Shutting it behind her, she felt the handle slick with her own sweat. Hossein was hustling out of the villa to greet her. And he was smiling—broad, cheerful, friendly. It sent her stomach into her throat, and she felt her neck growing flush. Could he see? Did she care? She did her best to smile back.

CHAPTER 21
Istanbul

GLITZMAN HAD SPENT the afternoon in the safe house with Rivka and the surveillance team, waiting, hoping, for Moghaddam to return to the villa. By the time he did, strolling in looking quite pleased with himself, Mossad had lost the guy for seven hours and thirteen minutes. Plenty of time for Moghaddam to accomplish just about anything: meeting a source, passing cash, weapons, phones, or committing treason against the Islamic Republic with another intelligence service. Glitzman's thread-pulling seemed to have run out of sweater. For the last hour he'd been on and off the satphone with Cohen, debating the merits of snatching Moghaddam. Amos had only just hung up on him, when, through two of the surveillance cameras, Glitzman watched a Persian woman walk into Moghaddam's villa.

Most of her hair was wrapped up in a hijab with a playful strand draped across her face. What had doubtless once been a nose with a wider, steeper bridge was now slightly pinched and sloped—though thankfully it did not resemble melted wax, as is so often the case with Persians, who can sometimes overwork the few scraps of skin that the Guidance Patrol permits their men to lust after. He thought the smile genuine—not a prostitute, then—and just before Moghaddam opened the gate for her, Glitzman was treated to a clear view of her face, straight-on.

"Holy shit, it's . . . I think that's . . ." Rivka trailed off.

Glitzman experienced a strike of disorientation, as if he'd woken from a deep sleep in a strange room. His mind was reeling, trying to place this woman, when it hit him: She'd been running, quite fast, clutching her daughter, stuffed lamb in the girl's grip, the imprint stashed in his mind for all eternity. He'd watched all of this through a camera mounted to a gunsight, because the last time he'd laid eyes on Roya Shabani, Glitzman had been tending to the murder of her husband.

CHAPTER 22

Istanbul

UPSTAIRS, ROYA WATCHED hossein open two bottles of mineral water, and they drifted toward the living room window with its wide view of the Bosphorus. Somewhere between her first shaky sips and the sight of a white boat with gold trim, Roya made up her mind. Her lips were cold with anticipation. No matter how much water she drank, her throat remained parched. They stood there for a moment. They'd hardly spoken since she had finished delivering her report on her stops earlier that day. Had he lost his nerve?

"I love this place," Hossein murmured, his eyes fixed on the water. The boat's horn moaned.

"It's beautiful," Roya agreed.

A stilted silence spun open. He was far-off. Bewitched by the water? Did he not know what to do, how to take a woman to bed? He is smooth, she thought, of course he does. He is not shy.

Drugs? She had wondered about that, on their last trip. But she did not want to think about drugs. She took Hossein's hand—she liked how it felt, tough and warm. He gave her a watery smile. Drugs, probably. Was it opium? *Shisheh?* Crystal meth? She snatched a closer look at his lips. Were they thin, lavender? The light was bad. She could not tell.

CHAPTER 23

Istanbul

HARD FACTS, GLITZMAN THOUGHT. Stick to hard facts, slim though they are.

Roya Shabani enters the villa at quarter after nine in the evening. What is she doing there? Don't know, can't know. Hard facts.

After thirty minutes, the surveillance audio—which was of a maddeningly low quality—indicated that the friendly chitchat inside the villa had ground to a halt. In its place was silence broken only by the hiss of opening bottles.

"Are they in bed?" Glitzman asked.

"Can't tell," said Rivka. "Maybe. Probably. Why else would she be there?"

"Meetings," Glitzman said. "Bureaucracy."

The cameras did not offer a view inside the villa. And the silence suggested to Glitzman that if they were in bed, either both were the silent, nervous type, or he was doing a terrible job. Glitzman went into the kitchen to put water on for coffee.

The kettle had just begun whistling when, over the microphone, he heard Roya begin to scream. Glitzman dashed back into the sitting room. Rivka was hunched over the computers, watching the video feeds. Glitzman was a man who, regrettably, knew the different flavors of scream. This one wasn't pain or surprise. This one was terror.

"What's she saying?" he asked.

"His name," Rivka said. They listened for a moment. "She's asking if he's all right."

He heard a smacking sound.

"What's the sound I'm hearing?" Glitzman asked. "That huffing noise between all the shouting."

"I think she's trying to resuscitate him," Rivka said.

The cameras revealed nothing—nobody was in front of the windows. Roya was stammering and shouting, though Glitzman couldn't understand anything besides her repetition of his name.

Hossein, Hossein, Hossein.

"Now what's she saying?"

"She keeps telling him to get up."

Now Glitzman could hear her crying.

"Might be dead," Rivka said.

"I should call Cohen," Glitzman said, more to himself, because he wondered if perhaps he should not.

"PACK IT UP, ARIK," Cohen said after Glitzman had tossed a suitcase of facts at his feet. Cohen's salvo was that most un-Israeli of operational instincts: reluctance. Glitzman was momentarily dumbstruck. As he listened to the tinkle of ice in Cohen's faraway glass, Glitzman weighed the benefits of fighting for permission against the risks of asking for forgiveness.

"We've got two connections to Colonel Ghorbani," Glitzman finally said, "and they are inside the villa. And you want me to pack it up? Amos, come, now."

"He's probably dead," Cohen sniffed.

"She's not. There is little risk."

"How much risk, would you say?"

"Little."

"Not none, then." Slurp of his drink.

"Maybe I should call back when you're not drunk."

"Shit, Arik. It's Coke."

"Fine. Well, show me an operation with zero risk," Glitzman shot back.

"Arik, enough, I—"

"And I will show you—"

"Stop, stop—"

"—analysis. Analysis, Amos. That is a desktop exercise, not an op."

Cohen heaved an exhausted sigh. "Arik. Sit tight. Keep an eye on the villa. Then we can see how we wind it down." Then he hung up.

After he'd kicked over one of the foo lions, and sulked with his cup of coffee, and upon further reflection, Glitzman thought he could work with that.

"We will wind it down," he explained to Rivka. "But first we will wind it up a little."

THE VILLA'S FRONT GATE was defended by an electronic lock which Rivka took down in under a minute. The front door itself sported a pin and tumbler that Rivka examined with the piteous look one might offer a beggar. Seven seconds later, the door was open.

And then Glitzman was all movement, taking the lead as he trotted up the staircase, stun gun in hand, peering into an empty sitting room that Meir would have known how to describe. To Glitzman it was a bunch of Ottoman shit heaped around. He could hear Roya crying and sniffling in another room and began to shuffle down the hall, in the direction of the noise, Rivka right behind. They padded down a hallway until they came to the entrance of a larger living room. He paused and unconsciously rubbed his nose. Glitzman harbored no ill will toward the woman. Quite the opposite: he felt some sympathy for her position and wished there was a gentler way to do this. But he did not feel a tickle of remorse for what he was about to do.

He stepped into the room, moving fast.

Roya, seated in a chair, looked up at him, her eyes stricken by fear. She had just begun to scream when the fangs of the stun gun bit into her shoulder. She made a sharp noise, then went rigid and convulsed, slumping onto the floor beside the unmoving Moghaddam.

In a half second they were in a pile, struggling to bind Roya. Glitzman pinned her thighs to the floor while Rivka zip-tied first her arms, then her legs. Glitzman taped a sock over her mouth. Rivka, checking Moghaddam's pulse, shook her head. Glitzman had seen plenty of dead bodies, and this was definitely one of those. But still, for insurance purposes, they bound him.

Roya was trying to scream through the gag, and they absolutely could not have any more screams, not in a neighborhood like this, where residents weren't afraid to call the police. Glitzman tore at Roya's manteau and when, after a few violent tugs, he saw the skin of a shoulder peering back, he jabbed in the needle. They heaved her on the divan and Rivka held her down until, in seconds, the ketamine took effect. Rivka was about to smack the needle into Moghaddam's shoulder when Glitzman stopped her arm. Did she doubt the man was dead?

"No reason to fuck up the autopsy," he said.

CHAPTER 24

Istanbul

GLITZMAN COULD NOT FIND any wound of significance on Moghaddam's body. There was no blood. No weapon. No evidence of a struggle. Heart attack? He thought so. Maybe nudged along by drugs. Rivka and the surveillance team could not find any cameras, which did not surprise Glitzman one bit. In his experience the Qods guys didn't want the cameras turned on them.

Had Glitzman been a normal person, he might have thought about what the hell he was going to tell Cohen, since forgiveness for the unauthorized breaking-and-entering was very clearly not going to be in the offing, not unless he succeeded.

Instead Glitzman, looking down at the Bosphorus, latched onto another question: What had they missed during the seven hours when they'd lost Moghaddam?

His best—correction: only—thread to pull was Roya Shabani, his living, breathing connection to whomever had killed Meir and Yael and was doubtless coming for him. And for this thread pulling he required time, time without the Iranians believing anything amiss.

Glitzman knelt by Moghaddam's body. Turning it this way and that, he conducted a more detailed check for further trauma, and found none.

It might work, he thought. It just might.

THE CALL WITH the Mossad toxicologist to determine the proper quantities and proportions had been pleasantly straightforward. The discussion with Nene's grandson about the shopping list had also gone well, and when Glitzman dispatched him to purchase, among other things, "three or four handles of higher-end whiskey, scotch, gin, vodka, et cetera," "pornographic magazines, the nastier the better," and "a collection of garish dildos," the young man had just nodded along, which Glitzman interpreted as the response of a steady, unshakable asset, and Rivka took as proof that the man knew his way around a sex shop.

The first resistance to Glitzman's plan came, as he had expected, from Ankorion, at the Consulate, on whom he had to lean for a few of the medical items on his wish list. There were grumbles about the rapid blood type tests, syringes, a wheelchair, wigs, pressure bags ("What the hell are those?" Ankorion had asked, annoyed, and Glitzman had explained it slowly, as if he were speaking to Oriana), tourniquets, swabs, angiocaths, IV tubing, blood bags, Stericups. A loud grunt arrived at the mention of a "lighter big enough to be a small blowtorch," followed by the first real objection at the last item on Glitzman's list: crystal meth.

"Meth?" Ankorion said, his tone in the borderlands between incredulity and insubordination.

"Meth," Glitzman repeated.

"Most of the rest of this we have here in the Consulate or can buy at a drugstore, but meth? Where am I supposed to get meth, Arik?"

"We're collectors of intelligence, Ankorion. Secrets don't just sit around offering themselves to us. You've doubtless got some freak here in Istanbul who can collect drugs for us, yes? We've got to—"

"Oh for fuck's sake, Arik. Fine."

Glitzman heard a beep and then the silence of the dead line.

GLITZMAN'S SHOPPING LIST arrived in a few hours, courtesy of the support asset and one of Ankorion's people, who left quick as he'd come.

The blood-typing kit determined that Moghaddam was O positive, and—hark—so was Glitzman. "After all," Glitzman said, rolling up his sleeve, "it is the most common." Following the toxicologist's recommendation, Glitzman drained three units of his own blood, while Rivka, using the small blowtorch, liquefied meth in the Stericups.

"You want a cookie?" Rivka snickered at Glitzman, who, feeling embarrassingly lightheaded, had sunk down onto a divan in another sitting room to collect himself. "Or maybe some juice? Or you need this blood back? Last call," she said with a grin, then punctured the first blood bag with a syringe and began injecting the meth. Glitzman watched, fascinated, feeling less twisted in his own reaction seeing her lips pursed in a tight smile. The lightheadedness subsiding, he rose to his feet and they carried the bags to Moghaddam's body. Rivka found the antecubital vein opposite Moghaddam's elbow and speared it with the angiocath. Using the pressure bags as rudimentary pumps, they took turns filling Moghaddam's veins and arteries with the doped blood. Squeezing the last pressure bag empty, Glitzman said, "Who would have thought? In death we've converted him. His blood's nearly as Jewish as ours."

The surveillance team scanned for hairs; they cleaned and wiped down surfaces they assumed the woman had touched. They opened Moghaddam's phone with his lifeless finger and could not find any apps for a video management system, or portals to unseen cameras, thank god. There were doubtless loose ends, but what could they do?

When they assembled for a final review, Glitzman, to his great satisfaction, found he could spin the story. Moghaddam had a drug problem, he said aloud. Look at the liquor in here, in the kitchen of this villa paid for by the Qods Force! A few of the bottles were half-drunk, the whiskey was nearly drained. One glance in the cabinets, filled as they were with tourniquets, syringes, swabs, and Stericups, and it was clear the man was an addict. Like so many Iranians, when in Istanbul, Hossein Moghaddam partied.

And on top of it all: Moghaddam was a pervert. A fiend who sowed corruption on earth.

The evidence?

The final detail Glitzman saw on his way out was one of the items on the illicit shopping list. It was perched on a shelf on the far side of the bed, benefiting from a sturdy suction cup on its base. Its girthy green mass gave a droopy bow, its one eye regarding Glitzman warily as he slid shut the bedroom door.

SANTA CERVANTES and his surveillance team got on just fine without knowing *why* they were following a rabbit. So when Santa stood before Glitzman, reviewing a map for the countersurveillance run to the fallback safe house, he did not put that bothersome question to the boss, who, in addition to seeming temperamentally unwilling to answer such drivel, was also screaming at a man named Amos, his phone fastened against a brick-red ear.

"I am hearing you say yes," Glitzman was saying over the screams. "Amos, I am taking this as a yes."

Leaving Glitzman, Santa joined his crew outside and they dispersed into Bebek, this time trailing not a rabbit but searching for telltale signs of other crews: tradesman vans, drones, cars parked wheels out, ready for action, like his own Renault, idling two blocks west. After an hour they had not spotted repeat pedestrian or vehicular traffic circling the villa. The radio frequency scanners hadn't turned up the buzz of any comms activity. Santa called Glitzman and said they were good to go.

They waited.

Under the smog and the clouds, eating chips and fish sandwiches and drinking tea from thermoses, the surveillance team waited.

After another hour, a gray Sprinter van pulled up outside the villa. A moment later, through the light of the streetlamps, he saw Glitzman emerge, pushing a wheelchair holding a gray-haired woman whose neck wobbled like jelly. There was no sign of the rabbit, Moghaddam. A gust of wind snatched the old woman's gray hair, sending half of her mane skyward, exposing a shock of black beneath. The cameras did not offer a clean view, but someone had swung open the van's side door and the woman, still in the wheelchair, was heaved inside. Santa asked none of the half dozen questions soaring through his mind, first among them this: *Why* are you taking the woman? It was better not to know.

CHAPTER 25

Istanbul

THE MOON HAD NEVER RISEN, the sun had never set.

Roya remembered her first hours in captivity as lit by perpetual twilight, though later she would wonder if this was only because that's when they backed off the drugs. A line of hazy orange light split the gauzy curtains. Her mouth was so dry it felt like her tongue might crack, and the world was so quiet it felt that the slightest noise would crack it, too. She resolved not to move.

But then came voices, noise. Water on her lips, then coursing over the dry ravines of her tongue. Shapes appeared above, moving here and there, disappearing quick as they'd come. The orange light was fading to gray. The water refreshed her, but in its wake came the dull pain of consciousness, and then the realization that a cuff fastened around her wrist was also fastened to the bed, that there was an IV in her arm and a bag of clear liquid on a drip into her body.

Roya managed to sit up. She was alone. Where was she? An investigation seemed beyond her powers—she was winded from merely sitting up. And even if she'd possessed the energy? Well, she jangled her wrist, shaking the cuff against the metal bedframe. If Roya had been pious, she would have prayed for deliverance, but she did not. Instead Roya tried to orient herself. Surely in a matter of hours, days at most, someone from Qods or the Consulate would come knocking. Her sister would call . . .

"Hossein?" she cried out. This time her voice was louder, firmer—she was sure of it. "Hossein?"

Then she remembered.

ROYA AWOKE TO THE low moan of a boat's foghorn in the distance. She smelled coffee, and when she sat up, she saw a woman sitting across the room on a red velvet divan. She wore jeans and a leather jacket and tennis shoes in brilliant white, and she sipped coffee from a small glass cup. Roya had the impression that she had been watching her for some time. The cuff was gone, as was the IV drip.

"My name is Zahra," the woman said, smiling, in flawless Persian.

And though Roya sensed she was still delirious, she managed a sad laugh at the obvious lie.

"A Qods Force officer is dead," Zahra said, stealing a sip of her coffee.

Dead? Roya tried to remember, but all she could muster was the memory of standing by the window with Hossein before he keeled over. Had they killed him?

Roya could feel Zahra examining her. The woman spoke a little like a Tehrani, Roya thought. But not quite... there was a lilt to the accent she could not place. It did not make Roya feel better. It made Zahra more frightening.

Roya shut her eyes. She thought of Alya, of home. She had never felt such fear and despair, even in the wartime days following Abbas's murder. And thirst. It was crackling—her tongue so dry it felt shriveled like paper in a flame. She began to weep. "The world is a witch," Roya mumbled to herself. "The world is a witch."

"My maman read that poem to me," Zahra said, "when I was little." Zahra plucked a bottle of water from the floor and offered it to Roya.

Roya gulped down the entire thing, watching Zahra from the corner of her eye. The woman's face was a cold hearth. Roya knew women like her in Tehran. Women who drifted through life under pressure.

"You killed Hossein," Roya said.

"No," Zahra said curtly, "we found him dead. But that's a problem for you, isn't it, Roya? You were the last person to see him alive. There are messages on your phone. On his. That raises questions. Hard questions."

"Where am I?" Roya asked. "What do you want with me?"

This made Zahra smile, not unkindly. "Your name is Roya Shabani. You were working with Hossein Moghaddam on a team inside the Qods Force. You have a daughter, Alya, who will turn six next month. Your husband, Abbas, is dead. And, most recently, you were present for Moghaddam's bizarre death at his villa. Perhaps this was a lover's quarrel? I wonder what Colonel Ghorbani will think."

"What are you talking about?" Roya hissed.

"Maybe you killed him?" Zahra suggested, with whimsy. "He had other girlfriends, I'd bet. You wanted him to yourself. It's understandable, even if you'll swing from the gallows wearing a starchy chador for it."

They are Jews, Roya thought. Who else could this be, other than the Mossad? They had shot Abbas on the way to Alya's birthday dinner and now they'd kidnapped her in Istanbul. The Jews had her phone, of course, had probably opened it with her fingerprint when she'd been sleeping. What *had* they done with Hossein's body? What had they done to the villa?

"I want to go," Roya said. She was at the window, looking across the water to the sparkling villas like shoeboxes planted across the hill. She thought she was on the Asian side, though she was not certain. "This is illegal. I demand to see the Consul General of the Islamic Republic of Iran."

"Let's talk about Hossein Moghaddam instead," Zahra said. "Who was he going to meet in Istanbul?"

"I don't know."

"How will you explain this when you go home?" Zahra said. "What is your plan, Roya? I have a way to help you, but I need answers first. And I can't do anything unless I know who Hossein was planning to meet, when the meeting was to take place, and where. That's where we start."

They hung in a hateful silence. Roya did not know how to convince these people to let her go, and she was not sure what she would do if they did. Confusion reigned.

"Let's start with the timing," Zahra said, as if this were a perfectly reasonable place to begin. "Hossein was here to meet with someone. When was that meeting scheduled?"

The meeting had already happened. Friday afternoon, in the rental she had stocked. "I don't know."

"I see," Zahra replied. "And where was the meeting to take place?"

"I don't know."

Zahra pursed her lips. "For an intelligent woman, you don't know so much. How about this: Who was Hossein planning to meet with?"

"I don't know." Here Roya spoke the truth, though she immediately felt that it was less satisfying than lying.

Shadows fell across Zahra's face, and in a sharp tone she said: "There is a clock here, Roya. This will go badly for you if these answers do not change. And quickly."

"It's already going badly!" Roya heard herself yell.

"You fool," Zahra said. "It could be so much worse for you. We can do whatever we want with you. Don't be stupid. Think of Alya."

Roya went to the window, trying to think of Alya smiling and drawing, but she could only remember those terrified screams from the backseat of the car on the evening Abbas had been murdered.

More than the sight of it, it was the noises that haunted her. "I can't see, I can't see," he had cried out between the burst of gunfire that wounded him, and the second that would kill him.

"Think of Alya," Zahra said again.

"Were your people thinking of Alya when they murdered her father, my husband?" Roya asked. "*Bilaakh.*" Fuck off.

Zahra tilted her head to the side. This creature had just said something curious.

Roya tapped a knuckle against the windowpane and found it thick. Looking down, she worried the drop would not kill her.

"Think of Alya." Zahra could think of only Alya. "Your daughter will be alone."

"Yes, she would," Roya said. "Because you, Israel, the Zionists, killed her mother and father."

"What does Israel have to do with anything?" Zahra said, the only clue to her lies the strange accent, which Roya still could not place.

"You're a coward," Roya muttered, "you won't even admit it. Or maybe, for such an intelligent woman, *Zahra*"—the name soaked with pure venom—"you don't know so much."

"I cannot help you unless I know when the meeting was to take place," Zahra said. "You have many problems, but the most basic one is this: Your boss is dead. A male. An officer in Qods. And if they were to review your text messages..."

Don't be a whore, her sister had said.

And look at where that advice had landed her: prisoner of the Jews.

The heat of Zahra's stare, though, strangely gave her courage. Roya could not remain here; she could not see what this woman might do. At once she saw the narrow path to freedom. If Roya managed to escape and reach the Consulate, she could explain that the Israelis had killed Moghaddam, captured her, and then interrogated her. Her eyes searched the room and found nothing she might obviously conscript for a weapon.

"I can improve your chances of survival upon returning to Tehran," Zahra said.

"You're the one putting me in danger," Roya cried. "You!"

"That's why I can help you out of it. You are being difficult, for a woman with so few options," Zahra replied. "And that is not a threat, Roya. It is merely an observation."

"I want coffee," Roya said. Zahra raised her glass to one of the cameras hung in the corner, and with the other hand extended two fingers.

"I see two paths," Zahra said. "Two options." She'd sunk into the divan to wing her arms across the back. "First one is you return to Tehran without my help. Take your chances. In that case you have a dead body to account for, and the sad reality that you were the last to see Hossein Moghaddam alive. In this context the text messages become sinister, illicit details, wouldn't you agree? There will be troubles. The second option is you answer my questions and then we write a plausible story. In this scenario the dead body is linked to an accident, I think. Maybe it is found floating in the river, maybe mangled in a car that skidded into a ditch and wrapped itself around a pole. Maybe, just maybe, his blood is swimming in drugs. Maybe you were never there."

Roya, though, was no longer listening.

She had decided she would rather be killed by Iranians than work with her husband's killers.

The door opened and a man entered, carrying two glasses of Turkish coffee. Roya's instinct was immediate; she sprang up, hammering a clenched fist into the side of Zahra's face. The woman cursed loudly in a tongue that Roya assumed to be Hebrew and fell back onto the divan, offering Roya space, precious space, to bowl into the shocked man standing near the doorway.

She was past him, out the door, and into a hallway. At the end was a stairwell. From downstairs she heard a commotion. Searching this way and that, it seemed that the only way out was down. There was a small table at the end of the hallway and she picked that up and dragged it to the top of the stairwell, and when the first one turned the corner, reaching the landing, she tossed the table on him and heard him cry out, cursing, again in that same language. A single step onto the stairwell, and hands were yanking her shoulders and pulling her to the floor. All around her was noise: Hebrew, shouts in Persian for her to be still, the moan of another horn out on the water. Her hijab had come off in the struggle, it was now a blindfold over her eyes. Above, Zahra's firm voice: "Think of Alya, think of your daughter. We want to help you. We want to keep you safe."

Roya wept. There was shame in it, she knew, but she could not stop.

"You are monsters," Roya said, softly, through her tears and her tussled hijab. "You murdered him. Them. Both of them. Abbas. Hossein."

Roya felt a prick in her shoulder and saw Zahra looming above her. Blood ran from the woman's nose and mouth. She stared longer, harder, at Zahra's blood. A few drops spattered nearby on the floor. The blood made Roya happy. When I am freed from their prison to one of mine, she thought, I will tell them I resisted. I drew Zahra's blood. Roya became very dizzy, the hallway around was growing dark. Hadn't the sun already set?

CHAPTER 26

Istanbul

LATER, GLITZMAN WOULD SAY that the idea came to him while he watched Roya on the cameras, after the brawl. She had shrugged off the ketamine and was now lying on the bed, cuffed, blinking at the ceiling. Glitzman was mesmerized. Even while she was peacefully reclined, he could feel the hatred on her. Whatever they thought of Jews, plenty of Persians despised Israel. Oh, they had their conspiracies and their reasons, each one as absurd as the last and essentially boiling down to this: we exist. Roya Shabani, though, had a damn good reason for her hatred. Israel—Glitzman and Caesarea, in point of fact—had killed her husband.

If Rivka cannot pull it off, he thought, what then? Render Roya to Israel? No, no, what will we get? Middling intelligence, most of it garbage, all of it stale. Roya's value to the Office plummeted outside of Iran, away from whatever she was doing for Colonel Ghorbani. His trophy for disobeying Amos? A useless, shattered Persian widow. Had to destroy the whole family, didn't you, Arik? Glitzman could practically hear his friend's jibe, probably jotted down on one of his goddamn Post-it notes. Glitzman mentally sketched out the arguments for killing Roya and decided the cons had it, then did the same for letting her go and he wound up right back with Amos turning him into the butt of a joke before sidelining him.

Or... might he give her a purpose married to his own?

Would Amos approve? Glitzman thought that perhaps he would not tell him—at least not straightaway. Here, the breaking-and-entering business was instructive. If you failed, even after securing the proper approvals, you still got your ass booted out the door. The approvals didn't matter so much. In Mossad you could get away with anything if it turned out to be successful. These thoughts were interrupted by Rivka's appearance on-camera.

ROYA DID NOT LOOK UP when the door clicked open.

Nor did she look up when she heard Zahra's soft footfalls drawing near.

Zahra lingered for a moment, then coolly pronounced: "You are out of time."

Roya sighed. But what did this woman mean, anyway? Without raising her head to acknowledge Zahra's presence, she shrugged, then said, "Am I?"

"Who was Hossein meeting?" Zahra's voice was patient and clinical; it was terrifying. Roya made a derisive noise.

"Look at me, Roya."

When Roya finally lifted her gaze, she was staring down the barrel of Zahra's raised handgun. Outside of movies she'd never actually seen a gun, even the one that killed Abbas. She was cold and then hot and then she was cold again.

"When is the meeting going to take place?" Zahra took a step closer.

"I don't know," Roya said. Her shaking hands shivered against the sheets, and she dropped her gaze again.

"Who was Hossein Moghaddam going to meet here in Istanbul?" Zahra gently screwed the gun tight to Roya's forehead.

"I don't know." She blinked furiously.

Zahra's hand gently cupped Roya's chin. The woman raised her head until Roya was staring at her straight-on. Roya's teeth were clacking madly, and she clenched her jaw and bit down to make them stop. Zahra pinched Roya's lower lip as if she were a fish and whispered, "Open your mouth, Roya."

"No," Roya mumbled. "Please."

Then Zahra slid the barrel against Roya's front teeth and said, quite gently, "If you don't, I am going to break a hole through those pearly whites." She gently tapped once, twice. "Open wide."

Her teeth were clacking so wildly she could barely open her mouth, but it didn't matter. Zahra pulled down her lower jaw and Roya felt the barrel on her tongue and her teeth chattered across the metal like a clockwork toy.

"Final chance," Zahra said, finger dancing along the trigger. "Where was the meeting to take place? The address? And with whom?"

Roya felt like she was going to vomit.

"Where do you think you'll go when I squeeze the trigger?" Zahra asked. "Have you made peace with the mullahs' god?"

She hadn't. God, she hadn't, not like they wanted.

Grasping Roya's hijab for leverage, Zahra muscled the gun deeper into Roya's mouth. She was gagging, and she realized Zahra wouldn't need to shoot her: she was going to throw up and choke to death on her own vomit—over an address. "Wait," she mumbled. "Wait."

Roya gasped as the gun slid from her mouth. But it was still pointed at her head, strings of her own saliva dangling off the barrel.

"The meeting happened on Friday afternoon," Roya said, hating herself. "Three o'clock. I think that was yesterday. You missed it."

"Where did it happen?"

Roya gave the address.

"Who was he meeting?" Zahra asked.

"I don't know. Please—"

The gun went back into her mouth.

"Roya," Zahra said evenly, "I need names. Descriptions. Phone numbers. Emails. *Kunyas.* Whatever you have. Everything you have. Now."

"I don't know," Roya mumbled into the barrel of the gun. "I don't know."

The gun explored deeper into her mouth and then Roya was gagging and tears were running down her face.

"Who did Moghaddam meet?" Zahra shouted. Her eyes were wild;

it looked to Roya as if the woman were having some fun. Roya tried to look away, but the woman grabbed her chin, forcing Roya to meet her gaze. "Who?"—now it was a whisper, and she pulled the gun out so that Roya could answer.

"I don't know!" she cried. "I told you I don't know."

"That's a shame." Zahra sighed, then shoved the gun back in. Roya was struggling for breath now as she heard the sound of Zahra clicking back the gun's hammer. Then Zahra pulled the trigger.

Roya blinked furiously, shuddering, listening to a *click-click-click* that felt like it was in her brain, and when she looked up at Zahra, the taste of metal thick on her tongue, she realized she was still alive. Zahra withdrew the gun very slowly and took a step back, her brow furrowed, keeping close watch on something creeping along the floor, which she clearly feared might sully her tennis shoes. Roya had not felt a thing, but when she looked down there was a puddle spreading from her bedside. She had soaked her bottom and her legs.

"Happy with yourself?" Zahra asked, with an eerie smile and dead-eye wink. "Because you're a cunt for the mullahs."

Roya knew about the cameras, of course, but the last shreds of her honor dictated that she wait until Zahra had left, the door shut and locked behind. Her relief withered into pure hatred for this woman— and for herself. She wished the gun had been loaded, she thought as she smashed her face into a pillow and drew the covers over her head. Alone, she sobbed.

The Interrogation Room
Location: █████████████

Present day

KAM DOES NOT SLEEP much in prison, even if they spare him the music. Three, maybe four hours each night, or what he thinks are nights. There are no windows and no clocks. No time, really, between the writing sessions. It's been eight meals, he knows that much, since he last wrote for them. He is spread on his mat, and he's thinking about Roya when he startles at the click of the door. Kam used to feel a cascade of shame when this happened, but now he accepts it as a physiological reality, a reflex like a kick after a doctor swings a rubber hammer into your knee. This is simply what the human body does when a door opens.

The guards march him to the interrogation room, where the General is waiting. They lead him to his chair and Kam is crestfallen that there does not appear to be any tea. But there is also no sign of Colonel Askari. He's always found the General's beatings preferable to Askari's questions. The General's torture is somehow more honest.

"Your first two parts weren't dogshit," the General says, after the door shuts. In the General's hierarchy, "not dogshit" is top marks. Kam is riding high, having long since stopped caring why praise from a psychopathic torturer gets him going. It doesn't matter. He'll take what he can get.

"As always, honesty will save you," the General continues. "Keep giving us the truth and we'll let you keep the books in your cell. And the music off."

In Iran the truth only comes out when you're backed into a corner. And though he's certainly been cornered and then broken, there are pieces of his former self he's managed to hold on to. One of them is his secret. It's what sustains him. In his shattered state, he sometimes wonders if it *is* him. If it might be all that's left.

It's the reason he did not hang himself in his third prison, though Askari foolishly left him alone with a belt, exhausted from the lashing. It is the reason he did not slit his wrists with the metal shard discovered along the wall of his sixth and roughest jail cell. It is the reason he's never tried the blue-crayon-through-the-eye-and-into-the-brain finale.

Kam would rather die than hand over this secret.

And this business of drafting a final confession? Well, he figures the General will soon oblige.

Speaking of: The General is calling for paper and pen. (He means crayon, everyone knows this.)

The smell of rosewater comes first. Askari has opened the door. He sets down the papers and the box of crayons. He lingers, curling his long business fingers around one of the chairbacks.

The General grunts. Kam imagines the disappointment across Colonel Askari's face, but he's fixed on the table. The colonel leaves.

The General taps the top of the paper stack. "Next part. Start with Glitzman's summons to Istanbul. Back to your con."

"Yes, General."

The General leaves. Soon as the door shuts, Kam sorts through the box for a workable crayon, wondering again about the ending. It probably doesn't matter. They'll kill him before he gets there. And if it's the same ending as always? Perhaps that won't be so bad.

النجاه فی الصدق
بخش سوم از شهادت‌های من

.... Number
.... Date
.... Attachment

The power
is with
those who resist

The Islamic Republic of Iran

In the name of God
Honesty will save you
The third part of my sworn confession
— Kamran Esfahani

CHAPTER 27

Stockholm / Istanbul

Three years ago

COME TO ISTANBUL IMMEDIATELY. *We will figure compensation here. Absolutely no delays. NONE! 630p direct Stockholm to Istanbul on Turkish Air. Book 3 nights hotel Witt Istanbul in Cihangir. From hotel come directly to meet me at bus stop near north end of Bebek Park.*

It's been three years, so I'm sure I've got one or two words wrong, but Glitzman's message went something like that. I felt an immediate jolt of excitement, followed by a pang of irritation that he always knew whether I was in Sweden or Iran. And then I would be grateful that Glitzman's intelligence probably was no more specific than that. (Though now I wonder.)

Because when the message arrived I was sitting on—but not using—the toilet in the downstairs powder bath of my brother's cavernous home in Stockholm.

It was a bright spring Saturday afternoon, and I was in Sweden to visit family and celebrate Maman's birthday the following week, which meant I had spent most of my time searching for reasons to avoid them, at least before happy hour. In his efforts to become more Swedish than the Swedes, Sina has adopted most of their cultural paraphernalia (country house, high-fiber diet, preference for long spells of silence), but thankfully not the strange attitude toward booze, that anxious Swedish blend of shame and lust. After five it's rare to see him without a drink in hand, or pushing one into yours. The message landed around one p. m., well before I'd dosed the liquid courage required to face the chaos of his home, which that afternoon presented as a rolling confrontation between his daughters over who was borrowing clothes from whom. My nieces, I must always remind myself. They are your nieces. The fight had spilled over into the kitchen, where I'd been searching for a snack. I took refuge in the powder bath to doomscroll social media and wound up logging in to check for messages from Glitzman.

The summons was unusual for two reasons. One: besides the training in Albania, I'd never been asked to travel. And, two: the urgency. Leave now, today?

What would I tell Sina? How would I explain cutting my trip short by three days? Missing Maman's birthday? Well, I'd probably be back for it, I reasoned, and decided that would be the truth.

His girls began screaming at each other again, this time it was something about sharing makeup. Your nieces—I reminded myself, possibly aloud. I flushed the toilet (for cover, there was nothing in it), and decided I'd manufacture an excuse. Sina was aware of the vague business opportunities I was pursuing to import medical equipment into Iran, and, further, he was not keen to ask questions because I think he may have suspected I was violating sanctions. Plus, his wife would not be disappointed at the early departure. She wasn't fiery or hostile, she was merely frigidly Swedish. And Swedish captivity, let's face it, was a kick in the balls. Of course, Glitzman also had me by the balls, but it was profitable and often thrilling, even if it came with incredible risk.

In the months since Amir-Ali's death, I had learned that when my mind turned to him, I could turn it away, to California.

GLITZMAN WAS NOT a reasonable man, but his fanaticism had physical limits. He was not prone to working the graveyard shift if it could be avoided. As it happened, though, it could not: I wouldn't sleep more than a wink over the next few days.

It was well past midnight when I arrived at my Istanbul hotel, but I remember being wide awake, running on adrenaline and the six cups of coffee I'd consumed on my flight. My journey to meet Glitzman at the park involved a circuitous combination of taxi and walking. I knew from the prearranged codes that I would receive a garbled French text message from a random number if at any point I should abort.

I never did. Glitzman was waiting for me at the bus stop. We exchanged no more than a nod, and then I followed him back to his hotel and up to the room. The door was open a crack and I walked in to find a crowd. The carpet I crossed was green as a tennis court and the consistency of artificial turf. Through the open window was a balcony, and beyond that a few lighted boats swayed in the Bosphorus.

Despite the vacation vibes, the room felt tense. Glitzman plunked himself down in the sitting area, half-hidden by a sparkling bar cart forested by bottles. Rivka was pouring coffee for herself in the kitchenette, and I got a nod from her when I entered, and another look at those eyes, which I was learning were either dead as doornails or shining like torches. Aryas and Kovan were sitting across from Glitzman, and when they looked up and saw me, I could tell that they were equally clueless about our mission.

While we made small talk Glitzman stood to open a few more of the sliding doors, which I took as an invitation to fix myself a smoke. The Israelis followed, then the Kurds. We all sat there in a conspiratorial cloud. Glitzman now passed me a folder, which I opened.

I looked at her picture for a moment. It was, I now know, a photo snapped by Rivka during the intake: Roya was delirious and unsmiling, though her mouth was open slightly as if she might do so at any moment. This, I later assumed, was an aftereffect of the drugs. There are many things about Roya that filtered through that picture, but most of all was this: I did not want to look away. Soon as I had, I was thinking about going back. Her eyes were double-colored. One was brown, the other gray.

"Her name is Roya Shabani," Glitzman said. "From Tehran. She was married to a Qods scientist, who unfortunately died earlier this year after we shot him. Do you know her?"

I took a closer look. "No, I don't know her."

"You looked at it awhile, like maybe you recognized her," Glitzman said.

"I wanted to be sure," I replied. "We killed her husband?"

"That's right," Rivka said. "And you didn't help us out on this one. In case you're wondering. Separate crew."

"How about you two, do you know her?"—this, from Glitzman, went to Aryas and Kovan, and their answer was the same. No. Total stranger.

"It's really fucking important," Rivka said, "that if you know her, or if you've come across her in any context at all, any casual social situation, anything up to and including sidelong doe-eyed glances on the streets of Tehran, that you tell us right now. So take another long, hard look and tell us again that you're sure."

All three of us did, and we said that we were sure.

Glitzman and Rivka studied each other for a moment until they silently agreed that we were not lying.

"Good," Glitzman said, his teeth clamped around the cigarette. He puffed for a few beats, folding his arms around his chest as if gathering thoughts to himself, deciding which he would share.

"Your last operation gave us names," he said. "Two of them. One: Hossein Moghaddam. Two, a colonel, his boss: Colonel Jaffar Ghorbani. Do you know them?"

We all said no immediately—after all, none of us ran with Qods goons—but Glitzman patiently searched our faces for traces of doubt before continuing on. "Ghorbani is running an assassination squad from Tehran. And now he's killed two Mossad officers"—here the Kurds and I exchanged dark glances—"both murdered by a kamikaze drone. Flown into their goddamn study in Jerusalem."

I'm not sure what I felt at the moment, I certainly had nothing noble to say, so I said, "Oh god." The Kurds mumbled something similar. I could tell that whatever emotions Glitzman felt about this, they were now gone. He spoke of Ghorbani and his work clinically, as if the man were a tumor to remove, a germ to eradicate.

"We followed Hossein Moghaddam to Istanbul two days ago. He's dead. And not by our hand. Heart attack, we suspect."

I exchanged a skeptical glance with Kovan, which drew an irate glare from Glitzman, though he said nothing.

"We broke into Moghaddam's apartment immediately after," Rivka said.

"What did you find?" I asked.

Glitzman tapped the picture of Roya. "Her."

CHAPTER 28

Istanbul

THE BLOW-BY-BLOW Glitzman gave me, detailing their Istanbul adventure, ended with this punch line: Mossad had visited the address Roya had provided—and everything was gone. Roya was the only remaining lead. In her purse was a boarding pass for an Iran Air flight back to Tehran on Monday afternoon. We had one night to work. And there was so much to do.

Rivka briefed a written assessment from Mossad's psychologists that, among other things, described Roya Shabani as a *headstrong individual*, who, despite her *present adverse circumstances* (read: widowhood at twenty-seven courtesy of the Mossad; kidnapping, detention, and "light interrogation" at the hands of the Israeli government), remained *stubbornly in control of her faculties and, most of all, her sense of self-worth*.

"She is intelligent but naïve," Glitzman said as he set the report down, his voice rich with disappointment. Looking directly at me, he added: "But she is a strong one."

Then Glitzman gave us the pitch. For a very long while, we discussed the roles that Aryas, Kovan, and I would play in what was to come, and what we absolutely must collect. We spoke of Iran's Ministry of Intelligence, the Vezarat-e Etela'at, VAJA, reading through Mossad briefing packets on its structure, culture, customs, and role. We watched videos—I had no idea how Caesarea got them—of VAJA officers addressing training classes and delivering testimony to the Iranian

Supreme National Security Council. I paid close attention to the officers' speech, dress, and body language.

We spoke about my practice, about my clients and my apartment and my social circles inside Tehran. Then we repeated the process for Aryas and Kovan. It was all part of confirming their network mapping—to understand if, as the operation progressed, Roya might be able to uncover our true identities. If one of her uncles knew one of my second cousins, in a matter of days we could be compromised. All the while, Rivka scribbled copious notes, though I wondered why. They'd doubtless mic'd up the room.

Kovan was walking Rivka through one of the branches of his family tree when Glitzman motioned for me to join him on the balcony. He slid shut the door behind, separating us from Rivka and the Kurds. I accepted a cigarette from Glitzman.

"But you should know better," Glitzman chided, soon as I'd taken it. "Your smile is your livelihood."

"You're the patient here," I said. "You get that mouth guard made yet?"

He laughed, and I looked across the water, waiting.

"You've gotten good at not speaking first," Glitzman said. "Bravo."

"Thanks."

We watched the shadows of boats gliding by.

"What do you think?" he said.

"I think it's a major revision to our arrangement," I said, in the evenest tone I could manage. "I think the risk is higher than anything I've done for you before. Driving your people, accepting and collecting packages... that's low-risk compared to impersonating an intelligence officer. If I'm caught, I'm dead."

"And what's new there?" His voice had grown less chummy, more commanding.

"Both victims worked directly for you?"

"They did. I mean, how the fuck?" Glitzman looked more offended than sad, as if their deaths, however tragic, had matured into a professional slight. "Who's carrying Ghorbani's water in Israel? Who's smuggling shit in for them? Who's flying the goddamn drone? Who are they targeting next?" Glitzman had wrapped his hand around the balcony railing to choke the life from it.

"How do they know who's on your team?" I asked, reasoning that if the Iranians knew about Glitzman's officers they might know of his agents as well. Were they coming for me?

"I don't know."

Sensing my agitation, Glitzman tried to reassure: "I don't think the Qaani operation is, specifically, the common denominator."

"So what is?"

"They're almost certainly after Israelis who have conducted operations against Iran. Could be a coincidence."

Now it was my turn to treat Glitzman to a rare look of pity. He sheepishly surrendered with a turn toward the water.

"The woman," Glitzman muttered, "Roya Shabani. She is our thread. She pushes paper for Ghorbani. She does not have the full picture, only the details that form it. Flights, money transfers, safe houses, on and on. But she will not share it willingly. She needs to swallow the right story. You—" He took a paternal swing, touching my shoulder and treating me to a look of pride. "You can tell a good story. You know people. Hell, you recruited Amir-Ali to our cause. You understand how they work. You can burrow into her life and uncover her dreams. Dreams she may not even know she has. Find a way to make her think she can have them, whatever it may be. Love. Sex. Ego. Thrills. Money. Power."

"Revenge," I added.

Glitzman concurred with an amiable grunt and we watched the cherry glow of his cigarette float into the water below. "The State of Israel killed Professor Abbas Shabani," Glitzman said. "It was all legal. Procedural. Rivka was working a robotic machine gun we'd smuggled into Tehran piece by piece; she pulled the trigger via satellite uplink in Tel Aviv. But yes, you are right. I gave the order. I was watching. Israel killed him."

"Why *him*?" I asked.

"Abbas was their top drone-cladding expert. Materials guy, had a Ph.D. thesis that impressed even our people. We'd watched him for a while, and we all sort of liked him, I'll admit. Good sense of humor. Family man. Should have taken a postdoc opportunity in Paris when he had the chance. Instead, he was inside Qods working on science that would permit the regime to sneak hordes of armed and invisible drones past our air defense systems. They want to turn Tel Aviv into Kyiv? Fuck them. Guy had a load of knowledge in his brain and we spilled it across the street on his way to dinner."

Glitzman lit another cigarette and shared a meaningful glance with Rivka through the window that I could not decipher. "It was also a message," he went on. "Considering working on drone-cladding? Look what happens. You go out with your wife and little girl and the birthday celebration hasn't even started before that gigantic brain of yours is painted across the sycamores and the garbage-clogged drainage canals. Don't care for that lousy ending? Find another job. Take the postdoc in Paris. Go work on plastics you can put in the microwave."

"She could be seduced by the feeling that she is taking part in avenging him," I offered. "That she is fighting back against the people who killed her husband. There's loads of hatred for us to work with."

"Buckets," Glitzman agreed.

And it was a strange sensation, just then, because his voice softened but the gaze he'd fixed on me was steel. "I'll consider you in, then."

I let that sit a moment, thinking about how Glitzman had fucked up a bit here, offering details that could only drive up my price, or perhaps convince me to bail. I'd never seen him so worked-up. I didn't usually have Glitzman by the balls, it was always the other way around, but I certainly had a grip here. Problem was, I didn't quite know whether to squeeze or run.

"Arik," I said, "it's very risky."

He looked at me with a volatile mixture of great loathing and respect. I turned to study a freighter moving through the dark water.

"Do it for Amir-Ali," he said.

That thought, circling since the beginning of Glitzman's speech, now went through me like a blade. I might deliver vengeance for my friend. Who gets such an opportunity? I did not think too hard about what Amir-Ali would have said to this, because I knew he would have told me to forget about it, to let him go. No, that's not right. He would have told me to raise the price. So I did.

"My friend Meir," Glitzman said, "used to say that we had to pay double or triple for everything in Persia because we were foreigners. I fucking hate it."

"You're worse than a foreigner, Arik," I said. "You're a Zionist."

The laugh was joyless. "Tell me what you're after."

"My payout," I said.

Now Glitzman was giving me the same astonished, offended look I'd just given him.

"But not straightaway," I said. "Not for nothing."

"For what, then?" he replied.

"For results. I run the woman, Roya. We deliver Ghorbani. We deliver his people in Israel. Then you pay, and I'm done."

"There will have to be blood to justify such a quick payout, just so you understand. Arrests of accomplices. Ghorbani and maybe a few of his comrades rendered to Israel. Or shot dead in Tehran." He blinked, looked off, scratched at the bridge of his nose, and then tugged at his ear, which meant he was thinking. "No bodies," he said, his voice rising again to a military timbre, "no cash."

He looked at me, I looked at him. "I understand, Arik. Bodies."

"Good," he whispered, jerking a slight nod. "Done. One condition."

"What is that?"

He turned to the water and made it clear that I should, too. "It stays between us," he said. "Aryas and Kovan are certainly wondering what we've been chatting about out here. They're Kurds, and so you'd think I should be able to play them off each other, but they're also brothers, and... well, I can assure you there's not enough cash in the pot to make this deal three times."

GLITZMAN AND RIVKA LEFT once we'd agreed on the next twenty-four hours of choreography. My focus had shouldered aside my fatigue; I had a great deal to memorize before I saw Roya.

"What do you think?" Kovan asked me, near dawn. He had his feet up on the chair where Glitzman had held court. Smoke curled from his nostrils.

"I think it's clever," I said. "Maybe too clever."

"And too fast," Aryas said. "Rushed."

I thought about that for a moment. "The greatest risk is if she begins asking after us in Tehran. If she's got a cousin who works inside Etela'at, or—"

"They don't think she does," Kovan said.

"They don't know," I snapped. "How could they, really? We'd be wise to keep that in mind."

LATER, AFTER I had reviewed a final batch of surveillance photos showing VAJA headquarters in Tehran, I returned to one of Roya's pictures. And I stayed there, for one of those moments that soon becomes several. Roya, I thought, looked like somebody that I would like to know. And I believed that she would like to know me, too. That she would appreciate some of my confidence.

So little of what came later was true, at least in the conventional sense. But that much was, General. And I must believe it still is.

CHAPTER 29

Istanbul

I AM A TALKER, a people person, not a specialist in what Glitzman once called "the dark art of separating Persians from their heads." Up to that point I had never carried a weapon during an operation, not even when we had kidnapped Qaani. Weapons had been the Kurds' department. Now, driving across Istanbul, I could think of nothing but the specially outfitted handguns Mossad had procured locally, snug in their cases on the backseat floor.

The leafy block in northern Üsküdar was lined by grand old Ottoman homes, sticking their brightly colored wooden necks out for cleaner views of the water and the hills across the foggy strait, where the patchwork of lights and the suture of roads resembled the anarchy of smoldering coals in a dying fire. As we waited outside the safe house, raindrops began to smack the car. It was two minutes to eleven o'clock on a dreary Sunday evening. Light was pouring through the safe house windows. In the backseat Kovan lifted one of the black cases from the floor, popped the latches, and removed suppressors and the special magazines from their foam inserts. Kovan handed a suppressor to his brother, then to me. I screwed it in and smacked in the special magazine, trying to feel confident about my confidence. Then I watched the front door.

After a few minutes a man came outside. The rain had picked up but I could see him with little trouble: At our eye contact my adrenaline spiked and time seemed to flow quite strangely. He was one of Glitzman's, maybe one of the surveillants, though I never did learn his name.

"Let's go," Aryas said.

I felt for the reassuring chill of gunmetal snug in my waistband, then rolled my jacket down, and we exited the car. I approached the man, and in English I asked for a light. In broken English he replied that he was done for the night. Here, time seemed to shake and quiver before bending back to its normal rhythms, and then I kicked him, hard, in the shins and drove my knee into his groin and I had the gun barrel jammed into his neck. "Open the door," I said.

I don't know how the separate parts of a face can synchronize such mockery, but his did, and I tried desperately to avoid the eyes of the Kurds. As per Glitzman's instructions ("Part's for authenticity, for realism, and the other is to show the Kurds you can run this. Don't hold back. The Office's insurance plans are top-shelf"), I drove my fist square into his nose, then again, shoving his back into the wall of the villa. Though he was clearly in pain, I would say he was still smiling. I'd not wanted to be the first in, of course. But the con demanded it.

"Open the door," I said, in English, in a tone I hoped was befitting an officer of the Etela'at.

The man coughed and blood gurgled down his chin and I wondered if it was a pained laugh. He entered the code for the door. Following the buzz inside, we began to ascend the staircase. The man led, hands limply held in surrender, my pistol wedged in his back, Aryas and Kovan behind. My knuckles were on fire, and the only thing I'd broken was perhaps my hand, not his nose. As we climbed to the third floor, I found myself absorbing useless details: the smell of barbecued meat and coffee; the tingle of dust in my nostrils; the tang of a droplet of blood that had shot from the man's nose to land on my lips, where it was discovered by my tongue.

Then we were outside her holding room.

The lock had been rigged on the outside. Murmurs and a bar of light seeped from beneath the door. "Open it," I commanded. With my left hand I gripped his shoulder and with my right I forced the barrel into the side of his temple. A key went into the lock, and when it turned I was watching my father die in the passenger seat of my car, on a mountain road approaching the Caspian Sea.

The man opened the door, time flooded back, and I shoved him inside, the gun screwed so tightly into his head it could have been fucking his ear.

Roya was sitting on the bed, inching back toward the wall. Aryas and Kovan fanned in around us. Rivka, who she knew as Zahra, stood from the divan.

"You will let her go," I told the woman in Persian. "Now."

"Who are you?" Rivka said.

I jerked the gun toward her, then jammed the gun back to the man's head.

A silence spun open; I met Roya's eyes, and I have never seen such terror written across a face. The man jerked his left elbow as if attempting to strike me. I took a half step back and glimpsed him mashing his hand into his left pocket. I aimed there and pressed the trigger. He screamed and bent down to clutch his leg, which ran with blood. Too much blood, in retrospect. You'd have thought his leg had been sliced off, from the way it was gushing through his pants. I shot him again in the leg and he keeled back onto the floor. Aryas, or Kovan, I am not sure which, shot him again, and then a few more times for good measure or because they were having fun, I wasn't sure.

Rivka was hustling toward me. I really do wonder if she wanted to kill us.

I shouted for her to stop but she did not and time was blistering ahead. I pressed the trigger, then again, and she fell a few steps in front of me. Blood pooled out from beneath her chest. She coughed and moaned and Kovan must have shot her five times more in the back before she was silent.

"Who are you?" Roya shrieked. "Who are you? Who are you? Who are you?" Her back was smashed against the headboard; her hands were in front of her face and they were shaking, as were mine when I limply held up the gun to the ceiling to signal I meant no harm.

"You are Roya Shabani, yes?" I said in the Persian lilt of a native Tehrani. Which I suppose I am.

She nodded, blinked, looked to the bodies before returning to me with a glassy stare of shock.

"We are with the Intelligence Ministry," I said. "We are here to bring you home."

CHAPTER 30

Istanbul

IN THE CAR I chewed a piece of gum loaded with a hundred milligrams of caffeine and kept my eyes on the road, though I occasionally shot anxious glances back at Roya and the Kurds. I'd practiced the drive three times that day but never in darkness, much less folded in sheets of rain. The only constant was the traffic, easily as bad as Tehran's.

Each stop and honk had me scanning for police. Listening for sirens. Had a frightened neighbor heard the earlier shots? Were Istanbul's traffic cameras tracking us?

The latter risk Glitzman's people in Tel Aviv did not think likely. They had a map of the cameras courtesy of an asset in Turkish intel, and it was only a couple months old. We'd chosen our destination because an algorithm Glitzman called only "MOSHE" had informed the analysts that if you drove from the scene of the crime to this new house, there were four potential routes on which an intrepid driver might disappear from the cameras. I was white-knuckling it on one of them. We also considered the risk of police manageable because the Israelis back in Üsküdar would be well positioned to field any questions about noise, seeing as they were quite alive, having only been shot by our blanks. I expected they had already managed to mop up the chemical blood. And, further, their Iranian hostage was gone.

The house Mossad had hastily procured was a concrete pile on a crumbling street down in İnönü, chosen because the suburb had once been farmland. Why, I had asked, did that matter? "The lots are larger," Glitzman had said, "so if she runs you'll have more time to catch her."

The house was behind a chain-link fence draped with workman's canvas. There was a large Judas tree out front, which resembled a gnarled hand clawing out of the soil. We hustled inside through the driving rain. Aryas and Kovan held her shoulders, just in case.

The inside of the house was a theatrical production. We were fully on camera—every room, bathrooms included, this was all too important for dignity or modesty to concern us—had been wired for audio and video—and the interior had been thoughtfully arranged to appear as though we'd been camped out here for a few days. Churned-up bedsheets and air mattresses were visible through the door to the bedroom. The kitchen had been stocked for the spartan tastes of three Etela'at officers sent to Istanbul outside normal channels to follow a juicy lead. The teakettle was yellowed and dented. The trash can groaned with Styrofoams and foils stripped from greasy food bought on the go. Boxes of sweets sat on a table. Next to that a few packs of cigarettes. They had told me Roya privately enjoyed a smoke. I did not ask how they knew, but I suppose they had learned this while surveilling her family in preparation for killing her husband.

I invited Roya to sit in one of the green overstuffed chairs in the living room while I made tea. She had not spoken a word on the trip here, and I suspect she was still in shock. She barely managed a nod. I brought the box of sweets and the cigarettes. The silence was total until the kettle began to sing. I steeped the tea, filled four mineral-stained glasses, and rejoined them in the living room, where we sat for a few uncomfortable seconds. The glass shook in her hand. Once she brought it to her lips but stopped partway, and held it there for far too long before lowering it to the table.

"My name is Major Esfahani," I said, "and these are my lieutenants"—I gave the Kurds throwaway work names. "We report to Colonel Hashemi inside the Vezarat-e Etela'at. Civilian, not the Revolutionary Guards. Hashemi runs a department called Internal Security. You know it?"

She shook her head and did not otherwise respond, nor did she make a single move toward the tea, to say nothing of the sweets or cigarettes.

After you tell her who you are, what is the first thing she will want to know? Glitzman had asked me in the hotel room.

Why I am here? I had said. She will want to know why I am here. What I want.

Wrong, Glitzman said, making an awful noise like a buzzer. Totally, utterly wrong.

"I know you have a daughter," I said, taking great care at this tender moment to emphasize my vowels like a Tehrani. "And I must imagine you have not spoken to her in a few days." I put her Turkish cell phone on the table and slid it her way. We'd snatched it during the last act of our theatrical rescue. "Please," I said, "as you wish. But I must beg you not to tell her—yet—what has happened. We have things to discuss first."

Roya blinked at the phone as if it were a mirage. Then she picked up the tea glass, but her hand was shaking so much now that half of it went overboard. She did not even look at the mess, nor did she wipe her fingers.

"I do not think," she muttered at last, "that I can speak to Afsaneh or Alya right now without worrying them. And it is also very late."

"I understand," I said, making a show of leaving the phone on the table. She must feel choices, options, at all stages, I had argued.

I asked Aryas and Kovan to go outside and keep watch. We had purportedly killed two Mossad officers, after all. We had to be on guard.

"I am sorry that we do not have a woman to debrief you," I said, after they had gone. "The program I am running is quite . . . small. I hope this is fine. Are you hungry?"

She shook her head.

"Would you like a cigarette?"

She nodded. I slid the pack and the lighter her way. The tremors in her hand gave her some trouble flicking the lighter. When she finally succeeded she leaned back in her seat, the first small step to letting down her guard.

"The people holding you tonight," I asked, "do you know who they were?"

"They are dead?" she asked.

"We had no choice. Did they happen to say who they were?"

"No. But I . . . I think . . ."

I waited. I wanted her to say it aloud. She demolished the cigarette, stubbed it into a cup on the table, and examined the pack hungrily, though I was pleased to see she was awaiting my permission.

"I think they were Israeli," she said. "They did not tell me. But I believe it is so."

"It is true," I said. "The woman is, was, a Mossad officer. Her family has roots in Tehran, which is one of the ways we know of her. After the Revolution her Zionist parents fled to Occupied Palestine. The other one, the man, is another Mossad officer. We have been paying close attention to them, listening. They have been up to no good."

"She told me her name was Zahra," Roya said. "What is it, really?"

"She is a liar," I replied, though instead of a name I handed her a cigarette from the pack. She accepted my light and sat with her elbows on her knees, taking drag after drag. I joined her, and we smoked together in a silence that grew more comfortable with each passing moment. She now had a phone, cigarettes, and an audience with an Iranian official. Whatever the mullahs say, Paradise is a fluid concept.

"How did you find me?" she asked.

"There are parts of that I cannot answer," I said. "Suffice it to say that my unit has been watching those two Israelis for months. They run spies inside Iran. We came to Istanbul hoping to catch one."

Her gaze, which had been thawing, now iced over again. Whatever mental pictures were clicking through her head were doubtless jammed somewhere between Moghaddam's villa and Glitzman's holding chamber.

"Roya," I said, "are you sure you are not hungry?"

She looked at the sweets but again shook her head.

"You're in shock," I said, giving a name to it. "And I'm sorry about this, but I need to speak with you before too much time has passed. It must be tonight, when everything is fresh. I imagine you have many questions for me. But perhaps I will go first? I won't start with questions, though. Only a story."

CHAPTER 31
Istanbul

I HAD A GREAT DEAL on my mind, and a lot to do—I should have been taking ground in the conversation. But I was momentarily distracted by this: a few forelocks of Roya's dark hair had spun out of her cornflower-blue hijab, and she had not bothered to tuck them in. In Sweden I never stop to admire a woman's hair, but as soon as you cover something, well, you sit there listening to the drum of rain withering to the gurgle of drainpipes, wondering what's beneath. Roya smoked in a puddle of light cast from the floor lamp hunched over her chair. The bags beneath her double-colored eyes were thick and puffy, but did not diminish her high cheekbones, accentuated by the smoky light. She had brought her feet onto the chair and pulled her knees into her chest. Her strength was returning, her composure along with it.

Focus, I said to myself, you've got a story to tell.

"My team and I have been coming to Istanbul for several months now, after some extremely sensitive intelligence indicated that the Israelis were running a ring of agents inside the Qods Force. They have been meeting these people here, in Istanbul. This time, with some help from contacts in Turkish intelligence, we were able to track the two Israelis, the leaders of this ring, and follow them here. They led us to the meeting with Hossein Moghaddam, which led us back to his villa, which led us, well, to you."

"You were watching his villa?" she asked, giving me a curious look. I had the sinking feeling that she was on to me. Roya's government, employer, dead boss, and official god had spent most of their time spinning lies for her—and she had probably spent most of her time pretending that they were the truth—so she must have been uncommonly attuned to the sound of a falsehood. But I was not them, and she had no other options, and at any rate there was nothing to do besides sell the lie.

"We staked out the villa," I said. "We knew Moghaddam would eventually show up. We were planning to break in and collect evidence of his treason. Then we saw you arrive, head inside, then . . ."—her body bristled and she curled up more tightly on the chair—"then strange visitors arrive. They are inside for a few hours. They brought you out in a wheelchair. You had a shawl over your shoulders and a faraway stare."

She looked unwell.

"Please, Roya, what happened? Your answer will stay between us."

Her sudden, clipped laugh was humorless; disdain for such promises escaping in the form of noise. "Please," was all she said. Her head shook, gaze drifting to the smoke curling into the ceiling. "I don't know how he died. We were . . . he just fell over."

"Did he use drugs?"

"I don't know," she said. "Maybe. We never talked about that. Why did the Israelis come? I don't understand."

"Why don't you let me finish my story—"

"No. I have a question," she said. The sudden firmness of her tone took me aback. I should not have cared for it, but I found I did not mind. I rather enjoyed the spark. "Why did a gang of Israelis kidnap me?" she asked.

"Hossein Moghaddam was working for Mossad," I said. "He was a Zionist spy."

CHAPTER 32
Istanbul

I WAITED, WATCHING ROYA tick through a predictable sequence: surprise, disbelief, anger, a flicker again of disbelief. The anger shone brightest because of the hint she might be an accomplice, an implication I was in no hurry to dispel. A potential agent under the twist of coercion or blackmail, even if the threat is unspoken, must never believe that things will return to the way they were. There must be, as Glitzman was fond of saying, an *overhang*. Something that might crash down on them to punish rule-breaking. What hung over me? I knew something was there, and I knew I didn't want it to fall. Proof, I suppose, that the concept works.

And, though the setting was casual, what with the cigarettes and sweets and a phone on the table, I had carefully hoisted two massive weights above her. One: she had been the last to see Moghaddam alive. Two: she had collaborated—knowingly? unknowingly? —with a traitor. But these were left unspoken. Instead, I asked again if she was hungry. This time she said yes.

BUT FIRST I INSISTED she call Afsaneh.

The messages Caesarea had sent from Roya's Turkish phone (one each on Saturday and Sunday afternoon) had been designed to convince her sister, Afsaneh, that all was well in Istanbul. Busy crazy trip and no time for a call, et cetera, et cetera. What we could not know was whether Afsaneh had grown suspicious, or worried, or if she'd contacted the Iranian authorities, or the Consulate in Istanbul. Whatever concerns her sister may have about the lack of a phone call over the weekend will be soothed immediately by the sound of Roya's voice, Glitzman had said.

"I have missed two nights of phone calls," she said. "That does not happen when I travel. It has never happened."

"Well, look at the kind messages Mossad sent to your sister. You did not disappear, not to her. The Israelis would run this no other way. They held you because they wanted to know what exactly had happened to their asset, and once they did, they wanted to know what you knew about *them*. They had no interest in alarm bells ringing in Tehran.

"Call your sister," I continued. "Speak to your daughter, even if it is late. But keep it normal, normal, normal. Tell them how busy everything has been. Tell your sister about the food you are eating, the sweets and *simit* and the fish sandwiches and the thick coffees. Tell them you are sorry for being unreachable."

She did not ask for privacy, which was nice, since it wasn't an option. Afsaneh answered right away, chatty and carefree, and after a few minutes she offered to wake Alya, she'd gone to bed late anyhow, and Roya did not say no. I watched the tears, which she kept secret from them, wash her cheeks, and saw her entire body shudder when Alya shrieked into the phone.

"Maman!"—shouted joyfully, her daughter's volume turned all the way up despite the late hour. "When do you come home?"

"I will see you tomorrow afternoon, my love," Roya said, and because time is a haze to five-year-olds, they spent a few minutes discussing how long that was when measured by naps and sleepy times.

The Mossad report summarizing Roya's "light interrogation" had featured three paragraphs on the topic of *"maternal/paternal attachment,"* but it was really simple: She loved her daughter, and her daughter loved her. And though Roya had not so much as sniffled through her tears, though her voice remained bubbly throughout, I could see that this was that rarest of social systems: the happy family.

When Roya had said a few dozen goodbyes and again explained to Alya that she would be home after her nap tomorrow, she hung up and the phone clattered onto the table. Her body convulsed, and she began to sob. I knew then that whatever she believed, she was not a fundamentalist about it. She was not a true believer. Roya was a typical earthy Persian: She loved the things of this world, her daughter most of all. She had thought she would die, and she had not. "You rescued her," I remember Glitzman insisting, emphatically jabbing his chubby finger into my shoulder. "Remember that in the Book of Roya *you* are credited."

I sat beside her, and Roya's head slumped against my shoulder, and she put a hand on mine. We sat like that until she had stopped sobbing.

She smelled of salt—the tears, I suppose—and I noticed the heat of the places where her body met mine. I found myself noticing the noticing when I should have been thinking ahead. I liked her head on my shoulder. I liked our hands knotted together. We sat together for a moment once she'd stopped crying. I returned to my seat and said I was sorry for what had happened to her.

"You have killed people before?" she asked.

A strange first question. I was reminded of Glitzman's verdict on Roya: brilliant, but naïve. In any case, being thought a hero could only help my cause.

"Yes," I said, trying to imagine that I had been responsible for Amir-Ali's demise. The lie seemed to land, probably because it was partly true.

"You shot them," she said. "The two Jews. You and your men shot them."

"They kidnapped you. One of them was trying to pull a gun. It happened very fast. I did not think about it."

"Thank you. For coming for me. For saving me from them."

In some gloomy recess of my brain I saw Glitzman stand, smile, and begin, very slowly, to clap. "You're hungry," I said, snatching a look around. "And I promised you something to eat."

GLITZMAN'S PEOPLE HAD scouted a *lahmacun* joint a short walk from the house, away from the water and up the hills toward the cemetery. The MOSHE algorithm had designed the route to avoid cameras, though I wished we had solved for drainage instead. The rain had turned much of the route to lagoons. With a nod to the Kurds, whom I ordered back inside, Roya and I strolled with hands in our pockets against the windblown cold. When our path became puddles, I would offer my hand to help her dodge the water. By the time we approached the restaurant, she had accepted the offer.

The meal was one long companionable silence. The restaurant was cramped, the tables were scarcely large enough to hold two plates, and most were illuminated by small candles. Ours was not burning, but when I asked in my broken Turkish for a light the only thing that came was a roll of the waiter's eyes so abusive it seemed to rock his entire head. The size of the table meant there was no way to avoid knee-knocking. She had more Turkish and more charm than I did, so she ordered. Hers with garlic, mine with spiced beef. Two glasses of ayran, which earned from the waiter a not-so-subtle frown because the drink was refreshment for hot afternoons and the night was cold. *Simit* to start, then *pide*, a canoe of flatbread stuffed with cheese. Her hunger had at last arrived with safety, a fellow Persian, and the connection with Alya. Despite my feelings on the service, and the looseness of the cultural code on such matters, I left a reasonable tip. You never do know where you might need a friend, but I did know that I didn't need any enemies.

On our walk to the safe house we kept our hands firmly in our pockets.

I was disappointed to see how quickly the puddles were drying.

CHAPTER 33

Istanbul

"MY TURN," Roya said.

I had passed her another cigarette. After I lit it, she sank back into the chair, huddled deep into her manteau. The cold had settled into the house; into my bones. I felt Glitzman's gaze on me, through the hidden cameras, heard his judgments warbling in the clandestine microphones. I was ready to slip back into Tehran, where his all-seeing eye clouded from crystal clarity into a milky haze.

"Your turn," I affirmed. "I will answer what I can."

"You said Hossein Moghaddam was an Israeli spy. What was he doing for them?"

I considered answering, then pivoted: "Do you understand who I am?"

"I thought it was my turn to ask questions."

"A suggestion," I said. "Start with that one."

"Ask who you are?"

"Yes."

She pursed her lips, then ran her tongue across her front teeth like a windshield wiper, clearly annoyed. "Who are you?"

"An Etela'ati."

"You told me this."

"My team is not a typical one, Roya. We are handling a highly sensitive matter: Mossad's penetration of state security organs, in particular the Qods Force. May I say I am surprised you work there?"

"And why is that?"

She wasn't looking at me then—something in the kitchen had her attention—but I could feel the conversation compress like a spring at maximum tension.

"The Qods Force," I said, "it's a... fervent place." Then I pointed to her lit cigarette; I pretended to tug on a forelock of my own hair, snaking invisibly down my face. My smile said I understood her predicament. At the time I wasn't sure I was being effective, but watching the tapes later I almost believed my own lies.

Roya tucked a stray cord behind her ear—though not under her overworked hijab—and considered the cigarette thoughtfully. Then she took a determined pull, and when her eyes again found mine they were smiling defiantly. "My husband is dead," she said. "I have a daughter to raise, bills to pay. Qods helps me pay them."

"And you do what for them, precisely?"

"I work—worked—for Hossein Moghaddam. Administrative job. I run the office. Boring."

I lit my own cigarette and hunched forward, elbows on my knees. "In the past three years alone, twenty-one men—scientists, engineers, security officials, soldiers—have been killed in Iran. And all of them worked either for the Qods Force or the Revolutionary Guards. Your husband, of course, was one of these victims."

Roya's mouth twitched. She said nothing, gave only a sickly nod.

"A month ago," I went on, "we collected an intercept of your captors speaking about a meeting in Turkey with, and this is a quote, *'one of the friends.'* The Mossad officers use code names for their sources, and they mention two more working directly with Moghaddam. One is, and this is also a quote, *'on his new team.'* There is an Israeli network under our noses in Tehran, Roya. Deep in the Qods Force."

I let that sit.

"My group?" she eventually mumbled.

"I would like to show you a video from Hossein's villa. I know you don't want to relive that night, but you should see it for yourself."

IN OUR FRENETIC PREPARATIONS, Glitzman had insisted that Roya should experience an "abundance of realness" in our first hours together. My words were critical. They would be an invitation to betray her country under the blissful ignorance that she was actually serving it. But there also had to be cold hard facts. Two dead Israelis were one of them, of course. We'd shot them, hadn't we? Spilled plenty of their blood. Before I put the thumb drive into my computer to show her the surveillance video from Moghaddam's apartment, I told her a little more about the nonexistent Colonel Hashemi, chief of Internal Security. I gave the Ministry's address and his office location and wrote down his secretary's open line number—these were backstopped, and would be answered by Glitzman's people if Roya pried. I folded that information into Roya's hands. I showed her my passport, the name and picture my own. Further proof that I was who I said I was. All of it said: *Trust me.*

She watched the video created for just this moment. She saw herself entering the apartment, greeting Hossein. I fast-forwarded. Glitzman and his people went in. They wheeled her out.

"Enough," she said at last. I snapped shut the laptop. I fixed more tea and tried to appear calm, though I was frantically ticking through my mental checklist.

"You haven't told me how he died," I said. (Glitzman said it was a heart attack, and then I was skeptical. Now I believe him).

"I don't know how Hossein died," she said. "He just keeled over."

"What did they do with his body?" she asked. She could not look at me.

"I don't know," I said. "We couldn't search the villa. We trailed the Israelis to their safe house, looking for you. I wonder if they left the body where it lay. It's what I would have done. In any case, I can assure you that they will do their best to make it look like an accident. Whatever the truth may be."

"What does that mean?" she said.

"It means that you are the only one who knows what happened." *A rough spot for you to be in, Roya,* I did not say.

She said, "Make it look like an accident? Why? How can you be sure?"

"The last thing Mossad wants, even with two of their people dead, is to trigger investigations and spy hunts in Tehran, especially since Moghaddam is not the only spy in his unit. The Israelis have every interest in sweeping this under the rug. I do not know how they will go about it, but I would wager they will try to make it look like an accident."

"What if . . ." Roya trailed off.

I waited.

"What if . . . what if they do not believe me?" she murmured. "In Tehran. What if they think I killed him?"

"Oh," I said. "Well, I expect Mossad could lay a trail of bread crumbs for investigators suggesting a heart attack, or a suicide, probably with boatloads of drugs in his system to explain it. I don't see why they would frame you. What do they gain?"

This speculation was Roya's ticket home, and the slight softening on her face showed that she knew it, too.

"I am exhausted," she said, her voice wavering. "I need to sleep."

"Do you understand what it means if I am right about this?" I asked.

"I don't understand anything," she said. And when she punctuated that sentence with my name, I interpreted it as yet another murmur of the trust growing between us.

"It means," I continued, "that the people who know Hossein Moghaddam is dead—us, the Israelis—have no interest in pursuing the matter further. As far as Tel Aviv is concerned, the case is closed, at least for now." I made the point with a wipe of my hands.

"Hossein was a spy," she murmured, beginning, to my immense satisfaction, to tell the story alongside me.

"Precisely. And I want to hunt the rest of Mossad's network in Tehran, inside the Qods Force. I would like the Zionists to stop killing our people, murdering them, like they murdered your husband. And I could use your help."

Turns out that describing how someone might change the world—say, by avenging your dead husband—is quite simple, but convincing them that it's possible, selling that fantasy, is really the trick. Because obviously, in reality, no one changes the world.

"My help?" she repeated.

"You worked closely with Hossein," I said, "in this unit with Colonel Ghorbani. And I know you are not one of the spies, Roya. They killed Abbas. They kidnapped you."

"What would I say happened to Hossein?" she asked.

"Well," I said, "nothing. You would say nothing. You ran your errands before the meeting, Hossein asked you to come over and run another errand for him. We will invent one. You will call his phone now, maybe. There will be no answer because it is in the kitchen over there, and soon I am going to break it to bits. You'll call three more times. Do you have an emergency number you can phone back in Tehran?"

She nodded.

"Good, yes, you'll ring that number and note that Hossein is not responding to your calls. I will send people to your hotel to collect your things. The Israelis might be lurking around. We cannot take the risk. You'll sit tight here, and fly back to Tehran as planned."

"And work for you?"

"*With* me."

"Why?"

"There are Israeli spies inside the Qods Force, Roya. They helped kill Abbas, and you can help me find them."

She blinked. "How?"

The conversation had devolved to one-word responses. When the questions become that simple, it means a choice has been made. It means nothing will ever be simple again.

FIRST UP, what Glitzman wanted most of all: an address for Ghorbani's operation. It was a residential home in Niavaran, one of the more pleasant neighborhoods in north Tehran—she knew it by heart, she had been the one to arrange it, she said. How? I asked. Qods money. Next was the names of everyone on her team. There was the leader, Colonel Ghorbani. Major Shirazi and his strange and secretive room, filled with computers and monitors, where she had seen views of a mysterious city that she believed to be Jerusalem. There was Mina, the analyst-cum-housekeeper, and the major's lieutenants. Roya the administrator.

"Small group," I said. "What is it actually doing?"

"I don't know," she said. "I really don't."

I believed her. Why would she know? Ghorbani gained nothing by telling her. She had joined nine months earlier. She could remember the date Hossein first approached her because she'd been fighting with Qods about Abbas's pension and the martyr's bonus.

"Does anyone at Niavaran communicate with anyone in Qods proper?" I asked, sensitive to the specificity now marking our discussion.

"No," she said. "Colonel Ghorbani prohibits it. The network at Niavaran is separate. There isn't a connection to headquarters."

"How do they communicate outside of Niavaran? Or do they?"

"There is a WhatsApp group," she said. "It's for simple messages. Come to the office. Don't come to the office. Roya, show up at seven to make breakfast. That sort of thing."

I tapped her Turkish phone, which was still spread on the table. "Do they ever contact you on this?"

"No."

"You don't have your Iranian phone anywhere?"

"Hossein forbade me to travel with it."

I had her write down her Iranian phone numbers. "For when I am in touch," I said, folding up the paper. "Back in Iran."

Roya's eyelids were stitching together; she was fading.

"You have no idea what Major Shirazi is doing in his room?" I asked, hoping the exhaustion had loosened her lips.

She yawned. And shut her own. "Can we stop for now?"

"Certainly," I said.

"Thank you again, thank you," she said before drifting off. "For finding me. For saving me." And again she said my name. I wish I could hear her say it again.

CHAPTER 34

Istanbul

SLEEP, THOUGH, did not come for us.

In the few remaining hours of that long night, I snatched glances of Roya spread across the couch, staring, unblinking, at the pattern embossed on the blue wallpaper of the safe house, sun-stained and fraying and bubbled. I must have dozed off, because next thing I recall is that the lamp had been flicked on, its light pooling around Kovan, playing watchman in the chair. I heard the shower running. It was 6:18 in the morning.

"She wanted to clean up," Kovan said.

A yawn escaped with my nod, and my attention landed on a damp spot on the couch, where Roya had been sleeping. I frowned and stooped over for a sniff.

"It's sweat," Kovan said. "Not piss."

I pulled back the blanket, which was also damp. The stain ran the full length of both cushions. "It's been a rough couple days," I said. "How long has she been in the shower?"

Kovan shrugged. "A normal amount of time."

"What does that mean?"

Sighing, Kovan checked his watch. "Maybe ten minutes."

That felt long to me, but I also didn't have a woman in my life to calibrate. I counted to thirty and then knocked gently on the bathroom door. "Roya?"

I scratched at my nose. No response.

"Roya?"

I counted to three. No response.

"Roya?" I yelled.

"What?" she replied, the water shutting off. "I'm fine. I just... I'm fine. Let me finish."

"Take your time," I called back, in a voice that made clear she should do no such thing.

Aryas, armed with Roya's key card, had gone to her hotel to collect her case. When Roya appeared she was dressed in a manteau and gray pants. Despite the shower, sweat was beading along her upper lip and where hijab met hairline. She'd sat right back down in her own sweat and didn't have a word to say about it. I asked Kovan to give us a few minutes, and claimed the chair under the lamp.

"How do you feel?" I asked.

"Not well."

"Are you going to be sick?"

"No. I don't think so.

"Can't I just tell Colonel Ghorbani what happened?" She wiped the sweat from her lips and left it on one of the cushions.

I will be much more at ease with this sordid business, Glitzman told me the night before, if you can remind her that she is owned by you, that the consequences for betrayal are grave, and may include her daughter. Think of Alya. But I thought this approach would backfire. I was different. I was a friend, even if I owned her.

"It has not been easy for you," I said tenderly. "You've watched Hossein die. You've been kidnapped and interrogated by the Zionists. I fully appreciate the stress you are under. But"—here my voice sharpened—"I must reiterate: my team knows that Hossein was working for the Mossad. That there are other spies inside his group. This is a matter of the utmost national importance. I need your help, Roya. If you mention anything to Colonel Ghorbani, it will be viewed as collaboration with the Zionists. But I am not worried, because you are a loyal citizen, and also because, well, why would you do such a thing? I want to catch the men that killed your husband. Help me. Help me unmask them. Help me avenge Abbas."

She raised her eyes to meet mine. "How much do you know about how Abbas died?"

"I know Abbas was targeted, with help from the traitor Hossein Moghaddam, because your husband was helping Qods design materials to make drones invisible to radar. I know he was shot by a robotic machine gun fired from Israel on the night of Alya's fifth birthday. I know that your eyes are now double-colored because of the blast—the Zionists fitted the gun with explosives to destroy the evidence. And I know the evidence was not destroyed."

Her mouth opened a little. We looked at each other for a long time.

"How?" she asked. "How? Qods kept it a secret."

"It's my job to know their secrets."

"He did not die right away," Roya said. "I can still hear his voice. He told me he could not see. He opened the door and fell out of the car and then the shooting started up again. And—" She just stopped. There was no energy for hysterics, not after a night like this.

"I did not know him," I said. "But I am told he was a kind man. Funny. That he was always showing pictures of Alya to his friends around the office. That he had a secret handshake with her. So secret, in fact, that I don't even know it." That drew out a thin smile.

Aryas poked his head out the door of the bedroom and the look I gave him sent him back inside. I leaned forward in my seat.

"The Mossad officers I mentioned to you," I said, nervously veering off-script, "the ones whose calls we've been listening in on: they know the man responsible for your husband's death, the author of the operation. He has a little girl the same age as Alya, I hear. He murdered Abbas on Alya's birthday, then he went home to play with his little girl. His tentacles are deep inside Qods, Roya. Help me cut them off."

I was looking at Roya, and Roya was looking at me. There might have been noise in the background, traffic or construction work or birds, but I would have scarcely noticed a truck driving through the living room.

Did she trust me? Did she believe? Though the jerk of her head was barely a nod, I thought she did.

"Good," I said, standing. "I'll fix tea. Then you'll make a few phone calls."

THE CALLS WERE the first brushstrokes of an alibi. Glitzman, who'd been monitoring my progress, had sent instructions for the precise order. First, Roya called Hossein's Turkish phone—Monday morning, checking in with the boss to see if he'd had a good weekend and did he need anything before she flew out? An hour later she called him again. Then, thirty minutes later, three more calls, minutes apart. After that, the emergency number Hossein had given her. She left a voice mail asking someone to call her back straightaway.

We waited for fifteen minutes. Her phone rang, and she let it ring for a while. When she picked it up it was with a whiff of disgust, as if it had been dropped in the toilet.

"Hello," she said, putting it on speaker.

"Roya," Ghorbani said, "what's the issue?" She mouthed, to me: *The colonel.*

"I've called Hossein several times," she said. "I've checked at the villa, but there's no answer. I wanted to be sure he didn't need anything before I left today, but I . . . he—"

"You don't know where he is?" Ghorbani snapped.

"I don't. Do you, Colonel?"

I hoped he could hear the edge of fear sliding through Roya's voice; though she was acting here, I figured it was real enough.

"I will ask the questions."

"I'm sorry. Of course. What should I do?"

"You prepped everything? The meeting went off?"

"I did. It happened on Friday. He told me right after that everything was fine."

"When is your flight?"

"This afternoon. Should I take it?"

"You absolutely must take it. What's the flight number?"

After Roya had found her ticket, she said "Iran Air 091." Ghorbani hung up.

SHE HAD A HARD TIME ACCEPTING—though she must, deep down, have known—that she would land at Imam Khomeini under clouds of paranoia and suspicion. That someone, probably Colonel Ghorbani himself, would be waiting for her at the airport and he would want her story immediately. We had worked on it, of course, what she'd done that weekend, what she'd bought—Aryas and Kovan had fetched gifts, including a stuffed lion for Alya—and how she'd seen Hossein briefly on Friday evening before he'd gone missing over the weekend.

I'd given Roya instructions to contact me once the situation had settled, which I defined as being back at work, with the belief—even if unproven, because how, really, would she know for certain?—that Ghorbani bought her story. We downloaded a crossword app on her phone. We created a profile (*KhanumGoogoosh71436*) and worked out a few simple codes we would use to communicate. We agreed on Laleh Park as our meeting spot. She often brought Alya there on the weekends, or in the evening after work.

"You will be on the flight?" she asked, in near-desperation, as we were mulling how best to discreetly put her in a taxi.

"I have business to finish here for a few days," I said. The safe money was on someone in Ghorbani's shop using Hossein's disappearance as an excuse to take a good hard look at the comms, particularly Roya's, in the days to come. There was going to be some heat, and we had to wait it out. She looked like she wanted to argue, she wanted me on that plane to administer a few sharp doses of moral courage, but she had to be alone, and this wasn't a debate, I was in charge, and I could see that Roya, smart girl, knew better than to plead with a representative of the Islamic Republic who'd made up his mind. It would only signal weakness. We did not speak anymore.

I walked her back up toward the *lahmacun* joint and hailed her a taxi.

She was still sweaty, her gaze was harried and strung-out, but I took heart that she'd retreated from the threshold of a panic attack. Some of the fear, I thought, had given way to resolve. Though not all of that fear, which cheered me greatly. You wanted an agent to show some fear, which meant they understood the risks. If they didn't, they were as good as dead or blown.

I wanted to see Roya once more before she disappeared, but the cab sputtered off quickly, turned the corner, and vanished. If Roya could keep herself alive—if I delivered those bodies—I might win the race that had begun, in one sense, when Glitzman had taken his seat in my dental chair, nearly three years before. In another sense, of course, I'd been on this journey all my life. I was distracted, in the clouds, on my walk back to the safe house: I had a great deal of money on my mind.

CHAPTER 35
Istanbul

OVER CELEBRATORY WHISKEYS at his safe house command post, Glitzman delivered a brief speech about the valiant agent behind enemy lines, the nobility of waiting and waiting well, the dish seasoned with stories of Roya's grit under pressure (which he had applied), and pride in her determination to avenge the sins done to her (which he had committed).

Had I seen Glitzman happier? No, it was not possible. He was sloshing whiskey in everyone's cups, cracking jokes, a few of which were delivered in Hebrew, earning blank stares from the Kurds and me, and looks of regret from Rivka, who had greeted us coldly, perhaps because the last time we'd seen her had been the theatric rescue, and I think one of the Kurds may have hit her quite hard. In the mania of his victory Glitzman would frequently wander onto the balcony to blaze through cigarettes. During one of these intermissions, Rivka with him outside, I asked the brothers what they thought of Roya.

"Great ass," said Kovan.

"Oh fuck off," I said. "I'm serious."

Kovan smiled and, feigning great offense, slid his hand to his heart. "So am I. Problem is, my friend, you just don't know how to properly surveil a Persian girl for her saddlebags. You've got to know how to see through the chador."

"X-ray vision," Aryas said, his hands twisting to goggles, which he pretended to focus on his brother's crotch. Kovan made a show of positioning himself so his brother would have a good angle, and then told us a story about how, when he'd been twelve or thirteen, they'd gone for a picnic by a river in the countryside east of Tehran, and a woman had walked into the water on the opposite bank, and even through her chador, which was not tight, he claimed, it was a bag, yet somehow he could tell she had curves, he knew it, and she'd pulled the fabric up to wade farther out, and he'd seen the pale flesh of her ankles, and it had been too much for him, those fine porcelain ankles, and—

"And where were you during this very lovely scene?" I cut in, glaring at Aryas.

"I was minding my own business, swimming in my chador," he said, blinking behind his imaginary X-ray, and the brothers erupted in laughter.

These fucking morons, I thought. Aryas pulled his drink onto his knee and began tracing the rim with his finger. "You conned her," he said. "Why don't you go first?"

The balcony door whooshed open, and a Glitzman chuckle was the first thing through, followed by a campfire of smoke, parting for the two Israelis, who joined our conclave. "What are you talking about?" Glitzman asked.

"Roya," Kovan said.

The furrow of Glitzman's sweaty brow, the wipe of his chin, the great swoop of his arm across the top of the couch, the shift of his gaze off to the middle distance—I recognized preparations for a speech.

But it was Rivka, in her fearsome efficiency, who got there first. She spoke into the dry bottom of her cup—all offers of refill had been rudely refused. "She is young. Energetic, emotional, and remarkably vulnerable; a twenty-seven-year-old widow with a young daughter and no living parents. In Iran." Rivka clicked her tongue. "And her first attempt at intimacy since her husband's death ends in the death of her would-be lover before they can begin. Vulnerable, and unlucky to boot."

"How do you know it was her first attempt at love?" Kovan said.

"I know," Rivka said, with such confidence that we all let it drop.

"Also: Israel found her," I said to Glitzman.

"Not so lucky," Glitzman murmured, "indeed."

"Let's hope she finds a little luck," I said, raising my glass.

"Hear, hear," Glitzman said. With a sigh, he narrowed his eyes thoughtfully. "She is prone to delusion. Her sore luck, her powerlessness, they stir cravings for fantasy."

I was blind then, General; unwilling to stare down the terrible risks and choices littered across the paths before me. But when it came to Roya? I saw, with crystal clarity, the roads she might travel: every turn and bump, the great cliffs on either side.

"She is young, sure," I said, "but not a fool. She could put her head down, find a new husband, care for her daughter, probably make a few more of them. In one light it's a cage, in another it's a noble life."

"And you could have remained a mere dentist," Glitzman said. "Found a Swedish girl, settled down. Noble? It's noble to serve Israel. To not waste your gifts as a dentist."

In the moment, I neglected the obvious implication of Glitzman's remark. Had he not been so fully immersed in celebration, Glitzman would never have veered so near the damning conclusion that Roya and I were both fantasists. That I'd built a theater for her, just as Glitzman had assembled one for me.

CHAPTER 36

Istanbul / Stockholm

BUT ON THAT BOOZY NIGHT it all seemed promising.

What was waiting for us was thrilling adventure in service of a noble cause. What had happened to Amir-Ali would not happen to me. We all had a few more drinks at the safe house, said our goodbyes to the Israelis, and then the Kurds and I spent the rest of the night getting very drunk in the bars off Taksim. By the time I'd sobered up I was deplaning at Arlanda. There was no sun, the ground was covered with discouraging piles of April slush, and I accidentally stepped in a puddle the color of milk chocolate by the taxi stand. I called Sina on the ride to his house.

"He lives," Sina said, his Swedish upbeat and demeaning all at once.

"I'm back in Stockholm," I said.

"Now?"

"Just landed, and in the cab. Made it back for Maman's birthday. Just like I promised."

"Lucky you," Sina said. There was an awkward pause. "What do you think about Frantzén?"

Frantzén. I almost laughed. It did not take much to tangle up a conversation with Sina. The mere mention of Sweden's only Michelin three-star had blown a cloud of smoke right over our chat.

"You already have a reservation."

"I think ahead."

"You're on the hook for the table."

Though I said nothing in this regard, I was curious why he thought our maman, a woman whose culinary beliefs were so doggedly pro-Persian they veered toward racism, might enjoy such a place.

"It's not your birthday, Sina," I scolded, trying to keep my tone breezy, though I was knocking dangerously close to the heart of things.

"It will be good for Maman to be out," he said. "And I'll treat"—here, in what must have been his subconscious urging him to stop there, he admirably paused, but then found he could not help himself—"of course."

Of course? There was the knife. And from what Sina knew, or assumed, of my finances, he wasn't wrong. A recreational root canal is a more pleasant experience than discussions of money with Swedes or Persians, two cultures that, though nothing alike, breed masters of silence, stonewalling, and dissembling on such matters. There's a hierarchy, all right, in Sweden and Persia, and though we all know it and feel it, only fools talk about it. We're all equal, like in *Animal Farm*.

And, really, what was there to say? Sina had ascended to the level of wealth where one loses all perspective on the rest of us down below.

The line was silent.

"How was Istanbul anyway? Good? Did you visit that Turkish bath I recommended, the one by the Blue Mosque?"—he could stand it no longer. If my brother's plunge into the Swedish pool has been deeper and fuller than my own, he has never matched my gift for that most Swedish of pastimes: passive-aggressive silence.

I thought of Glitzman. The staged rescue, the guns, the fake blood, the ensuing theater. I thought of Roya headed to Tehran and then decided I didn't want to think about that. "It was a great trip," I said. "Didn't have time to squeeze in the bath, though."

CHAPTER 37
Stockholm

IT WAS UNSPOKEN that I would be the one to collect Maman for dinner. Sina did not like to come here, and I felt guilty enough for being away that I did not like to press him on it. We both agreed, though, that it was fortunate sometimes Maman did not know where she was.

When I arrived to collect her, one of the caretakers (a Serb, I thought) was waiting with her in the lobby of Värboca Phase 2. As her dementia accelerated, Sina and I had been forced to treat her just as the Islamic Republic had: we kicked her out of her apartment. But this was for her own good, we both insisted, and perhaps even believed. Värboca, it must be said, was top-notch: sparkling parking structure, a courtyard with *pétanque*, and staff that had all been thoroughly certified, as per the generous signage, by the "Dementia Academy." The walls were as white as the residents, the scent was institutional baked-cod and chemicals, and the décor was Scandinavian minimalism with a health care twist, which is to say: Värboca Phase 2 was a Persian version of hell.

I went in to kiss her cheeks and she asked why I was there.

"It's your birthday Maman," I said. "We're taking you out."

Despite the flight of her mind, or perhaps because of it, my mother devoted gobs of time to her dress, hair, and skin-care routines, somehow maintaining her old rhythm of visiting her hairdresser every other week. The hair was spiraled up into a beehive—the look had been popular in Pahlavi's Tehran—fixed in place by pins and an ungodly amount of hair spray. Despite forgetting it was her birthday, she—likely with an assist from one of the Serbs—had dressed for it. A stylish slash of kohl rimmed her eyes, and she wore a silk blouse the color of ivory over a long A-line skirt, with sharp-toed boots that looked to have been stolen off a much younger woman, perhaps on a mountainside. I led her on my arm to my car, and on the drive she explained that a recent dinner had been a great success, seeing as the Homayouns had joined, and Mrs. Homayoun had complimented her pomegranate chicken, which was a real treat because Mrs. Homayoun was a mean bitch.

The only bit of Maman that I was glad to have lost was her internal censor, vaporized by the dementia. I stifled a laugh and nodded my head in agreement that yes, Mrs. Homayoun was indeed a wretch. The Homayouns, also uncommitted Jews, had fled Tehran for Los Angeles shortly after we had departed for Stockholm. Maman had not seen Mrs. Homayoun in over thirty-five years.

"I cooked that chicken last summer, Maman," I said.

"For who?" Maman asked, delighted. "A party? A girl?"

"For me," I said. "Just me."

"Alone?" Maman gasped. In her ruling there was no social value to cooking for yourself.

I turned on some music to pass the time.

In one of the restaurant windows was a small golden statue of a rat. I pulled alongside. Sina was outside on the curb, glued to his phone. He opened Maman's door, helped her out, and I went to find parking. On the walk back, I anxiously smoked two cigarettes and then, outside Frantzén, I smoked another one while staring at the rat, hoping it might bestow some kind of courage upon me. I rang the doorbell—this was the sort of restaurant with a doorbell—and waited for a moment, picturing myself the unwanted houseguest.

Our table was upstairs. A bottle of champagne was on ice. Maman was picking at a plate of canapes.

"Happy birthday Maman," Sina said, in Persian, raising his champagne.

"Happy birthday," I said, clinking mine to Sina's.

"I need to use the bathroom," Maman said. Sina showed her the way, and when he returned I asked, in Swedish, "No Frida?"

"She didn't want to come."

I nodded and snatched a cheese canape.

"You head back to Tehran next week?" Sina asked.

"Probably."

"Probably?"

I spotted Maman veering from the bathroom toward the elevator, and I went to fetch her.

"What were you talking about?" she asked when I brought her back to the table.

"Tehran," Sina said, and this careless reference in Maman's presence made me wonder if he was drunk. I certainly wanted to be, but I had to drive. I was going to have to watch him drink.

"Your father has been gone too long," Maman said, her face darkening, her eyes glazed.

"He has," I agreed.

"Three weeks now," she said. "Three weeks in Tehran. We will never get our house back. What is he doing? He sees his patients and then stays on fighting over the house. The stinking mullahs will never give him back a single brick! Give a Jew back his house? Please!"

She had delivered this speech, for the first time, a few months after Father had died. More than a decade on, and her mind's clock was still broken.

"We weren't even Jews in Tehran," Maman said, casting a judgmental eye on the scallops presented for the first course, "not really. We didn't go to synagogue. Barely celebrated. Quiet Passover in the home, who did that hurt? We certainly weren't Zionists! We are Persians! We are Iranians! And look what they did . . ."

Sina and I ate our scallops while Maman spoke at us, or around us, or to herself. When the time came for the next course, my mother's scallops sat untouched. The waiter asked if the food had been to her liking. Her eyes flashed, she clicked her tongue to her teeth. Persian translation: *Hell, no.*

"Everything's great," I said, handing the waiter my empty plate. "I'll finish these." I slid Maman's in front of me.

"That house," Maman murmured, when the waiter had gone. She shut her eyes. "That house. We slept on the roof in the summers and you could see the peaks of the Alborz in the moonlight. We knew each other, we knew our neighbors. You"—she pointed at Sina—"could watch him"—she pointed at me—"and cartwheel through the whole neighborhood without fear." Neither of us interrupted to correct her that I'd not passed a year in that home; there had been no cartwheeling. "Not like here, where everything is locked all the time." Maman's fingers were busying themselves with her earrings, an absent-minded smile played on her lips. "And the colors, we had carpets hanging in closets that were brighter than Khomeini's soul, I'll tell you that much. What did he say on his flight back from exile? They asked him what he felt on returning to his native land. What was it . . . ?"

"Nothing," I replied. "Khomeini said he felt nothing."

"Nothing," Maman said, as some beef thing arrived. "What kind of Persian feels nothing? All we have are feelings. He makes my skin crawl. He hated us. And not just the Jews. All of us. Our whole living room was covered in carpets and paintings. And there were balls! A social season. Then do you know what? We all went to bed one evening in the year 2537, which is how they had the calendar in those days, it—"

"I know Maman," Sina said. "It—"

"It dated from the coronation of Cyrus," Maman said, steamrolling him, "2537! Persia was advanced, the future. And then we woke up next morning and that snake Khomeini had changed it. Now it was 1357 on the Islamic calendar. Overnight, we went back in time over one thousand years!"

"This wine is nice," I said, taking a sip.

"It's a Cos d'Estournel," Sina said. "I didn't catch the year."

"And of course with these shits"—Maman's language again—"it always drifts sexual. The Shah bans the hijab, Khomeini makes it mandatory. Can't have you men aroused by a strand of my hair, can we? No. So when Mrs. Homayoun and I go to the baker, now we're sweating, matted, and greasy under these damn chadors and hijabs looking like two bowling pins hobbling down the road. And I'd never thought much about being a Jew, but the mullahs won't shut the hell up about it. Zion this, Jew that, well, what can you do? The Shah's secret police was in bed with the Zionists. Boo-hoo, I say, you tossed that bastard out, didn't you?"

The long vowels and hard consonants of my mother's formal Persian had painted her profanity-laden speech with the gloss of an epic poem, the type she had read to me when I was very young. Sadness slid through me. I couldn't bear to tell her the truth about Tehran today, that there was nothing for her there. Maman's Tehran had sunk beneath the waves of history.

I DROVE MAMAN BACK to the assisted living facility. She was tired, and most of the ride passed in silence. But at a stoplight, she did manage this: "I was thinking about you the other day."

"Oh," I said. "What about?"

"There was a story from the Torah that I told you boys when you were fighting. Joseph and his brothers. Do you remember when I would read it to you?"

"I do, Maman. What made you think of that?"

"One of the nursing assistants encourages us to write down stories. You and Sina were always looking for a quarrel. And usually you found one. In those years your father was not home. He was working two jobs. I had to referee, I had to make peace. I liked the story because . . . well, I wanted you to stop fighting. I couldn't take it . . . I needed you boys to forgive each other. We had no room for fights. Our apartment then was nothing—paid for thanks to the state and a janitor's salary! Two tiny bedrooms. You remember it?"

"Some things," I said. "The stove, kitchen floor, I don't know why. An old green couch. Sina and I had a lava lamp, didn't we?"

"I don't know. Probably."

We had reached Värboca. I parked in one of the visitor spots, unbuckled my seat belt, and opened the door. I had one foot on the pavement when I noticed Maman hadn't budged. She was staring at the pale yellow light of the lobby in pure disgust. Lucid moments were rare. I swung my foot back into the car and shut the door. I put my hands on the wheel and sat with her until she was ready to speak.

"When we first left Iran and came here, I didn't resent your father. After all, things were bad for the Jews and getting worse. And here in Stockholm, well, he was a janitor, but at least he wasn't dead or in prison. I was grateful for that. But as the years went by, I began to hate him for it. We could have stayed in Iran and died or been shorn of our belongings in honor. Or not. Maybe it would have worked out? We'd all be in Iran now, we'd have made peace with the Islamic Republic. Instead we're here. But what is this? It is not home. It is exile. It was exile when we left and it is exile now. I should have packed up and left this place when your father died. Before I got . . . before . . ."

I had to interrupt. Conversations about her dementia usually ended in despair or anger, or both. So I asked: "Where would you have gone?"

"Oh, who the hell knows? Back to Iran. To California. Anywhere but here. I think I remembered the Joseph story because I've been angry with your father. I wondered if writing it down would help. Probably not. It usually didn't work on you boys. A half hour after the ending, you'd be at it again." I thought she might laugh, but instead she was grinding her teeth, staring bitterly through the windshield, and though I will never have young children, I could sense that those years had been so brutal that three decades later she was still incapable of summoning nostalgia for them.

"Our apartment," I said. "Mostly I remember how quiet it was. Other than the fights, of course."

Maman laughed, and I was thankful to see her shove open the door. "Tehran was many things, but it was never quiet. But this place . . ." She paused for a moment, staring at the looming silence of the Vårboca lobby. "I hate it here."

If she'd been speaking of the despised facility, it would have lit my usual fires of shame and guilt. Thankfully, I knew what she meant.

After all, I felt the same, and—

The Interrogation Room
Location: ███████████
Present day

THE BLUE CRAYON SQUIRTS from Kam's fingers at the buzz of the door.

You might think that's frowned upon, and you'd be right, but what really turns those frowns to beatings is standing up to go after it. Kam sits, watching it roll, butt cheeks clenched tight as they'll go. The door swings open a bit, then falls back. Outside there is faint conversation.

But there's no hint of Askari's rosewater. And it's not the General, either. It's a guard he doesn't recognize, but he could be on the team, who's to know? Three years in Iranian prisons, and he's spoken to a lot of people through hoods.

"Done for now," he says. "Let's go." The guard gathers the paper and two more men come in. Kam breathes a sigh of relief as they lead him to his cell: no one saw the rogue crayon.

He is brought food and his prison copy of the *Shahnameh*, which he's read countless times, and though it is printed on simple paper, and the cover is yellowed and fraying, he finds it as beautiful as Rashida's illuminated version, which he once saw with his father on display at the Golestan Palace. Hushang has just cleaved the black demon's body in two when the lights die without warning. Kam scrambles to his mat and lies down.

The darkness does not bring nightmares, but it does bring memories, and they are more intrusive in the cell than when he is writing. The crayons offer some control, some protection. In the cell he's unarmed.

The memories that torment him most are not what you'd expect.

They are not about Colonel Askari, nor the General's pipe, nor the Chicken Kebab.

On many nights, or what Kam figures for nights, he remembers this...

"I DON'T LIKE BEING APART from her, Abbas"—Roya is speaking.

This line marks the first stirrings of the memory. When it comes, Kam knows there's no sense in fighting. His recollections are sourced from a package of intercepts, video, and notes Glitzman sent him after Istanbul, in preparation for running Roya in Tehran. In the months before Abbas was killed, Glitzman had spread a surveillance blanket over the Shabanis. Before the inevitable communications scrub following Abbas's death, before the Qods Force confiscated all of their old electronics, Glitzman had Roya's phone. Kam gets that line of Roya's through a recording off its microphone.

Glitzman's notes mention that Roya and Abbas have been squabbling over whether Afsaneh might take Alya for an afternoon each week. Afsaneh adores the girl, Roya is tired, and Abbas, thoughtful husband that he is, believes she might enjoy a quiet house for a couple hours. So, with Roya's desire unheeded, the Tuesday before the killing Alya is deposited with Afsaneh for a few hours. Take a nap, Abbas said. Go for a walk, read a book, go shopping, anything you like.

Roya goes straight home and spends the first half hour sitting in the unnerving stillness of their apartment. Then she goes into Alya's room and there's no video, but Kam hears rummaging through dresser drawers, opening and shutting, opening and shutting. Closet thrown open. She's huffing around.

Roya's face suddenly fills the screen. The phone is on the kitchen countertop and she's looking at a recipe, studying the screen while she collects ingredients from the refrigerator and cupboard. Saffron. Rice. Olive oil. A few other cans and jars. Her movements are frantic, she's humming but the tone is harsh and stressful—it's like shouting at yourself to relax. She's opening and reopening cupboards and it feels like she is retracing her steps, forgetting why she went to a cupboard only to remember after she's shut it. *Smack*—turmeric, Kam can read that one because it's right by the phone. Barberries. She's making *zereshk polo morgh*, he thinks. The ingredients are spread across the counter. There's a pot on the stovetop and she's probably starting the tomato paste sauce— that's where Maman begins—when she clicks off the heat. She leaves the room for ten minutes and thirty-six seconds.

Back into view of her phone's camera in the kitchen. She fills a glass with water, scrolls the recipe again, and gives the microwave clock a guilty look. She lights a cigarette, expelling the smoke up into the fan above the stove because Abbas hates the habit, hates the smell. Glitzman notes they've had a few fights about this, and Roya has told him she's given it up. This is one of the few lies she tells Abbas. *She and the girl are coconspirators*, Glitzman writes. *Only Alya knows the truth.*

Roya is studying the ingredients with the gleeful shame of someone desperate to surrender to temptation. She lights a second cigarette, and when Kam next sees her face it is one that has made decisions. At 2:11 in the afternoon, six days before she will be widowed, Roya scuttles dinner, returns the ingredients to the cupboard shelves. Then she disappears. When she returns she's lugging a heavy case. With great effort she heaves it onto the table. She fixes herself another cigarette. The surveillants said she was fond of one, maybe two each day. She's on number three, and by the time she's in the street the count is five.

The surveillance team picks her up on camera outside the apartment. Kam doesn't know who they are, of course, but Glitzman confessed to him that, after Abbas was killed, a handful of support assets had to be smuggled out of Iran. It's probably those guys behind the camera.

The team follows her, building pattern of life for someone whose husband is about to die, searching for any vulnerability in the routine, and the notes show the drudgery that accompanies planning a murder. First stop: fabric store. She is inside for just over twelve minutes and purchases three meters of something and then something else the microphones don't quite hear.

The phone logs show that Roya was checking the time constantly, just about every two minutes. She jogs home with the bag, and here the surveillants immortalize their puzzlement in the logs, wondering why in the hell she is running. Maybe because she shirked on dinner, time to get cooking.

At home, back in the kitchen, for a while the video is black. Phone in her pocket. But what does Kam hear? Silence broken by the occasional grunt, mild curse, swishing, and the flick of a lighter, all accompanied by the whir of a mysterious machine.

Thus passes one hour and forty-one minutes. Kam is fast-forwarding...

And here, at least initially there's a bit of confusion in the surveillance logs, because she's left her phone inside. The team outside picks her up on camera and the parabolic mics snuggled in one of the vans. Roya forgot her phone but not the cigarettes, which she's blazing through in the clear light of day, taboos be damned. Then she searches her purse and pats her manteau. She's realized the phone is missing. A tremor of panic seeps across her face, and she looks backward, then forward, and back again, deliberating over whether to retreat or press on. She's in a tunnel, walking briskly, agitated, clutching her purse. Where is she going? the team wonders. Confusion bleeds through the notes. Another errand? Afsaneh said she would bring Alya home, and they aren't due for another hour. Maybe she's going out for food? She abandoned the dinner, after all, and even though Abbas said she should do what she wants that afternoon, well... what's for dinner, exactly?

She asks a passerby for the time. She must look a little tweaked, because, the surveillants note, the passerby, an older woman, is reluctant to give it. When no response comes and the woman walks right on by, Roya hisses at her, says what's wrong with you, I'm looking for the park, my little girl's at the park and I'm on my way, I left my phone at home, you hag, what's the matter with you? What time is it? Surveillant's note: *the woman kept on walking, and did not give Roya the time.*

Roya hustles faster now. She's almost at a jog. Her skin is glistening. She's running. She's cursing herself. Her face is drawn tight like a woman expecting bad news. She bumps into someone, apologizes, keeps on jogging.

She reaches the park and runs, faster now, toward the benches. She hugs Afsaneh tight, it's a surprise, and her sister's hands are down at her sides. Initially there is some frustration across Afsaneh's face: *What's wrong, you didn't trust me with Alya?* But that doesn't survive contact with Roya, because whatever stress had her disfigured on the walk to this park, it's vanished, the cameras make that plain. There is pure joy pouring from Roya's face. She hugs her sister again, and Afsaneh looks around, flabbergasted, watching her baby sister march toward the slide. Alya, at the bottom, has spotted her maman.

Roya scoops her up and kisses her neck and the mics pick up her saying that she came for Alya because she had something special for her, she has just made it today, and could not wait to give it to her. Alya's face perks up and they clasp hands and run for it. Run, run, run. There's a swing in their stride like they move to the same beat, they hear the same music. Back to the bench.

Roya pulls a pink tulle skirt from her purse. Alya shrieks in delight.

"Remember the one you lost?" Roya says, breathing hard. "Remember, it was just like this? I made you one, love. There, we can just slide it on right over your dress. There you go. How does it fit? Good? It looks good."

"You look beautiful, Alya," Afsaneh says, but she's looking at her sister, and it's with hopeless curiosity, someone who knows they are not going to get to the bottom of things.

Alya twirls. Twirls and twirls and twirls, and Roya twirls her again. They all sit down on the bench and the two sisters speak for a few minutes and the mics catch none of it. Then, quite clearly, Afsaneh says she brought the car, she'll drive them home, but Roya says no, they'll walk, it's a fine day, maybe a little wind, but it's a skirt meant for the wind, after all. Roya hugs Afsaneh again, and you can see on the tapes that her sister wants to ask if everything's okay, but the answer to that is obvious, at least to me. Everything is perfect. This is exactly what Roya wanted to do with her free afternoon, and maybe Abbas was right to suggest one after all, because if she'd been with Alya all day, there wouldn't have been a surprise.

They walk home, and much of the tape is fuzzy, or they drift in and out of the frame, but what's clear is that they're laughing and for bits of it they're running, Roya is chasing her, and when the mics do pick things up it's their own language. It's Persian of course but nonsense to anyone but them. There's a puddle of something outside the apartment door and Alya lifts up her skirt while Roya carries her across and they're inside.

Up in the kitchen, Alya asks what's for dinner. Roya laughs, but her phone's in her pocket again, and there's no video. You can hear the flick of a lighter and then a *sshhh* and Alya giggles.

"What's for dinner, Maman?"

There isn't a sound, but Kam knows Roya is smiling. Is that the whir of a stovetop fan? He believes it is.

"What do you think about your maman?" Roya says. "What do you think of me?"

Alya doesn't say anything; here, Kam always imagines confusion spreading across the little girl's face.

"Do you think Maman is too strict?" Roya said. "Do you think she keeps the house nice? Do you think she's a little crazy?"

Alya giggles, there is a sound like the smacking of lips on a cheek. "I think you're pretty," Alya says.

I hear the squeak of a chair on the floor.

It is silent for a full thirty-eight seconds. The mics pick up their breathing because Roya has pulled Alya into a hug, and her phone is in her pocket, snug against them both. There are little shudders, too, and I can't quite tell what those noises are until Alya says:

"Why are you crying, Maman?"

"I might never do much of anything," Roya says. "But I made you."

AS ALWAYS, when the memory finally lets Kam go, he's awake in the darkness and he knows that the operation was fucked from the get-go.

The idea, as Glitzman liked to say, was to give Roya her dreams. Well, that's a tough one, isn't it, trying to sell someone something they've already got?

In the morning, or in what Kam figures for morning, they collect him from his cell, and soon he is back writing. The memory is not gone, but with the crayon in hand, he stands a halfway decent chance of warding it off, at least for a while.

شماره:
تاریخ:
پیوست:

النجاه فی الصدق
بخش چهارم از شهادت‌های من

Number		
Date	The power is with those who resist	The Islamic Republic of Iran
Attachment	1979	

In the name of God
Honesty will save you
The <u>fourth</u> part of my sworn confession
Kamran Esfahani

CHAPTER 38

Värnamo, Sweden

Three years ago

GLITZMAN'S SUMMONS CAME one week after Maman's birthday.

He had rented a house in the countryside outside Värnamo, an hour or so from my family's old summer cottage, a property my father had purchased once the dental practice had at last taken off, in yet another fruitless attempt to show that we, too, could be Swedish. On our first weekend at the cottage, while in town to buy groceries, one of the neighbors approached my father and asked, in addition to the house caretaking, did we offer lawn and garden services?

Now, in a slushy spring that refused to arrive, a thin blanket of snow was pulled tight across the lawn, the roof, the patio. Smoke curled from the chimney. I sat in the drive, car still running, hands on the wheel. I sat for a long time. Once or twice I even put it in reverse. Finally, I killed the engine, grabbed my bag, and, finding the door unlocked, I went inside.

Glitzman and Rivka were sitting in front of a crackling fire. The place smelled smoky, like the flue wasn't fully open, and also of something warming in the kitchen—cinnamon and nutmeg and walnuts, and the smell nearly made me cry. Both officers stood at the creak of the door, glasses of brown liquor prayerfully in hand. On a small table by the fire sat one for me.

"Hungry?" Glitzman asked. "Food in the kitchen. Rivka made it. Some kind of Iranian stew. Smells like soul to me."

"*Fesenjan*," Rivka said.

Maman liked to make it for my birthdays, which I suppose they had learned while spying on me. It was touching, it was violating—it was my relationship with Glitzman and his Office in a pot. We moved to the kitchen, served the soup, and gathered around the table. I'd only just got the spoon to my lips when Rivka said, "It's time to go back in. Roya's in the clear."

"She hasn't sent me any messages on the crossword app," I said. "How do you know?"

Glitzman, taking his first puffs on a cigarette, hacked smoke from his mouth with his laugh.

THE FIRST PIECE to slide into place, Glitzman said, was an intercept of a report filed by the Turkish police and shared with the Iranian Consulate. Hossein Moghaddam had overdosed, meth and booze, etc., no hint of foul play, at least according to the Turkish investigators, Glitzman explained, with obvious pride at his handiwork. The Istanbul surveillance crew had been staking out the villa, 24/7 physical coverage in shifts, plus four fixed cameras, and apart from a visit from one Iranian official—who Glitzman said was a diplomatic lackey, not a security man—alongside a crop of Turkish cops, there'd been no Persian fingerprints on the place. Same for the safe house Roya had rented, and her hotel.

"This was reason for optimism," Glitzman said, dipping his own spoon into the soup. "But not enough to risk your life in Tehran."

"I'm sure you'll get there," I said.

Rivka laughed—it was the first time I'd heard one from her, and it was more delicate, hesitant, than I'd expected. I suppose she didn't have much practice.

"You put that malware on her phone?" I asked.

"MEDUSA," Rivka said. "It's a nasty bitch."

I had worked with the malware briefly during our training in Albania. Mossad could send a text message or email laden with it and the recipient didn't even have to click on it for the Israelis to take control.

Because Roya had written down her Iranian phone number for me in Istanbul, well, I imagine the Israelis had harvested every scrap of data: photos, videos, location records, texts, emails, web searches, passwords, call logs. MEDUSA would also enable Mossad to infect other phones in contact with Roya's. Like Ghorbani's.

"Her phone did not travel to Niavaran for a week," Glitzman said. "She was probably on ice while Qods figured out what the hell happened to Moghaddam in Istanbul. Roya was doing normal things: taking Alya to the park, a visit to a mechanic."

"It looked like she'd been given the week off," Rivka said.

I thought of the paranoia that must have accompanied all these normal activities: nail-biting, watching Alya swing, sweat dripping while negotiating the price of new tires.

"And at last," Glitzman said, "on Ghorbani's command, she returned to the Niavaran office two days ago."

"Back to work," Rivka said.

"Are the Kurds back in Iran?" I asked.

"They will be tomorrow," Glitzman said.

"We have most of the police and Etela'at and Rev Guards fiber-tapped," Rivka said. "And there's been no interest in you, your apartment, or the dental practice. Camera feeds don't show any evidence of surveillance teams. Only patients agitated at your long Swedish vacation."

"I'm not on any watch lists?" I asked.

"None that we see," Glitzman said.

"Do you see all of the watch lists?"

"I'd say most of them," Glitzman said. "The ones that matter."

"The Islamic Republic is inept," I said, staring right at Glitzman, "except when it comes to killing its own people. Then it's a well-oiled machine."

Glitzman put his spoon in the bowl and wiped his lips with his napkin. He folded his arms on the table and looked into my eyes like he wanted to peel them. "The machine is not looking for you. You have my word."

I nodded. What could I say? For a while after that the only sound was the clink of busy spoons. Halfway through my second helping I became convinced that this was actually my maman's recipe. That they'd lifted it off my phone or computer, probably using MEDUSA. Glitzman left the kitchen when I stood for a third bowl, and when he returned he was carrying an envelope, which he kept beside his plate.

"Money is nice"—he slid the envelope my way—"but vengeance is better. And this is our chance for vengeance on Ghorbani. Believe me. Take it from me. Yes, I can see it written across your face. Tell me I'm wrong."

"Amir-Ali was my friend," I said. "The regime, Iran, Ghorbani, whatever we call it—it killed him."

And they both looked at me with a profound understanding. Like my answer was good enough for them.

LATER, UP IN MY ROOM, I opened the envelope and found the escrow statement from Cayman National Bank & Trust. Thirty-five months at ten thousand American a pop. Not enough . . .

A payout of $250,000 when Glitzman got his bodies . . .

Sale of the practice in Tehran, my apartment . . .

Would it be enough?

I daydreamed for a moment about my feet in the Pacific. Then I mindlessly scrolled real estate listings near Corona Del Mar before shifting to more reasonably priced inland properties, which were still insanely expensive. To start I was going to have to find a property I could rent out for a chunk of the year to cover the mortgage.

I spent the rest of the evening reviewing Mossad's prior surveillance notes on Roya, in preparation for Tehran. That night was the first time I witnessed the tender afternoon in which, instead of kicking loose, Roya had made a skirt for her daughter. When I was done watching, I lay down on the bed and realized I'd forgotten to brush my teeth. I also wasn't tired, so I went downstairs, found a beer in the fridge, blinked at it, and set it back on the shelf. I bundled up to take a night walk and then, halfway down the drive, abandoned the idea and retreated inside.

I wound up flat on my back in bed, lights out, phone brightening my face as I doomscrolled social media and more real estate listings. I'd never gotten around to brushing my teeth, but now I couldn't summon the energy to rise from the bed. Reviewing those properties had become my reality check. The reality was that any path to L.A. went through Glitzman. And the cash was beginning to feel like blood money.

NEXT MORNING, THURSDAY, I woke late, angry at myself because I'd stayed up until two a.m. for no reason, and I was going to be exhausted for the drive back to Stockholm. I rolled over and checked my phone. There was a little red number one in the corner of the crossword app. My heart began to gallop. The notification was an invitation to begin a game with *KhanumGoogoosh71436*. I accepted. I put down the phone and when I'd showered and dressed I checked back and saw that she'd filled in several answers correctly. I took an unsuccessful swing at 31 Down. Then she filled in three more while I watched, waiting and wondering how much time would pass before Glitzman knew about these messages. Then she typed into the chat: *I'm getting the hang of it!..*

Two periods at the end. Roya Shabani's raised torch in the darkness.

Translation: *I am through the fire.*

I went outside to smoke and ponder the blend of fear, regret, and excitement coursing through me.

As I lit my second cigarette, I heard Glitzman, in the kitchen, shouting for joy.

CHAPTER 39
Tehran

GROWING UP, I had visited Tehran at least once each year, sometimes in summer, sometimes around Persian New Year, and always kicking and screaming because, at least once Papa was working for a larger dental practice, he had six weeks of annual vacation and I wanted to go to the beaches in Spain or Thailand like everyone else. Anywhere but Tehran.

Resentful though I was, I'd always arrived with the certainty of someone who belongs, or at least could fake it. After all, I had been born here. My family had called Tehran home for three generations. There was our appropriated house, and the Jewish cemetery in Damavand where dozens of my relatives are buried. There are connections, even if they are only monuments and memorials. More recently, since returning to the city, at Glitzman's urging, to open the practice, I'd grown numb to the danger. I'd convinced myself Amir-Ali's death was a freak accident. Certainly nothing that would happen to me.

But this time, with far more dangerous work in front of me, Tehran felt like it was watching me, and the sensation still lingers, here in this room. It is a buzz of anxiety, a turning in my guts that never stops, never goes away. At passport control I was sweating and my hands were shaking.

In the usual grind of traffic from the airport, instead of commiserating with the taxi driver I imagined the flash of sirens and the rough hands of police dragging me away.

That first night I lay there in my bedroom waiting for a knock, tossing and turning, and didn't get a wink of sleep.

Around dawn I went out for a walk, thinking it would clear my head, but I had to turn around because I thought I was having a panic attack. It seemed as though every passerby were watching me. The ubiquitous cameras were craning their necks for a peek. Every black Peugeot belonged to the real Etela'at, sharpening their knives for my arrest. I wondered if Roya was laying a trap for me.

I CHANGED INTO A BLACK SUIT, tailored here in Tehran, and not made of polyester, which would mark me as a man of some class and status. Our hope was that I would look not like the Basiji knuckle draggers who terrorized the oppositionists and artists and gays, but like a more elevated thug, an artist uncommitted to thuggery and violence as ends in themselves, but perfectly comfortable with them as tools to get there. The black Peugeot 405 with tinted windows that had been parked three blocks from my apartment, its keys sent in the mail, completed my look as a true Etela'at man. They all drove one.

As I stepped into the car, my throat burned, and my eyes stung badly from the apocalyptic smog, but otherwise, as I drove toward Laleh Park, I felt focused, dialed in. When I'd first returned to Tehran, even after I'd brought a good friend into the game, I'd figured that when the dust settled we'd have some extra cash, and a collection of thrilling memories to boot.

Said differently: Everyone wins. (Except, Amir-Ali had lost.)

This time, folded into a far more intricate and dangerous conspiracy, I understood that no such thing was possible. If I won, Roya lost. This was plain to me, lurching through the snaggle of traffic that afternoon, and I accepted it, not as a problem to be solved, but as a trade to be made. And yes, I had my selfish motives, but I had other reasons, too, did I not?

She was working for the Qods Force, wasn't she?

Those Jew-killers.

Colonel Ghorbani was the exact brand of theocratic, fascist, racist Persian who'd pushed my family out of Iran—our home for thousands of years, so, who the fuck does he think he is? —and who was now laying siege to Israel, that great fortress for other Jews, in the hopes of burning it to the ground with seven million of them inside. I did not realize it then, but somewhere along the way I'd bought into Glitzman's logic: I was going to help get a few people killed to save countless lives.

I pulled the car into a spot on the curb a couple blocks from the park and sat there for a moment, going over everything in my head. Sweat? No, my hands were now surprisingly bone-dry, and they were also steady. Heartbeat? Normal. Vision? Watery, but that was the fucking smog. I wiped my eyes once more and stepped out of the car and buttoned my suit. I had matured, I thought. I knew the rules of the Game and I accepted its consequences. At the time this felt like something quite near to wisdom, though I will admit, three years on, that it also sounds chillingly cold-blooded. But are those two things always so different?

CHAPTER 40
Tehran

THE PARK RANG WITH the joyful shrieks of children and the *whump-whump* of kids kicking around a ball playing *gul-kuchik* in a patch of grass. I spotted Roya sitting on a bench and sat down beside her. For a minute, maybe two, we sat silently watching the kids playing on the playground. I had not met her daughter in person before, but I picked her out when Roya's eyes tracked a pink-clad girl with brown pigtails and a glittering tiara as she moseyed around the swings and started climbing the ladder to a slide. So this was Alya.

Reaching the top, the girl waved to her mother. Roya waved back, and Alya shuffled to the incline before letting herself drop. Even at a distance, I saw the rapturous mix of joy and terror on her face as she shot down the slide so fast her tiara fell off. At the bottom she stamped into the dirt, clapped her hands, and shrieked in glee. Picking up her tiara, she started running to her mother. I remember thinking she must have had to go to the bathroom, she was running so fast, but now I realize that Alya was incapable of walking anywhere unless her mother was forcibly holding her hand. The girl loved to run.

Roya held out her arms and swooped up her daughter into a hug.

"Did you see me, Maman?" she asked.

"I did, Alya."

"I went fast!"

"Very fast."

Then Alya looked at Roya's purse and yelled, "Snack!" Roya nodded, plopping her on the bench, the side opposite me. She handed her a bag of roasted melon seeds.

"Did you see me?" Alya had leaned forward, mouth full of seeds, to be sure I understood that this was meant for me. She chewed with overgrown white teeth and stared me down with her visionary eyes. In all my years of cleaning kids' teeth, I'd never met one who could hold eye contact like Alya.

"I did see you, Alya. You were going very fast."

She looked shocked: this stranger knew her name.

Roya delivered her explanation with a tired tone that suggested Alya asked lots of questions. "He is a friend of Maman's. He is saying hello."

"Why?"

"To be friendly."

"Why?"

"Because it is good to be friendly," I interjected, "especially to little girls in pink."

She smiled and, apparently satisfied, went back to her snack for a moment. "Can we go home, Maman?"

"Not yet, sweetheart."

"Would you like to see something interesting?" I asked Alya.

Her smile was some cross of mischief and curiosity; she looked to Roya, whose nod signaled to Alya that she should feel free to nod herself.

"Come here for a moment, in front of me," I said.

The little girl hopped down from the bench and bounced over to me. I removed a five-thousand-rial coin from my wallet and held it between the thumb and two forefingers of my right hand, tilting up the face so she might see.

"What do I have here?" I exclaimed.

"Money!" she squealed, her hands covering her mouth in anticipation.

"Yes, a coin," I said. My left hand swooped and I snatched the coin with my thumb in front, fingers behind. I closed my palm. "Give it a smack."

Alya gave it a pop and took a precautionary step back, as if it might explode. I thrust open my left palm and showed her it was empty. She gasped. "Perhaps you took it when you clobbered my hand," I suggested.

"I did not!"—she was still happy, but her voice carried a trace of indignation.

She pounded my knee with her fist, and her eyes went wide. Then she opened her palm. The coin, which had been lodged inside, plinked onto the bench. I picked it up and repeated the same flutter. The coin was gone.

Roya made a startled noise.

Alya's eyes were wide; she looked around for the coin. "How did my hand get it?" Alya asked.

"Magic."

"Where is it?

"It has disappeared," I said.

Alya looked at me, then at her mother, who was, I could feel, staring right through me. The girl retrieved her snack bag and regarded me with equal parts suspicion and wonder until she said to her mother: "Maybe it's with Papa."

I was looking at Alya, not her mother, but all the same I could feel Roya begin to chill.

"Run along and play," Roya said, her tone firm. At once the girl understood, and her own countenance grew serious. With half a glance back at me—right at my hands, perhaps hoping for a glimpse of the rogue coin—she hustled toward the playground. When she'd reached the slide, Roya joylessly smiled. "She is so happy. All the time."

I suppose most people would have merely agreed, accepted it as a breezy pleasantry, and moved on. But the op would only be as successful as my read of the mark, and I'd seen something just now. "Her happiness," I said, "sometimes you do not like it."

She looked at me, and for a fleeting moment she was not beautiful. "No," she said, "sometimes I do not."

From her perch atop the slide, Alya waved. Roya waved back, and I followed suit, and when the little girl had reached the bottom, I saw her mother trying to smile as she bared her teeth.

"Tell me what's happened," I said.

Colonel Ghorbani, she said, had greeted her at the gate at Imam Khomeini. There'd been an interview, right there at the airport, some writing, but no mention of Hossein, other than it had been clear to her that they did not know what had happened. One of the colonel's men, someone she'd not met before, had confiscated her purse, luggage, and Turkish cell phone for a few hours. Finally, they'd given it all back, put her in a cab, and Colonel Ghorbani told her to go home, he would summon her when the time was right. She told me she'd sat at home for one week, struggling to sleep and barely eating. On her first morning back in the office, there'd been another interview with the colonel, who had been cold and occasionally hostile, as all such interactions with him tended to be.

I stole a look at my phone, to see if I had any messages from Aryas or Kovan, who were out there, circling, checking to see if she'd brought surveillance to the meeting. There was nothing, so I continued. "What did he ask you?"

"He wanted me to run through everything I did in Istanbul," she said. "It was the airport interview all over again. He was checking my story."

"No new questions?" I asked. "Identical script?"

"No, not quite the same," she said. "He asked if I thought Hossein had used drugs."

"And?"

"I said I knew he liked opium, everyone knew this, but that I didn't think he was an addict. I had an uncle who was, and his lips were lavender-colored and thin as reeds. Hossein did not look like that. Then the colonel asked about meth. I said I didn't know. And the colonel said, well, how would you? His voice then was dangerous. So I conceded the point, and spluttered out something about how of course, Colonel, of course I wouldn't have known. And right then there was a long and awful moment where it was like we were standing opposite one another, like on the bank of a river, and dozens of burning questions are floating by, and I wanted to ask a few of them—"

I must have shot her a questioning look, because she put her hand to her heart and said: "Believe the breath from my mouth. I didn't. I swear."

Alya returned for another handful of seeds, then ran off, quick as she came.

"Then he told me Hossein was dead."

"And what did you say?"

She looked up angrily, and I couldn't blame her. She was, after all, experiencing yet another interrogation. But I just stared right back at her until she looked off, at Alya up on the slide again, and said, "In the best of times, I don't know what to say when someone tells me about some tragedy. I didn't know what to say to myself for months after Abbas died. So I said, 'Oh no,' or something like that, and looked sad, which I was. And am. I asked what had happened to him. Colonel Ghorbani said there'd been an accident, it seemed. They were still looking into it. We went through the rest of my time in Istanbul, and I gave him the chronology you and I agreed on. I talked about shopping. The gifts. Sleeping a lot." Her left foot had begun tapping the sidewalk in a frenzy, and she'd hunched forward, folding her arms on her lap, as if the lies made her want to shrink, to present the smallest possible target.

"Do you think Colonel Ghorbani suspects anything?"

And she looked quite intentionally at me, and said no with a firmness that felt so out of step with her obvious anxiety that I wondered if she had practiced the delivery at home that morning. I was unconvinced, but I also knew it was the best I would get. Roya was almost certainly unconvinced herself, but she did mention what I considered to be the supreme mark in her favor, which was that her responsibilities back at work were the same, as was her access. "I have my computer," she said. "My phone. I am on the WhatsApp group. First day back, my colleague Mina came to me with another request for money, to buy data. I did so. I still make the tea. I brought tea yesterday morning into Colonel Ghorbani's office. It's all the same, except Hossein's gone."

"No replacement?"

"Not yet," Roya said.

"What data did Mina purchase?"

"I don't know. I just handled the payment."

"How does Colonel Ghorbani seem? Any changes to his moods? Anything new?"

"He likes shouting. He orders everyone around. All the same."

"There is more to go through," I said. "We will need time. I will come to your apartment tonight. I would normally bring you into the Ministry for such chats, but you understand that on such a sensitive matter, it is simply not possible."

I believe she wanted to say why not and yes and no and maybe and fuck off all at once. She wanted me gone, she wanted revenge, she wanted to disappear with her daughter, she wanted her old life. So little of it was truly possible. She was quiet, watching Alya.

She'd not given me her address in Istanbul, but I was Etela'at—I knew it, of course, even if my source was Glitzman, who knew it because he'd killed her husband. I spoke the address aloud, plus the apartment number, and said I would be there by eight, she should mind the hallway to be sure neighbors weren't snooping. The consent Roya offered was far looser than any case officer would prefer of their agent: she was quiet, though she did not say no.

CHAPTER 41

Tehran

ROYA OPENED THE DOOR with the resigned look of a prisoner standing aside for an impromptu search. The apartment was spacious but more joyless than I would have thought: few pictures, only a handful of visible displays of Alya's art; the furniture could have come from a hotel. This was the sort of place where one crumples up after tragedy has struck. I had two friends in Stockholm who'd found similar apartments after their wives kicked them out. Cheap furniture, bare walls—an air lock before onward passage to whatever misadventures life was preparing for them beyond.

The smell of the food, though, was delightful. It had been cooked and dropped off, I would learn, by Roya's sister, Afsaneh, who, lacking that ultimate Persian currency, children of her own, seemed to trade instead in hospitality.

"The magician!" Alya shouted, and I was dragged off for a tour of her room. I took her offered hand and we trotted down the hall into her den of pink. The room even emanated a pink glow, thanks to a neon light. Her walls were taped-over with drawings. She was on the floor rummaging through a basket of dolls and stuffed animals.

"Do you like dogs?" she asked.

"Yes," I said.

"Do you like bunnies?"

"Yes."

"Do you like lambs?"

"Yes."

"Which is your favorite?"

I thought about that for a moment. I must confess, I was not thinking of the detail from Gltizman's story about killing her father, otherwise I wouldn't have said: "Lambs."

Her face flooded with joy. "Mine, too!" She handed me a floppy stuffed pink lamb. "He will eat with us?"

"Certainly." I smiled, and to Alya's great delight, I hoisted the lamb up for a piggyback ride and followed her to the kitchen.

There was tangy salad rich with mint and dill; eggplant and celery-flocked beef and warm rice floating on plates, capped by the crispy burnt *tahdig* of rice. The lamb sat between me and Alya at the dinner table. We ate in the pleasant absence of adult conversation—only Alya asked the questions. Though I never wanted kids, I think they're delightful to be with. For one, they don't lie. What you see is what you get. And with Alya it was pretty much pure joy. Her father had been murdered in front of her, on her birthday. And there we were, talking to a stuffed lamb, not about the murder, but about whether he liked the rice. Alya had dumped a spoonful onto his head.

Alya's first question: "Why did you come to dinner?"

"Because your mother invited me, and I am her friend." I heaped more of the exceptional salad onto my plate.

"Why are you friends?"

"Because he and Maman are friends." Roya's tone was stern, as was her gaze, but Alya did not see, or did not notice, or did not care.

"Why?"

I laughed.

"Eat some rice, Alya," Roya said.

"Why are you and Maman friends?" Alya asked again.

Kids, well, you'd think they'd be easy to trick, wouldn't you? Adults see what they want to see. Kids see what's in front of them—they are tough marks.

"I am friends with your maman," I said, "because I think she is interesting."

"Why?"

"Well, I can't explain it yet," I said. "But I think that's pretty interesting, Alya. Do you think your mother is interesting?"

"I think she is pretty," Alya said.

"Your lamb is also pretty, Alya."

"He's a boy!"

"Handsome, then."

"Will you be here tomorrow?"

I shook my head. "I am going to leave after dinner. I will have to see you some other time."

Alya scowled. "You're disappearing?"

"No," I said, looking to Roya for some support, and finding her energies consumed by her eggplant. "I will not disappear. I will see you again."

"You promise?"

Why did I feel a tremor of guilt, that it might be a lie? What did I care?

But I did promise, in the end, feeling it had been sworn in the best of faith. Her lips were pursed and she gave me a stony-serious nod.

Then there was a fight over whether Alya would take a bath that night, and if a certain pair of pajamas were clean. There was a good deal of shouting while I picked at my food.

Finally surrendering, Alya dismounted her chair and collected her lamb. She hustled around to my side of the table. She could not wrap her arms around me for a hug, so she instead placed her head on my shoulder.

Alya looked up at me: "You know 'Lili Lili Hozak'?"

"Of course. My maman . . . " I'd started a fib about how my mother had played it with me, but I found it did not suit. The lie was sand on my lips.

She held up her hand.

I looked over to Roya and saw a tangle of wonder and despair. She nodded. I took Alya's hand and sang:

Lili lili hozak
Little little pool
The chick came to drink water

But fell into the little pool!
This one pulled him out of the water and saved him

Alya giggled. I wiggled her pinkie finger, gently bent it down.

This one dried him up

I did the same for her ring finger. I stole a glance at Roya. She was smiling, but her eyes were watery and sad.

This one gave him bread

Middle finger down.

And this one gave him water to drink

Next the pointer finger, sticky from the eggplant.

And then someone said:
"Who threw the little chick into the little pool?"

I tapped her thumb and cleared my throat in preparation for my best bully voice. Even though Maman had not sung this to me, it was obvious the thumb was the bad guy.

This one said,
"Me! Me! The bigheaded one!"

I wiggled her thumb, made a noise, and gruffly said: "Poor little chick!"
Then she ran off, a peal of delightful laughter in her wake. Roya, following her daughter, said she would be back in a few minutes, and soon the bath was running, and they were singing songs I did not know. Roya knew how to be happy, this was plain. Which meant she had been,

once. But now? It was painfully clear that Roya was aimless, probably depressed, and that her daughter's joy might be all she had going in this entirely unexceptional life.

She'd also left her phone in the kitchen with me.

Almost an invitation, I thought. After all, it was right over there, out on the counter.

CHAPTER 42
Tehran

BATHWATER RUNNING, Roya and Alya's voices alternating between conversation and crazy songs, I snatched up Roya's phone, shucked it from its pink case, and removed a compact pouch snuggled in my jacket pocket. Inside were a few cables, a phone identical to Roya's, and a computer no bigger than a cigarette pack. I plugged Roya's old phone into the computer, which, after a few moments, created an identical copy. Next, I put the new, modified phone on the table. This new phone—a match to hers, except for the cosmetics—had been outfitted with software on a partitioned hard drive that would enable it to receive and transmit large quantities of data, say, for example, while it sat in the cubbies outside the secure areas at her office in Niavaran. I copied the old phone's data onto this new, donor phone, then ran another software program that would reconfigure the new phone with the old one's serial number. Last, I took the SIM card from the old phone and slid it into the new one. I put the whole thing back in the old case. In the bathroom Roya and Alya were loudly singing "Lili Lili Hozak," Roya urging Alya to hold still, you'll get shampoo in your eyes.

I returned the new phone to its spot on the counter, packed up the kit and the old phone, and slid them into my jacket. I cleaned up the dinner, washed the dishes, and did my best to straighten the kitchen.

WHEN ALYA WAS at last settled in bed, Roya returned to the kitchen to find me sitting at the table. I could see that she was surprised—though *shocked* might be the better word—by the cleanup.

"I have known other security men," she said, joining me at the table. "My husband was surrounded by them. You are not like them."

"Etela'at requires all types," I said, aiming for a shrug in my tone.

"She is usually shy, you know," Roya said, standing to flip on an electric teakettle. She collected glasses and a box of mint tea and sugar cubes and dainty silver spoons.

"Alya?"

"Yes."

"That girl, shy?"

"Sometimes she won't look people in the eye."

"Kids are fun," I said. "And they trust me."

Do you? I wondered. I was not sure, but I do believe that she trusted too quickly, and too easily, even if it must come soon in Tehran because there is so little space to develop it naturally.

The kettle screamed, and Roya began to fix us tea.

"Why are there no pictures?" I asked.

"What?" she replied.

"On the walls."

"Pictures of what?" She frowned.

"Of anything."

She inserted a sugar cube between her teeth and drank some tea. "Pictures make you remember things."

"Most widows want to remember their martyrs," I said, because that's exactly what a self-righteous Etela'at officer would say, if for no reason other than pure sport.

"You know, they did take one of me and Alya during the secret ceremony," she said, and there was a dark amusement spreading through her, as if she were recalling a cruel joke told at her expense. "One with a bouquet of tulips. Alya was smiling because she didn't know any better.

They didn't let me keep the picture, though. Not even the flowers. Then, I was angry. But now, I'm maybe grateful."

"You're trying to forget?" I asked.

"I wouldn't have figured you for one of the death-obsessed," she said.

An artful parry, I thought. Bravo, Roya.

"Oh, I'm not obsessed," I insisted. "Just aware."

"I wish I weren't," she said. "I'd like to live my life with death at the end, where it belongs, not jammed into everything else, too. It's exhausting. Half our streets are named for martyrs. Shia are good for bleeding, are they not? That's what makes us Shia." She paused and looked at me as if for permission. I didn't move a muscle, so she just went on. "But do I need the constant reminders? When the Americans murdered Commander Soleimani, there was a digital billboard of his smiling face for weeks above Vali Asr Square. May tulips grow from your blood, they say. No, thanks. Keep your picture. Keep your tulips."

You may not want their tulips, I thought, but what if they'd given you a sword?

She stood to refill my tea, and I said: "I have a question for you, it may sound a bit strange. In Istanbul you told me that you saw a few screens in Major Shirazi's room. Could it be possible that they display video from a drone?"

Her brows furrowed in a look of suspicion.

"I ask," I said, readying a bit of a lie, "because we gathered some very interesting information. A few months ago a drone flew into a home in Jerusalem. Supposedly, it was intended to explode. It did not. Hossein and his collaborators sabotaged the operation."

To deceive someone, especially on a longer play, the hook must be set with real meat. You've got to whet the appetite with something real, even if it's mixed up in the lies. "Have you heard of something called Stuxnet?" I asked.

"No."

"Years ago the Zionists and Americans cleverly implanted a digital worm in a system at one of our nuclear plants. Our research requires thousands of centrifuges, Roya. These are the machines that spin to enrich uranium. They are run by what are known as programmable logic controllers—computers that manage machines, assembly, and the like. The worm caused the centrifuges to spin outside the optimal range of speeds, delaying enrichment, and wrecking valuable machinery. There are many ingenious facets to this operation, but the one I found most clever, and damaging, is that the worm did not just break our enrichment capacity, it sent messages to our engineers and technicians that all was operating normally. That the machines were fine. It ran for years before we discovered it. I am telling you this because I think we have found a similar worm at Niavaran. Not a digital one, though. Flesh-and-blood. A worm that has convinced its masters in Qods that it is hard at work, flying kamikaze drones into homes in Jerusalem and meeting with mysterious sources in Istanbul. And all the while it is wrecking us from the inside. The drones are sabotaged. The so-called sources in Istanbul are, in reality, their Zionist masters."

Roya had been rubbing her temples while I spoke. We believe things not because they are true, but because we want them to be. She desperately wanted to believe me; her mind was working out whether it would permit the indulgence.

"Did you ever meet these so-called sources, or informants?" I asked.

"I told you in Istanbul: no."

"No names, faces, phone numbers, anything like that?"

"No."

"That's because they don't exist, Roya."

"How?" she said. "How could they not exist?"

"Here's how. Hossein Moghaddam required an excuse for travel to Istanbul to meet with his Israeli handlers. We know a great deal about Mossad's tradecraft, and they do not like to meet their sources face-to-face inside Iran. They prefer the Kurdish areas in Iraq, Baku, Dubai. And yes, Istanbul." I took a long sip of tea and watched her face grow pale. "Moghaddam and his accomplices have worked their way into this elite group of assassins. And that is helpful to Zion, is it not? They have a preview of who is on our kill list; if any of the loyal operations officers get anywhere close to recruiting someone in Israel who can participate in or lead an attack, well, the Zionists have the jump on them, don't they? And if nothing else, just like those logic controllers that seemed to be working just fine, this group can make it appear as though they are working hard, striking Jews, when in fact it's all compromised from the start."

Roya's attention swung to the doorway.

Alya was there, clutching the lamb to her chest. "You are still here." She sounded pleased.

"Alya, go back to bed," Roya said, though she was too exhausted to make it a proper command. The girl stayed put, watching us.

"Yes, I am," I said. "I've been talking to your maman."

"Time for bed, my sweet," Roya said. "It is very late."

"Show me the coin again," Alya demanded. The lamb was pulled up into her chin.

"Then off to bed, okay?" I said.

"Okay."

I fished around in my pocket and found a coin, which I disappeared again—it's a technique called the French Drop, for the record—but this time I did not ask her to knock on my hand. "Open your palm."

Her eyes widened at the sight of the coin.

"Now blow across it, close your palm, and make a wish."

She did. She'd also shut her eyes, and when they opened, bright and lively, she said: "I wished—"

I cut her off. "Now, now, Alya. No telling. It's your secret. If you tell us, it won't come true."

She opened her palm: nothing. I showed her my empty palms.

"How?" she shrieked, laughing.

"Magic," I said. "Now listen to your mother. Run along to bed."

Roya kissed her cheek, and when the girl had gone, she said: "I've done everything you asked. Tell me what I need to do to be done. Please. I am so tired..."

"We need to find these traitors," I said, quite vaguely.

From my coat pocket, right beside the other pouch, I removed an Ethernet cable, on which, like all mundane technologies, our fates hung. The cable was the last plank in our digital bridge. Once connected to

Ghorbani's computer, a clandestine Wi-Fi antenna hidden on the doctored Ethernet cable would pipe data to the partition hidden on Roya's new phone, which sat in the cubbies outside the secure workspaces. From there, it would bounce to a computer in the listening post soon to be established by the Kurds, and the hopscotch would continue until the data had bounced across a dozen or so servers, landing, at last, in Tel Aviv.

"Sometimes you serve tea to Colonel Ghorbani in his office," I said. "You told me in Istanbul. And tonight you told me it is still true. Yes?"

She might not have been listening; her frightened eyes had fastened onto the cable. "What is it?" she asked.

"Roya," I said, my tone hardening, "if you can replace the cable that runs from Colonel Ghorbani's desktop into the wall with this"—I poked the cord—"we can determine if anyone inside is scraping information from the network for passage to the Israelis. Large pulls of data leave a signature. I plan to start by examining the data before Abbas was killed. Which, I believe, happened shortly after Ghorbani and Moghaddam first established the cell. You didn't have the Niavaran house, of course, but if I remember your chronology correctly, by that point those two had begun work. We might find evidence of their role in Abbas's death."

Her eyes hadn't left the cable. She took it into her grasp and, running fingers across it, she said: "There were no suspects in his murder, they said. It was a mystery." Her eyes had traveled to the indifference of the wall, searching for courage, or perhaps a way out.

"It's embarrassing," I agreed. "Our people butchered like this, and in broad daylight, no less. The leaders try to keep it quiet if possible. It's sensible, I guess, in a cunning sort of way. And it's also inhumane."

"They took my life away from me. For what?"

"We are in a struggle, Roya," I said, "with a particular breed of pharaonic Jew who believe they cannot merely live in our region, they must rule it, too." I had lifted the line from a long-ago dinner with Maman, figuring a rough mirror of the Israeli position ("We are in a fight with despotic Shia") was just the thing that would wash here. I went on, "They kill us for the crime of defending ourselves."

"We had a nice life back then," she said, still to the wall. "I was a person, and Alya had a father, a future. They're always out there, talking about justice and vengeance."

"I can help you with that," I said, really wanting to believe that I could.

And also wanting to believe that Roya actually wanted vengeance, in the end.

CHAPTER 43
Tehran

THIS WAS WHAT Glitzman was after, as I remember it:

One week of 24/7 surveillance video covering the Niavaran compound.
The daily schedule and rhythm—times of arrival/departure, regular meetings, etc.
A sketch of the property, including its entrances/exits.
Vantage points nearby with views of those entrances/exits.
If keypads or padlocks are present, the codes to any gates or doors.
Notes on whether the neighboring properties are commercial, residential, government, etc.
Are children, women, civilians regularly nearby within a fifty-meter radius of the Niavaran home?

"That last one," Kovan said. We were reviewing the list from my apartment. "That's a..."

"A blast radius," I said. I pulled up one of the satellite photos appended to the list and the three of us spent a moment looking at the neighboring properties. The logic behind the Niavaran location had been immediately clear: The street was purely residential. No government buildings, certainly nothing obviously linked to Qods or any security service. On a walk past the home later that week, Kovan would hear children kicking a ball in one of the neighboring courtyards. I could imagine the state-drafted press release ("Zionist Bombs Flatten Home, Kill Family") and the inevitable pictures showing the bloodied death masks of the kids next door.

"It's residential up there," Aryas said. "The answer to his question is an obvious yes."

"They won't bomb it, then," I said.

"Won't they?" Kovan shot back.

"No," I said, "they won't. Ghorbani tolerates collateral damage. Glitzman will not."

WHILE WE WAITED for Roya to do her work, I began taking regular trips to Niavaran. There was a nearby bookshop that I visited on the Friday morning, and on my way home I drove by the house. The Kurds had booked a room at a hotel, a three-star south of Niavaran Park. In a bag on the floor I had a phone fitted with an antenna just like the one I'd passed to Roya. Idling outside the house for a minute, I sent a burst of data from the phone to a laptop in the Kurds' hotel room. After a few minutes I had a message from Kovan: *It's working.* Test successful. We had our listening post.

On that quick run past Niavaran, I collected our first on-the-ground video using subminiature video cameras rolling from a concealment in the side mirrors. One of those included a close-in shot depicting the locking mechanism on the front gate. Later, in light disguise, Aryas walked along the streets and alleys bordering the house. There was a small gate leading into the alley. A larger one for vehicles, maybe leading to a garage or parking spots. Keypads on both. The next day the Kurds, wearing sunglasses fitted with cameras, walked through the neighborhood scouting for places where we might install more permanent, unblinking eyes.

IN MY APARTMENT, snug inside a safe concealed in my oversized dresser—the one I told you about in our first discussion, General—was an arsenal of surveillance equipment, which included handy items such as strontium-powered cameras the size of a small bolt, tailor-made by

Glitzman's artisans to fit into all manner of interesting concealment devices, including mimicked electrical boxes, false rocks, discarded aluminum cans, and a pigeon carcass taxidermized to resemble roadkill. (Regrettably, I never found a valid operational reason to use the pigeon.) Over that weekend, on visits to the bookshop and a nearby café, I placed magnetized electrical boxes fitted with cameras on two streetlamps, a weather enclosure at a bus stop, and a road sign. All had clean views of the house.

At randomized intervals, the cameras lobbed encrypted blobs to a computer in the hotel room, where the Kurds streamed Netflix through a VPN, an alibi to cover the massive amounts of moving data. From there it zigzagged through a managed attribution system that bounced the video along servers in about fifteen countries before they landed in Israel.

On Sunday we watched Mina enter the code for the side gate while taking out some garbage. That night we debated searching the trash but decided it was too risky.

Where do they all park? Glitzman asked.

On Monday we saw a black Lexus enter through the vehicular gate. Analysis of the video gave us the gate code and the identity of the driver: Colonel Jaffar Ghorbani. A few moments later Major Shirazi arrived (late, and, we would learn, uncharacteristically so) in a white Peugeot. We determined that there was a parking hierarchy at Niavaran, as there is in all offices, and it was exactly what you'd expect: the gravel patch inside the gate, which could accommodate two cars, was reserved for Colonel Ghorbani and Major Shirazi. Everyone else had to fight for spots out in the chaos of the unwashed masses. The only exceptions were days when you would come for visits, General, and Major Shirazi would make room for your staff car by relocating his to a spot on the street.

Does he have a security detail? Glitzman wrote us. *A driver?*

Three more days of video, and the answers were: no, and no.

"Seems odd," Aryas said, sitting in my kitchen as we typed out another report for Glitzman.

"It is a little odd," I conceded. "But the whole point of Ghorbani's operation is to fly under the radar. No, no, rather it's to be off it entirely.

Driving into a residential neighborhood with a convoy of black cars would raise his profile. So would having a driver."

"Plus," Kovan said, "he wants to keep it all tight, doesn't he? Limit the number of people the Zionists can compromise."

Overall, Glitzman was pleased with our progress, but he was quite snippy in his messages, and sometimes even angry. Once he became very agitated, and typed a few unkind words aimed at Kovan, because we could not work out how to map the interior floor plan without asking Roya, and we could not ask her without suggesting the possibility of an assault on her office. We worried that could send her running to Ghorbani, and if that happened the operation would be killed. And so would we.

The video was useful not only for mapping the comings and goings, the rhythms of the place, but also for answering other exotic questions Glitzman tossed our way, such as: *Does anyone visit other than the people listed by Roya? At what day and time is the property most likely to be empty?* That last one is useful for break-ins, of course, but its opposite (*When is everyone there?*) can be queried if the goal is instead a killing. Or a kidnapping.

Which did Glitzman want? I pondered that question while we worked.

To answer that, we'd need access inside the house, and for that we needed Roya.

While terabytes flew on encrypted wings to Glitzman and Caesarea, I waited for her call, or for a signal from Glitzman that she had installed the cable. And though in those weeks I often found myself worrying about Roya—which worried me as much as the actual worrying—there was nothing I could do.

I wanted to see her again, if I am being honest.

And after all, it is honesty that will save me—

The Interrogation Room
Location: ███████████

Present day

KAM NEARLY DROPS THE crayon as the General swings open the door. His last word has mutated into a long blue squiggle across nearly half the page. There's no eraser, of course, and, dammitall, Kam is going to have to throw out this sheet and—

The General joins Kam at the table and says, "I didn't say stop writing."

Kam nods uncertainly, sets the paper aside, snags a fresh one, and starts over at the top. The crayon tip—this one is dangerously near a nub—has barely kissed the A4 when the General shouts, loud as he can: "Stop!" He slams his hand into the table.

The crayon goes flying. Don't move, Kam reminds himself. Don't chase after it. Kam tries to stuff his shaking hands out of sight, in his lap. The General can tell the difference between the jitter of a muscle cramp and a tremor of fear. Kam does not like to let the General win these little intimidation sessions, ridiculous though they are, and terrified though he is. Kam is losing the bigger battles, why lose the small ones too? You can't win, but it's an option not to lose. And here not losing means the General's not sure if you're terrified. He's got a little doubt, and doubt spoils his fun.

The General is not interested in Kam's hands, though. The General is flipping through the papers.

"How far are you now?" he asks, frowning.

"The surveillance work on the Niavaran compound," I said.

The General had been rapt at this part of the story in the early drafts, demanding every little detail, but Kam lately has wondered if the old psychopath has lost interest. He already found all the cameras, of course, and Kam's already opened the messaging program on his phone, showed them how to access the partition, given them the codes, read them Glitzman's questions. The General even sent a note to Glitzman a few years ago, though Kam's got no idea what it said.

"You're not to the botched escape?" the General asks gruffly. "To their deaths?"

The General smiles because he knows talking about that night is the purest form of torture he can administer. Kam would rather submit to the pipe, the Chicken Kebab, even to Colonel Salar Askari himself, than talk about watching those two drift beneath the waves.

Guards are summoned to bring Kam to his cell.

The General enjoys punctuating their sessions with this memory, working on the theory that it's a sort of autopilot for the pain, a way to keep the torture rolling even when the General is fast asleep, or at home scarring his children, or the poor Mrs. General, if any of them exist in the first place. Unfortunately, the General's theory is correct. Until Kam comes back here to write, he won't be able to think of much else.

CHAPTER 44
Tel Aviv / Rosh Pinna
Three years ago

GLITZMAN, ON THE DUTY SHIFT, was wide awake on a cot in his office, fantasizing of smoking guns. The encrypted data from the tap on the fiber line at Niavaran would soon be pouring in—Roya would do her work with the cable any day now—and whenever that happened a group of techs, analysts, and Persian linguists were going to climb the mountain of data. When Glitzman got up he logged in to find a message which said that Roya had been called off work that morning—no reason was provided—and the cable implant in Colonel Ghorbani's office would be postponed. *Nothing*, Kam wrote, *will happen this weekend. The house is quiet.*

Glitzman kicked over the cot. He considered making coffee but instead sat at his desk and stared at the ceiling until his open line rang. The phones were ancient, you couldn't tell who was calling, but Tzipi was the only person who had this number. He also knew what she wanted to talk about, and he could not believe he'd just been stripped of his only reason to say no, at least without lying. But truthfulness was a habit Glitzman embraced at home, not for ethical reasons, but for the coldly practical: he wished to stay married.

WHAT HAD BEGUN AS hints had evolved into requests, then urgings, and finally, in recent weeks, had risen into full-throated demands. Tzipi wanted to spend a weekend out of town, at the family's second home up in Rosh Pinna. "Tel Aviv is a prison," was her trusted and most predictable line, "I want to breathe freely up north. And Lebanon is quiet. No missiles! Think of Oriana. Think of me."

Tzipi.

Oh, Glitzman sure as hell did think of Tzipi. He suspected—knew!—she would use the getaway as fodder to haul them all away from Tel Aviv for good once he'd retired. I will sell dresses, Arik, Tzipi would say. And Glitzman wanted to reply that he did not believe any retail property in Rosh Pinna, save for maybe a few of the more high-end *zimmers*, generated any cash flow whatsoever, but when he would consider this retort he would regard the shifting shine of her eyes, and he could practically see the ledger calculating his absolutely gigantic debt to the family accrued over a twenty-six-year career in the Mossad. Missed birthdays. Forgotten anniversaries. The vanishings, as Tzipi liked to call them, when a phone would ring and Arik Glitzman flew off somewhere for a few days, weeks, or months, and which had happened mere weeks earlier when he'd flown off to Istanbul with about an hour's notice. Tzipi managed the house, raised Oriana. She was sharpening her knife for life after Mossad, when she would exact a most gruesome revenge: Rosh Pinna.

The Glitzman family drove up that Friday afternoon.

Two hours north of Tel Aviv, a crop of Glitzman's forebears had arrived from Poland (at the time, it was technically Austro-Hungarian Galicia) in the 1890s and settled here, on a piece of land granted originally to Baron Rothschild. The home was up in the older neighborhood of the city, just below the Lookout, and its backyard and balconies boasted wide views of the Hula Valley and the snowcapped peaks of the Golan and Mount Hermon. The air was sweet. The streets were built of cobblestones hauled in on Rothschild credit. And they were deserted. Quiet.

Too damn quiet for Arik Glitzman, who, like the murdered Meir, was congenitally unable (unwilling, Tzipi would say) to stop and enjoy the briefest moments of peace. The quiet was noise to his soul.

On Saturday morning Glitzman had only just finished tangling with a piece in *Haaretz* about another fucking corruption inquiry on yet another goddamn snake in the Knesset when Oriana appeared.

"I have a request, Papa," she said. Tzipi had coached her daughter to describe any and all demands as *requests*. How could a request be anything other than reasonable?

"What is it?" he asked, hiding a smirk.

"I request," Oriana began, and she cast a sidelong glance into the hallway, offstage, where her mother was doubtless mouthing the lines, "a Papa day! It will be fun!" It could be fun, but Oriana's tone made it sound like a threat. Also: Glitzman liked to improve his negotiating leverage by refusing up front, no matter the request.

"Papa has work to do." He said it loud enough for Tzipi to hear in the hall. Bracing himself, he flipped into the International Section and pulled the paper in front of his face. He could not see how her face contorted, but she made a noise that he would have believed required far larger lungs, followed by a deluge of foot-stamping and tears, the wicked little actress.

Out the window a strip of haze had settled across the valley. All around him were open spaces, and yet Glitzman felt the walls closing in.

THE "NEGOTIATION" ENDED with Glitzman giving Oriana exactly what she wanted: a walk to the springs. Glitzman packed chocolate bars and cookies and filled water bottles. Hand in hand they trotted downhill until they reached the synagogue. Behind it was a stone staircase that bent down to the stream, the water now little more than a trickle with the summer approaching. They chose the furrowed path, cutting through groves of pine and wild olive and patches of wildflowers, which Oriana stopped frequently to pick. She wore a pink backpack. Her nails were painted bright pink. She'd chosen a pink tutu over tights (also pink) and had fought bitterly against the larger coat—an unfortunate beige—which Tzipi had insisted she wear and which, once they'd reached the staircase, Glitzman had permitted her to stuff into the pack. The day was bright, clear, and cold for late spring, and Glitzman was chilly, even in his coat. But not Oriana. The golden skin of her arms and shoulders was bare to the wind and she did not mind in the least. Across the wooden bridge, and they were in a meadow of pines.

"Chocolate?" Oriana said. He had not seen more hopeful eyes.

Glitzman unwrapped two chocolate bars, gave one to Oriana, and ate one himself, in four manic bites. He lay down in the grass, listening to the nonsense of her songs. When he sat up the chocolate bar appeared to have been transferred to her face and hands. He wiped her clean with a cloth before setting out again. Here the stream began to dry out and the path marched upward into rocks and the complaints began.

"I'm tired," Oriana said. Then: "Uuuggghh." Her little shoulders stooped; she stopped.

"The hill cannot be conquered if there is no grave on the slope," Glitzman said, smiling to himself.

"Papa, I'm sooo tired." Oriana sat in the dirt.

"Should we go home?"

"No!" she screamed. "Not yet."

"But you've stopped." He wrinkled a threatening eyebrow, but now she had her hands up, fingers flapping into her palms. He looked up at the ascent and then at Oriana and he considered the risks of his blackened lungs popping or maybe his heart wheezing to a stop with an additional twenty or so kilos riding on him.

Notwithstanding the trauma for Oriana, he decided this was a fine place to die and, assuming the risk, swung her up onto his shoulders. He huffed on, enjoying the sweat seeping through his arms, the plotless banter of his daughter, the rustle of pines, the clean air. Glitzman had not enjoyed anything in a long while and he found to his incredible surprise that he was having some fun. He began to sing nonsense songs, and she would sing them right back. He forgot about work. He forgot about Iran and the mark on his head. The blackness in his gut, that constant companion, seemed to drift away for a few glorious minutes in which the Glitzmans were at peace and he—somehow—had found a way to enjoy it. Oriana was an old woman, Glitzman was long gone, and Israel was still here, vibrant and Jewish and free. Oriana lived in Rosh Pinna and visited his grave at the military cemetery and her sons and daughters were farmers and vintners like his great-great-grandfather had been. He was pulled away from this pleasant vision only once, when she blindfolded him with her little hands, nearly causing them to trip over stones littering the path. He looked down at the valley below and made up more songs and walked under the shade of pines and cypress. After a while, they came upon the crossroads where the Blue Trail met Green.

Here, with Oriana still mounted on his shoulders, he looked out across the Galilee. The Sea was a flat satin carpet stretching beneath the gnarled heights of the Golan, tawny as lions in the sun. Beyond was the Syrian meat grinder—as the crow flies they were nearer to Damascus than Tel Aviv—and perhaps a dozen or so competent Arab militias that would be keen to sack Rosh Pinna and to murder every man, woman, and child if given the chance. To the north was Lebanon and the menace of Hezbollah. Of Tehran. Israel: turned on itself, engaged in eternal bloodletting with the Palestinians, and now, surrounded by Persia. The future was again a nightmare. They'd taken the hill, left graves on the slope, and now they were digging them on the summit.

Rosh Pinna was a crumble of white stone and orange roofs in the hillside below. He looked at it for a long time.

"Where's our house?" Oriana asked.

Steadying her with his left hand, he pointed with his right. "You see the synagogue?"

"Yes."

"You know the synagogue, Oriana?"

"What?"

"The synagogue. The big one down there."

"Okay."

"Well, count six houses up from that one."

"Why?"

"To find our house."

It took a good while. Glitzman helped.

"One of your great-great-grandfathers built that house," Glitzman said. "The first bricks of it, at least."

"Why?"

For much of the past year Glitzman had sought to distract Oriana from her Socratic methods. He'd gotten nowhere. She was like her mother—the best way out of a jam was through.

So he answered: "He needed a new home."

"Why?"

"Some people made him leave his old one in Poland."

"Why?"

"They didn't like him."

"Why?"

"A good answer to that question, sweetheart, and we Jews could be on our way to a better and brighter future. Haven't gotten a workable response from the opposition yet. Maybe you can get one? You could fix things."

The word *fix* conjured for the little girl images of housework, of responsibility. So she said, flatly: "No."

"Please?"

"No."

"Pretty please?"

She said no, but he could picture her up there, a little smile cracking through.

"Extra pretty please?"

"Okay." The smile surely widened a bit, but she spoke in the same sullen tone she used to agree, with extreme reluctance, to make her bed.

They turned back, and for a while walked in silence, though Glitzman could tell she was thinking hard on something. He was thinking about his great-grandfather and how he would have seen Arik Glitzman's peaceful stroll with his daughter through the woods outside Rosh Pinna as nothing other than total victory. Glitzmans on the slopes of the Galilee, alive, prosperous, multiplying.

She giggled, and little hands made the world go dark. He gently pried them off and scolded, "No, Oriana. You must stop."

"Why?"

"You will kill us," he said, his tone warm.

CHAPTER 45
Ein Shiloh Settlement, West Bank

FROM THE BENCH outside the yeshiva, Haim watched the white pickup bounce up the hillside through the fading light. The air was dry, the spring wind cool, rustling through the olive trees on the slopes, and up the hill through his sidelocks. The next gust blew off his black woven kippah, which he rearranged as he lost sight of the car. To the east, beyond the Arab village of Tal Ammus, the Jordan Valley glowed the color of bone. The lights flickered on as darkness began to swallow the hills.

Those lights angered Haim—there had been no electricity, not even a paved road, before the creation of Ein Shiloh and a string of her sister villages, inhabiting the holy flesh of Judea and Samaria. Or what Haim's sister back in Tel Aviv would have called "the West Bank."

His sister, who did something or other for a technology company in Herzliya, who had her own apartment, who took the pill to avoid the consequences of her sin, she said that the Land belonged to the animals down in Tal Ammus. But he was here, wasn't he? Ein Shiloh was home. It was *his*. It was his sister's, too. But she would not claim it.

Two girls marched past the yeshiva, their long hair fluttering in the evening breeze. Haim waited until he heard the door of the girl's trailer slap open and then shut.

Haim watched the truck crest the last rise, its headlamps now illuminated. It rolled to a stop outside the yeshiva.

The school was the largest building in town: a low-slung pile of concrete blocks that Haim had helped build with his own hands.

Itamar stepped from the truck, clutching his purple kippah against the wind. Was it the same truck Haim had driven to Jerusalem? They embraced warmly. Haim almost had to stand on tippy-toes to plant kisses on the large man's cheeks. When Haim shook his hand, it felt—as always—like warm leather. Where had Itamar's family come from? Haim thought his skin was dark as an Arab's, but he'd never had the courage to ask. And what was that Hebrew accent? At times it almost sounded American. Itamar made no sense to Haim's worldly instincts. And yet, he thought, what holy man had ever made sense to the world?

He examined the truck and decided that it was different, though the color was the same weather-beaten white. This one was a Toyota. Haim thought the truck he'd driven into Jerusalem had been a Nissan, though he'd been so anxious then that his memory did not inspire confidence.

Haim followed Itamar into the office in the back of the yeshiva, where they kept the crates. Haim felt Itamar's large hand settle onto his shoulder, then gently squeeze. Haim went into one of the classrooms and read from Yehoshua for what might have been an hour.

He sensed a presence in the doorway, and when he looked up he saw Itamar bow his head and tap his knuckles on the doorframe. Together, Haim and Itamar lugged a crate into the bed of the pickup. There was a strange mechanism with a small keypad affixed to the wood, just as there had been on the crate he'd delivered to Jerusalem. Then, Itamar had said it was a lock, and Haim thought that was partially true, because he'd shamefully read a few of the articles in the aftermath of Jerusalem—though the rabbi discouraged them from consuming such filth—and some of the security officials, those Hellenizers, had said that the crate had been flung open by remote control, and Haim had wondered . . .

Crate inside, Itamar slammed shut the doors of the truck's camper shell. For a moment they looked off at the shadowed outlines of the valley, down to the lights of Tal Ammus. The wind had returned, colder now.

"The rabbi says your studies are coming along well," Itamar said, "that you are making great progress."

"The rabbi is a great teacher," Haim said.

"He loves you," Itamar said. "The rabbi loves you. And he loves this place. When I come here I feel the love of the Lord on this hilltop."

Haim could sense what had drawn the rabbi to Itamar. Here was a man you would follow, though Haim could not quite say why. His fear of God, certainly, which glowed through him, bright as a torch in the night. But deeper, in the darker corners of his heart, Haim thought the man was full of magic. A wizard.

They got into the truck, but this time, as before, Haim was in the driver's seat. Itamar clicked on the Garmin and showed Haim the coordinates where he was to leave the crate. Then, from his pocket, Itamar withdrew a slip of paper. He clicked on the cabin lights. They were looking at a picture taken by a satellite. They'd done this before Jerusalem, and though he'd had so many questions, Haim had only asked one, and because of how Itamar had answered, now he knew to keep quiet. He would listen, and calm the anxiety flooding his heart.

"Same as before," Itamar said, tracing a thick black line along the picture. "Whatever the GPS says, when you get close, you follow this route. I've marked the cameras here, just in case, but they won't see you if you follow the line." He traced it again, then stopped, and stared coldly at Haim. "Yes?"

"Yes," Haim said, fighting down this question: *How do you know where all of the cameras are?*

"This," Itamar said, bringing a knuckle to rest on a blue circle, "is the precise coordinate. See this cluster of rocks? You drag it in there. There are gloves and a fresh pair of shoes back there. You wear those, yes, understood?"

"Yes. Understood."

"Good. Drop it, then go here." Itamar showed him a second set of coordinates on the Garmin. "When you get there, you call this number." Now he turned the picture over, where Haim saw, in Itamar's script, a phone number he did not know. Haim nodded. Itamar handed him the paper, which he tucked into the cupholder.

"I am proud of you," Itamar said.

"I am a vessel," Haim replied.

For a moment they stared out across the darkening valley. "Remember," Itamar said, "remember and take heart, that these men do not fear our Lord. They have betrayed him, betrayed his people. Betrayed us. They call themselves Jews, and yet"—he raised an accusatory finger toward the lights kindled by the Arabs down in Tal Ammus—"they've given our Land to these dogs. If you are pulled over, what do you do with that?" Itamar gestured to the paper with his map.

"Eat it," Haim said. "Quickly."

CHAPTER 46
Tel Aviv

SINCE RETURNING from Istanbul, Rivka and Glitzman had established Caesarea's war room in one of the stucco guesthouses on the Office's headquarters compound. The property was a white Bauhaus cottage trimmed in sea-blue, with a large swimming pool. For years the guesthouse had been a favored hideaway for visitors seeking a private word with the Israeli security services. If the property had maintained a guest book—and it most assuredly did not—it would have shown a colorful cast of Saudi princes, Jordanian security officials, and Kurdish warlords, to say nothing of the more humdrum visits from CIA. Rivka had once heard a rumor that Leonard Cohen had spent a weekend upstairs.

With Glitzman up north, Rivka had answered the late-night call. There'd been a sudden technical glitch with the managed attribution system used to patch the surveillance team's video feed from Tehran to Tel Aviv. Near one a.m., and she was sitting with a cluster of the tech guys in the downstairs living room, her feet up on a table covered with snack wrappers, shot glasses drained of espresso, and cans of Red Bull and BLU, the kosher option for those in need of a buzz. In the kitchen the electric kettle whistled and one of the guys sprang into action, answering the call.

"Ten-minute break," Rivka said. This had the feel of an all-nighter. She went outside onto the patio for fresh air, shutting the slider behind her. She walked around the pool for a brilliant view of the moon glowing above the Mediterranean. The air raid sirens began whooping and she watched as fireballs popped through the sky, each one a Hamas rocket destroyed by Israel's Iron Dome.

The guesthouse had one of the concrete-reinforced safe rooms required by law, but she did not move. And neither did anyone inside—her team, in fact, barely looked up from the computers. The explosions sounded just like fireworks, and these would be just as harmless. The sirens no longer made Rivka fear for her own life.

Mostly they brought rage, the hot kind that made you want to put your fist into a wall—rage that the night sky testified to Israel's encirclement. She heard her mother quoting Balaam's pagan prophecy about the Jews: They are a people that shall dwell alone and not be considered among the nations. Alone, Rivka thought, listening to the crackle and pop of the Iron Dome knocking more rockets from the sky. We are alone. When the sirens had stopped, the loneliness and dread coalesced into a kind of steely resolve. And she heard a hum like a distant lawn mower.

Then she saw the green lights. The noise grew louder.

"Get b—" she shouted. She managed to turn toward the house.

The drone rocketed past and through the sliding door, which collapsed like an ice floe falling into the sea. The shock wave from the blast hurled Rivka airborne and then into the pool. Underwater she rolled there for a moment in a womblike trance, eyes shut. When she got them open, she paddled to the surface and sucked in a deep breath. Smoke was billowing from the wrecked window. A handful of blackened ball bearings plinked across the stone and splashed into the water. Hauling herself out of the pool, she saw that her arms were bleeding, but she did not feel much pain. Someone was screaming. Hobbling inside, Rivka saw that one of the analysts had been shouting. He was reaching for a black Converse sneaker, which held one of his legs, up to about the knee. As the carnage came into focus, she saw that pieces of her friends were everywhere.

CHAPTER 47

Rosh Pinna

GLITZMAN WOKE TO an insistent tap on his shoulder and rolled over in his sleeping bag.

"I'm thirsty."

He blinked a few times and checked his watch. One-thirty. He looked around.

Oriana was inside her pink sleeping bag, nestled alongside his on the floor of his office. She tapped his shoulder once more and cleared her throat. "I request some water."

The day had ended with a sleepover. A hike *and* a sleepover to boot. Quite the Saturday. Glitzman had grumbled about it but not too much, mostly because he was having fun.

Unzipping himself from his bag, he picked up her pink plastic cup for the shuffle downstairs.

Standing at the sink, groggy, he felt cool water running over his fingers and looked down to see the cup overflowing. He dumped some back into the basin. Shut off the tap.

Then came the explosion. The house rumbled, the ceiling shook, dishes tipped off the counter. His bones juddered. He dropped the cup and started running. Later they would find blood streaked across the kitchen and the stairs because he'd stomped straight through shards of glass. The smell upstairs was acrid: a smoky bite like scorched almonds that plunged him into the muck of Lebanon. Tzipi was screaming. Was that Oriana crying out, too?

"Oriana!" he shouted. "Oriana!"

He flung open the door to his office. Looked around, and there were tattered ribbons of pink sleeping bag across the carpet and glued halfway up the wall, and he realized that he'd imagined her little voice. Glitzman made a long bleating noise, and his legs failed him.

CHAPTER 48

Tel Aviv

ORIANA AND SIX OF HIS Caesarea officers were not a day in the ground before Glitzman was again living in his office. There were rumors his first visit had been a midnight sit-down with Cohen to secure assurances he might remain on the operational team, though no one, not even Rivka, would ever confirm if such an audience had occurred. What was certain was that just before the critical intelligence arrived from Tehran, Glitzman was seated calmly at his desk, shirt rumpled as always, fielding a tense phone call on the open line from Tzipi. This was not unusual.

For years it had been a near-daily occurrence inside the Caesarea Division. But though these chats had centered on topics as mundane as the dinner menu, and though their tone had always been joyless, akin to a debate over funeral planning, this time eavesdroppers were immersed in greater darkness because that was very near to what they were doing. There was going to be a reception at the synagogue in Rosh Pinna and Tzipi had remained behind to plan. She cried frequently on these calls, and Glitzman found in those painful days that he was not capable of it. Outside their wrecked home, with a herd of techs and police and soldiers and the first few security men from the Office crawling around inside, the forensics appearing identical to Meir's fate—kamikaze drone—he and Tzipi had determined the essential division of labor that would provide the only source of distraction from the cloak of despair settling around them: Glitzman would find and eliminate the people who had killed Oriana. Tzipi would handle everything else. He noticed Rivka prowling outside his office at the tail end of the conversation with Tzipi, and waved her in after they'd hung up.

So far he and Rivka had discussed the twin attacks in purely operational terms, vacuumed of all emotion. Feelings were to be buried. They would increase the risk of being sent home, or put on psych leave. Ghorbani was targeting not Jews, not Israelis, not Mossad officers, but officers of the Caesarea Division itself. By now he'd killed eight, plus Oriana. There was going to be vengeance. A kill order. And Glitzman could not have a few tears or a misplaced shout endanger his participation. When Rivka sat down she winced and put a gentle hand over the bandage on her left arm. Her pain was obvious, but she'd said nothing about it. They felt the same about such things.

And she was smiling. She did not often smile, certainly not in the past few days. But she was almost beaming.

"Our dentist came through," Rivka said. "Roya swapped the cable. Data is piping in from Tehran as we speak. Technical guys say Ghorbani's team is using the same encryption as the rest of Qods, so they can break it."

"A lead," Glitzman said. "Holy shit. How long do they need?"

"They said give them until early morning."

GLITZMAN CALLED THE BRIEFING for four-thirty a.m. He stepped into the makeshift conference room, and jerked nods to Rivka and two of the technical people whose names, on better days, he might have remembered. One of them, the male, had a weepy nose he was blowing into a pack of Kleenex like a trumpet. The girl looked no older than twenty. Both of them were puffy and red-faced like they'd been crying, and they probably had been. Six of their teammates had just been murdered.

"Give me a percentage," Glitzman demanded. "How much are you through?"

"Most of it . . ." the girl began.

"Above eighty?" Glitzman said. "Yes or no."

"Yes," Rivka cut in, and Glitzman waited for an argument, but they were either too tired or too wise, and one never materialized.

The guy said, "As we expected, they are using a local area network for their secure commo; we don't think it's connected to any other network inside Qods. There are five machines on it, and we've had a look at a lot of that data, plus the personal phones we've compromised with MEDUSA. What we have not yet found is communication with anyone in Israel. Several files hint at a source they are running, but we can't find anything beyond the code word IBEX and records of crypto payments and other expenses in a few spreadsheets. There's bookkeeping, as expected, but it's not giving us targeting leads. A least not yet."

"This IBEX," Glitzman said. "No connections to a country? A place? A handler inside Colonel Ghorbani's group in Tehran?"

"Not yet," the girl said.

"What about the drones?" Glitzman demanded. "There must be video of their flights? Messages about where to place them? A list of targets?"

"Not yet," Rivka said. "It's also possible, Arik, that there is a second network inside the Niavaran house. One that's separate from the five machines we're tapped into now. One on machines that Roya can't access..."

"She did mention that goddamn room," Glitzman said, "didn't she? Major Shirazi's fief. All those fucking screens. The drone command center. It's not on this network?"

"Maybe. She told us that she can't go inside," Rivka said. "Might mean they've got another network in there."

"Multiple networks, all hived off from Qods, and they're running this IBEX sticks-and-bricks," Glitzman murmured. "Those clever fucks."

"It's tight," Rivka agreed.

Glitzman saw his fingers curling up into fists, unrolling, curling up again, and he was briefly mesmerized: he'd lost control of everything, even his hands.

"The surveillance logs suggest that Ghorbani holds a weekly meeting with everyone on Tuesday mornings," Rivka said. "There is an argument for dropping a bomb on the house during the next meeting, or flying a kamikaze drone into it."

Glitzman shook his head. "We need to identify IBEX. The only people who know who it is are inside the Niavaran compound. We kill them, we lose our only leads. We kill them, and maybe there is some fucking backup record somewhere, and the Iranians find a replacement for Ghorbani, reestablish contact with IBEX, and we're in the same fucking spot."

Rivka nodded in agreement. "Here's my theory, Arik: Moghaddam meets with IBEX directly, in Istanbul, probably to pass along orders and money and commo gear. No digital trail. Colonel Ghorbani probably has hard copy in that house, in file cabinets and safes, like they did in that south Tehran shithole where they'd filed everything on the nuke program. And they've probably got all the hardware and software for the drone ops in Major Shirazi's lair. And we've probably got none of that here."

"Probably," Glitzman repeated, his tone dangerous. "Probably, probably, probably. Fucking probably." He pumped his left hand into a fist.

"If IBEX is a source or group of sources facilitating killing operations inside Israel," Rivka said, "Colonel Ghorbani would be a fool to sprinkle digital crumbs around unnecessarily, even inside his own group. He, more than most, would understand just how much we own them from a SIGINT perspective. So, yes, Arik: fucking probably."

Another Caesarea officer flung open the door. He marched to the table, dropped a short stack of papers in front of Glitzman, and pointed at a line on the first page. "This is off the network at Niavaran," he said breathlessly. "Just now decrypted and translated."

Glitzman read it, blinked a few times, and could not quite name the frantic emotion consuming him, some half-breed of laughing fit and panic attack.

GLITZMAN HAD NEVER much cared about his annual performance reviews until he found them all sitting on a Qods Force computer in Tehran. He did not read them so much as stare in wonderment, until, worried he might be sick, he went to fetch water. When he returned, he looked at the papers for a long moment and then gulped down half the glass.

He was looking at a document of the Russian SVR, their foreign intelligence service, originally written in Persian. There was a blue stripe in the upper right-hand corner. The cover page explained the document to be Moscow's answer to a request for information sent from Colonel Jaffar Ghorbani. Mossad databases hacked by the Russians, it said, were being passed to Tehran as part of this package. And with those, some analysis of the group Ghorbani was most interested in: the Caesarea Division. Glitzman turned the page. He was looking at the Russians' approximation of his org chart. He was on there. Meir. Yael. Rivka. The technical people. Everyone except for a few of the newcomers—though undated, it was maybe a year old. He was reading his own short bio. They had his birth year wrong.

"Fucking Russians," he mumbled.

He came to a satellite photo of the Mossad campus, also passed by the Russians. The guesthouse, where the Caesarea war room had been, was circled. There was an SVR commentary on the right-hand side, and the gist of it was that this is where Arik Glitzman's people plan and run their killing operations.

"Fucking Russians," he said again. He picked up the phone to call Cohen.

In a few hours the techs would tell him that they believed that Moscow had compromised two different personnel databases, though whether they'd purchased them on the dark web or hacked into them, no one yet knew. The analysts suspected that the Russian information and the compromised databases had been complemented by intelligence-gathering inside Israel, probably by IBEX or IBEX subsources.

Everything had been collated into a targeting database that now lived in the Niavaran network's secure share drive, in a folder titled "Data." Inside was an Excel file with a far more descriptive name: *Zionists Who Must Live Secretly*. Each row was a member, current or former, of Glitzman's own Caesarea Division. The columns? Addresses, phone numbers, driver's license numbers. An embarrassment of options for fucking Colonel Ghorbani. Who was next on the kill list?

Glitzman began to flip through the translated printout of the database.

He was looking at the address of his homes in Tel Aviv and Rosh Pinna.

He was looking at Meir's badge photo. He was looking at Meir and Yael's address in Jerusalem.

Last: his own badge photograph. It had been snapped just shy of five years ago—he remembered because he'd sat for it the day before Oriana was born. Only five years, he thought. It could have been fifty. And here, though he was still a good way off, was the nearest Glitzman would come to crying.

CHAPTER 49

Tel Aviv

ALL THAT DAY and late into the night, they planned and argued, whispered, and shouted. Cohen's office was a revolving door for much of the evening, his overworked executive assistants playing air-traffic control for the now-Office-wide effort to grind Colonel Ghorbani's operation to dust. For much of the day, the team had clung to the hope that, in the intelligence trove secured from Niavaran, they might find something—anything—that would generate a lead inside Israel. A phone number. A bank account. Hints at a location. A flight number. A passport number. A photograph. A physical description—of anyone. A name or an address would have been glorious, but Colonel Ghorbani was no fool. A nickname, Glitzman thought, a nom de guerre, was that too much to ask? It was.

Around dinnertime—though no one was thinking of eating anything for dinner—Glitzman barged into Cohen's office uninvited, took a seat, and said, "Amos, we have threads. The threads are in Tehran. We have what we need to stitch together a successful operation."

Cohen, sliding his finger along the adhesive stripe of a pink Post-it note, regarded him closely. For a moment he seemed on the verge of speaking, and something in Cohen's hesitance tipped off Glitzman that this wasn't going to be about the operation.

"Arik, please. We go back years, I love and respect you. And no, hold on, hold on. I need to say this, to say something. I'm . . . she was—"

"Amos, I begged you. You swore to me. Stop that, it's—"

"Arik, let me, it's important—"

"Enough," Glitzman shouted. "Amos, enough. Enough! You swore! I don't—"

"Goddammit, Arik, hold on—"

"Goddamn you, Amos!"

"Arik, goddamn it, you—"

"Enough, Amos!" Glitzman, standing, had made a few threatening steps toward the desk. "Enough! Goddamn you. Enough! You told me, Amos. You swore. You said I could run this! I told you I would be clinical about it. So enough! Fucking enough!" Glitzman put a hand to his mouth, then to his hip, and he looked at the ceiling for a moment before retreating into his chair.

Cohen's finger was now sliding maniacally across the post-it, as if he might blend it into the wood grain of his desk. One of his people opened the door. With a brief glance at each man, he backed right out, leaving the two sitting in a prolonged, painful silence.

When Cohen stood, he made two espressos from his fancy machine and handed one to Glitzman, who accepted it without so much as a nod. As they sat there, quietly sipping, Glitzman remembered sitting with Cohen after news had reached Amos in Lebanon that his older brother had been killed by a suicide bomber at a café back in Tel Aviv. Glitzman was not fully certain—more than thirty years had passed—but he recalled having the good sense not to offer his condolences, nor to say much of anything at all. What he did remember, with striking clarity, was sitting there with Amos for a very long while. Then, they'd been in fatigues, drinking beer they weren't allowed to have on duty in Lebanon. Now, they were in jeans, drinking Amos's espresso. It was all the same, it was all different. He looked at Amos. Amos looked at him.

"Oriana is worth more than all of them," Cohen said.

Glitzman, defeated, lowered his head.

"Draw up the Red Page," Cohen said, "and bring it back to me tonight."

GLITZMAN HAD NOT EATEN in a day, had not slept in two, and the scotch-colored urine filling the toilet suggested he was way behind on his water. He wanted to call Tzipi, to hear her voice, but he worried if he did, he would not be able to stay away, and he had responsibilities here. He would be useless by her side. He had names in Tehran. He had an address. He had codes for the gates. He had patterns from the surveillance logs submitted by the dentist and his Kurds.

In the silence of his office, a memory of Oriana's face sprang to mind. He thought about how he had not spent much time with the girl, had always wanted to spend more, but usually when given the chance he had not. He'd said he was busy. Had he been a father in anything more than name? Now, though, he felt like a father. Now that she was dead, his fatherly shame was unbearable. They'd had so much time; just days ago there'd been so much of it. She was five. He didn't need to be a present father now. They had years ahead of them. He made a small noise, squeaky and pitiful, right into his hands. He'd reached the end of himself.

He was going after the guilty ones, but in truth he'd have killed a million innocent Persians if it would bring Oriana home, and probably a similar number even if it didn't.

Glitzman waved Rivka in.

"The shrinks have raised some concern about the dentist's involvement in the raid," she said.

"To Cohen?"

"To me," Rivka said. "But it's not in writing. At least not yet."

"What are they saying?"

"They worry that Kam is too close to Roya," Rivka said, "that it will be difficult for him. Emotional bullshit, Arik, but they think there is risk. You know how it is with the shrinks. You saw what they wrote up after Kam's friend, Amir-Ali, died during the kidnapping."

"He's not friends with Roya," Glitzman said. "They're not even having sex. These same goddamn shrinks looked me square in the eyes and told me he was in the Game. He was fine."

"They've gone through all the video from Istanbul, plus the audio from the meetings in Tehran, and they have concerns."

"What the fuck does that even mean?"

"Dr. Gafni told me, and I quote . . ." Rivka sighed, shut her eyes, and, as if ashamed even to deliver the news, turned her head to the ceiling: "It is his professional opinion that Kam has demonstrated a number of worrisome signs of emotional attachment, to include an obvious desire for physical contact, a warm connection with her daughter, Alya, and—god, Arik, you know their mumbo-jumbo, so don't take it out on me—something about how the combination of body language, eye contact, and voice intonation suggested something or other, blah, blah, blah. Kam is fond of her. That's the headline."

"Kam's fond of her?" Glitzman said, and it was the nearest he'd come to a genuine laugh since his daughter had been killed. "Kam's fond of her," Glitzman repeated. Now he did laugh, then he was shouting again: "We need hands and feet in Tehran! Hands and feet! So what if he's fond of her? Fond! Holy fucking shit!"

"Arik, don't shoot the fucking messenger, I agree—"

"I'm not shooting the messenger, Rivka. I'm merely giving her the message. I'm shouting it, for emphasis, so you can deliver it the same way to the fucking shrinks, before they put something foolish in writing that will delay us further, and which I know they will deeply regret. So here it is: This raid already has too many Israelis on the ground for my liking. And I will not put any more of us at risk than is necessary."

"Kam's a Jew," Rivka said.

"Not an Israeli," Glitzman said, in irritation. "Which puts him, in my book, one step above the Kurds. One below you, me, and the operators. It's cold, but there it is."

Glitzman had flung open one of the safes.

"What do you want me to tell the shrinks?" Rivka asked. "I'll try to head them off before Gafni goes to Cohen, or the other way around."

Glitzman was rifling through the assessment files. "Ah," he said. "Aha! Here." He bashed his fist into the paper. "Dr. Gafni wrote this after Kam's friend got shot while we were kidnapping Qaani. Which could fuck with your head, I suppose, seeing that our dentist recruited him in the first place. So I asked Gafni, didn't I? I said, Doc, I want to know if this guy can compartmentalize it all appropriately. Can he be clear-eyed, maybe even a little cold about this? And Gafni gives us this clinical jargon, doesn't he? Do you remember?"

"I remember, Arik," Rivka said.

"I said, Dr. Gafni, I've got one simple question for you. I get that this guy is cold enough that he can shoot a dog. Hell, almost any of us could grow the balls to shoot someone else's dog under some circumstances, right? Neighbor dog bites your fucking kid, you'll shoot it. What I want to know, Dr. Gafni, is if he can shoot *his own* dog. And what did Dr. Gafni say?"

Rivka blinked.

"What did he say, Rivka?"

"He wrote that the subject exhibited—"

"No," Glitzman said. "No. I said, what did Dr. Gafni *say*. Not what did he *write*. Do you remember? You were there."

Rivka cleared her throat. "He said that Kam was capable of shooting his own dog. He wouldn't want to, the doc said. But he would."

"Damn straight," Glitzman said. "I told Kam when he agreed to this charade that if he gave me bodies, I'd give him his cash. And there are going to be bodies, Rivka. We've got names on the Red Page the Prime Minister is going to sign in a few hours." Glitzman pointed at the wall clock, then wiped spittle from the corner of his mouth. "And I've got an assessment from Gafni that says Kam wants nothing more than to flee to California and fall in on himself like a goddamn neutron star. A dentist capable of shooting his own dog. You go to Gafni, you tell him there's no risk because, if Kamran Esfahani was willing to shoot his own dog before"—he mashed a finger into the assessment—"well, he'll be even more inclined now, because we're going to pay him handsomely for the service."

THREE HOURS LATER, in Cohen's office, Amos handed Glitzman a single sheet of red paper bearing the Prime Minister's signature.

"All the usual concerns and caveats," Cohen said. "But he signed. I consider it an insurance policy. Protection, in case things go bad."

Glitzman grunted. "The bodies will be warm when we bring them back. We've got questions."

"Warm and breathing," Cohen said. "But you're a go. Execute the operation, Arik."

Glitzman looked again at the Red Page. He had written more than a few of them, but this was the first time he'd felt any semblance of joy with the red paper in his hands.

The Interrogation Room
Location: █████████
Present day

THIS TIME the interrogation room is empty when the guards lead Kam inside. He sits at the table for a long time, avoiding the merciless gaze of Khomeini's portrait. Dreams are not so common here, but last night Kam had one where he died. Or felt that he had. The details are fuzzy, but he woke with a foreboding sense that the day was bringing horror. Yet even with this vague dread, Kam takes heart that he has not yet finished writing the story. The General is not the type to abandon projects: he will keep Kam alive to reach the end. And Kam is close. He is approaching the part that he does not like to write. The part that floats into his secret and the memory that has tortured him since he was last here writing.

How long ago was that?

Months, he thinks.

Maybe.

At this point it's a guess because Kam has embarrassingly lost track of his only clock: his meals. He is a little ashamed of this. Following the passage of time was a minor rebellion. And in here, rebellions that don't lead to punishments are delicacies to be savored. They'd taken everything else, his life and freedom, of course, and they'd even claimed the sun and the moon and the stars and his watch and he hadn't seen a clock in three years, but by counting his meals he stood fast. Kam never surrendered the time. He kept it right under the General's nose. But now it's gone. He thinks the specter of his execution and marination in that ghastly memory are to blame. He's beginning to give up.

The General swings open the door and even in the moment Kam thinks it significant that he's not twitched or jumped, though he certainly doesn't know what that means. Is that surprise on the General's face? Amusement? Kam quickly breaks eye contact. A guard puts paper and crayons on the table and leaves. The General is staring at Kam. He seems preoccupied, anxious. He does not sit. "Start when you found out Glitzman's daughter was dead," he says. "And go right up to the end." The General seems to consider adding to the prompt, but then he turns and slams the door shut behind him.

Kam slides a piece of paper from the stack. Then he catches a glimpse of the crayons.

They're red.

Kam blinks a few more times. Red.

Red?

Red.

He turns a mass of them over in his hands, desperately searching for a slash of blue.

Red, red, red.

He holds up the box and gives the camera a plaintive look that says: *Need I say more?*

But no one responds.

"There is no blue," he stammers to himself, rifling through the box. "No blue." What to make of this? Whatever it is, it cannot be good. He sits there for a moment, running his hands over his mouth and face and bringing them to rest on his head. His palm has left a sweaty imprint on the first page.

What the hell is this? The General wants this story in two colors?

Kam sorts through the crayons for a while, wondering, if he draws out the selection process, maybe the guards will grow impatient and bring him the blue ones. But of course the point of prison is that it will wait you out. Red, it seems, is what he's got. Kam picks one up and begins to write. The tip snaps right off, two letters in.

النجاه فی الصدق
بخش پایانی از شهادت‌های من

.... Number

.... Date

.... Attachment

The Islamic Republic of Iran

In the name of God
Honesty will save you
The <u>fifth</u> part of my sworn confession
    Kamran Esfahani

CHAPTER 50

Tehran

Three years ago

I FLICKED OFF the vacuum at the buzz in my pocket and dared a glance at my phone. A deep drag demolished most of my cigarette. I had a notification in the crossword app. A sharp pang of fear had me momentarily staring up at the ceiling, where the smoke detector had been, before I yanked it out—I cast a spiteful cloud its way. Roya was asking for a meeting at Laleh Park, around lunchtime. Three periods at the end meant it was urgent. I said I would be there, messaged Glitzman, and alerted Aryas and Kovan, who would run a shoestring countersurveillance operation, checking her for coverage on her journey to the park.

In the kitchen I lit another cigarette with the old one. Roya had swapped the cables, and though I had little beyond the basic confirmation that information was flowing out of Niavaran, it was always possible they'd discovered the tap, and blamed her for it. Was this a trap? If it was, I was about to find out. I brought the vacuum to life for another run through the hall.

ROYA WAS CLEAN, the Kurds said.

I'd arrived first, and in costume: my not-polyester-black-suit of the Etela'at officer. My park bench faced an imposing wall of neatly trimmed thuja topiaries, and though it was Thursday, first day of the weekend, the gray skies conspired to thin the crowds.

A few minutes before noon Roya approached the bench, stroller crunching through gravel. The look of alarm on her face made me tense up and, despite the Kurds' assurances, I began to feel watched. Alya was smiling at me, completely oblivious to her mother's anxiety, chattering away from the stroller.

"The magician!"

"Alya," I said, "I'm so glad to see you. But let me quickly talk to your Maman, okay?"

"Okay," she said, but I could see that was not what she meant. "Can you tell me a story?"

"A story?"

"When you're done talking to Maman?"

"A story? Uh, we'll see," I said, like an idiot, not understanding that to a child of five "We'll see" might as well be a blood oath.

Roya put a phone into her daughter's hands, flipped on a cartoon, tugged headphones over her head, and I filed alongside as we walked under the sycamores.

"Tell me," I said.

"There was an operation last night," she said. "An attempt."

A lone man had appeared on the path as we turned a corner. For a few seconds we did not speak. Her face was puffy, there was a haggard quality to her then, a mix of mania and fatigue that I remember seeing on Sina's wife in the first months after the birth of a new child, and which I've also seen on shell-shocked soldiers. The man had drifted out of earshot.

"Last night..." she tried. The muscles on her face were straining against tears. "Last night..." She'd brought the back of her trembling hand up to her mouth. I took over the stroller-pushing with my left hand and nudged her with the elbow of my right. On instinct we locked arms and walked in another silence, made even more brutal by the insistent slaps and stings of the dirty wind.

"You told me," she said. "You said that they would fail."

"Roya," I said, "I don't understand what you mean."

"You said there were Israeli spies in Colonel Ghorbani's group, and they wouldn't let an operation succeed. Last night they flew a drone into a home. I don't know where it was, or who they were after. I don't know anything else. But the operation did not go well. Whoever they were aiming for, they missed."

"Who said all of this?" I asked.

"Colonel Ghorbani," she said.

"And how did you hear it?"

"They went into the conference room right after. Colonel Ghorbani was furious; he gets angry a lot, but I've never seen him like this. He yelled at me to prepare tea, the General was coming. Surprise meeting."

"General?" I asked, and she told me your name, General, and I made a noise of recognition, though we'd not yet met.

"The General was there in twenty minutes," Roya said. "He bulls in, and he's yelling, before he's even to the conference room. I'm finishing the tea in the kitchen and the General is shouting that he wants to know how Colonel Ghorbani and the team managed to miss the mark on a target he had personally selected. They'd killed his child, and now they'd never get him, would they?"

"A child," I repeated. "You don't know who they were targeting?"

"No. And then the General, I think he noticed me, he got quiet. I set tea in the conference room. The General, Ghorbani, Major Shirazi, and his men all take their seats. I was sent home. On my way out, I heard the General angrily musing if the fault lay with something to do with a satellite or just incompetence. The very last thing I heard was the General asking Major Shirazi if he'd screwed up the piloting. He was almost out of his mind. The General is out there again today. They told me to stay away for the weekend. Said they would fix their own tea. I . . . I am struggling. I do not understand."

"Which part?"

"If there is a spy in Niavaran . . . the child. They killed a child."

"You are sure they said 'child'?"

She was looking at Alya. It was quiet for a few moments, until Alya giggled at something in her show.

"Roya?" I said. "How do they know it was a child? Do you know?"

She shook her head. Wiped her face.

"Maman," Alya said, raising the phone to her mother, who clicked into another show.

"You overheard all this?" I asked.

"Yes, in fragments. They were fighting yesterday even before the General arrived. The colonel blames the major for what happened. And the major blames the colonel. They didn't say anything in front of me, but it was in the air. They were so angry. And afraid of the General."

I was grateful, yet again, that the pervasiveness of real conspiracies among the Tehrani security men made the fabrication of one for Roya's consumption a much simpler task.

Alya had poked up her head. "Can the magician eat lunch with us, Maman? He promised a story!"

CHAPTER 51

Tehran

WE WALKED SOUTH from the park to a café near the university. I had tried valiantly to continue the debriefing, pleading with Alya that I had to speak to Maman, could we do a story later, maybe another cartoon? She was tired of the show, she shouted, and things soon devolved into a full-blown tantrum that drew unwanted attention and made it impossible to debrief Roya in the first place. I racked my brain for stories to tell Alya, and in the end, on the threshold of a complete meltdown, I borrowed one from Maman.

"DO YOU KNOW THE STORY of Joseph?" I asked. I knew it was in the Quran, but some parts were different from the Torah.

Alya, wiping her tears, shook her head.

"I'll tell you the story, but you must be quiet and listen, okay?"

A smile instantly materialized and she nodded.

"Joseph," I said, "was a shepherd. He worked with his brothers, and—"

"How big is Joseph?" Alya asked, slurping apple juice through her straw.

I was recalling the story on the fly, and modifying some of it to resonate more with a little girl, so I thought about that for a moment. "Well, about your age, I suppose."

She cracked a tremendous smile. "And what did he do?"

"Listen to the story," Roya said, "and we will find out."

"Joseph was mean to his brothers. He said mean things about them to his father. But Joseph was his father's favorite. He even got a fancy coat for a present."

"It's pink?" Alya asked.

"All the colors," I said, though I think that was the Broadway version.

"How many brothers did Joseph have?"

I thought about that. "Ten," I said (and yes, I know now this was incorrect). "And so his brothers hated Joseph. Joseph even told them that he'd had a dream he would be their boss. He was going to tell all of them what to do when they got older. No one liked that, and everyone was mad at him. One day Joseph's father sent him out to check on his brothers in the field, and they decided to kill him, and..."

I trailed off, wondering if perhaps she was too young for this part, but she was rapt, Roya was distracted, and I pushed on. "... kill him and tell their father a wild animal did it."

"What animal?" Alya asked.

"A lion."

She nodded: right answer.

"But one of his brothers said, let's not kill him, let's just throw him into a well out in the desert. But soon a caravan appeared, and the brothers decided to sell him instead. So they did, and the caravan took Joseph away from his family. And his brothers killed a goat, and dipped Joseph's coat in its blood, and then they went home and showed it to their father. He was so sad. He started crying. He wailed and tore his clothes and said his son was dead."

"Like Papa," Alya cut in.

I turned to Roya, and saw that she was crying.

DESPITE ALYA'S SHRILL protestations, I did not finish the story, not then. In the telling I'd come to realize I'd forgotten good chunks of it; I was pretty sure I didn't even remember how it ended. I paid the check and we left the café. They had walked, so I loaded the stroller into my car and drove them back to Roya's apartment through a spitting rain and a squall of Alya's tantrums.

That evening I saw the message. I was in my kitchen, laptop open, picking at a hunk of bread. Like all messages from them, it was unsigned, but Rivka's voice carried through the spartan prose. Glitzman, for all his stoicism, was more lyrical when it came to cable-writing.

The cable, which of course did not use anyone's true name, said that Glitzman's home had been targeted by a kamikaze drone, his daughter Oriana the only casualty. A Mossad facility had also been hit, killing six. I stopped there, set down my bread, my hunger subsumed less by grief or sadness, and more by a renewed sense of danger. In the space of three months, eight Mossad officers had been killed, and the young daughter of one of the most vaunted operators in Caesarea Division had been slaughtered in her home. And this had happened after, or during, our big breakthrough inside Niavaran.

I imagined the knife fights in Israel: we have a source inside the group, we've got their fiber tapped, and still, still, we can't prevent an attack? Mossad would not be patient. Not now. I kept on reading, and when I saw my instructions, I knew that people in Tehran were soon going to die.

CHAPTER 52

Tehran

WHILE I WAITED, I vacuumed. This time I was back in my bedroom, on hands and knees, working on a few of the rugs I'd not cleaned since yesterday. If you shut your eyes it was easy enough to imagine they were filthy, that this was time well spent.

My anxieties, usually below the surface, were in those weeks rising well above the waterline, and at present manifesting in the form of a primo Miele vacuum that I'd had sent in from Dubai. It was curry-yellow, specially fabricated for delicate rugs, and cost almost sixty million tomans, including the cut for my fixer. Pure retail therapy. Other signs of distress were the long periods I would go without eating, only to punctuate these hunger strikes with a snacking binge or, on one or two occasions, cooking a gigantic meal from Maman's recipe book and plating the food on my table as if hosting a ghostly dinner party. I spent an ungodly amount of time on social media, all the while cursing the unreliable VPN coverage.

When I was finished vacuuming the bedroom rugs, I went out into the living room looking for fresh targets. I probably put a few kilometers on the vacuum that week. I was also working through a compilation of the poetry of Hafez and had not managed to clear more than a page or two each night, so distracted was I by . . . by . . . what, exactly? I was waiting, waiting for the thud of the bodies I'd promised Glitzman. There was nothing to do but wait.

Handlers, of course, must think constantly about their assets. I had reasons to think constantly of Roya—yes, I did—because for the entirety of those long waiting days, outside of my bursts of cooking, and doomscrolling, and rearranging, and vacuuming, well, I'd thought of little else. And I have solid operational reasons for this, I would tell myself, while cleaning lint and hair from the Miele's filter.

What was Roya thinking? What did she want? And how would it end? I had no answers.

So I went for small things: random facts, a useless question that I could not answer, social media posts, newspaper headlines. These I could consume.

Even questions from Glitzman about the surveillance operation fell on this list, so long as they were details. So long as the chunks were bite-sized, void of complexity, calories, meaning of any sort. I was in a dark tunnel and it was absolutely useless to consider all the ways I might have avoided it, if there were other paths up and over the mountain. Or around. Useless. Better to bounce through social media until my eyes were sore and my brain felt like it was going to bleed. Better to doomscroll southern California real estate . . . but then I found that it felt so distant, so unattainable, that it forced me to think of the bigger picture. And I hated that.

Better to memorize a few helpful facts.

After Albania, Glitzman had given me an escape plan out of Tehran: there was a phone number, prearranged codes. I studied the information, thinking about the circumstances under which I might use the escape, and whether, with the intelligence flowing from Niavaran to Mossad, my obligations to Glitzman were complete, and I'd have my money regardless of whether I stayed inside the country for a few more weeks. Fantasies, I will admit, held a certain appeal in that rough period. You're sitting there, waiting, thinking, hoping. It's natural to get carried away. After I'd vacuumed one of the rugs in my office again (I swear it was actually dirty), and even though it was late, I decided it was time to go see Roya.

ROYA LET ME INTO her apartment, though I'd not told her I was coming, and the reasons for my appearance were so thin, I hoped she would not ask. The place was quiet. Alya was fast asleep. She fixed tea, but the bowl of sugar cubes slipped from her fingers before it reached the table, spilling across the wood. With fingers vibrating like a tuning fork, she plucked the cubes from the table and plopped them in the bowl. I snatched the one nearest me and tucked it into my mouth and watched her standing by the counter, one knuckle clamped in her teeth, staring at a dishrag. I sipped my tea. She put another knuckle against her teeth. I waited.

"I'm a fool," she murmured, "a fool."

"I don't understand," I said.

"What will I say when they find out?"

"Find out what? And who is they?"

"That I was there for Hossein's death! I didn't do anything wrong, but I was there... I could have told them. That I put a cable... oh, I'm going, I'm going to be sick..."

She put a hand to her mouth and stooped over the sink. It was barely a dry heave, but she seemed convinced of her illness and stayed there for a few minutes, hacking up nothing but spit. Her cheeks were twitching. She rinsed her mouth and spat again and joined me at the table.

"You are playing a critical role in an operation to discover and apprehend Israeli spies," I said. "The head of the Ministry knows this. My boss, Colonel Hashemi, knows this. You will be decorated, Roya."

I felt heavy about the lie, though in the moment I could not have said exactly why—up to that point I'd told so many, what was one more? She looked at me, believing me and also not quite believing. I was holding eye contact with her, breaking it only once to snatch an unfortunate glance of one of Alya's drawings pinned to the fridge; it was a chaos of pink and purple, maybe a horse, and it made me feel like I'd slipped into an icy sea.

"You've been honorable," she said, "though I can tell you've not always wanted to be. I'm a widow; to survive I've had to study the looks of men. I know. I know what it looks like."

"I feel like we are having a few different conversations," I said.

"Are you married?" she asked.

"No."

"Have you been married before?"

"No. Roya, why these—"

"You're not an honorable man," she said. "I can tell... I don't know how, but I know. It's all over you. It's the dim light pouring through your eyes, it's something in how you look at me. But you've behaved honorably... or acted the part."

"To do otherwise," I said, "would have violated the rules of my organization."

She laughed. "You're the only one who seems to follow those rules. And do you know what that makes them? Exceptions."

Why had I come here tonight? I could not have told you, but by then I was wondering if it might have been for no reason other than to bed her. I was certainly considering it, thinking that perhaps not only would it be wickedly fun, but also reassuring. Keep her calm and on course for the path ahead. The operational logic was sound. Would Glitzman approve? I thought not. He wouldn't even have approved this visit.

"I'm a fool," she said, head in her hands. "I'm in danger. And for what? What good is revenge?"

"There is no need to be ashamed of revenge," I said, quite firmly, because what I was saying was true. "It's one of life's joys. Like eating a fine meal."

"I've never been trapped after eating a meal."

Though her reaction was absurd—Persian mealtime hospitality is quite often a trap—she had the nub of it right: she was stuck.

And at that moment, as I had for the past few weeks, I wondered how this very ordinary girl was still standing, after all she'd been dealt. That thought was why, after a grand and solitary dinner in my apartment, I would light a cigarette and stare despondently at the waiting dishes and think about Roya in Istanbul, legs crossed, the two of us smoking together in conspiracy, forelocks of her hair dripping down her face, my hand on hers during the walk to the *lahmacun* joint. I would be processing the surveillance videos, or waiting in line at the bakery, thinking of "Lilli Lilli Hozak" and her bathtime chatter with Alya, and my heart would begin beating violently. Dozens of solid operational reasons for such a physiological response, I would think, and in time, just you wait, Roya will live on as nothing more than a few scattered memories.

I am driving, the Pacific out my window, and Roya and Alya are people I knew once, a long time ago, in the dim passageway of the old life that birthed this new one. I cannot picture Roya's visionary eyes. I no longer sense the steel beneath the skin of this supposedly unremarkable widow. I will think of Alya, but I'll remember her in theory. She was a happy girl, I'll think; smiley. But I cannot picture Alya's bright face, I cannot hear her wondrous laugh. I'm sure it is for the best, I say, hands on the wheel. We all die, don't we? In my childish nihilism I say that there were a few billion years before you got here, there will be a few billion more after you're gone, so what does it matter if you depart a few years earlier than scheduled? Dust to dust, etc., and if that's so, the universe has already judged us all, and sin is nothing more than the wash of the tide. And what's more, no one suffered. All is well, isn't it? Yes, yes. The sun is bright. The top is down and the ocean roars at the bottom of the cliff. It has been roaring for all time and it will roar for the rest of it. There's some comfort in that, isn't there? Alya is fine. Roya is fine. I am fine. There are not all sorts of things between us. How could there be? My memories of them are light as pillows.

We are not bound up by fate, I say. I am not silly enough to fall for a story like that, am I?

I had hawked that most elusive and addictive of drugs: meaning. She'd bought it, and I saw now that she did not want what I'd sold. Now the one thing she desired, I could not give: Roya wanted out.

For a long while I tried to console her—I told her that she was brave, that Abbas would be proud of her, as would Alya, when she was older and understood what her mother had done. That in the future she would be proud of herself, for not merely sitting back to accept what she was given. For pushing past the limits to make a difference. She fixed more tea, and we talked around and around, and when she seemed no longer to have the energy even for despair, she said, "I've done what you asked. And I'm stuck. What now? What do you want from me?"

I wanted to take her to bed, and I could see that she wanted it, too; most of all, for a promise. And though it is true that it would have been simpler to let my body say the things that my mouth was then too cowardly to speak, you don't get forgiveness in bed, not before you tell the truth. You get it afterward, on your knees, if you ever get it at all. We looked at each other for a long moment. Her eyes were different colors, one brown, one shimmering gray. I'd never known a bomb to leave anything beautiful in its wake. Suddenly I saw that there were vital organs outside of myself.

"What do you want from me?" she said again.

"Nothing," I said.

And it was only partway a lie, because even if Roya had offered the thing I wanted from her most, I could not have accepted, not then, not for words, an expression—for free. Whatever was flickering my soul to life did not come cheap. Love comes with a knife, my mother would say, reading to me from one of her worn collections of Rūmī. It seems free, too good to be true—and it is. Love is the king of all cons. Outside the kitchen window a pale strip of dawn was rising to challenge the darkness.

CHAPTER 53
Tehran

BECAUSE THERE WEREN'T yet bodies, I still had options, though truly I only see that now, after a few years and a hundred drafts of this story. There were other roads, there had to be, even if the instructions from Tel Aviv made it seem as if the path had narrowed to one. And I must have had some inkling of this, because on the appointed morning two days later, before I went to meet the Kurds, I took one small step away from the life I had wanted toward the one I deserved. For an accomplished fantasist I sure was struggling to imagine a clean way out.

When I walked outside, I wondered if I would ever see my apartment again.

I suppose there were indeed operational reasons for the circuitous, zigzagging route I followed to link up with Aryas and Kovan, and in prior drafts I've tended to emphasize the tradecraft, or to reference the maps we built together, General. The reality is that I wanted a glance at my parents' old house. When I had reached it, I looked up at the window of the room where Maman had nursed me as a baby, in those few brief months before we left Tehran.

Grandfather bought the place in '46. The front is watched over by admirable sycamores, which the pictures attest must have been young when grandfather first moved in. Most of these venerable houses have disappeared. The lucky ones were taken over by museums or art galleries or philanthropic organizations. Ours was confiscated by the Islamic

Republic, the keys handed over to the Sheep Butchers' Union when my parents fled.

From an open window came the chatter of the SBU men; from what I could hear it was decidedly mundane, a conversation about slaughterhouse prices, and I imagined Papa gritting his teeth out here, listening to them drone on inside his house. He had spent years vainly trying to recover it—working every bureaucratic angle he could, inking endless paperwork, slinging bribes. We were never going to get it back, but in the moment I convinced myself that I was making a grand trade, and I took heart in knowing that Papa would have cheered me on. I still do.

By the time I set off, the SBU men had drifted into an argument about an auction schedule interrupted by the angry honks of cars snarled in traffic and the distant baying of sirens, probably rushing to scrape the remains of a pancaked pedestrian from the concrete. I was nearly clipped by a passing motorbike as I stepped out to cross the street.

CHAPTER 54

Dasht-e Lut

(the Plains of Emptiness)

I CURLED ALONG VALI ASR until I saw the white Toyota van outside a bakery. I slid open the door, tossed in my pack, and jumped in. Aryas was driving. Kovan, in the passenger seat, fiddled with the GPS. "It'll be just like Albania," he muttered by way of greeting. "Just like Albania."

"They locked us in a shipping container," I said. "It would be great if this were different from Albania."

Aryas laughed as he pulled the van into the stream of cars.

Soon the concrete wasteland of Tehran's industrial ring loosened its grip, and we were cruising south on the 7 toward Qom. There, after topping off the van with petrol, we turned east, toward the desert, our silence snapped by the crackle of the roasted wheat and melon seeds we snacked on mindlessly.

I stared out the window as we drove. The Dasht-e Lut, the Plains of Emptiness, is a scorching moonscape of salt and rock and dunes and furrows that most Iranians would visit only if delivered by a plane crash. I'd actually come once before, with Papa, and in a car, because he'd been here once, on a car trip with Grandfather. Even in May the place feels like a kiln. It looks the part, too: everything, far as the eye can see, is the color of baked clay, of rusty Mars. Papa told me that the locusts are cannibals because there is so little to eat. The afternoon was nearly gone. The hills and dunes were now paling to salmon in the gathering dusk.

"What are you going to do with the money?" Kovan asked. It had been hours since anyone spoke. I assumed he was addressing his brother, so I said nothing.

"Well?" he said, turning around.

"What money?" I replied, speaking to the window because my head was slumped into it.

The brothers chuckled. "We're going to Germany," Kovan said, turning back to face the road. "Open a restaurant."

"German girls hate me," Aryas said. "And you know what? I like that. I don't know why."

"You don't have to travel that far to find girls who hate you, brother," Kovan said. "Plenty in Erbil."

"I like German teeth," Aryas said. "I don't know why, but the teeth need to be straight. Bone-white. Maybe a little on the big side—the teeth, I mean. Remember that wasted blonde we danced with in Hamburg? Sloppy mess, great teeth." He jerked a thumb my way. "The dentist would have approved."

"Did Zhina have nice teeth?" Kovan asked. "I don't remember."

The mood in the van soured at the mention of Aryas's great love, Zhina; I'd heard the girl mentioned only once before, in passing. Aryas's knuckles shifted and his grip tightened on the wheel. "Zhina had a little gap between her two front teeth. Otherwise they were perfect. When she was thinking, she would poke her tongue into it."

It was plain that Kovan had a lewd joke at the ready, almost certainly about other things that poor Zhina might have let slide through the gap in her teeth, but there was defeat all over his brother and, in a rare display of restraint, Kovan sank back into his seat and said nothing.

"A restaurant?" I prodded, trying to lighten the mood. "What the hell do you guys know about cooking?"

"We'll hire a chef," Aryas said, brightening. "Maybe a Lebanese guy. Do some Lebanese food. Germans already think we're Lebanese. Or Turks. But Lebanese food's better."

"When we get out of here," Kovan said, "when we're clear of the Israelis and the bank accounts are unlocked and all that, I'm going to buy a case of champagne and rent a chubby blond girl with big tits and I'm going to take her up to one of the ski resorts in the Zugspitze for a nice long weekend. Hell, maybe we'll stay for a week."

Aryas, in his usual, serious voice, said to me, "Do you really not know what you're going to do with the money?"

"What money?" I said, a ham-fisted effort to avoid a discussion of *how* much. And this time their laughter was tinged by frustration, not amusement. With a shrug, they turned their attention to the darkening desert highway.

Of course I knew. Or I had known. But with Roya constantly on my mind, and after listening to the brothers' fantasies, I felt a prick of embarrassment. Would my own dreams sound as ridiculous as what I'd just heard from the Kurds? We're sacrificing Roya and Alya for what? I thought. For ski weekends with chubby German hookers. For a California house that wouldn't fit in my grandfather's old courtyard.

For Israeli lives, Glitzman would have said, and he'd be right, of course.

The mountains and dunes were now the navy-blue color of the night itself. I hadn't seen another vehicle in over an hour. When we'd reached the coordinates on the GPS, Aryas pulled off to the side of the road. The moon was a sliver.

The temperature had plunged with the darkness, and we slipped on jackets. We shone lamps across the sand for a few moments until I spotted the well-worn ruts of the path. Nomads use it, Kovan had said. And so do desert adventure excursions, which was our cover if we chanced upon anyone. Kovan entered another set of coordinates. I would be driving one of the cars out, and I'd not driven this road before, so they put me behind the wheel for practice. It was slow going and bumpy; I only lost the trail twice, and both times we stopped, got out, shone our lights around, and found it within minutes. In an hour we reached the new coordinate.

Much of the Plains of Emptiness is sculpted by the whisp of star dunes and the crenellations of *kaluts*, massive rock corrugations formed by the freakish winds that rip across it during the summer. But there are pockets of salt flats, and some of them, like the one before us, stretch out across what Glitzman's message called *a comfortable 1.2 klick Visual Runway*. And if the organization you work for happens to possess a constant-stare satellite capability over much of the vastness of Iran, you might be able to muster near-real-time images of a dozen or so potential landing strips across the Plains of Emptiness, just to be sure no tribesmen are pancaked by your plane when it lands. After all, a C-130 can land just about anywhere, as long as the runway's got about 1.2 klicks.

Glitzman called our technique a box-and-one. Double-checking that we were parked at the proper coordinate on the salt flat, from the compartment of the van I removed three blue infrared beacons, positioned them in a cluster, and flipped them on so they were blinking. This was the one. From there we drove north along the ghostly runway, stopping a little beyond a kilometer at yet another coordinate, one of the four remaining. This was the box. At each, we placed a cluster of green IR beacons, until, at this end of the runway, opposite the blinking beacon, there was a box, a near-perfect square, fifty meters by fifty meters.

We parked the van up on the bank of a dune to wait. The clouds were shoaling high, well above the cliffs and crags spreading their legs into the salt flat. You could have read a book in this desert at night under the glow of a full moon, and we certainly didn't want that attention, but neither would Glitzman's planners have desired no moon at all. When we had practiced this once, in Albania, we'd been told that the C-130 pilots flew with night-vision goggles, which required that a small amount of light be magnified to work at all. And when you were flying a C-130 low, over Iranian mountains, well, you'd rather not be blind in the clouds. The pilots don't want the last thing they see, when the clouds part, to be the face of a cliff.

I could hear the low hum of an engine out there in the darkness, south of the first beacon.

"Any minute now," Aryas said.

Kovan had come alongside me. "Is there anything we need to know about?"

I gave him a blank look. "What are you talking about?"

"You went to her apartment two nights ago."

"Huh," I said. "We didn't have surveillance scheduled."

I couldn't really see his face, but I could feel his pity through the silence. I wondered why Glitzman hadn't told me.

"I'm her handler," I said.

"Ah," Kovan sneered, "so did you handle her?"

We stared at each other with *what-the-fuck* faces while the noise of the engines grew louder. Sand whipped into my eyes, from the wind, not the engines—they were still too far off—and I had to look away from him.

"It's too late," Kovan said, and when I was done madly blinking, I saw that he was wiping his face, too. "It's done."

"What are you talking about?" I snapped.

"Are you sleeping with her?" he asked, shouting now. "Is that why you went to see her?" The dark outline of the plane roared over the top of the crag to our east, making for the lights that marked the start of the runway.

"No, I'm not," I shouted, though in truth it was far worse than that. "Where the fuck is this coming from?"

The ghostly plane drifted down, down, down until it kissed the salt flat just beyond the first beacon. It rolled into the middle of the box and then taxied off, making room for the next.

Kovan inched closer for a good look at me in the darkness, and I could see his face drawn tight, which was deeply disconcerting. That sort of look was normal on his brother, not him. "We've been watching you two since Istanbul," he said. "And I don't like how you're looking at her. It has me worried."

"Me, too," Aryas said.

"What the fuck are you two worried about?" I hissed.

"If you can do the next part," Kovan said. "If you're up for it."

"That's the question," added Aryas. "That's what we're worried about."

I looked back and forth between the brothers. I took half a step toward the van, but Aryas snagged my arm. His grip, though sure, was sufficiently chummy that I complied.

Aryas said: "We don't want to involve them"—he nodded toward the plane below us, which had come to a stop—"but we will if we need to. We can't have you getting us killed."

"Back in Istanbul you were cold as steel," Kovan said. "What happened?"

"I really am not following this," I said.

"Tell us you're up for this," Aryas said. "Tell us that Roya and the girl... tell us you can deal with it."

The buzzing noise was back—second plane inbound. There was one correct answer to this question and at that point I thought it might still be the truth.

"I'm up for this," I said. "I can deal with it."

The brothers exchanged glances. Kovan sighed, Aryas said let's get down there, and the tension dissipated at the demands of flashing the far recognition signal—three bursts from a red flashlight—down toward the first plane. From inside the cockpit the same flashes came back. We repeated the process with the second plane, and then loaded into the van to meet the Israelis at the landing zone.

We were trundling down the dune, Aryas clenching the wheel as we bounced over a hump of sand, when he said: "You should know, neither of us can tell when you're lying."

"I'll take that as a compliment," I said.

CHAPTER 55

The Plains of Emptiness

THE TWO C-130S that landed on the Dasht-e Lut salt flats that morning had departed from an air base in the Negev. The planes were painted matte-black and piloted by men who looked too young for facial hair, though one of them did tell me that he had flown the Lut Express, as he called it, more than fifty times. Sometimes it was to bring in a car, sometimes weapons, sometimes people. Common factor, he told me in English while bumming a smoke, watching everyone unload, is I don't know shit about what's actually going on. The route, a hopscotch across what the pilot called the "Arc of Misery," cut from their Negev air base out across Syria and Iraq, zigzagging across a well-trod route through central Iran to avoid the radar. Sometimes, near Tehran, this took the plane above seven kilometers, and at others it glided no more than fifty meters above the Plains of Emptiness.

Inside the first C-130's cargo bay were two heavily modified Toyota Hilux pickups, each bearing legitimate registrations and paperwork linking them to a tour company, a Mossad front. A loadmaster removed the wheel chocks, chains, and tie-downs securing the vehicles, both of which sported camper tops. Later, I would find out what was inside, but at the time I only thought it mildly curious that Rivka insisted we pack the breaching gear into the back of the Toyota van, and not the pickup beds. The Kurds would each drive one of the pickups back to Tehran. I would pilot the van.

During our brief introductions, the Kurds and I were handed push-to-talk radios, and I learned that each of the six-man assault team were YAMAM operatives. They wore civilian clothes, mostly jeans and jackets, and I suspect they were more lightly armed than they'd have preferred. I do not recall what YAMAM stood for in Hebrew, but it was something vague and anodyne, along the lines of the Special Central Unit or some such. The taciturn assault team leader told us they'd taken a vacation from rescuing hostages in Gaza to now take a few in Iran. Though he said this without smiling, I believe that he was having great fun. I never learned his name, but he was bulky and towered over us, and I now think of him as only the Tree.

Outside the planes, while helping load water and food rations into the vehicles, I watched one of the YAMAM operators slide a Negev light machine gun across the floor of the backseat, which would be used, as he put it, in case we had to tear something's ass off on the way in or out. In the movies everyone's running around with an Uzi because it looks cool, but in a real fight, they told us, with long guns aimed your way, well, you might as well be shooting BBs. A duffel bag holding a few Galil rifles went into the back of the van, within arm's reach in case things went sideways on the road to Tehran.

I was surprised to see Rivka, who, after acknowledging me with a tepid handshake, told me Glitzman wanted a word.

Glitzman. Was he here? Rivka pointed to one of the C-130s.

Of all the shocking things—and the list was growing—his presence surprised me most. I am not an employee of the Mossad, but I would have guessed that his superiors would have opted to let Rivka or someone else run this, seeing as we were less than a week removed from the death of his daughter, and this very operation was aimed at her killers. I hiked up the cargo ramp and found him fiddling with a pocket-sized satellite phone on one of the seats. He did not look up. I did briefly consider offering my condolences—it would have been only human—but I felt that Glitzman would despise such useless sentimentality, and also probably me for engaging in it. I did nod solemnly his way, but he didn't even look up.

"How many times is this for you in Iran?" I said.

Glitzman, pushing a few of the buttons, laughed, but still had not looked up. "How does it feel to be leaving it for good?"

I'd not yet come to terms with that reality. I didn't really want to think about it. "I feel fine," I said.

A silence spun open between us. Glitzman fussed with the phone for a few moments while I stood there. "Fine?" he asked. "We're on the cusp of smashing Colonel Ghorbani, and you're merely fine?" *Tap-tap-tap.* The phone made a noise, then so did Glitzman, and he finally looked up at me as if he were surprised I was still there. "Ask your question," he said.

"What do you mean?"

"I can see it all over you. Just ask."

"What will happen to my agent and her daughter?"

"Exactly what I wrote in my cable."

"You didn't mention them in the cable."

"Right," Glitzman said. "Which means I don't know."

"Don't know, or don't care?"

Glitzman took a moment to think about that. "Ghorbani has killed eight of my people. And my daughter." His focus drifted to the phone. "So it's both."

CHAPTER 56

*The Plains of Emptiness /
the road to Tehran*

THEY WANTED IRANIANS at the wheel to deal with problems: roadblocks, cops, or civilians, if there was an accident, or a need for words. We collected the beacons because the exfil site was nearer to Tehran than the infil here had been. It had to be, because when we were done it was far more likely someone would be chasing us.

I drove the Toyota van, the Kurds the pickups. The Tree rode alongside me, in the passenger seat of the lead car, two of his operators in back along with Glitzman. We left the salt flat landing zone at first light. Everyone who wasn't an Iranian wore light disguise over their civilian clothes: wigs, eyeglasses, jackets, makeup. Rivka donned a chador. The drive was stunning: clopping through the ruts and furrows of the nomads' trail, then through open desert stretching away from the road in every direction until the flat sand met high wispy dunes or jagged towers of rock. But I did not enjoy the scenery; instead, I dwelled on the insanity of what I was doing. I thought about ways it might go wrong. I considered asking for a weapon, so I could shoot myself if things went haywire, but I knew how that question would be received, and I held my tongue.

The YAMAM operators, I suspect, were not thinking such things. I knew little about the unit, other than it had spent much of the war in Gaza rescuing hostages, killing Hamas commandos, intercepting terrorist suicide bombers, and sometimes, at least as could be gleaned from the scant press coverage, all three at once. The operators were quiet but alert; they each had a pistol, I think they were Glocks, either on their person or at the ready in a pack at their feet. They sipped energy drinks in silver cans without labels and when I asked if they had an extra to spare, before handing me one from his bag the Tree inquired, with his classic humorlessness, if I had any heart conditions. That thing must have had the caffeine content of a few liters of coffee, because, a few minutes after I'd finished, I could feel my heart beating on my ribs and could not stop my left foot from tapping the floor, or my fingers against the steering wheel.

A few hours clear of the landing zone, on the side of a remote stretch of desert highway, the Tree had the whole convoy pull over, and he gave me, Aryas, and Kovan our tasks for the operation. To my great surprise, he also gave me a gun, a Makarov, practically identical to the one I'd fired so poorly on the Albanian range, long ago.

"I'm not sure that's a good idea," Glitzman told the Tree, right in front of me.

"Why not? the Tree asked. "All hands on deck."

"He's the worst shot I've ever seen, that's why."

The Tree whispered something to Glitzman, who nodded. Then the Tree looked at me. "Don't use that on anyone but yourself."

"Got it."

The Tree unfurled a few maps and gave the three of us our orders. His team, of course, had already rehearsed everything in Tel Aviv. This was about looking us in the eye and making sure we knew what the hell to do. He used Rivka as translator, and I do not know if the directions were intended to sound simplistically insulting, or if that was merely the messenger. In any case, on the map of Niavaran, the Tree told each of us where to position ourselves for overwatch (we knew this already, we'd picked the spots), how to communicate if we spotted anything amiss, and what we were to do at the end, once given a few basic signals. He looked at us like a father hoping for the most exaggerated signs of understanding, and we gave them: nods, thumbs-ups, grunts. We could all say, *Got it*, in Hebrew and we must have said it a dozen times. When the Tree at last seemed confident that we three ragtag Iranians knew up from down—and also that I could properly handle and appendix-carry the handgun—we loaded back up for the final leg, into Tehran.

I suppose all such men, like athletes, have different routines for getting into the zone, but the Tree and the two men in my vehicle, at least, were the silent type. I do not think of Glitzman that way—if it had been he and I alone, we would have had some chatter, at least every now and then. But he did not speak, either, and I still wonder if this sprang from deference to the operators—it was the Tree, after all, who was in charge here—boredom, or the deep pool of rage, grief, and exhaustion in which he was doubtless swimming. Glitzman looked straight ahead and sat quite still, as if he'd opted to pass an airplane flight without in-flight entertainment or reading material. On the drive I did not know that Glitzman had been the one to find his daughter, and now I understand why he could not shut his eyes.

CHAPTER 57
Tehran

BY FIRST LIGHT we pulled into the empty loading dock of an abandoned distribution center outside Shams Abad. The metal gate was rusted, the high concrete walls were whipstitched by razor wire. There must have been a grain-processing facility nearby, because the smell—one I will never forget—was that of wheat cereal. There were faded numbers painted above the loading docks and a graffiti-flocked logo across the metal rolling doors that I think was a cheetah. MEDUSA had infected the personal phones for everyone on Ghorbani's team, which meant that someone in Tel Aviv could watch in real time as they left their homes and apartments to converge on the Niavaran office.

Glitzman kept us updated through the satphone. The analyst, Mina, was first to arrive, followed by Roya. Then Major Shirazi's two lieutenants, their arrivals separated by a few minutes. The Major himself pulled his car through the gate at 7:22. Colonel Ghorbani was not yet there, but we had to leave soon if we wanted to arrive in time to disrupt the meeting. Initially I experienced a wash of relief—Colonel Ghorbani was the key. If for any reason he did not go into the office, might Glitzman and the Tree call it off?

And when I realized that I felt hopeful the operation would be canceled, which meant there wouldn't be bodies, which meant I wouldn't get paid, well, I knew that I'd forded a great river in my mind, and, worse, that it was only the beginning.

The Tree clicked the push-to-talk.

The three squelches told us it was time to drive.

CHAPTER 58

Tehran

OVERWATCH MEANT monitoring the compound's perimeter for the unexpected; deliverymen, unannounced arrivals, or the neighbor kids who, during our surveillance, had once knocked because they'd kicked a soccer ball over the fence. There was also risk of what the Tree, in his short roadside brief, had called "squirters"—people inside the compound who, at the sight of the YAMAM assault team bursting into the staff meeting, might somehow squirt loose and dart out into the neighborhood.

We took up our assigned posts. I parked the Toyota down the street with a clean view of the front gate. Kovan's pickup was on the other side of the home, keeping tabs on the gate outside the driveway. Aryas headed for the alley that ran perpendicular to both of us. There, he parked near a rusted, shambling side gate that led out through the garden. We'd never seen anyone use it, except to toss garbage, but who could know the mind of a squirter?

Time's pace was quickening; the slow tedium of the drive had accelerated into the sight of traffic hurtling around me as I drove, at the Tree's direction, up the sycamore-flanked road toward the compound.

Glitzman, from the back, put down the satellite phone and said to me: "Is there anything on the crossword puzzles? Anything about the meeting being canceled?"

Why was he asking me? MEDUSA let Mossad see everything on Roya's phone (and surely on mine) up to and including the crossword app messages. I wondered if maybe the person monitoring her phone was in Israel, and there was a delay. Glitzman was also a paranoiac. Forget squirters, who could know the mind of Glitzman?

So, though I had checked the app about fifty times that morning, including as recently as two or so minutes before, I duly checked again. "No," I said, "nothing."

I found a spot outside the main gate and time slowed back down while I watched the traffic slide by, waiting for word from Tel Aviv. Ghorbani's apartment was in Velenjak, which was not far, but if he did not leave soon, he was not going to make the meeting. Would it be canceled?

The satphone beeped. Glitzman picked it up, listened, then set it down with a grunt of acknowledgment. "He's on the move," he told the Tree, "ETA between 9:44 and 9:51, depending on traffic."

GHORBANI'S BLACK LEXUS snaked by the front entrance at 9:46 before turning right, toward the driveway. "Gate is opening," Kovan said over the radio. Then, a moment later: "Green One is inside . . . and . . . gate is shut."

"Nine-fifty on the dot," Rivka said. "Plenty of time to get tea before the meeting starts."

The meeting had been the answer to this question from Glitzman: *When is everyone most likely to be inside the compound?* We knew from the surveillance that the meeting almost always began on time—Ghorbani was a punctual man, and a stickler for the trait in others. Sometimes the meeting went on for twenty minutes, sometimes thirty. Never longer. Colonel Ghorbani did not like meetings.

Based on the information, the Tree had sensibly decided to breach the entrances at ten minutes past the hour.

It was now five past.

In one sense I'd been waiting for this moment all my life, but now buyer's remorse pummeled me, and I hadn't even left the store. What was so bad about being a dentist, really? Who cares what Sina's got? Don't like the Swedish winter? Get a fucking heavier coat! Instead...

And though I was overwatch for a Mossad assault team preparing to conduct a brazen kidnapping in the heart of Tehran, my shot-through nerves had less to do with what was going to happen next, and more with what was coming after.

CHAPTER 59

Tehran

I HAD STOPPED BREATHING, I am sure of it.

A vein in my neck was pulsing, squeezing me like a tentacle. There was a salty ball of saliva in my throat and I could not work it down. Every passerby was a policeman and they were all looking at me, sitting in the van just outside the house.

In English, Glitzman asked for an overwatch update.

There was nothing, we all said. Nothing is happening. It was a beautiful spring day; the sun was shining and the smog was light. Even Tehrani drivers seemed to be in good moods. The usual music of angry honks and screeching brakes was instead a pleasant hum of activity on the street. Everything seemed quiet and normal, and that's exactly how all those scientists felt, how Abbas and Roya felt before he'd had his eyes shot out by a robotic machine gun. It was how Glitzman must have felt, curled up on his last night with his little girl.

There was a series of names, each repeated three times over the radio—Ari, Ari, Ari, Yoni, Yoni, Yoni, Artem, Artem, Artem—with clicks before and after each as they moved to the breaching points.

I could not swallow. That slippery ball in my throat would not go down.

The Tree and another operator, wearing jeans and light jackets, now exited the van, walking quickly but not too quickly up the sidewalk toward the front gate.

Through the radio came what sounded like another synchronization in Hebrew. Two would go in the main gate, two over the back wall, one in through the rusty garden door. Behind them, one in each entrance to dam up any squirters.

"Your source said that they do not carry weapons at the staff meeting?" The Tree had put this to me, on the ride in from the desert, and though I'd known him for only a few hours, I knew enough to understand he was deadly serious, and I would regret my lips parting into a smile.

"Right," I said. "There's been no mention of weapons on the compound."

That brought the first creases of a smile over the Tree's lips. This was peak amusement, his version of rolling on the ground in laughter. A compound without weapons? Insane.

"If your source is right about that," he said, "when we get back to Israel I will buy you a beer."

"I'm not going to Israel," I said.

One of his eyebrows rose slightly, and he said, "I will drink it for you, then."

"How long will it all take?" I had asked, deciding the unexpected camaraderie opened the door to a question.

"From which point?"

"From when you get inside the compound. In the front door. Over the walls."

He'd put a few melon seeds in his mouth and scraped at something behind his ear, which he'd been working on for the entire ride, and which I did not think was there. "Start counting," he said, and shut his eyes.

I gave him a doubtful look, but he could not see, and also his face was stone. I began: "One, two, three, four, five, six, seven, eight, nine, ten, eleven, twelve, thirteen—"

"Thirteen seconds," he had said. He opened his eyes and put down a good deal of his energy drink. "Similar places in Gaza take ten. But Gaza is a shithole, and the homes are smaller. Here, it will be thirteen."

CHAPTER 60

Tehran

FOUR SQUELCHES ON the radio meant go.

I began counting aloud, in the vain hope it would help me breathe. Glitzman was in the back of the van and I did not care. I held the steering wheel in a death grip, and I counted.

ONE . . .

A grunt from the Tree, in Hebrew—

TWO . . .

A buzz. The slam of metal on concrete, and I cannot breathe, but somehow I can count to—

THREE . . .

The knock of boots and heavy breathing—

FOUR . . .

Did I count it? I don't know. I can't hear anything anymore—

FIVE . . .

I try to swallow and I gagged instead—

SIX . . .

Doors fly open but my throat will not, and if the number escapes my lips it cannot have gone fa—

SEVEN . . .

A woman's scream drowns the boot-knocking. Mina. I know what Roya's scream sounds like—

EIGHT . . .

I hear, in Persian: Put up your hands! Put them up!—

NINE . . .

A miserable swirl of thuds and curses, and I just think, No gunshots, no guns, please, no guns—

TEN . . .

"Fuck you, Jew! Fuck you!"—

ELEVEN . . .

"Green One secure! Green One secure!"—

TWELVE...

Roya screams in terror, and—

THIRTEEN...

I try to say something, but there is a bubble of air caught in my throat and it will not go down—

THERE WERE MORE CLICKS on the radio and Glitzman hustled out of the van.

Ninety-seven...

I am still counting.

SOME TIME LATER, minutes, seconds, I do not know, the Tree clicked the radio. He said my name three times. Leaving the car, I entered the gate code, but I did not hear the buzz, because my ears are ringing, and I'm walking inside—

CHAPTER 61
Tehran

AT OUR ROADSIDE BRIEFING, Glitzman asked me to be the interpreter, so I went inside to find him.

Rivka spoke excellent Persian, but Glitzman predicted there would be a great deal of shouting and gutter language best interpreted by a native speaker. There was really not much time for a proper battlefield interrogation, so there could be slipups, no room for misunderstanding or misinterpretation.

I moved toward the screams and on the way there was no mess, no blood, no sign of a struggle. I'd wondered what the house looked like inside, and now I had my answer—for the most part it looked like a normal, well-appointed home in north Tehran. Ornate carpets covered the floor and most rooms were lit by large chandeliers. Everything was gaudily decked out in crystal and gold, which the Persian part of me insists is classy, though my Swedish sensibilities beg to differ. An ashtray sat on a table beside a sofa, smoke still curling from the remains of what I presumed had been Shirazi's cigarette, left unfinished to make the meeting.

I stepped over a few bloodstains on my way into the conference room. The blood must have belonged to Major Shirazi, whose face was covered in it. The chairs were overturned, papers were scattered across the floor. The major, Colonel Ghorbani, and the two lieutenants had been bound with zip ties across their hands and feet, blindfolded, and arranged in a row along the wall. Hoods were thrust over their heads. Mina and Roya, also bound, were propped against the opposite wall, though not yet hooded. I looked away from Roya.

The assault team hustled here and there, dragging computers, boxes, filing cabinets, phones, backpacks, and notebooks—anything they could carry—out to one of the waiting pickups, which Aryas had brought through the gate and into the driveway after the Iranians inside had been secured. I watched one of the YAMAM operators scrape every sheet of paper and notebook off the table, cram it into a box, and then drag that box outside. Out in the hallway two others carted a safe on a hand truck.

Colonel Ghorbani, slumped against the wall, was cursing the Jews.

Glitzman and one of the operators hoisted him up to take him upstairs for a brief chat.

I had avoided looking at Roya, but now our eyes met. She made a desperate noise, and her chin drooped to meet her neck.

A hopelessness slid through me, dull and painful as a wrecked blade.

When Roya lifted her head she said, to Rivka, in Persian, "You died in Istanbul. You died when he rescued me."

"A rescue," Rivka said, bemused. "Not quite." Then Rivka motioned to the operator who had the medical kit. On the table he opened a small plastic case; he withdrew a pack of syringes and vials.

"How?" Mina screamed at Roya. "How do you know them? How? How, how, how? What do you mean, rescue?"

One of the operators pinned Roya to the wall, tugged off her manteau, ripped the sleeve of her shirt. What are you doing, she screamed, what are you doing, what are you doing? No, no, no. I watched as she jerked her head around, trying to see, and it was getting a little out of control, Mina was shouting, too, and there were neighbors, after all, so the operator shoved her down and straddled her while the medic jabbed one of the needles into the skin the first man had uncovered on her upper arm. Roya was squirming, kicking.

"Please," she yelled. "Please don't."

The operator's hands were on her neck. She was an animal. She was certainly no longer a person. She would not look at me. She tried to sit up as the drugs kicked in, and she was unsteady, her head like a block of concrete attached to the thin straw of her neck. Her eyelids shut for a moment, but before she passed out, Roya managed one last raise of her head. She forced her right eye, the gray one, open to a narrow slit and looked right at me. She blinked a few times and I saw her nostrils flare. Her double-colored eyes were usually hiding something, but not this time, and I had to look away. Thankfully, when I dared glance back, they were shut. Her breathing was slow, rhythmic, almost peaceful.

Upstairs, Glitzman was calling for me.

CHAPTER 62

Tehran

IT WAS A MARK OF Glitzman's psychotic professionalism that, having moved heaven and earth to capture the man responsible for killing his daughter, he had no plans to harm him. I do believe he would have drawn some joy from it, but I am certain Glitzman hoped it would not come to that.

The Tree had dragged Ghorbani into a small office on the second floor, where, still bound but now unhooded, he sat in a desk chair with Glitzman facing him. I took a seat on the edge of the desk and realized it was Roya's office—there was a picture of Alya smiling right at me. I was sorely tempted to flip it around, but that would have raised all manner of suspicion, so I looked out the window, convinced that once we started the debriefing the nausea would subside. Down in the courtyard I saw two of the YAMAM guys begin unloading what, during the briefing, the Mossad team had called the Escape Pod. The Tree left us.

Glitzman set his hand on Ghorbani's leg. In English, he said, "We've been searching for each other, Colonel. Do you know who I am?" He nodded for me to translate, but before I could begin, Ghorbani said, quite firmly: "Arik Glitzman."

Glitzman sat back in his chair, and they studied each other like two men who'd known this was coming all along, the uncertainty only in who would have the upper hand. It felt like they hung there for a long time.

"That night, I went downstairs to get Oriana a glass of water," Glitzman said. From his pack, Glitzman removed a folder of surveillance photographs, snapped, I knew, by the Kurds, and placed them like floor tiles at Ghorbani's feet. One of his parked Lexus. One of the entrance to his apartment building. One of Ghorbani's wife, Fereshteh. One of his son, Mehdi, walking into a store, holding hands with his mother.

"You have a network operating inside Israel," Glitzman said. "Surveillance. Smuggling. Moving drones. Maybe flying them, though with your setup downstairs I wonder if you fly them from here. I want names. Addresses. Selectors. Everything."

Ghorbani's defiance briefly buckled to despair. He stared at the picture of his son. He must have been holding much of the conversation in his head, because, without another word, he said, in Persian, "What good are Zionist promises?"

I translated.

And Glitzman said, "Well, Colonel, shall we find out?" He made a show of checking his watch. "I have your personal phone and a finger of yours to unlock it." Glitzman leaned forward and tapped the closed fist of the colonel's bound hand. "I could send your wife a text message asking if the whole family might have lunch around here. There is a pizza place just up the street that I am sure Mehdi would like. They come. I send another message saying you are running late. They take a table outside. My people in Tehran slap a magnetic bomb on the underside of their car." Glitzman slapped a photograph of Fereshteh's blue BMW on the floor. I translated.

"You are a monster," Ghorbani said.

"My Oriana was five," Glitzman said, his tone clinical. "You murdered her. And eight of my friends. Monster? Colonel, please. Your organization works day in, day out to hasten the destruction of the only Jewish state. You kill Jews at random around the world. You'd have preferred the Shoah succeed, Colonel, though, bizarrely, you would also probably deny it ever happened. You're a bagman for a crop of corrupt medieval mullahs who've run Persia into the ground—"

I put up my hand, and in English told Glitzman that I really should translate this before I forgot anything. With an affirmative grunt and wave of the hand, he sank back into his chair and stared right through Ghorbani.

While I spoke, I think it struck Ghorbani that I was a native Iranian, and though he kept quiet, something began to shine in his eyes and I saw that he hated me. And do you know what? During that short conversation I put all of my misfortunes on his shoulders and found that I loathed him, too. When I was done, Glitzman told me to let the colonel respond. There was so little time.

"You." Ghorbani looked around the office, his tone hardening with each breath. "You, Arik. *You* murdered my friends. Two years ago, Israeli jets murdered my brother—air strike in Syria. You kidnapped and killed Captain Ismail Qaani. And last year you murdered the husband of the woman downstairs . . . look, that's her daughter in that picture, there on the desk. You killed that little girl's father." He jerked his head toward the photograph of Alya, and I couldn't look.

"You're complaining about combatants," Glitzman said, shaking his head. "About me killing your soldiers in the middle of a war, is that right, Colonel? What the hell was your brother doing in Syria? Training Jew-killers, that's what. And this woman's husband?" He snatched up the picture of Alya and shoved it against Ghorbani's nose—"This girl's father was designing drones so you could glide right through our air defenses to kill more Jews. You and your friends in Hamas and Hezbollah kill civilians. Noncombatants. I'm after your soldiers, Ghorbani. I could have dropped a bomb on this goddamn house, but unlike you and your death-worshipping mullahs, I—"

"Arik," I said, shifting my weight on the desk, "I'm going to forget bits of this if—"

Glitzman dropped the picture on the floor. I shuddered when it cracked, fighting the odd thought that I should right the picture on the desk, though I was relieved it had landed face down. Glitzman knifed an agitated hand through the air: *Get on with it.* He and Ghorbani stared through each other while I spoke. Their eyes were filled with a calm, steady hate, and I think it was the purest hate there is: the sort that comes not from misunderstanding, but from intimacy. For an excruciating moment after I'd finished no one spoke.

"Soldiers," Ghorbani repeated. "How about the thousands of Palestinian women and children you've bombed or shot or starved? They're soldiers in your book, Arik, eh?" Ghorbani's gaze dipped down to the photo of his son. "Mehdi is eight. He's a soldier?"

I was afraid to translate this, but as I did, the Tree stuck his head in and told Glitzman the assault team had collected everything they could. The fresh C-130s were an hour out.

"You are running an operation right now in Israel," Glitzman said. "I want names. Phone numbers. Addresses. Everything. You give it to me, Fereshteh and Mehdi live. You don't, and they don't."

Ghorbani looked right at him. Then at me. "You," he said to me. "You translate this for Arik, word for word."

I nodded.

"You are a Zionist son of a dog," Ghorbani shouted, "you fucking Jew!"

He paused there, seemingly wanting me to translate this productive preamble, so I did, and it made Glitzman smile at the floor while he feathered the toe of his boot over one of the photos of Ghorbani's son.

"What's the Mossad motto?" Ghorbani continued. "Divided, we rule. You pour water in every line and fracture in our society and wait for winter to see the cracks. Well, Arik, you know what? The Zionist entity is under similar stress, is it not? You've got your Arabs, sure, but, even worse, because it's close to the heart, you've got fascist Jews. We found a few of those. It was not hard to find young hopeless radicalized Jews happy to help sow chaos in Israel. What do you call them, Hilltop Youth? The ones who believe your government is as corrupt and evil as ours in Tehran. Who—"

"Colonel," I said, "let me stop you there."

Glitzman was expressionless as I translated. When I was done, he nodded for more.

Ghorbani went on, "We found Jews who might help us fly a drone through your fucking windows, long as they believe they're reporting to Yahweh and not the Mahdi. You've got yeshivas as radical as a Saudi madrassa and we found a man who could recruit at one of them, a Jew who's more Persian than Jew who convinced three of those slaves to the Torah that they were doing God's work when they set drones in enclosures, or took receipt of explosives. The irony, Arik"—he was shouting now—"the irony of a bunch of Jews delivering explosives and modified drone parts, all smuggled into Israel by Hamas. Weapons fabricated by Hamas, transported by members of what might as well be the Jewish Hamas." A paste had collected on his lips, where it mingled with the snot running from his nose. "This is what it feels like, Arik, for your nation's guts to be turned inside out by your faraway enemies. Remember it."

Glitzman was now standing over Ghorbani, nose twitching. In Persian he said: "Names, Colonel. Now."

"We do what you've done to us," Ghorbani murmured.

Glitzman tapped the toe of his boot onto the photo, blotting out Ghorbani's son. "And I promise you, Colonel, that we'll do it right back."

Then, on Glitzman's command, together we manhandled Ghorbani and hijacked his struggling finger to unlock his phone. Glitzman dictated the message to me. It required a few tries because I was shaking so badly. I read it to Ghorbani, then handed the phone to Glitzman. His finger hovering above the keyboard, Glitzman began counting down from ten. I translated. When we got to three, Ghorbani told us to stop.

CHAPTER 63
Tehran

HE WROTE DOWN FIVE NAMES. He claimed that he did not know the phone numbers from memory, but Glitzman would find these in the files being looted downstairs. Where specifically? Glitzman asked. The safe in Ghorbani's office. Glitzman asked him who Hossein Moghaddam had been meeting in Istanbul and Ghorbani circled one of the names. Glitzman asked: He is IBEX? Ghorbani, momentarily confused, seemed keen to ask how Glitzman knew of IBEX, but he did not. He just nodded, then explained that IBEX was a Persian Jew with an American passport who'd been recruited in Turkey and sent to Israel, to live and work among the settlers. If Glitzman was surprised by any of this, it still did not show. He was note-taking like a mesmerized student, and in a few moments, the Tree knocked to say it was time to go.

I had expected Glitzman to say something at the end, perhaps a comment about Oriana, or his closing argument about who occupied the more righteous hill. But instead, Glitzman shoved his notes in his pocket, gathered up the photographs, and stood, leaving without a word. Outside, the Tree was calling for one of his men to join. I was alone with the colonel.

This should have been the climax of the spy story, the part where I had words for the defeated bad guy. I was going to tell Ghorbani that this was vengeance for Amir-Ali, that the good guys were winning. But instead I felt the futility of revenge, to say nothing of my guilt for Roya, and that insatiable thirst for atonement made me hate Ghorbani even more. I saw how absurd my words would be. As useless as trying to shame a lion for its kill.

The Tree and one of his operators shoved past me, lifted Ghorbani to his feet, and slid the hood back on his head. And then they hauled him out. Though I couldn't see Ghorbani's face, I pictured him smiling.

CHAPTER 64

Tehran

I STOOD THERE for a moment, and I imagined Amir-Ali alive again. A different life.

In this brief fantasy I am not preparing to flee Tehran forever. I have no foreknowledge of the strange aircraft that will soon fly over the city.

In my daydream Amir-Ali and I talk about the stories that will doubtless be circulating that evening about this strange pod. There'll be a citywide debate over whether it was the Jews or maybe aliens. Rumor moves through Tehran at light speed, plus there is no smog today, so there'll be loads of cell phone videos. There'll be other theories, too, endless chatter and conspiracy, that great Persian pastime. Some new toy for the mullahs flying through the sky? A gift from the Russian military? Maybe it was CIA. MI6. An Anglo-Saxon conspiracy. The Jews and the CIA and MI6, all in collaboration. No, no, wait—all of that, certainly, but that's an alien spacecraft, isn't it? Aliens are also working against Iran. We Persians are already surrounded by enemies, and now we've got to worry about the aliens. Amir-Ali and I would have a laugh over a few whiskeys, just like old times.

I knelt and picked up the picture of Alya, plucking the broken glass from the frame. I looked at her for a minute. Then I placed it back on the desk. Looked at it again. Was that where the picture had been? I did not think so. I tilted the angle a little, toward the window.

CHAPTER 65
Tehran

DOWNSTAIRS, Glitzman was calling my name. Passing the conference room—avoiding a glance at the unconscious Roya—I swept into the office where they'd stashed Major Shirazi and his two lieutenants. They were seated, hands bound, their backs to the wall. I stood by Glitzman, who was hungrily reviewing them as he might items on a grocery shelf. There was a gun in his hand.

Glitzman turned to me: "I want you to ask who was flying the drone here in Tehran. Who piloted it, and if that changed depending on the operation. I also want you to confirm they flew it from here, by satellite."

I put these questions to Shirazi, whose answer was to spit on my shoes.

Glitzman was unfazed. "Tell him if he doesn't answer, I am going to kill the man to his right."

I said this. Shirazi peered up at Glitzman in hateful defiance. Glitzman raised his gun and the lieutenant in the crosshairs began babbling about the operation, how he and the other guy helped with the computers, and technical issues, and Shirazi flew the drones, and he would be happy to tell Glitzman everything if he'd just let him go. Please! Please, let me go!

"Shut up, you fucking dog!" Shirazi commanded. "Quiet!"

And then the lieutenant was, because Glitzman shot him in the head.

Gore spattered across the wall and Shirazi's face. Then Glitzman shot the other lieutenant through the forehead. Then he put a round into Shirazi's foot.

The major screamed. His mouth was contorted, a bit of his tongue was lolling out, and I think he'd bitten through it. "I'd have done this to Ghorbani," Glitzman said. "But he's needed in Israel. And you were the one who pulled the trigger, as it were. The one who killed my friends. The one who killed my daughter."

Glitzman shot Shirazi in the knee.

Shirazi moaned, then, shivering in pain and rage, he cried out, "One less Jew, Glitzman! Your daughter is one less—"

Glitzman emptied the magazine into Shirazi's head. *Click, click, click.*

I stood there for a moment reviewing the carnage. In the moment it felt like a dream. I had never seen so much blood.

I looked at Glitzman. The gun was now down at his side. He was giving Shirazi's corpse a thousand-yard stare. Glitzman brought the gun up once more, aiming at what was left of Shirazi's head, and when he squeezed the trigger there was another click, and he gave the gun an agitated look, as if he'd forgotten that seconds earlier he'd gotten the same result. We left the room. Glitzman shut the door gently behind us, as if a business meeting were still going on in there. The Tree was looking hard at Glitzman—after all, there'd been a lot of gunfire.

"We had two spots on the Pod," the Tree said.

"We only need one," Glitzman said.

Outside, a chain saw snarled to life.

CHAPTER 66
Tehran

FRUIT IN SEASON is to Persians what wine is to a Frenchman, and now, out in the courtyard, two operators wielding small chain saws were committing a sin that in France would have been as grievous as pissing in a freshly uncorked bottle of Bordeaux: they were chopping down the fruit trees.

The satellite imagery had shown ample room for assembly and vertical takeoff, hidden from view inside the high walls of that courtyard, but only if the trees were felled. The fig and cherry trees had already succumbed. Morbidly fascinated by this unexpected yet tremendously insulting violation, I watched as they finished the mulberries, and hauled them off to the side. The neighbors might wonder about the noise, but they could not see in, and that would buy us the time required.

Then, from the bed of one of the pickups, two of the Tree's men hoisted up what appeared to be an aircraft fuselage. The cockpit had a tinted black windshield, and the whole thing was covered in a carbon-fiber-and-Kevlar composite, stretched tight over supporting bars like skin over the wing of a bat.

Next off the other pickup were what looked to be stubby wings, covered in the same material as the fuselage. Then two long aluminum rods coated in black oxide, followed by four smaller carbon fiber rods, each sporting two sets of rotors apiece. Felled trees aside, and though the scale was much larger, the courtyard was beginning to feel like a living room in the throes of boxed furniture assembly. Two of the operators inserted the longer aluminum rods through guide holes in the fuselage, and then they slid on one wing at a strange, downward angle before twisting it upward, locking it in place. While they repeated the process for the second wing, two other operators had begun fastening the rotors to the first, using a tool that resembled an electric torque wrench, but had most certainly been fabricated in Israel for this task alone. They repeated the same process on the second wing, and one of the operators began conducting mechanical checks on the eight rotors.

The courtyard was a frenzy: loading, unloading, clearing. And yet, there was no instruction manual, everyone knew their role. It was quiet except for the clink and thunk of drone components, the thud of metal on concrete, and the bursts of the torque wrench.

One of the operators had taken the pilot's seat—I saw now there were two seats in there, back-to-back. In Hebrew the pilot barked at a few of the operators who were gathered around a small opening cut into the fuselage. I could see a circuit board of some kind in there, along with a nest of wires. The Pod, an electric vertical takeoff/landing craft, powered on with a slight hum and the blink of small red lights on each rotor.

I watched, transfixed, as Ghorbani, now unconscious from a heavy dose of ketamine, was fitted with an oxygen mask, weighed on a rollaway, collapsible scale, and then slid into a box that, intentionally or not, resembled a coffin. Two of the operators, along with Rivka, were stuffing the computers and other hardware from Major Shirazi's room into another box, which was then weighed. Finding it overloaded, the Tree issued a few snappy directions. His operators removed two cabinet drawers and carted them into the newly available space in the bed of the pickup. Then they unbolted a panel on the back of the fuselage and slid the box with the documents and computers and files inside. Ghorbani, unconscious and oxygenated in his own box, went in next. One of the operators fastened the panel shut. The Pod held two prize boxes for exploitation back in Israel: one material, one human.

Once complete, the whole thing looked like a bat with stubby wings extended.

I had once seen a YouTube video of a joystick-operated drone that carried a single person over a forest. But it had not been stored in the bed of a pickup, unfolded, and assembled in about ten minutes, and it surely did not fly at three hundred kilometers per hour, as the Tree had said this would. Two C-130s were going to land on a sparse plain one hundred kilometers outside Tehran in about thirty minutes; Glitzman wanted Ghorbani and the most critical intelligence on the first bird, and he wanted them out of Tehran fast as they could fly. I saw Glitzman, on the satphone to Tel Aviv, passing along the names from Ghorbani's confession.

In the hubbub I ducked back inside to check on Roya. She was right where I'd left her, unconscious and flex-cuffed beside Mina in the conference room. Kneeling, I found her pulse normal, and I wondered again if she might be just fine. Someone was behind me. I turned. It was Glitzman, and I believe he was reading my mind.

"She heard Roya," I said, glancing at Mina. "Before she was drugged."

"What did she say?' Glitzman said.

"Roya recognized Rivka, mentioned the phony rescue in Istanbul."

"That's unfortunate," he said, and his tone had me thinking that he meant it. "You believe we should kill her? The analyst?"

I tried to feign surprise, but he had it right.

"And even if I did that," he said, "it goes badly for Roya either way. Why didn't they shoot you? they'll ask. They shot the other woman. She is clever, she might make up a story, but this . . . this is a terrible breach. She is going under the microscope, and she is going to crack. She'd probably crack even if she weren't guilty, but she knows she is, and so she'll crack even faster. They won't punish Alya if she cooperates. And she'll cooperate."

Glitzman put his hand on my shoulder while I watched her breathe and said: "Now let's walk away. There we go. One step at a time. There we go."

And we were outside in the courtyard, just in time.

Over the radio the Tree confirmed with Aryas and Kovan that all was clear, and the driveway gate, which we'd shut to conceal our work in the courtyard, began to creak open. Aryas hopped into his Hilux alongside Rivka and three of the assault team operators. Kovan took the other, alongside Glitzman.

It was to be the last time I saw Arik Glitzman, and though he'd successfully intuited my emotions that morning, I do not think he understood just how far gone I was. There was no parting missive; there was not even a last look. We were set to leave on separate exfil routes, after all. There would be time later to talk it all through. At the tinny hum of the rotors, I watched the Pod rise above the compound, bearing Colonel Ghorbani, unconscious in his black coffin. It levitated above the top floor for a fluttering moment, the rotor wash delicate, like the rustle of wind through the trees. And then it rocketed off, bound north, for a flight path away from the city, up near the base of the mountains. We'd been in the compound less than twenty minutes. When I turned back, Glitzman's pickup was gone.

I looked around the wrecked trees littering the courtyard. I looked back at the house. I should walk out the front door now, I thought. Get in the Toyota, drop it where I'd been instructed, and make for the exfil into Iraq.

I didn't know who it was back then, but at that moment Colonel Salar Askari's car bumped into the driveway. The gate had been closing but, sensor tripped, it now swung back the other way until it was open. My first impression of Askari was, I think, the essence of the man: a gate was shutting to a place where he was unwelcome, and still he drove right through.

I have lived plenty of moments in your prisons, General, in which I second-guess what I've done, wondering if there were other, wiser paths. But as I made my first eye contact with Askari through the windshield of his car, standing there among the felled fruit trees in that courtyard like some criminal lumberjack, I realized I had but one path in front of me. The way out was through, and that's where I was headed. I turned and ran inside.

CHAPTER 67
Tehran

I RACED INTO THE HOUSE and took up a spot behind a couch in a sitting room, where I had a clean view of the hallway leading to the back door. My heart was in a stampede as I unzipped my pack, reaching inside for the feel of gunmetal on my fingers. I fantasized that this new arrival might be a mere lookie-loo, curious about the drones that had shot from the courtyard like alien spacecraft, and that perhaps after a few rattles on a locked door he'd give up, maybe call the cops. The police move quickly for bribes and little else. I'd have an hour, maybe seven.

Askari had been sent to the house once before, he would tell me later—during some of his blade work—to deliver a message from you, General, to Ghorbani, but this had preceded our surveillance, and we'd never once seen him. That morning he was there, unannounced, to do the same.

The buzz and the click—he knew the code—had my fingers cold as the Makarov they were vibrating against and I was back in Albania, aiming a gun just like this, and it was shaking about as bad. I was on that range with Amir-Ali and the Kurds, and the brothers were ribbing me as I missed everything, our instructor was treating me to a withering headmaster's stare, and I was telling myself it was fine because in what possible circumstance would I need a gun? I'm a dentist, I would tell myself, with each hammering thump of a round hitting the sandbags wide of the target.

Askari stepped boldly into view. I was actually raising my gun to slide the barrel against my own skull. It was the one shot I wasn't likely to miss, the surest way to excuse myself from the unpleasantness to come. Askari, of course, interpreted this as a threat.

"Who the fuck are you?" he said. He raised his gun as I did the same, but I bumped into the couch, and was too slow.

Askari's first two shots went high, lodging into the wall behind me.

Turns out it's hard to kill yourself in the middle of someone else trying. Something instinctive must kick in, and you start to defend yourself even though a second earlier you and your assailant were practically on the same team. I got one shot off and it sent a spray of plaster from the wall, about a meter to the left of the colonel, who momentarily scrambled back into the entryway. Then, in one of those classically Askari moments, he began running toward me.

I popped my head above the sofa, brought up the gun, and squeezed off two more rounds, both of which went high. He dove up onto a staircase, clear of my sight line. For a few seconds nothing happened, then I said, in my most desperate military voice, "You are interfering in a Qods Force operation. We are under the command of Colonel Jaffar Ghorbani, and you will answer to him if you don't leave immediately!"

"Who the fuck are you?" he asked. "Where is the colonel? Where is everyone else?"

"If you don't get the fuck out of here," I commanded, fidgeting around with another magazine, though I did not yet need to reload, "you'll be answering to Colonel Ghorbani." I dropped the magazine, and as I watched it clatter onto the floor, I thought maybe I should give suicide another try.

"I'm a colonel, you motherfucker," he said, huffing for breath. "What happened to the trees out there?"

Two squelches on my radio, then my name murmured twice, *Kam, Kam*. Translation: *What the hell is going on in there?* I was about to respond when the colonel sprang out, gun raised, and fired another three rounds in my direction, again missing so high that a few of them shattered a chandelier hanging nearly two meters above my head. He swore and ducked back into the stairwell. Tile chips went flying when I put a few rounds into the floor at the foot of the stairs. Askari's curse made me wonder if he'd gotten a few shards in his eyes, and I decided to press my imagined advantage, abandoning the cover of the sofa to scooch along the wall until I reached the foot of the stairs, which were just around the corner. Even over the rocking adrenaline I'd seen that Askari was a terrible shot, worse than I am. I had a chance, however slim, to win this thing.

I could hear the creaky sounds of his weight on the stairs, and I thought he was ascending, near the top. But when I sprang around the corner, he was less than a meter from my face.

We both shot rounds past each other's heads.

I could feel the slurp of pressure from my ears, and then our shared shouts were swallowed by a high-pitched ringing. Askari bowled into me, the guns clattered onto the floor, and it was a scrum until I finally got a clean grip on his neck and started to choke the life out of him.

His eyes went wide, his face purpled, he was still trying to reach the gun for a shot into my chest, but this time I smacked it hard and clean with my free hand and it skittered farther across the floor. But that was all he needed: taking advantage of my distraction, he'd rolled off me, freeing his neck from my grip. I clambered to my knees, but he kicked my chest and I slumped back to the floor, where he pounced, mounting me, trying to choke me, but missing each time I deflected his large hands away from my head.

Frustrated, he began to pummel my face. I heard something crack, and then my mouth filled with the taste of blood. I reached over for his gun and nearly wrapped a finger around the barrel, but he caught me and dealt a hammer fist into my extended elbow, which sent my fingers spasming. But my other hand now had some room to work. I swung up for purchase on Askari's face and gripped his nose, careful to avoid his gnashing teeth, and then jammed at his eye, trying to wiggle it in there, as if I were a rock climber using that cavity as a hold to lift myself from the floor. Soon the pain was too much for him and he fell off me.

Dragging myself to my feet, I saw bloody fluid leaking from his face, running through the cracks in the cup of his hands. He looked at me and I looked at him. Then I stomped on the side of his head. There was a loud snap, and some blood pooled beneath his mouth. I hoisted my leg to stomp on him again, but my adrenaline had become too much, because I lost my balance and fell into the stairs, where I landed hard.

The commotion would have earned us plenty of attention, but the other living occupants of the house were, at that point, flex-cuffed and deep in their ketamine dreams. Things were quiet, except for my radio, where the squelches and murmurs meant Glitzman was going wild, demanding an update. He'd not heard any of the shooting, but someone in Tel Aviv could plainly tell that the Toyota was still on the street outside the compound, when it should have been long gone. Standing up, I felt a rush of blood to my head, I could hear my heart in my ears, and I thought I was going to faint. I put a palm on the wall to steady myself.

I slid two fingers to Askari's neck and registered the thin pulse. I considered putting a few rounds into his brain, for purposes of insurance. I even picked up my gun and pointed it at his head, but I could not bring myself to do it, General. I could not. I bound him up with flex cuffs one of the operators had discarded after the melee, smashed Askari's phone to pieces, dragged him into a bathroom, and shut off the lights, perhaps because in my mania I stupidly imagined he would sleep longer in the dark.

I could trace my movements to bind and stow Askari along the maze of bloody spatter I'd left in my wake. When I examined myself in a bathroom, I saw a man staring back who might have taken a few long drinks directly from a bowl of blood. It covered my nose and mouth and chin and chest, and now it was all over my hands. I rinsed off in a sink. Angry splotches had already appeared on my neck and face and I figured they would be blue-black in no time, but in the adrenaline rush I still felt little pain.

I did not know how long it would be before someone came looking for Askari, or any of the others, or if the Pod had been linked to the compound, or if a neighbor had called the police at the sound of chain saws biting through fruit trees in an otherwise tranquil Persian garden, but Askari's appearance at the house gave me an explanation I could use with Glitzman. Up to the gunfight, I'd not known what I would say. Now, for the first time, all I had to do was tell the truth.

CHAPTER 68

Tehran

I RAN INTO THE conference room and, though I knew Roya was there, the sight of her, unconscious and bound, still cut me deep. Like a childhood memory, or a great trauma, that image is still branded into my mind, and I know it never will leave.

I stooped down. Listened to Roya breathe.

There was a voice still at work inside me, and it said to run. Run! Think of yourself.

But I also knew that if I didn't do this, I was going to be so badly corroded on the other side that there wasn't going to be any point in getting there. How had it come to this, a world where the only good thing I could do was going to lead me straight through hell?

I hauled Roya up.

Then I slung her over my back and carried her out to my car. I was lucky. We passed only one old man who stared blankly at us and said nothing. The street was quiet except for him—he was still watching us—but I felt that stuffing her into the trunk might have him reaching for a phone to call the cops. In Tehran no one really *wants* to call the police, but decent people have their limits.

I gently slid Roya into the front passenger seat, and when I'd jumped in myself I positioned her head against the window, like she was sleeping. I caught my reflection in the side mirror as I backed out. My face was brick-red from Askari's blows; I wiped a spot of blood from the corner of my mouth. There were three dead Qods officers in the house, two unconscious, and one passed out in my car. Through the radio I heard Glitzman curse me, shouting for an update. Roya's head slid away from the window and I thought I heard mumbling. How much ketamine had they given her?

CHAPTER 69

Tehran

I PUT ROYA IN MY BED to sleep off the drugs, unable to work out a way to retrieve Alya without her mother present. Their apartment was empty—the girl was with her aunt—and I thought that meant we would have some time, though not much. If the ketamine did not wear off soon, things were going to get even more dicey. I flipped through several of the state-run channels, scanning for any alerts about Zionist infiltrators or kidnappings or flying spacecraft. Nothing, besides interviews with bitchy Tehranis complaining about food prices. I turned off the television, then shut door to the bedroom. I turned the radio back on.

I pushed the talk button twice and then said: *Arik, Arik, Arik.*

Within seconds Glitzman said, "What the fuck?"

"Someone showed up after you left. Right after."

"Who?"

"I don't know," I said. "Drove his car right through the gate, just as I was headed out. Said he was a colonel."

"And?"

"He's not in great shape."

"Is he dead?"

"He wasn't when I left."

The line crackled during a long silence, then: "You're okay?"

"I'm fine," I said. "Cuts and bruises."

"He saw you?"

"We fought."

"That wasn't my fucking question."

"He saw me."

I'd wondered if Glitzman might order me out to his exfil site, but that was foolish: he would not want my face and car speeding toward an Israeli C-130 landing strip outside Tehran. If I'd been made, he'd want me as far away from them as possible. I was a Jew, not an Israeli, and there was a bit of a pecking order to this exfiltration, even if no one ever said it.

"You're farther behind the Kurds than I'd like," he said, his tone bitterly angry. "You'll miss the car to Iraq."

And probably bring loads of attention along with you, he did not say.

"Your programmed exfil," he mumbled. "You've got what you need?"

"I do," I said.

"I'll let Tel Aviv know," he said. "Good luck."

I wished him the same, but there was no response. It was the last time I heard his voice.

THERE IS AN olive-green chair in the living room that, most unusual for a piece of Tehrani furniture, was fabricated in a warehouse outside Tel Aviv. I didn't use it much, for two reasons. One is that it wasn't very comfortable.

The other?

I threw off the seat cushion and searched the cambric for the six pins. Which was easy because after almost two years of use the spots were well-worn and, in a sloppy piece of tradecraft, visible to the naked eye. Any investigative team worth their salt would find this if they ran a deep scrub on me, but taking delivery of a new concealment device was a hassle, and I'd been putting it off. The pins were arranged in a hexagon— you compressed them in order, starting at the top left and working clockwise. *Snap. Snap. Snap. Snap. Snap. Snap.*

Pop.

I tugged away the cambric undercover and was staring at a safe with an electronic lock. I entered the combination and flung open the door. Inside were my passports (Swedish, Iranian, and the French one they'd made for me, just in case), along with stacks of rials and dollars and kronor and euros. I had not counted in a while but I figured in each currency I had maybe eighty million rials. Which would be enough for hotels and flights and all the bribes that were going to be necessary. A stripped-down medical kit. A Makarov pistol—never used. A few magazines. I slid what I could into the concealed compartments of my backpack, which were now bulging, and poorly concealed.

Back in my vacuuming stress haze I'd memorized the exfiltration details, so even though I had a card in the safe with the relevant information, I did not need it. The phone number had an Isfahan area code. Glitzman had told me that if you or your people ever dug into it, General, your investigation would turn up a tour operator and travel agency, Isfahan Excursions. I dialed and, as expected, no one answered. I was invited to leave a message.

"Hello," I said. "I would like to book your Silver Package. I've had some vacation time come up and I am keen for a tour. I'd like to do this as soon as possible. Please call me back at your earliest convenience."

Four cigarettes later, the call came through. "Hello?" I said.

"You called earlier about booking the Silver Package?" I did not recognize the male voice, but the accent was strange.

"I did. Do you have availability tonight?"

I heard a soft click, and then it was silent. I wondered if we had been cut off, until I heard another click and the sound of labored breath, as if in the interim the nameless voice had either sprinted up a flight of stairs or been shouting at someone.

"Can you please tell me why it is so urgent?" the voice repeated.

"I need a few days out of Tehran," I said. "Everyone here is breathing down my neck."

"Understood. Well, seeing as you already have a profile with us, we can arrange everything. Our guide will have a red sticker on the door of his Land Cruiser."

"I am looking forward to it," I said, and hung up.

I REMOVED ROYA'S FLEX CUFFS and dragged a chair over to sit by the bed until she stirred. I could give her another half hour to wake, then I would have to wake her. We had maybe six hours to reach the exfil site, maybe less; it's not wise to test the patience and goodwill of Azeri smugglers. Roya woke groggily after another fifteen minutes, blinking and rubbing the sleep from her eyes. Her mouth would have been dry and her head would have felt like someone had swung it into a wall. When she saw me sitting there, a look of pure loathing crossed her face. I would have seen that hate gleaming in her eyes, but they shot away from me to focus on the wall.

"Can you sit up?" I asked. "There is a glass of water on the table."

She did not reply, but after a few moments she did manage. The motion must have required some energy, because she stopped there, elbows on her knees, head in her hands, making a low pitiful groan while she rubbed her temples. "Where is Alya?" she asked.

"She is fine," I said. "She is still with Afsaneh. They think you are still at Niavaran. You have"—I checked my watch—"two hours until you said you would pick her up."

She took a sip of water. Then, with a frightful intensity, she flung the glass at me. It narrowly missed, popping against the wall like a firework. She seemed to be contemplating more violence, but, exhausted, she said: "I trusted you. I'm a fool. I trusted you."

"I know," I said.

"I am going to die," she said, her voice quavering. "They are going to find out what I've done—what you tricked me into doing—and they are going to kill me. I have no future. Alya has no future. We are done. We—" Her voice was cracking; she put a hand over her mouth as if this might steady her.

I picked a few shards of glass off my shoulder. "There is a way out."

"I'm not going anywhere with you. I am leaving. I need to get Alya. I—" Standing had not worked. She collapsed in a heap on the floor. I crunched across the glass, knelt down, and offered my hand. She smacked it away.

Leaving her there, I fished a few things from my backpack. The

Makarov. A magazine. And then the stacks of money. I arranged it on the bed. She had heaved her arms onto the mattress to pull herself up. When she did, I put the gun in her lap.

"Take it," I said. "Take it and shoot me."

By the way she looked at me, I could see that she wanted to. But she set it on the comforter and managed to stand. She went to the kitchen and poured herself a glass of water. She drank it all and then she filled another and drank that, too.

"Who are you, really?" she demanded, filling a third.

"I work for the Mossad."

"Your name?"

"It actually is Kamran Esfahani."

She didn't buy it, but she also didn't fight it. Or maybe she no longer cared. "What happened?" she asked. "What were they after?"

"They kidnapped Colonel Ghorbani. He will be taken to Israel."

She hurled the glass into the sink, then snatched another from a shelf and did the same. She put her head on the refrigerator door. For a moment I watched her hand slap the stainless steel, then she curled it into a fist and hammered, and hammered, and soon her hand fell limp and shook while she softly cried. I stood there. It was one of those long tense moments when all you can really do is stand there.

"How can I believe anything you say?" she murmured. "I don't believe you. I can't."

"You can't," I agreed. "But you were in that room. You saw what happened."

"I also saw you shoot two people in Istanbul," she said. "And that was fake."

"This time Colonel Ghorbani was there," I said. "Unless you think he was involved—"

"Enough!" she shouted. "I am leaving."

She started toward the door.

I put up my hand, shifted my body to block her path. "Hold on, I—"

CHAPTER 70
Tehran

SHE SLAPPED ME across the face. She stamped her heel into the top of my foot. She spat and it flocked me right above the eyes. She kicked my shins. I put my hand on her shoulders and she threw it off and landed another slap and I decided I wouldn't touch her again. She slapped me again. Again, and again and again, getting the hang of it, each one sharper than the last until my face was raw. I was reeling in pain, but I stood my ground, and my resistance enraged her. She shoved me, and my back slammed into the door. She did it again.

"Move!" she screamed. "Let me go."

I did not move. Instead I put my palms out, then my hands up. "Wait," I said. "Just wait. Just listen. Please. Please."

She balled up a fist and smashed it into my nose and there was more warm blood rushing into my mouth. I raised my hands higher, not even trying to block her. She drove another punch into my jaw and yelped as if she'd hurt her hand, and her next punch was soft and tentative, and on the delivery she screamed in pain.

Drawing closer to me, with her left hand she put jab after jab into my ribs until, exhausted, she grabbed my shoulders and tried to throw me away from the door. I braced myself and did not budge. When I looked down, I saw drops of blood splattered onto my carpet.

Roya took a step back and said, "You are a coward. You are a liar. You are an impostor. You are a traitor. You are the devil."

I dipped my head and stretched my hands higher, and this sign of defeat seemed to brighten her rage. She swung a glancing blow off my nose. Screamed and screamed until her screams became tears.

I knelt down in front of her. When I bowed my head, more blood *plip-plopped* onto the floor from my nose, and I saw that some was also dripping from her wrecked right hand. "We are going to die, aren't we?" Roya said.

"There is a way out," I said.

"Liar," she sneered. "You are a fucking liar."

"Not this time," I said. "Not anymore."

She lifted her hand to slap my face again, but, quivering in midair, instead she brought it to cover her mouth, and I thought she might be sick, but then her hands fell to her sides. She slumped her back into the wall and slid to the floor and brought her knees into her chest.

"What's your plan, Roya?"—still on the floor, on my knees, I was whispering, careful not to shout. I inched toward her. "Here is how I see it. The people back in the house are waking up around now. Mina heard you say you knew the Israeli woman, Rivka. There's no way around that now. No going back. Ghorbani has been kidnapped. Shirazi and his lieutenants shot. The house was looted. And you've admitted to recognizing one of the kidnappers."

"I can take Alya and go to the airport. Get out."

"Sure, you could. But the first thing Qods does when they find out what's happened is put your name on a list. They are going to put you on every watch list in the Islamic Republic. You think you fly out of Imam Khomeini on a commercial flight to Istanbul? No. They detain you at the airport. That window has closed."

"I could turn you in," she said.

"You could," I said. "And I would let you if it would help. But it won't. It'll make things worse. Because, as happy as they'll be to have me, it will raise tough questions for you. How did we meet? What did you think I was? Oh, you thought he was an Etela'at officer, did you? What did you do for him? They won't treat your treason differently just because you didn't think you were committing it."

"I could kill you," she said. "I should kill you."

"Gun is in the bedroom," I said. "But you'll be in the same spot, or worse."

"I hate you," she said. And then, standing, she hit me again.

CHAPTER 71

Tehran

MY FATHER WAS FOND OF saying that hate and love, being opposites of apathy, were in the end not so different. In that moment I must say that none of it rang true.

When Roya had tired of hitting me, and I had still not stood aside, she took a few steps back and said, "You are a liar. A liar! If you care at all for me and Alya, you would have left me there."

Some of my blood was on her hijab, her cheeks. "No," I said. "You would have died. Mina would have told the investigators what you said. And even if she'd been killed... well, what would they have thought? You were the only one who survived? What happened? They'd have hanged you in the end."

"You." She curled an accusing finger my way, and it was shaking horribly. "You could have told me earlier. You could have warned me. You could have stopped this."

What could I say to that? I could have stayed a dentist. Could have said no to Glitzman.

Could have, could have, could have.

"I'm sorry, Roya," I said. "I'm sorry."

She sat down in a chair, curled her arms across her chest, and, turning to the side, vomited across the floor. We were so deep down into the shit that neither of us even acknowledged it. Wiping her mouth, she put the heels of her hands to her forehead and sat, rocking slightly. I went to the sink to clean off my face. The rag was soaked red after one swipe across my nose and mouth. I fetched another and brought it into the living room, standing there, wondering if she was going to run, and deciding that this time I would not stop her. This time I would take it as her decision, now that she had the facts.

"Why are you doing this?" Roya whispered. "Why did you bring me out?"

Even if I'd been able to explain it then, there was simply no more time. We had to go get Alya. "I don't know," I said, dabbing the cloth over my clawed cheeks.

The look she returned was the most complicated emotion I have ever seen on someone's face, and even now, years later, I am unsure how to describe it other than to say it was a jumble of hope and hate. Whatever you might call it, I believe it revealed a grim reliance on me, the man who had betrayed her and now, for reasons she could not comprehend, was neck-deep in an attempt to bail her out.

CHAPTER 72
Tehran

THE EXFIL PLAN gave us six hours to reach Chalus, up north on the Caspian. Standing in our way was the big fucking problem that, since Roya was up, the drugs worn off, that meant Askari and Mina were probably also awake and making a racket, if they hadn't already managed to break free. It would not be long before we had company. We had to leave.

I abandoned the Toyota van in my apartment parking garage and we took the Peugeot. On the way to her sister's she rode in the backseat and we did not speak because there was nothing to say—her presence was her decision, as was mine. I was thinking about what might be waiting for us at her apartment. Officers dispatched to find her would not be geared up for a massive shoot-out, but there would be at least a few of them, and they would doubtless be armed, even if lightly. I pulled to the side of the street beside a tree-lined median a few blocks south of her sister's apartment and put my head to the wheel for a moment. The afternoon had brought the smog, and I sucked in a huge breath of Tehran's toxic air: all exhaust, no relief. Ahead, on the busy corner, was the café I'd picked.

"Text her now," I said.

I was not checking to see what Roya was texting, and I didn't watch over her shoulder. She could have been sending an SOS, but this whole thing would not work if I were her captor. At some point she had to believe me; she had to feel that even though a man has lied to you constantly, it does not mean that his next words are a lie. I felt that back in my apartment we'd reached an unspoken compact in which her trust had been extended, on credit, until she'd reached safety, at which point not only would it have run out, but I'd still be deep in her debt.

After a minute Roya said: "She's coming down."

"Remember," I said, "if anyone tries to take you, you point back toward the café and scream and say I've kidnapped you." Quite honestly, I believed she would do this anyway, regardless of whether anyone appeared.

Roya went first. I followed, searching for any telltale signs of surveillance—black Peugeots, white vans, militias on patrol. There were black sedans with government plates parked up on a curb but they were empty. Could be Etela'at officers out for lunch. Could be something far worse...

I went into the café, milling around, trying to keep tabs on her out near the street. I checked windows in the building opposite, I listened for the screech of brakes, though in Tehran that was far more likely to indicate a car wreck than a surveillance van peeling out from the curb. Roya's arms were folded across her chest while she paced back and forth. She was not on the phone. She was not running. Even at a distance she appeared frantic. At the sight of Alya, she waved, and I thought she might cry, or run through the crowded traffic for the girl. But Roya, who had now lived through more than a few traumas, was cool enough under the pressure to stand still and wave back with an admirably nonchalant smile. Using the window's reflection, I slicked down the yet again churned-up waves of my hair. I did not want to frighten the girl, though I barely recognized myself.

Roya and Afsaneh spoke for a moment, in one of those conversations that means nothing to one person, and everything to the other. Alya tugged at her mother's manteau, the stuffed pink lamb swinging in her grip. Whatever Afsaneh's concerns about her sister's strange request to meet on this corner, whatever fear she may have seen playing across Roya's face, in a moment they hugged, and I saw that Roya's embrace was pulling at her sister's manteau, and they hung there until Afsaneh, smiling worriedly, pulled back and squeezed her sister's arms in assurance of something that I do not think either of them could name. Afsaneh kissed Alya and headed back across the street. As happens with so many moments that are actually goodbyes, I do not think Roya ever got to say one.

Roya stooped down and hugged her daughter tightly and her body convulsed, though when she stood her face was dry, and Alya was still smiling. They began to walk my way, and in a moment had passed the café, headed back toward the car. Alya was bouncing on her heels; it looked like she was singing.

I followed them to the car; I did not think we had surveillance on us yet. I also knew that, depending on the size of the team, I'd only know when it was far too late. Within sight of the car, where they were waiting, I spotted Alya and waved.

"The magician!" she squealed, raising the lamb, which I now recognized as the one that had eaten dinner with us at their apartment. The one she'd been carrying on the evening of her father's murder, the one Glitzman had viewed through a scope.

We hopped into the car. I drove, Alya and Roya sat in the back; there would be no distance from her daughter on the journey ahead.

"You are hurt?" Alya asked, pointing into the rearview mirror with a worried frown. I had a look. My nose was bleeding again.

CHAPTER 73

Tehran

WE DROVE NORTH from their neighborhood through the grinding crush of Vali Asr Square. The shops were open and bustling, the air drowning with the buzz and growl of engines, thick with choking exhaust. The sky above us was leaden now. Roya and I did not speak, but Alya chattered at a nonstop clip, demanding I finish the story about Joseph. "Soon," I said, "soon. The traffic. The traffic is terrible."

But the usual tangle on the roads that day unwound for a few brief and beautiful moments: I weaved and danced through the lanes, gaps opening across Vali Asr as if by providence. Around Fatemi Square, after we had turned westward, we ground back into a clot of traffic and honks on the Jalal Ale Ahmad. We crept along the highway, my heart thumping at a beat precisely inverse to the speed of my car. Through the rearview I saw the hairs that sprang from Roya's hijab were damp and spongy, as if she'd just emerged from a shower and neglected to dry off. The anxiety had us both moving constantly: shifting in our seats, grabbing handles, toying with our hands.

In the backseat Roya began to recite, in a low hum, this Rūmī, which Maman had read to me, and which had been passed down just so across the sweep of Persia for a thousand years:

Our desert has no bound, and our hearts and souls no rest
World within world has taken Form's image; which of these images is ours?

When you see a severed head in the path rolling toward our field—

I completed the verse while turning left: "Ask of it, ask of it, the secrets of the heart: for you will learn from it our hidden mystery."

"I am the severed head," she said.

"No," I said, though I didn't get any further than that because whatever I'd added would have surely been a lie.

"I am the severed head," she muttered again with a glare. "But I don't know anything, much less the secrets of the heart."

"I'm hungry, Maman," Alya said.

"In a bit, my sweet. In a bit"—this to her daughter, then she leaned forward and said to me, "I'm going to be sick."

"Hungry!" Alya yelled.

My nerves were also cracked. I was swirled in smog, jammed in Tehrani traffic, on the lam from the police and Qods and probably a few more security organizations I didn't even know about. And now we had a toddler howling about a snack. Like that head, we'd rolled to a dead stop. I'm hungry! I'm hungry! Hungry! Roya rolled down her window and vomited.

The sight of her mother retching yanked Alya from her tantrum. "Maman? What's wrong?"

"Nothing, dear. Mama is fine."

"Little ick?"

"Little ick, yes, sweetheart."

I am a natural pessimist—I have yet to meet a Persian who is not—and I had to assume the airports would soon be shut, the major roads in and out of Tehran clotted by checkpoints. The border guards would have her picture, and instructions, both of which would reduce the likelihood of skating through with a bribe. Not that our route was official. But a crew of Azeri smugglers running *shisheh* through the Caspian under cover of a crabbing operation were not, and are not, my idea of trusted associates.

Near the amusement park I exited Sheikh Fazlollah and cut north, away from Mehrabad Airport on Bakeri, hoping that the security presence might be less muscular up in the tony northern suburbs. Wind brought more smog and the sky was the color of concrete, same as the squatty buildings all around us, jutting into the air like anarchic teeth.

"Your nose again," Roya said, eyeing the rearview from the backseat.

I snatched a napkin from the console and tried to stanch the bleeding. We crossed Jafari and I saw the first checkpoint of the day, snarling the westbound traffic. It was manned by Basiji in their day clothes, a mishmash of shirts and jeans. And the checkpoint was fresh because they were still hauling out sawhorses, cones, and lights from one of the vans. Roya looked sick again; I felt sick. Alya had fallen asleep.

I exited on Sharabiyani, near the sports complex, and said, "From now on its side roads. And it'll be even slower."

We crawled through north Tehran in a tedious zigzag, snaking westbound whenever we could, the mountains looming over us while folding into banks of smog. The sound of sirens, which was frequent, made us jump. Once or twice we crept past parked police cars and I would swear that for those awful minutes neither of us would breathe. At times I was numb; at others I felt my heart was running so hot it would explode.

"I'm sorry," I said, climbing some nameless street north of Chitgar, "I want you to know that I am sorry. I don't want you to say anything, I just want you to know."

And she complied. She did not respond; she only looked at me and I honestly, even now, cannot say the first thing about what it meant. Alya blew raspberries as she snoozed. Roya stared out the window.

Skeletal cranes rose into the sky as the sun began to set. The new apartment towers did not gleam or shine; they were the same dull gray as the clouds.

I was hoping the sky would clear for one last look at the Alborz on our way out of the city. I knew the curve and bend of those mountains as I had known the cracks and creases of my father's face before his death, and I wanted one more look. Every moment holds a death, doesn't it? You lose something, even if it is only time. But in some moments you lose far more than that. I never did get that last look. We turned north and the mountains were quickly behind us, lost forever behind the smog and the clouds. That was when we hit the checkpoint.

CHAPTER 74

Tehran / the Chalus Road

I INSPECTED MY FACE in the mirror while we waited our turn and wondered if I was going to need an answer for the welts, bruises, and cuts staring right back. We were maybe twenty cars from the checkpoint, which I thought was manned by regular police, but from this distance it was hard to say for sure. Could it be the Revolutionary Guards? If it was, we were done. Roya was attempting to fix her makeup, but I wondered if it was doing more harm than good; her hands were shaky and she kept dropping her brush.

"If they separate us," I said, "you tell them I kidnapped you. You tell them you heard me speaking in a foreign language to someone on my phone. You tell them about Colonel Ghorbani and Major Shirazi. Understand?"

The left corner of her mouth was twitching, as if it were reaching for her ear. "I don't understand anything," she said.

Good talk, I thought, craning my neck out the window for a better look. Two cars were parked on the left side of the road; the third, with two officers still in it, probably drinking tea and mocking the line of traffic, sat off on the right. They were definitely police, not Etela'at or the Guards or the Basij or the Guidance Patrol. Police were always hungry for a few extra rials, so I dipped my hand into the Peugeot's console where I kept cash for satisfying their appetites. This was (hopefully) a more workaday payoff, maybe just a few bucks, no more than a speeding ticket, which in Tehran is dirt-cheap. I felt for the Makarov stuck just under my seat—the metal was oddly comforting on my fingertips, even though, as I counted what looked to be six officers, I realized it was going to be suicide to use it. Or, maybe, that's exactly why I was reassured.

Three cars back now. Roya folded every strand of her hair inside her hijab. The sweat from my hands had turned the steering wheel to slime. Luckily I had on a light jacket, because I could feel it pouring like a secret faucet from my armpits. You've got this, I told myself, look at what you've accomplished already today. The thought of defeating Colonel Askari momentarily bucked me up, but then I looked back and saw Alya, and my heart sank. Roya had applied her lipstick badly, smearing it into one corner of her mouth. She handed me her national identity card.

One car back now. Was this a dragnet for us? Or a run-of-the-mill roadblock searching for contraband, bribes, or merely something to do? There were no sawhorses or cones—just two policemen lazily clutching machine guns set off to the side, the other two in the road conducting the search. I had so many stories rushing through my head I could barely hear my own thoughts. Roya's face was sickly pale. I was manufacturing lies by the second and eventually decided I would tell them she was sick because she was pregnant. She was in the back because Alya wanted to rest on her lap. Whose child was it? Maybe I was the father. Maybe I was the uncle. I yanked my left sleeve up a few inches so he could see my Rolex. I balanced my wrist on the window as it rolled down.

I pulled forward.

"National cards," the policeman said.

The watch jangled on my wrist as I slid our documents into his palm. "Wait here," he said, after he'd pretended to look them over.

Not what you want to hear, but not necessarily the end of us, either. Roya feigned a thin smile as the police officers peered inside the car. Were they running the names and photos through a database?

I could see her chest heaving even beneath her manteau.

"Wipe the sweat from your lip," I hissed. "Pretend you have an itch."

I had become deadened to the smell of us but it could not have been a pleasant one—the putrid stink of fear filling the car across three hours of zigzagging the streets of Tehran, waiting for the net to fall around us.

I was better prepared for it than she was—and it was not my daughter in the backseat—but I still found my skin crawling as we sat there, the dusk sky brightening momentarily with the emergence of a pale aluminum sun from behind the veil of clouds. I suspect we sat for only two, maybe three, minutes waiting for that policeman to return, but in that tight space I considered, again and again, whether it would be best for Roya to shout that she had been kidnapped.

The policeman handed me the documents. Bent down and looked at Alya sleeping the backseat. "She is your daughter," he said. It was halfway to being a question. But I caught him looking at my watch.

"My niece," I said. "Her daughter."

"Step out of the car," he said.

I thought of the gun, but then I did as he asked.

"Open the trunk," he said.

Scream, Roya, I thought. If this goes wrong, you scream.

He searched the trunk, then unzipped my pack. The cash was in a concealed compartment, but anyone with a hankering and a good knife would find it eventually. Plus I saw over his shoulder that there were strange bulges and the concealed compartments weren't so concealed anymore. He tossed the clothes, first-aid kit, and granola bars across the bed of the trunk, confusion spreading across his face. He took a step back, thumb on his chin, and contemplated this strange haul as if he were delivering a verdict on a painting. "This is interesting," he said.

"I like to be prepared," I said. "Good to be prepared."

"We will need to have a closer look at everything," the policeman said. "You can pull over there"—he motioned to the other police car.

"Of course," I said. "But might you accept a tip for working late? And to expedite the review?"

From my pocket I produced what I thought was a reasonable bribe from a wealthy Tehrani. The amount mattered. Too small, and this got worse. Too large, and he would wonder what I was hiding, and whether he might ask for even more. The sight of the bills in my hand narrowed his eyes to contemplative slits and I worried I'd found the one honest cop in Tehran. Then he smiled. Like a magician (respect, where it is due), he deftly slid the cash into his coat pocket—the essential sleight of hand of the Iranian policeman. Under no circumstance could his colleagues know the true amount. When they settled up later, over tea, everyone would claim they'd received half of what they had. He was packing my bag up for me. My heart was settling back into my chest. He shut the hatch.

"Have a nice day," he said, and I am sure he meant it.

We drove on and for some length of the journey it felt as though we were driving through a dream and then we were on the Chalus Road, bound north over the swell of the Alborz, toward the sea. My father had died on this road, he'd been alive when we'd entered a tunnel and when we came out the other side he'd slumped into the window and by the time I pulled over he was gone. Still, I found the road beautiful. A Persian should hope to die ensconced in the mountains.

CHAPTER 75
The Chalus Road

BY NIGHTFALL WE MADE Siah Bisheh, the tiny throughway on the march to the Caspian, no more than a few shops and restaurants. I bought snacks and drinks while Roya and Alya found a bathroom. Above me hung the dark outlines of the mountains. Roya buckled Alya into the backseat and we set off again. From nowhere Alya said: "Can you finish the Joseph story?"

I looked back at Roya, who had her head slumped into the window. The psychotic adrenaline rush that accompanies the feeling of being hunted (or hunter, for that matter), is finite. At some point your body stops producing the endorphins necessary to hustle your way through the dark jungle. You sit down, rest, hope you don't die. That's where Roya was, and I wondered if she had even heard the girl. The chain of streetlamps above the highway did not burn brightly enough for me to see her face. Only in the tunnels could I see what she might be thinking. Now I wondered if she might be asleep.

"Joseph," I said. "Right... what was happening when we stopped? Do you remember?"

Alya thought about that, and so did I.

"His papa was sad," she said.

The road cut into another tunnel and light played across Roya's face. Her eyes were wide open. Her mind, I thought, would have caught up with the facts by now. She was alive. She had her daughter. And she was never going home.

"Ah," I said. "Yes. Joseph was gone."

"THAT CARAVAN," I SAID, "had taken him to Egypt."

"Where's Egypt?"

"Far away. And in Egypt, Joseph went to work in the household of a very important official. Joseph did a great job, but soon the official's wife wanted Joseph to do something bad, and—"

"What did he want Joseph to do?"

"Ehh... give her a big kiss."

"That's bad?"

"They weren't married." I checked her expression in the mirror. This seemed to have worked. "And Joseph wouldn't do it, and the official's wife was so mad that she made up a lie about Joseph, and he went to jail. Joseph had always been able to tell people what their dreams meant. And so when he was in jail, other prisoners would tell him their dreams, and he would interpret them. One of those prisoners was the personal servant to the king of all Egypt. Joseph told him what one of his dreams meant, and later, after the servant got out, he told the king."

"The king had dreams?" Alya asked.

"He did," I said. "He had a weird dream about seven skinny cows eating seven fat cows."

"What?" Alya shrieked. "That's crazy."

"It was crazy. And what it meant was that there was going to be seven years where everyone would have a lot of food, but then there was going to be a famine... that means there wasn't going to be much food at all. And Joseph told the king that they should store up food in the plentiful years so they could eat in the bad, and the king was impressed with Joseph, and he made him a very powerful man."

"Like a mullah?"

"Yes," I said, "just like the mullahs. Except Joseph didn't steal." I winked into the mirror, but this had gone over her head: she only blinked back.

"And sure enough," I said, "just as he had dreamed, there were seven years of lots of food, and then there was a famine. But there was food in Egypt because of Joseph's plan. However, back where his brothers and father were, there was no food. So Joseph's father sent his brothers to Egypt to get some. And when they got to Egypt, they went to meet with Joseph at the palace, but so many years had passed, they did not recognize him. And you know what? They bowed down to him, just like in the dream he'd had, back when he was young. And they asked for food."

Alya was mumbling sleepily from the backseat: "Does Joseph kill them?"

"Kill them?" I asked. "What do you mean?"

"The brothers hurt Joseph. They're mean. Tried kill him. Made him go away."

"They did," I said. "They did."

She went on, mumbling something, drifting further toward sleep.

I am a bad Jew and maybe a worse son, because I was forgetting how Maman landed the story. I was open to suggestions. A palace shootout wasn't the worst idea. Maybe he poisons the sacks of grain. Joseph slaughters his brothers for what they'd done. There was a grim finality I found appealing from the standpoint of finishing quickly.

Then I asked Alya, "Do you think Joseph should kill his brothers for what they did?"

The little girl had fallen asleep.

WE REACHED CHALUS after midnight, right on time. I pulled the car off the main road, bouncing into an empty lot behind a beachfront hotel, its white stone glowing pale in the shrouded moonlight. It was not quite the high season, and there were only a handful of cars. I pulled up next to a Land Cruiser and saw a small red sticker taped to the driver's-side door. Roya and Alya were still asleep. I got out and knocked on the door. After a few raps the guy shook awake. He kicked the engine to life and rolled down the window. He was a squat man with a jowly face covered with stubble. His hair was thin and wavy and he had the red wrinkled nose of a professional alcoholic. His eyes, however, were very kind.

"I'm looking for Aslan," I said.

When he sat up, a collection of trash crinkled at his feet, and he smacked the red sticker on the door.

"There are two more," I said. "They are asleep in the car."

Aslan frowned. "Two?"

"Two more," I said. "Three total."

"Well, that's a problem."

From the south, back down the main highway, I could hear a faint blare of sirens rising above the crash of the waves. Aslan's eyes widened as the sound grew louder.

"We need to get onto the beach," Aslan said.

CHAPTER 76
Chalus

THE BEACH WAS ROCKY, the tide low, the sky moonless. Glitzman's planners would have considered the weather perfect for an exfiltration. That camouflage of darkness should have lifted my spirits, but its vastness unsettled me, interrogating every decision I had made, back to and including my first chat with Arik Glitzman in my dental chair back in Stockholm, years ago. To call it despair would be an understatement: I was so drained of life, so morally exhausted, that I seriously contemplated having a seat on a rock and waiting until they arrested me. Roya and Alya were the only reasons I kept moving, and even those were just barely enough.

All the way down to the beach I had been arguing with Aslan: he would not bring the boat ashore with the authorities tightening the noose around us, and no, there was no bribe I might offer to compensate him for the risk of his certain death. The baying of sirens filled the air. Chalus was not a large place, and I suspected they'd found the Peugeot by now, and probably Aslan's truck. He could bill Mossad for that loss, but still, he was not amused. Cigarettes and *shisheh*, he kept muttering, they don't cause such problems. We hid in a pile of rocks.

Alya had begun screaming during the descent to the beach, sensing her mother's own terror and hearing the pounding of unseen waves. I had only seen such fright in a child once: Magnus, six years old, ten teeth pulled in a single appointment, and judging by his screams we'd misjudged the anesthesia. I held the girl tight, slid my hand over her mouth, and said, "Do you remember the story, how Joseph was brave when he was sold into Egypt?"

Alya had stopped shouting, but she was shivering horribly. Eyes locked elsewhere, on nothing. She could not muster a nod.

"He was brave," I said. "He just kept on going. And he was alone. You are not alone."

I didn't yet hear the slap of boots on the pavement above, or the murmurs of Guards or police or border patrol running their dragnet, but they were close, they had to be. They must have connected me to Roya, or Niavaran, and then found my Peugeot traveling north. How many cameras had we passed on the way? Too many to count.

I handed Alya to Roya. In spitfire Azeri, Aslan finished a call on his satellite phone. I'd caught none of it, but the tone was dour, and his eyes betrayed his thoughts, darting as they did from the rocks up to the furrow of another small path. I could not blame him. There was much to be said for abandoning us to our fate.

The bricks of cash appeared from my bag. I counted out twenty thousand American and then its equivalent in rials. I slapped ten thousand euros on top of it, and unclasped my watch. Like Papa, I thought, I'm going to die in Iran, I just won't have the watch. All of it went onto Aslan's lap. "I expect the Rolex will go for decent money in Baku," I said. "It was my father's. From the days of the Shah."

Blinking, Aslan rubbed his stubbly beard. He looked at Roya and Alya. He'd called the boat off, but now circumstances had changed, what with the watch and the cash bricks, and he was thinking through whether it offset his concern that we all might die or, worse, be captured. Above us, near the hotel, I heard the voices. The din of the sea made it impossible to tell how many they were, but what was certain was we were seriously outnumbered.

Aslan picked up the satphone. We all huddled together by those rocks while he made the phone call that would decide if we lived or died. Alya was shivering wildly and Roya had curled them both into a ball, arms wrapped around her daughter.

When Aslan hung up he said, "We will bring the boat in, but I will need the rest of it."

You always hold some in reserve until you are certain it is the bridge to yes. I rummaged through my pack, unzipped one of the concealed pouches, and handed Aslan the last twenty thousand American dollars. He thumbed through it and then, satisfied, zippered it inside his waterproof satchel with the rest of the cash, the gun, and his phone. As with pilots and surgeons, anxiety is not what you want to see drawn in the lines of your smuggler's face, but Aslan wore his fear brightly. I'd conscripted him into a real jam. There was no way around it.

"There is one more thing," I said, and I pulled him in tight for a whisper.

Did he hear me? In any case, he shook his head.

The voices above us were closer now. I could not tell if they'd started down to the beach, but if they had not, it would not be long. I heard a gunshot up there, or maybe it was the slam of a car door, and within seconds sirens were blasting again.

I whispered the instructions once more.

Aslan shook his head violently, but his voice, and our argument, was swallowed by the crash of the waves.

A gunshot cracked through the night sky. I extended my hand and Aslan shook it. I know that for Persians—and here I would lump in Azeris, who wish they were Persians—commitments come and go, that Aslan would not hesitate to give me his assurances, only to break them minutes later if convinced by the arguments of a gunsight or, perhaps, a fine knife. In his mind this would not be contradictory; there would be no betrayal. Circumstances change. The truth—in Iran such things do not set you free. But he shook my offered hand and that promise was as good as I would get.

"You follow me," Aslan said. He looped his pack over his back and tightened the straps. "The tides are strong tonight. The swimming will be hard. But not far."

I stripped off my jacket. Roya shed her manteau. We each tied our shoes together and looped them over our necks. The Caspian is famously brutal—Papa told me once that a member of Iran's Olympic team had drowned in it. We were going to need some luck.

"We are going into the water, Alya," Roya said, "for a little swim."

The little girl shook her head, and I was relieved I could not quite see her eyes.

I knelt down to her. "I am going to carry you on my back, okay? You hold on to my neck and do not let go."

I got a little terrified nod of acceptance.

I looked at Roya and she looked at me and the moment was stuffed so full that words would not fit. I took Alya in my arms and ran my hands comfortingly through her hair and Roya did not argue, did not fight. I hoisted the girl onto my back and helped her clamp her arms around my neck. Aslan went first, darting out across the rocks and sand, Roya right behind.

Then I ran. With Alya on my back, I ran.

I did not even feel the water when I reached it, running full-bore, fighting to stay upright and trudge through the stinging chill of the tides. Alya was breathing heavily in my ears. Roya was shouting. My thigh banged into a rock and later I would find it had punctured my leg, but then I felt only dull pressure, no pain. When the water reached my neck I began to shove my feet off the bottom for power, bouncing toward the surface for clean pulls of air, holding Alya's arms so tightly it is a wonder they did not break.

Each time I sank down, the currents beneath us surged, tugging me away from Aslan and Roya, who were farther out to sea. My head dipped under as a wave rolled over us, and Alya began to slip from my grip. I clutched her tight around my neck, pinning her arms to my chest. I kicked off the bottom, and when we broke to the surface I hacked up seawater and Alya was gurgling now, coughing, but breath—any breath, no matter how strained or weak—was a godsend and we went right back under, and when we came up again I tried to tread water for a moment and saw that spotlights were brightening the sea. Roya's head above water, she was paddling beside us now, her eyes wide with fright, like prey. She was shouting for Alya, Alya for her mother. Where was Aslan? Where was the boat?

From the beach came a crackle of gunfire. All I could see was Roya and the inky layers of the horizon, all painted a different shade of purple and blue and black. Aslan was gone. He'd been drowned, shot, captured, he'd abandoned us—I did not know. Another volley of gunfire hit the water around me like gravel thrown against a window. Roya yelped and began to flounder. She was screaming, and then water filled her mouth, and she was gurgling, and then...

The last I saw of Roya Shabani was the crown of her head dipping under the water, cords of hair swirling behind it. And she was gone.

I was having a hard time staying above the water myself. Your doctors told me that I was shot twice, General. Once in my upper back. The second time in my right knee, which had been kicking just below the surface.

While water poured into my mouth and lungs, my ears filled with Alya's gurgles and desperate cries. For a moment I could not see her, I heard only this, and it was so very soft: "Maman, Maman, Maman! Maman..."

Given that I was shot in the back, I believe that Alya must have been, too. The bullet probably struck her lung, because, though she was trying to shout, she did not have the air to do so. She drifted in front of me. Along with the life, the terror was draining from her eyes, and the last time I saw her she almost looked sleepy. I tried to put my hand out for her, but a wave crested above me, and when I came back up, Alya was gone.

My eyes were wide open, but the sea was a black wall. I never found them. I never saw them again.

In my delirium I thought of Joseph and his brothers, about who deserved to die.

And, as always, across every story I've ever written, I wind up here, at its one and only end.

The Interrogation Room
Location: Evin Prison, Tehran
Present day

THE GENERAL SHAKES HIS empty teacup toward the camera hung in the corner of the interrogation room and holds up two fingers.

How many times has he read this story?

A hundred, perhaps, a hundred times in the three years since they'd dragged this traitorous scum, near death, from the sea. And this is the last time. The General can scarcely believe it.

He lights a cigarette, leans back in his chair, and flicks a smudge of ash from his pants. The prisoner, as is his custom, folds his hands on the table and waits to speak until someone speaks to him. This was one of the first lessons the General taught him, and it has stuck.

The General has read every word of this final testimony—the stack of papers dwarfs his teacup—to say nothing of the boxes and boxes of case files. The General personally writes most of the reports sent to the Leader and the Supreme National Security Council. He understands why this is happening, but he does not have to like it.

Kamran Esfahani belongs to me, he thinks. The man is my property.

The General and Kamran have maintained a one-way intimacy impossible outside of the relationship between jailer and jailed. And because of that, depending on the day, the General either loves or hates him, and sometimes both at once. Today he is not so sure. Today he feels something more surprising: sadness. I will miss Kamran a little when he is gone, the General thinks. The days will be a bit more boring.

The General taps the stack of papers. "No more writing. We're done."

The prisoner is disappointed, he thinks, but he confirms with a nod and treats himself to another look around. "Where am I, General?" the prisoner asks, a question he put to the General three months earlier, when, at the Leader's direction, they'd begun this final testimony. The General, magnanimous in these last minutes, feels compelled to answer. And why not? Kamran's time is up.

"Evin Prison," the General says.

The tea arrives, carried on a tray by one of his aides. Two cups smelling of saffron, and piping hot. This is the second time the General has shared tea with the prisoner, and its arrival seems to have destabilized the man. His eyes have widened, he has licked his lips. And yet he also regards it with fear, believing—not wrongly—that this luxury is possible only because it is his last.

The prisoner sips gingerly at first. His throat, the General recalls, is still tender thanks to a rough strangling delivered by Colonel Askari. The prisoner's hair was dark; it is now washed charcoal-gray. And he now has a deep fear of water; he dealt poorly with the simulated drownings they had conducted during the heady first months of captivity, when the General hoped he might lead them to more Israeli spies. At the sight of the tanks or water buckets the prisoner usually urinates and the doctors say he will never swim again, not because of the broken bones, but because he will refuse to enter the water.

But judging by his latest confession, Kamran remains a person. A human! The General finds this astounding, and profoundly agitating.

Some days the General chalks this up to sociopathy, others to a store of resilience, certainty, and moral courage that he finds foolish, but admirable. In the early days, when the General had pressed the psychologists for a clinical answer, all they'd managed was to sniff that the prisoner exhibited *characteristics consistent with functional (i.e., constructive) narcissism.* "So he's a Persian, is what you're telling me," the General would say, and after that he blocked the shrinks from accessing the case.

At first the General was disappointed. He failed to break a man! But slowly his frustration has matured to wonderment at the sight of the man's soul blinking through his eyes. He has kept it. All along the prisoner has kept his soul. Sometimes, though the General never says this aloud, he wonders if captivity was required for the man to find one at all.

The General pops a sugar cube into his mouth and pulls on a long sip of the tea until he cannot feel his tongue. Then he says: "There is one last question I will put to you."

Kamran dips his chin toward the General.

"Why did you try to save them?"

"I had a change of heart."

"But why?"

"I don't know."

The General's eyebrows shoot upward, and his tongue clicks against the back of his teeth to register disapproval. Over the years it has become less common for mentions of Roya and Alya Shabani to affect the prisoner. Evidence: he has managed to write the final part of his testimony and confession without much emotion. But now the General sees a shadow cast over his face. The man is doubtless back in the Caspian, searching for them, his back and leg shot to pieces, bleeding to death while he slides into hypothermic shock. There are no tears, there never are with Kamran Esfahani, but there is a sad softness that settles over him like a mist. They look at each other for a moment.

"You really cannot say it, can you?" the General says, and the prisoner answers by snatching a retaliatory sip of tea, wincing, and rubbing his throat. They look at each other again.

"I could have finished the op, the con, whatever you like," Kamran says. "But I found out I didn't want to. I felt I should listen to that little voice, whatever it was, whatever it said."

"Maybe you shouldn't have," the General says. "Look where it landed you."

"Maybe," the prisoner agrees. "Maybe not."

The General's phone buzzes, and he scowls at the number. "We're done," he says, standing.

"When are you going to kill me?" Kamran asks.

Askari swings open the door. The General takes one last look at the prisoner and sighs. "It wasn't my choice."

IRAN
Present day

THIS IS HOW IT ENDS.

A hood is thrown over Kam's head and he is frog-marched from the writing room.

They will not hang him in public. He expects an empty concrete courtyard, a few officials in attendance, simple gallows. They wind through hallways; patches of light filter through the hood as they pass what Kam assumes must be windows. Once or twice they pass clusters of other voices that Kam does not recognize. Soon they tear off his hood. They are in a waiting room. A ring of chairs around the walls, bare coffee table in the middle.

Above Kam is the portrait of Khomeini. War! War until Final Victory!—Khomeini's slogan, and yet he did not see that the war itself was his final victory. That the only bright period of his Islamic Republic was its bloody birth. Kam looks away.

Kam is led out into the light. They hustle him into the windowless back of a waiting van and the engine coughs to life. He asks them where they are going and they tell him to hush, and he asks again, and this time they tell him to shut the fuck up. They drive for what feels like an hour. The smell of diesel and exhaust is pungent. The honks are constant, the van sits still for minutes at a time. This is all out of order. Before Kam dies he will suffer through hell: one last Tehrani rush hour.

In time the door whooshes open. The light is blinding. His minders jump out, drag him along. He hears the spin of idling jet engines, blinks at the concrete reflecting heat like an oven. His minders walk him to a weathered plane painted with the blue block letters and livery of Iran Air. An airstair leads to its cabin. One of the minders, a bald man with a thin patch of beard, shows Kam to a seat in the third row.

There are the two minders. There is an unsmiling male flight attendant built like a wrestler who spends the flight standing in the galley by the cockpit, staring at Kam. No one else is on board.

Where are they going? He assumes another prison. He has heard of compounds, like gulags, in the south, beyond the Plains of Emptiness. They are done with him in Tehran. Now he is meat and muscle for forced labor. The plane takes off. Out the window are the brown curves and crags of the Alborz in summer, jutting from the earth like the crown of Tehran. It has been three years since he last saw them, driving with Roya and Alya, and he never thought he'd get another chance. I am lucky, Kam thinks, but not really. The plane rolls and banks as it climbs.

Before the Islamic Republic, the buildings and country and people beneath him would have been aflame with color. Now it is a chessboard of grays and blacks and browns, all rightful Persian decadence papered over by a colorless government. Kam trains his eyes on the Alborz until the clouds take them from view.

THE MINDERS SHUT THE SLIDERS over the windows. They do not answer Kam's first few questions and they, like the General, are practiced at making faces that suggest it will go poorly for him if he keeps at it. They fly for hours, but Kam cannot sleep. Sleep is hard. Harder, now, than suffering through a beating or remaining awake for two days straight. The plane bounces through a choppy landing and slams into the runway with such force it springs open a few of the overhead compartments. Rain is pelting the cabin—he can only hear it, though, the windows are still shut. The bald minder throws a pack into his lap. "Change into this," he says.

In the back row, with all of them still watching, Kam puts on a suit, white shirt, and scuffed black shoes. The fabric is dusty and smells faintly of starch and embalming chemicals. The sleeves fall well short of his wrists. The creases in the white shirt are rough ridges. Kam knows straightaway that someone was hanged in these clothes. And it must have been a small guy: he cannot squirm his feet into the shoes.

"Maybe we should cut off your toes, then," the bald minder says, "make some room."

"I'll just take my slippers back," Kam says.

"They're gone," the bald minder says.

"They were just in my seat."

"They are gone now," the minder says, stuffing them into an overhead bin.

We'll skip the shoes, he thinks. He is hustled to the exit, where he hears the thunk of a docking airstair. The minder reviews Kam's suit, straightens his lapels. Gives those stocking feet a gleeful smirk.

Then he spits in Kam's face.

Kam blinks and tries to wipe it aside but the man spits again. "*Bilaakh*," he says. "Fuck off." He shoves Kam out the door, into the whipping rain, to walk down the stairs. An unmarked plane is across the tarmac and Kam thinks he cannot believe it, maybe his vision is playing tricks again, but no, there it is. My god, there it is. Two steps off the airstair, and Kam is drenched. He turns his head to the sky and the rain comes in sheets unfurling from the blackness. It has been nearly two years since he has seen rain; three since he has felt it. Kam could cry, but he is too numb. A man has appeared at the top of the other plane's airstair. He is hustling down.

Kam moves slowly toward him, hitch in his stride, like sand has been poured into his joints. Kam's blurry vision means he only sees who it is when they've nearly met.

It is Colonel Ghorbani. Unlike Kam, his body seems to work. He has gained maybe twenty kilos but he is still moving quickly.

They stare at each other, but do not speak. Later on, Kam will regret not tripping him. Ghorbani begins to run toward the Iranian plane. Kam walks fast as he can. He'd run if he could. Another man has descended the airstair, soaking in this beautiful rain. When Kam reaches him, he stands there for a fluttering moment, drinking the water that runs into his mouth. He will remember that rain until the day he dies.

Arik Glitzman helps Kam climb the stairs, but they do not speak.

There is nothing to say.

ISRAEL
Present day

THE MONTHS THAT FOLLOW will be the strangest of Kam's life.

Stranger, even, than his brutal torture and captivity because, in unexpected doses, the things that together form a life will be reintroduced to him, and each one will feel brand-new, as had that sweet Vienna rain. He is, again, a child.

It is his inaugural visit to Israel, but at first he does not see much of the place. Mossad puts him up in a guesthouse. For a few days he sits indoors and reads, eating only ice cream, until the doctors intervene to stiffen the dietary regimen. Most nights he finishes a bottle of wine all by himself, thinking it will help him sleep, though it never does.

Sina and Maman visit at the end of the first week. The reunion unspools like one of those hopelessly stilted conversations you might have with an old acquaintance if you'd left town and then, years later, passing through on business, you stumble into them again. In theory there is much to say—three years have passed!—but in practice there is nothing. It is worse than meeting strangers, who come without expectation. Sina and Maman are expecting the version of Kam that went off to die. Also Maman is having more problems.

After hugs and kisses, she calls Kam by his father's name. A few times she calls him Sina. On the table there is tea that no one will touch. She asks after his children, he feels the loss of her all over again, and from this painful shore they embark on a futile journey to make sense of what the hell he's done.

"It's good to see you," Sina says. "We would have met you in Vienna, but we didn't know you were alive, much less out, until they brought you here."

"It's good to see you, too," Kam says.

Now that it's been established that everyone is happy he's not dead, Sina says: "How are you feeling?" He has been stealing glances at those gray hairs. Twice his gaze has lingered on the bad leg, but he won't see anything gruesome on the outside—the problem's in the bones.

"Parts of me feel fine," Kam says. "Other parts like shit. Do I look better than you thought I would?"

"I'm glad you're in one piece," Sina says.

And that makes him think, briefly, of Askari, and the time he got carried away with the knife, and the General made him find someone to sew Kam's pinkie finger back on. He looks at the finger, wiggles it a bit, and says, "Me, too."

Sina tells Kam that the limbo went on for a long while after his disappearance. The Iranians didn't say they had him, nor did Israel wish to admit that he'd been working for them. Sina filed police reports in Stockholm. He'd met a few times with Swedish intelligence, but information in those chats went one-way: from him to them. After a few months, he says, it was clear: Kam is either dead or missing in Iran. Sina visited Tehran twice, he says, and both times was stiff-armed by Iranian officialdom.

Maman says that she needs to lie down. After she is situated in one of the bedrooms, the brothers settle back at the table.

"We actually had a funeral for you in Stockholm," Sina says. "Just last year."

"A big one?"

Sina looks a little panicked; his brother doesn't see the joke until Kam asks whether his picture made the papers.

"No," Sina says with a laugh, "of course not."

In truth Kam finds this response more depressing than hearing about his own, poorly attended funeral. By now he's paid so dearly in private that a little public notoriety was not only welcome, it was expected. Deflated, Kam asks what Sina did know.

There had been leaks in the press, of course, about a brazen Israeli kidnapping operation in Tehran, occurring right around the time Kam disappeared, but Sina says that the first bit of tangible news had come only five days earlier, when a man from the Israeli Embassy showed up at his office in Stockholm. "He had a picture of you. A few videos, which I imagine they took in Vienna. There was a big trade, apparently. The Iranians captured a bunch of American sailors in the Gulf. The Americans had some Iranian spies. The Israelis did, too. And of course the Iranians had you. We don't know how it all got worked out. This guy in Stockholm said that he would arrange for us to come see you in Israel. And here we are."

The moment is not comfortable. Kam has no idea what else to say, so he asks about Frida and the girls. They are fine, Sina says, all fine. "We'll throw a big dinner for you when you get home," and though that last word has it all wrong, Kam doesn't want to spoil Sina's pleasurable dreams of playing emcee to a hostage return. The tea is cold by now, so he puts a kettle on the stove.

"You should know that in Sweden you are legally dead," Sina said.

"Sounds like there is going to be a lot of paperwork."

"Mountains," he says. "Are you going to come home for good? What are you thinking?"

"I'm coming back," Kam says. "But I don't know how long I'll stay. I need to figure out what to do. I need a smoke."

"I'll join," Sina says, and Kam hopes his face does not show the disappointment.

There is a square patio at the back of the guesthouse with a table, no chairs, and a view into the empty living room of the next one. The June sunshine burns from all sides: above there is no shade, and below it rises in a sweltering shimmer from the concrete. Sina refuses a cigarette, but stands there with Kam in the sort of blazing wet heat that has you feeling, on contact, that you've been licked by a dog. There is something Sina wants to say, or ask, and Kam doesn't want to give him an opening, but Sina jumps in anyway.

"I know you don't want to talk about any of it," Sina says, "at least not now."

Kam blows smoke across his shoes and thinks a drink would be nice. A little early, but after three years sober there's no harm in opening the bar...

"I'm just wondering," Sina says, "I mean, I knew your practice wasn't exactly killing it... but I... I didn't, I figured, I... I was drinking a lot back then... but it's better now... we talked about money, didn't we? A little bit. I'm sorry. I—"

"It's not your fault I wound up working for the Mossad," Kam says, hand on the sliding door like it's an ejection seat.

"Was it about money?" he asks. "If it was, you should have asked me." Sina's now shoving his hand the other way to keep it shut.

We're brothers, Kam thinks, and yet he's as alien to me as he was when we were boys. Kam could say that the money was only one part of it. But he decides on a simple answer. One that is both true enough and will mercifully kill this conversation. His hand comes off the door.

"I don't know what I was thinking," Kam says. "I should have asked for help."

A scrim of despair rips through Sina's face. "I'm sorry," he says, his jaw tight and twitching all at once. "I'm sorry. I'm—"

For what? Kam wonders, but he's never seen his brother this wrecked, and he knows it does not matter what Sina wants, he will give it to him. They embrace for a moment, Kam's hands tight on the back of his brother's sweat-soaked shirt. He thinks of Maman's story about Joseph and decides to accept this blank check of an apology. He'll fill in the grievance later, picking from several.

SINA AND MAMAN STAY for two days before returning to Sweden. Kam promises to join them soon, though Mossad has not been specific about how long he must remain in Israel. He asks after Glitzman, whom he has not seen since the flight, and is told that he will pay a visit soon.

Kam never had nightmares in prison, and he does not have them in Israel. Humans are plasticky; he has learned how to ward off the darkness. He reads poetry and refuses to ruminate on what has been done to him. The Mossad psychologists find this frustrating. They expect fragility, but what they've got instead is indifference. More than anything he wants to get busy again. There are things he would like to do, he's just not sure yet what they will be.

The physical scars, though, well, you can't do much about those. Sometimes the blurred vision makes reading difficult, and his first short jog around the guesthouses ends after ten minutes, each slap of his foot on the pavement sending shock waves of pain up his legs.

At the end of the second week, Glitzman arrives, carrying a shopping bag that clinks with the pleasant sound of kissing bottles. On the plane in Vienna, Kam was so delirious and distracted he couldn't have told you what the man looked like after three years gone by. Now Kam sees.

Glitzman has lost at least ten kilos. The lumpy bags beneath his eyes have been carried off, either by a surgeon or generous sleep. Glitzman carries himself with the breezy confidence of a man with ready access to pleasurable sex. The guesthouse does not have a view of the parking lot, but Kam knows he is driving a sports car.

Glitzman withdraws two glasses from a cabinet and hoists a bottle of scotch from the bag onto the table. The brilliant smile suggests some serious chemical whitening. He fills their glasses and then says, "We're getting drunk. No arguments." Then he points up, to one of the can lights. "Turned off the cameras. Mics, too. This is a private chat. Decompression." He makes a show of taking a deep breath, and stretches his arms high into the air. His fingers are ringless, but then Kam cannot remember if he ever wore one.

Needless to say, this is not the midlife crisis Kam envisioned for Arik Glitzman. But it suits him.

"You look better than I would have thought," Glitzman says, raising his glass. Amen, Kam thinks. They clink glasses, and over a few more liberal pours of the scotch Glitzman asks if Kam's needs are being met. He asks about the food, the sleep, the doctors, if Kam would like someone to take him on a tour of Jerusalem. He's not grinding his teeth and now Kam wonders if maybe this new girl he's got is much younger than him. Does Glitzman even work for Mossad anymore? Maybe he's advising at one of the tech companies in Herzliya and he's just been brought in on special assignment to hold an old asset's hand.

"How have you been?" Kam asks.

Glitzman rubs his nose and takes a long drink of scotch and behind his eyes shine three years of life and it's obvious that he doesn't want to talk about it. So he does what any sensible person would. Glitzman tells Kam he has been fine, just fine.

While they drink, Glitzman confirms the basic outlines of Sina's tale: that the trade was part of a larger prisoner swap involving a group of American naval officers captured in the waters of the Persian Gulf. The Americans had a few Iranians to trade, but the Iranians had wanted Colonel Ghorbani, and Washington had squeezed Israel.

"I asked that you be thrown into the pot," Glitzman says.

"I appreciate it," Kam says. They toss back the rest of their scotch, and soon Kam is buzzed running to drunk and thinks Glitzman can't be far behind.

"How did you know I was still alive?" he asks. "They were moving me around constantly."

Glitzman smiles at this, says, "Special collection."

A euphemism for signals intelligence, intercepts. And it is obvious Glitzman will not share more.

"There was a debate," Glitzman says—from his drunkenness glides an effortless voice for business—"about how to deal with you." I'd thought the sack contained only booze, but now I see it's got a folder. He slaps it onto the table. "Various pieces of shit in the organization felt that we'd settle up with you by the mere act of bringing you home. I did not agree. And I won, though I got less than I would have liked."

Kam opens the folder. It's full of the monthly escrow statements, and he also sees that shortly after his release a lump sum of $500,000 was deposited.

"That's the monthly rate for every month you were imprisoned, plus what the fucking accountants call a Hardship Bonus," Glitzman says. "It's payment for our bodies, and I think enough for a fresh start. You're going to stay in Israel, yes?"

"No," Kam says. "Back to Sweden. At least to figure things out."

Glitzman frowns. "You hate Sweden."

"I know," Kam says. "I just don't think I can stay here. I need to go back, at least for a while."

Glitzman sports a look of paternal disappointment. Kam hopes he doesn't keep poking at this, because he can't explain his answer. Glitzman waves a hand through the air, and his drunken tone returns as he pronounces the verdict: You're on your own journey. Though he does weigh in once more in his business voice to explain that under no circumstances is Kam to share anything with the Swedes, and he nods and says yes, Arik, yes, I've been over all of this with your interrogators.

"Interviewers," Glitzman corrects.

"Interviewers," Kam says. "Right."

Glitzman heads to the bathroom for the third time. Kam sips at his scotch and finds himself thinking of Roya again.

"Who was it?" he asks Glitzman, after he's settled back into his seat. "Who were the Iranians running in Israel? Did you find the people Ghorbani was telling us about?"

It is the nearest they'll drift to the topic of Oriana, and before Glitzman answers, Kam can see him sorting through his memories so he may respond without using one of her. "There were four of them. The ringleader, the only witting one, was a Persian Jew from Los Angeles who'd been radicalized by a Shia cleric in Sherman Oaks. Iranians formally pitched and recruited him in Istanbul. Guy was an American citizen, not on any of our lists, and so Ghorbani ran him as a false flag. As a settler, if you can believe it. He came to Israel and joined one of the extremist yeshivas in the West Bank. Even with his broken Hebrew he's so magnetic he starts recruiting his own following. In the end we could confirm three of his Hilltop Youth played roles in the attacks. Mostly moving and placing the drones. They are all in prison."

"They didn't know they were working for Iran?" Kam asks.

"The ringleader did. The others? No. They are Jewish theocrats, like the mullahs. They thought they were fighting against an illegitimate Israeli government, doing the bidding of God. They were in the dark. Like Roya Shabani was."

Kam is worried what might happen if his thoughts of Roya and Alya come loose. He prefers to keep their memories inside, feeding in the darkness.

"You know..." Glitzman says, and then trails off. His tone has become nonchalant while he runs a hand through his hair, which is now darker, probably dyed, but it's also thicker, and Kam wonders how he managed that. Pills? A graft? He goes on. "On that subject, eh... well..."

"What subject?"

"Roya's death."

Kam's lower lip slides over his teeth. Doesn't Glitzman see the pain across his face?

"A strange thing happened about a year ago," Glitzman begins. There is more in his bag. He has produced a small box and arranged it on the table. "Another balloon had gone up in Tehran. We had to get someone out, and we moved them overland into Azerbaijan. I flew to Baku for the debriefing. Shithole flophouse. I arrive early, around daybreak. The asset is still asleep in the bedroom. The Azeri who drove him out is making breakfast in the kitchen. I sit down, we have some tea, start talking. And I notice something on this Azeri smugglers' wrist. It's a Rolex, a well-kept vintage one. And I start turning over the strangest thoughts in my mind."

Glitzman is not smiling, but it looks like he wants to. His tone is that of a parent who, with the fullness of time, has refashioned a traumatic experience into a humorous anecdote.

"This happens to be the same network we'd programmed for your exfil," Glitzman says. "And sitting there in Baku, I remember the hell we went through after you were captured. Oh, it was a shitty time in Caesarea Division, and the shit was flowing everywhere, on everyone. Cohen and I must have seen the then–Prime Minister every day for a solid month. These goddamn Azeri smugglers had nearly been caught in the dragnet that snagged you. They escaped, but just barely. And you know what that means, don't you?"

"The price went up," Kam says.

"The fucking price went up," Glitzman agrees, with genuine camaraderie. "I rib the smuggler a bit, ask if he bought the watch with his bonus. And you know what? All that Azeri bravado just drains from him"—Glitzman snaps his fingers—"like that. Which is rare with Azeris. He's kind of petting the watch, as if it's prickling his hairy wrist.

And I ask, on a hunch: We tried to get a man out a couple of years ago. It went badly. Were you there? And he gives me a little nod. A grim one, the sort of nod that's not lying to you, not yet, but one that's certainly hiding things. And I say, well, the goddamn reports said you never made contact with our man. That he got scooped up before your boat hit the beaches. At this point we were reasonably sure you were alive, so soon as the guy starts stammering about how he found the watch on the beach or wherever the hell, I put up my hand and tell him to stop lying. I tell him that in exchange for the truth, I won't tell his boss that he wore the watch in front of me, like a fucking fool. And do you know what he did then?"

"He told you a story," Kam says.

"A marvelous story," Glitzman says. "Miraculous, even if only half of it was true. Do you know it?"

"The story?"

"Yes," says Glitzman. "The story."

"How would I? I've never met the guy."

For a brief moment Kam thinks Glitzman might punch him, but the lupine look dissolves quick as it came, and Glitzman laughs.

Then he slides over the box, and when Kam opens it he sees Papa's Rolex ticking and shining. Glitzman has cared for it, as he cares for Kam—and Kam can't make any sense of that.

"How much of his story have you confirmed?" Kam asks.

"Just the true parts," Glitzman replies.

Kam is relieved to see that Glitzman is opening the bottle to refill their drinks. He smiles and yawns and what Kam sees in there cheers his heart: Glitzman's bruxism has not worsened. In fact, he'd bet that Glitzman finally got that mouthguard. Kam's glass is nearly full, but Glitzman tops it off anyhow. He has many more questions for Glitzman, and he believes that, for once, the Israeli might answer them.

"The true parts," Kam muses. "How did you confirm those?"

"Special collection," Glitzman says. And from his cheerful bag comes an envelope.

SWEDEN
Present day

AFTER TWO MONTHS in the Tel Aviv guesthouse, after Sina's lawyers have intervened in Stockholm, and after the Israelis have doubtless given Swedish intelligence something it wants, Kamran Esfahani is pronounced legally undead, and issued a fresh passport by the Swedish Embassy in Tel Aviv.

He flies out of Ben Gurion, and the waters of the Med are taken by the clouds. In Stockholm he rents an apartment without furniture, buys sheets and a mattress, and for a few days shutters himself inside to read Hafez and Ferdowsi and Shamlu and Rūmī and Farrokhzad. Kam, it seems, is re-creating his prisons. He visits Maman a few times each week to play backgammon and, though she is often lost, he is glad to repay her for sitting across from him when he was a lost child.

One pleasant, and rather unexpected, development—and these days he's looking for upside anywhere he can find it—is that the calamity seems to have leveled the playing field with Sina. His brother's got heaps of cash, multiples on multiples more than the Israelis paid, but Kam was a spy, and he's returned home from a Persian torture party installed with valor and heft well beyond his meager finances. Sina asks Kam where he wants to go. Anywhere, he says, anywhere on the planet, I'm paying. Pick your place.

Kam has an answer, but he cannot tell his brother, so he instead says: "Grenada."

They spend a long weekend getting soused in Andalusia on Sina's dime and when they come back Kam drops him at his house. They were still drunk on the plane, but now they're just hungover, and Kam sees Sina's wife Frida on the stoop, glowering, and suspects his brother made promises about behaving himself. The brothers look at each other in shared mischief and conspiracy, and Kam realizes that the things you never thought would change sometimes do. Frida embraces Sina sternly while Kam drives off, Sina smiling his way.

Some nights Kam weighs the likelihood of opening his door to the knock of a Swedish criminal brandishing a gun at the behest of Iranian paymasters. His internet research turns up plenty of precedent—in Paris, America, even here in Sweden, though he is usually able to convince himself that if they wanted him dead, the General would have obliged ages ago.

There are days when he misses his cell, when Kam desires the intensity and attention of the torture. What might happen if he flew back to Tehran and drove into the mountains for a picnic? Or went to find the General...

He did not tell the General the truth about that night.

He certainly did not confirm anything with Glitzman.

Kam can scarcely think of it himself.

When these thoughts take him, Kam wanders to one of the boxes on the floor and finds the envelope Glitzman gave him, and, though he has opened it and retaped it shut dozens of times, he will slide it open again to read the short lines, and let his imagination run.

ONE MORNING KAM IS READING Rūmī, bars of golden summer light shimmering through the slats of his bedroom blinds. He found a fine collection of his poems at an antiquarian shop here in Stockholm, full of verses he did not have in captivity. He reads one, and remembers Maman reading it to him.

Love comes with a knife...
You have been walking the ocean's edge

Holding up your robes to keep them dry
You must dive naked under and deeper under
A thousand times deeper. Love flows down

He has been waiting, stalling, hand-wringing. He was dead for so long, then he was a captive. And now he knows he must get on with it. Even if it comes with a knife.

HOME

KAM LANDS IN LOS ANGELES.

At the airport, he rents a Corolla and plunges into chaos, fighting his way south on the 405. Kam has dreamed of a life here for so long that everything is sugared in a surreal gloss. The palm trees are lush and green, the air is clean, every pedestrian fit for the silver screen. In truth the traffic is a snarl, the smog about as bad as Tehran, but Kam finds the air silky and fine. Perfection. Three, four years ago, fantasizing about this victory lap of a drive, he was headed for Santa Barbara, Corona Del Mar, maybe even Westwood. Not now.

Though the drive is not long, even with the traffic, Kam stops for a burger at an In-N-Out just off the highway. He sits outside so he can smoke. The air smells of cut grass and grease, and the bees are hard at work on the trash cans. A man walks by and in his slipstream comes the smell of tobacco and piss. He's tempted by a second burger, but it is certainly not the ambience—it's procrastination. Kam washes down the burger with his third cigarette. Near sunset he drives on.

He flips on nameless music, but it only churns his anxiety, and he shuts it off. The short drive passes in a clenching silence. He entertains visions of a heart attack, his head slumped forward, the car unpiloted, veering off to wrap itself around a streetlight.

He winds into a neighborhood of small ranch houses in the shadow of the 405. Many of the shoebox homes are shambling and unkempt, bastions of drunks or the elderly, but others are well-tended, even if they're rentals, and cheap ones at that. His heart is galloping, his soul is staring into the abyss. Kam's fingers are icicles hanging from the steering wheel.

The sight of the home conjures memories that get stuck in his throat. He's looked at pictures of the place a hundred times. He's run the numbers on the property. He's conducted every bit of research one might from distant Stockholm.

This can end like Maman's story, he tells himself again. Even before they'd come clean, those brothers had their violence repaid, not with more violence, but with full sacks of grain. Such things have happened this side of eternity, and surely they'll happen again.

His car's appearance in the driveway brings movement from behind the half-shut blinds in the front room. This is one of the more well-maintained homes on the block. Even the trash cans look clean, square and straight like sentries facing the road, and he's pleased that the three palms in the front yard are even mightier in person. The grass is lush and furrowed by a recent haircut. The flower beds are prim and dazzling with color: purples, reds, whites. And pinks.

So much pink.

The girl who runs outside is wearing a pink dress, too.

Her shoes are pink.

The last time Kam saw her, he was heaving her up into a boat alongside her mother. Those fingernails were painted that same color, but by the time he'd gotten her safely aboard, much of it was washed off by the waves of the Caspian. Though he has replayed that moment a million times since, he's always wondered if he'd imagined that detail. He'd been shot twice, right afterward. And then nearly drowned.

After a few reedy, desperate breaths, he steps out. The girl's curious eyes flicker to recognition and then, to his cosmic relief, to joy. She must be nine now, but her eyes are the same. They are only one color, but they are still her mother's.

Alya shouts his name.

Roya walks onto the porch. She is wearing a green shirt pockmarked with stains from potting soil. Her headband is pink. Her long hair cascades halfway down her back. She is carrying a glass of water. Her lovely skin is slick with sweat. Kam has never seen a woman who looks so much like home. He feels things in that moment that are going to take years to say. He starts with, "Roya, I am sorry to drop in like this."

He hopes that glass of water will slip through her fingers, it would certainly appeal to his dramatic side, but she only looks at him while he looks at her, and they hang there in a moment opened by the slow turn of fate. And then she takes a shaky sip, turns around, and disappears inside.

But Roya does not shut the door.

LATER, WHEN THEY HAVE talked some of it through, Kam and Roya sit outside in the draining summer light, and he decides that if he could write the end of the story, it would start like this.

ACKNOWLEDGMENTS

Writing continues to be the loneliest of team sports. This book—my fourth—was fortunate to have many, many friends on its team.

Tremendous thanks as always to Star Lawrence, my editor at W. W. Norton, who continues to believe in me and my writing and makes it all better. My gratitude as well to the team at Norton: Nneoma Amadiobi, Kyle Radler, Steve Colca, Elisabeth Kerr. And to Dave Cole for once again helping one of my books into the world, and for saving me from several embarrassing errors.

I must also thank my incomparable agent, Lisa Erbach Vance, without whom none of this would be possible. Thanks as well to Kristen Pini at Aaron Priest, whose diligence and attention to detail makes everything move smoothly and efficiently.

Dave Michael once again submerged the writing in a world of pain, helping it rise from the punishment cleaner and better for its suffering. As a sometimes Swede, Dave also graciously provided insight on Kam's life and times in Stockholm, pointing out dozens of spots where my American understanding of the Nordic world was woefully inaccurate.

As always, many former CIA officers provided insight and counsel along the way. Mike Stokes, Charles Finfrock, Glenn Chafetz, John Sipher, Marc Polymeropoulos, Don Hepburn, Jerry O'Shea, Meredith, Cooper, Ralph, Shakespeare, Ash, and Steve Slick—all were gracious enough to pick up the phone when this unreformed analyst called with a question of tradecraft, lingo, or queries about Mossad or Iran's intelligence services. Thank you.

Arash Azizi and Shahrzad and Sia J. brought Tehran to life, helping this decidedly non-Persian writer with the finer points of Persian language, politics, family life, culture, history, cuisine, nursery rhymes, and poetry. Special thanks to the Js for cooking a delightful Persian meal and letting me spoil the atmosphere, just a bit, by bringing along a notebook. Many thanks as well to Jonah and Cooper for their friendship and help with Persian poetry and slang.

Jay Leftwich, DDS, not only provided insight on Kam's dental practice, he also answered the phone on a Saturday morning when I was worried my seven year old had knocked a few of his own teeth out of position. Thanks as well to Peter Nordh for details on dentistry, and to Karin Linge Nordh for valuable corrections on Swedish spellings, meatballs, and eldercare.

Mike Green again served as the book's resident doctor (with an admirable assist on a particularly gruesome—and ultimately deleted—scene by Mike Doden). The characters are, as usual, much worse off after his ministrations.

I must also thank the incredible team across the Atlantic at Swift Press: Mark Richards, Diana Broccardo, Rachel Nobilo, and the always indomitable Lisa Shakespeare. It has been an absolute joy to be a Swift author—here's to many more books together. My gratitude as well to Caspian Dennis, who continues to make it all happen across the pond.

Jason Beighley was wildly generous with his time, helping me craft the finer operational details of Glitzman's daring raid in Tehran. Thank you, Jason, for help with everything from the psychology to the weapons to the impact of the phases of the moon.

Matti Friedman, Eitan Danon, and Etan Basseri provided an incomparable education on Israel and its culture.

I am indebted to Dylan Sullivan for providing tremendous insight into how Mossad's (fictional) Escape Pods might function, though, of course, all aeronautical, engineering, and design flaws are my own.

Several former officers of the Mossad were gracious enough to lend their time and expertise to scaffold some authenticity around Glitzman and Kam's wild adventure. Though their names will not appear here, I am in their debt.

As always I must thank the group of readers who help me turn the reader's draft into something, well, readable. To my dad, Jenny and Mike Green, Becky Friedman, Elisabeth Jordan, Anna Connolly, Kent Woodyard—thank you all for continuing to read my stuff when I send you hopeless Word documents.

And to my three wonderful children, Miles, Leo, and Mabel: each of you provide healthy doses of inspiration and much needed distraction, joy, and laughter throughout the writing year. I love you all.

And finally, to my wife, Abby, to whom this book is dedicated: first reader, loving critic, champion, muse. None of this would exist without you, my love.